Chapter One

YOU'VE BEEN THROUGH a lot of traumas in only four months. How do you feel about that?"

I stared at the therapist on my laptop screen, trying hard not to roll my eyes. Not because I found it irritating that one side of his white button-up shirt collar was tucked under his navy-blue pullover sweater while the other was out and askew, like he'd thrown the sweater on at the last minute and hadn't bothered to check his appearance in a mirror. Nor that his comb-over was so pathetic no one was buying that he had hair on top of his head, which meant he was hiding things, and poorly, which meant he was a shit therapist.

Physician, heal thyself.

No, it was his ridiculous question that was driving me insane.

Four months ago, I'd killed someone while working as a detective for the Little Rock Police Department. Consequently, I'd lost my job, my house, my money, and my reputation. My partner Keith—both personal and professional—had turned on me.

"Why don't you tell me what happened the night of..." he said, checking his notes. His gaze popped back up. "October 17th?"

"I'm sure it's all there in the paperwork," I said dryly, gesturing toward the screen. I couldn't stop the self-deprecating smile that spread across my face. "In case you missed it on the news."

A hint of impatience flickered in his eyes. "I'd rather hear it from you."

And I'd rather not repeat it. I'd told this story so many times, I practically had the verbiage memorized, which, I was sure, gave it an air of inauthenticity with each subsequent retelling. But if this was what it took to convince the department I wasn't unstable and that we could amicably cut ties, then I'd do it to cut the marionette strings.

"I was investigating a murder case," I said, sitting back in my chair. My gaze drifted involuntarily to the cabinet under my sink where I kept my bottle of Jack Daniel's. "I was looking for a witness, and I was told he worked the night shift at Durango's Liquor. When I walked up to the establishment, a teen was hanging outside. His name was Dylan Carpenter. I asked him how old he was, and he told me to fuck off. I told him not to enter the store and went inside myself."

"Did you identify yourself as a detective?"

"No."

"And then what happened?" he prodded.

I fought to keep from reminding him that therapists were supposed to let their patients tell their stories at their own pace. Did this guy have dinner reservations after this? I had my own plans, so I didn't mind hurrying things along.

"I noticed the witness wasn't at the counter and the clerk was checking someone out, so I walked around the store to see if I could locate the witness. While I was in the back, the teen came in and tried to buy a bottle of whiskey. I approached, asked him for ID, then he ran out the back with the bottle. I followed."

I'd relived that night so many times. So many exhausting times. And I'd let myself wonder what would have happened if I hadn't followed him. If I'd let him go. But the truth was I *had* followed him out into that back alley, and no amount of wishing or manifestation would change it.

I had to own up to what I'd done.

Then again, admitting to it wasn't my problem. My problem was living with it.

"And then?" he asked, glancing down. I realized he was looking at his watch. Maybe I hadn't been that far off in guessing he had plans.

"When I went out the back door, he had a gun trained on me. I drew my service weapon and told him to put the gun down. Instead, he took off running. I followed, telling him to stop. About twenty feet from the door, he turned and pointed his gun at me again and took a shot. I shot back. He missed. I didn't."

The therapist picked up a piece of paper and scanned it. "The report doesn't mention recovering a bullet or casing from the boy's gun."

"They said there was no evidence he'd shot a weapon, let alone had one. That I fabricated seeing a gun and hearing the shot because my mind couldn't cope with the guilt."

"And do you believe that?" he asked earnestly.

Did I? I wasn't sure what to believe anymore. One minute, I wondered if they were right, but the next I was willing to bet money I no longer had that the Little Rock Police Department was gaslighting me, not only about the shooting, but about the three break-ins at my house that had occurred within two weeks of the shooting.

It had been suggested to me that those break-ins were imaginary too, but there was no denying someone had stolen a photo of me and my sister that had been taken shortly before her kidnapping and murder. Just like there was no denying I'd seen the back of the man who'd taken it and chased him through my backyard and down an alley before I lost him. I hadn't imagined *that.*

"I don't know," I said, even though my gut churned at the thought of giving them what they wanted. Of admitting they'd made me start to doubt myself.

"There's nothing wrong with that answer," he said with a smile and a hint of triumph in his eyes. "No weapon was recovered, Harper. It's good that you're finally acknowledging that."

Was it?

But I bit back the retort on the tip of my tongue because that wasn't what he wanted to hear. He wanted to hear that everything was fine. Just fine, because that was what the Little Rock Police Department needed to hear from their once-exemplary detective. They needed to put this all to bed, and this session was the final nail in the coffin, my exit interview for my fourteen-year, formerly stellar law enforcement career.

"So tell me how you're doing," he asked.

"I've had my good days and my bad days," I said softly with a small smile. I tucked my shoulder-length hair behind my right ear, making myself look slightly vulnerable. Soft, but not too soft.

This wasn't my first therapist rodeo over the past four months, but I planned for it to be my last.

"And how do you handle the bad days?" he asked, a fake smile matching the fake concern in his eyes.

I wasn't about to tell him that I handled it with booze. Lots of booze, preferably Jack Daniel's, usually mixed with Coke. The Coke wasn't absolutely necessary, but he *definitely* didn't want to hear that.

"I journal," I said. "And take walks. Fresh air usually helps."

Lately, the only fresh air I got was on my way from my house to my car, and then from my car into a store and back again. And the only journaling I'd done was the occasional texts I exchanged with my friend Louise, one of the only people I'd kept in touch with from my Little Rock life. She was the police officer who'd responded to the last of my home invasions in Little Rock. Although she'd been a stranger at the time, she'd become a friend, partly because she'd *believed* me. She'd left the Little Rock PD too because, according to her, something was rotten there. I wanted to believe it. I wanted to believe the something rotten wasn't me.

As far as actual journaling went? I hadn't journaled since I was a teenager, when my sister was murdered.

But he didn't want to hear about that.

I'd made the mistake of spilling my guts early in the process, and I'd discovered the hard way that the court- or work-appointed counselors were just there to sign paperwork and make sure psychopaths hiding behind a badge weren't running around on the streets. Everything else was considered normal.

"Good, that's good," he said, jotting something down off screen. "And your move to your parents' place in…" He rifled through some papers then looked up triumphantly. "In Jackson, Kansas. How's that going? It's not always easy to go home after living apart from your parents for so long."

"That's Jackson Creek, Arkansas," I said, trying not to let my irritation show or he'd mark me down for anger issues. "There've been some bumpy parts, but over all, it's been okay."

By bumpy parts, I meant that my mother had barely spoken to me since I'd moved into their garage apartment two weeks ago, and that I had hardly left the four-hundred-square-foot studio since I'd moved in. "I'm actually going out tonight when we're done with this call." A genuine smile curved my lips. "I'm meeting a friend."

That was probably the first true thing I'd said in the past twenty minutes. I was meeting Louise, actually. She was now working for our county's sheriff's department.

"That's great, great," he said, writing something down again. "Socializing is important."

"It makes everything feel more normal."

"Normal is subjective, Harper," he chided, then looked up at me. "What do you plan on doing with your life since you're no longer with the Little Rock Police Department?"

"That's a good question," I said in all sincerity, but struggled hard to keep the sarcasm out of my voice. "I'm taking some time to explore my options."

AKA I had no fucking clue.

"Good. Good." His head bobbed as he smiled, probably thinking we were close to ending this call and he could shut down his laptop and get a beer. "Any more nightmares?"

I swallowed hard, my smile falling slightly. "They seem to be gone, thankfully."

Since I'd come home, my memories of shooting the kid had been replaced with memories of my sister's kidnapping. I wasn't sure which were worse.

"Don't be surprised if they resurface," he said, studying my face. "Change can bring them back. If you feel the need for any medication—"

"Then I'll contact a psychiatrist," I said adamantly. "So far, I'm good."

He glanced down again to take some notes, then looked up at me. "Well, unless there's anything else you wish to discuss, I think this concludes your appointed therapy."

"Thank you, Dr. Abalone. I'm eager to move on to a new chapter in my life."

We ended the call and I shut the laptop screen, every nerve ending in my body on fire. Without giving it another thought, I grabbed the open bottle of Jack Daniel's under my sink and didn't bother with a glass, drinking a gulp straight from the bottle. Who needed Prozac when I could self-medicate?

I screwed the lid back on the bottle, then closed my eyes and took a deep breath. Other than my trips to the liquor store up in Wolford, this would be my first time out in public since I'd come back to my hometown. In Little Rock, people either saw me as a poster child for the Thin Blue Line or a pariah. I had no idea what to expect here, but at least Louise and I were meeting at a bar.

Chapter Two

"YOU LOOK LIKE SHIT."

I gave Louise a sarcastic smile as I sat down at her table in the dimly lit bar. "Hello to you too."

Considering I didn't know her very well, I figured I must look pretty bad.

To be fair, I hadn't seen Louise in a few months, not since she'd shown up at my house as a Little Rock police officer to take a breaking and entering report in the dead of night. I'd been a detective with the department on paid leave after a shooting.

I'd thought I'd hit rock bottom back then.

That seemed like ages ago.

Before she'd left her position in Little Rock in favor of a job at the Lone County, Arkansas sheriff's department, she'd told me, *Even rats leave a sinking ship.* We hadn't talked about it much since, but I believed her. I wanted it to be true because it would mean I wasn't the kind of person who imagined guns and bullets. The kind of person who killed a kid by mistake.

"Interesting place," I said, glancing around. "Seems like an odd place for a bar, this far out of town." When she'd suggested we meet at Scooter's Tavern, I'd been surprised but also relieved. It was ten miles outside of Jackson Creek, which would hopefully be enough to save me from running into anyone who'd recognize me.

She gave me a smug grin. "It's next to the Grant County line." Lifting her bottle of beer, she added, "Grant County's dry."

It seemed crazy that in this day and age some counties in the state still refused or had strict limitations on the sale of alcohol, but the proof was just a few miles away.

She leaned in closer and lowered her voice. "How are you doing? *Really.*"

I'd just lied through my teeth with that therapist, but Louise was my friend.

Still, I didn't want to acknowledge how far I'd fallen. "I'm gonna need a drink before we get into that."

"Fair enough." She took my order—Jack and Coke, of course—and headed up to the bar to get us a round, giving me a chance to decompress. I'd been nervous about seeing Louise again, worried about what she'd think of me now—the disgraced ex-detective who would likely never work in law enforcement again.

She came back a few minutes later with a highball glass and a bottle of beer, and I caught a couple of men staring at her ass before she slid into her booth seat and placed the glass in front of me. Louise had always been pretty, with long dark hair that hung down her back, but she looked much more relaxed and happy than she had in Little Rock. The move to Lone County had been good for her.

Too bad I couldn't say the same for myself.

My mouth watered at the sight of the drink, and I had a sudden desperation to slam it down to ease my anxiety.

Instead, I picked it up and took a casual sip. "Tell me about your job," I said, eager to turn the conversation away from me.

She told me that while she loved the sheriff, some of the deputies were giving her a hard time. She was one of two female deputies in the department and some of the men had let her know they didn't appreciate her presence. The sheriff didn't put up with their bullshit, but he only knew about a quarter of what was going on, and she wasn't about to tattle.

"Okay," she said after answering my questions for ten minutes, her gaze on me. "How are *you* doing? Really. And not some bullshit answer. It's me you're talking to. The person who had your back in Little Rock when no one else did."

I wiped condensation from the side of my nearly empty glass and gave her another sarcastic grin. "Great. What thirty-six-year-old doesn't love living with their parents?"

She laughed. "I offered you a place to stay."

She had, several times, but I carried around a stink she didn't need associated with her. She was already facing an uphill battle in her new department. My baggage would only weigh her down.

"It's only temporary. Until I figure out where to go…" I shrugged. "And what to do."

We were both silent for a moment until she said, "What those assholes did to you wasn't right, Harper."

My thumb slid up and down the side of the glass, focusing on it and not the anxiety racing through my body. I took another drink, finishing it off. The burn in my stomach started to relax my tight muscles.

"Yeah, well…" I let the weight of my words hang in the air. It wasn't right, but there wasn't a damn thing I could do about it. I was lucky they'd just backed me into a corner and not a jail cell.

"Harper." Pity tinged her voice, making me flinch. I'd had plenty of people pity me over the years, and I hated it. Anger and frustration I could deal with. But nothing was as suffocating as pity. "I believed you then, and I believe you now. You know that, right? That kid had a gun, and someone made it disappear."

She'd told me the same thing four months ago, the night she'd shown up at my house after that final break-in, but it felt good to be reminded that someone believed me.

"I'm gonna get another drink," I said a little too brightly, making the words sound brittle. "Want anything?"

Worry filled her eyes, but she lifted her half-empty bottle. "I'm good."

I slid out of the booth and headed to the bar to place my order. There were more people than I would have expected for a Monday night. A few men were milling around the pool tables in the back, and some older men were hanging out at the bar. A group of young women occupied the table closest to the pool tables, their gazes drifting toward the men.

The bartender walked up to me, and his mouth ticked up in a smirk. "What can I get you?"

"I'll take another Jack and Coke."

He kept his gaze on me, forcing me to really look at him. Something about him rang familiar, but he was too old to be one of my former classmates. I guessed him to be in his mid-forties, but he definitely wasn't rocking a dad bod. The muscles of his arms filled out the sleeves of his T-shirt and his dark hair was thick and several inches long. A tattoo peeked out of the top of his collar. There were crow's feet around his eyes and his face was covered with stubble, giving him an *I can't decide whether to shave or commit to a beard* look. But his dark brown eyes unnerved me, like he could see right through me.

A shiver ran up my spine. I was in Jackson Creek to hide and lick my wounds. Not to be seen.

"Anything else?" he asked. "We serve food."

"Nope," I said with a false brightness, which thankfully sounded more genuine than it had with Louise. "Just the drink."

"Haven't seen you in here before," he said as he grabbed a glass and filled it with ice.

I didn't answer. Surely he didn't know all of his customers. If the place was this busy on a Monday night, it had to be crazy on the weekends.

He finished making the drink and set it down in front of me. "You want it on a tab?"

"Sure."

I headed back to the table, Louise's eyes on me the entire walk back.

As I slipped into my seat, she flashed a glance at the bar, then back to me. "I see you met James Malcolm."

I squinted at her. "Why does that name sound familiar?"

"Because he's *the* James Malcolm. The one who helped bust that international drug ring."

My jaw dropped, but I quickly recovered. "*What?*"

Amusement danced in her eyes. "I admit that I had ulterior motives for asking you to meet me here. Malcolm owns this place."

James Malcolm had made national news three years ago for his role in a sting operation in Fenton County, about a hundred miles southwest of here, that had brought down an international crime organization. No one knew exactly what had gone down, but the FBI had made a deal with him and then rescinded it. Malcolm had been in federal prison for months before all charges were dropped and he was released.

"What the hell is he doing *here?*" I asked, still in shock. I'd thought I was the most notorious person around these parts.

"Good question. He moved here soon after he was released from prison and opened this place."

"But why *here?*" I repeated. I couldn't fathom it. I knew the Arkansas state police had suspected he'd had ties to Arkansas organized crime syndicates as well, but nothing had ever stuck.

"I know," she said with a laugh, glancing over at the bar. "Seems like an odd choice, doesn't it? The sheriff thinks he's up to no good, but Malcolm's as slippery as they come. He can't find any evidence of wrongdoing."

I took a long sip of my drink, relishing the burn as it slid down my throat. This was my second drink in about a half hour—my third in an hour, if I counted the one I'd knocked back before leaving my garage apartment—and I was finally finding the sweet relief only alcohol seemed to give me these days. "You can't be dirty that long and suddenly go clean."

"Seems to me it can happen in reverse," she said, her gaze on me.

My face heated. Was she talking about me? After college, I'd gone straight to the police academy, then paid my dues as a beat cop until I worked my way up to detective six years ago. My record with the Little Rock police force had been spotless—exemplary—until it wasn't.

"Not you, Harper," she said bitterly. "Your partner. Among others."

Keith Kemper. Asshole. Bastard. He'd turned his back on me after the shooting. Tried to get me to take the fall.

The pain of his betrayal was the worst of all. Especially since we'd shared more than a working relationship.

"I don't want to talk about any of that," I said with a shake of my head, then took another long drink.

Over the last four months, the life I'd painstakingly built for myself had been turned upside down. The rapidity and finality of it had shaken me to my core.

The last time that had happened was when my fourteen-year-old sister had been kidnapped in front of me. Her battered body had turned up one week later.

Andi was the reason I'd become a police detective, and when I'd lost my job, it had felt like I was failing her all over again.

Louise reached out and placed her hand over mine. "It's gonna be okay, Harper."

I was glad she was so certain, because I definitely wasn't.

Chapter Three

LOUISE'S PHONE RANG and she grimaced as she answered it. "Louise Martin." She listened for a moment, then said, "I can be there in forty minutes." She hung up and gave me an apologetic smile. "I've gotta go. Rain check?"

"Yeah," I said. "Of course. Everything okay?"

"There's a bad accident on Highway 24 and some of the deputies are tied up with a murder north of town. They're short-handed, so they asked me to come in and help."

Murder? Last I remembered there weren't many murders around here.

I wanted to ask about it. But I reminded myself I wasn't a detective anymore and gave her a wave. "Go. We'll catch up later."

She started to get out of her seat but lowered her gaze to my half-empty glass. Her bottle was still only half-empty. "You're not planning on leaving soon, are you? I can drive you home."

My back bristled. "I'm good. I'll make sure I'm sober before I drive. Besides, I have a high tolerance these days."

She gave me a dubious look. "Harper, I know everything sucks right now, but it *will* get better. Okay?"

"Yeah," I said, trying not to frown. "I know."

She got out of the booth and hesitated, placing a hand on my arm. "Call me if you need to spend a night away from your parents. Or if you just need a friend."

I glanced up at her, hating the burning in my eyes. "Thanks, Louise. That means more than you know."

She nodded, her mouth pressed into a grim line. "I'm gonna go pay the tab for both of us. Let's try this again soon." She headed up the bar and settled up with a female bartender. Malcolm wasn't in sight.

I nursed the dregs of my drink until she finished paying. She gave me one last look before heading for the door. Less than a minute later, I was up at the bar asking the bartender for another drink.

The bartender—her name tag read Misti—shot me a sympathetic look. "Sorry. James says we have to cut you off."

My mouth dropped open. "You can't be serious. I've only had two."

"He said if you want another drink you have to eat something first."

What the hell? I wasn't even drunk. Was this some underhanded way of making customers spend more money? Fuck that.

Then another thought hit me.

Did he know who I was? The name Harper Adams was pretty infamous too these days. I was either a martyr or a murderer, depending on who you spoke to.

That was rich—a known criminal blackballing *me*.

I grabbed my purse and my jacket from the booth and headed out the door. I didn't plan to drive yet—I was smart enough to know my blood alcohol was over the legal limit—but I didn't plan on nursing a glass of water and a basket of fries while Misti watched me either.

I walked out into the cool February night air. Standing on the sidewalk in front of the building, I dragged in a deep breath to settle my ragged nerves.

Maybe this was a mistake. Meeting Louise. Moving into my parents' garage apartment. Maybe I should have...

What? Taken a job at Walmart or a car wash? I'd definitely needed to leave Little Rock. I was too damn notorious, whether people approved of me or not. I had no desire to be some poster child for the discussion about bad cops.

Moving home was penance...if I only knew for what.

I heard the roar of a motorcycle round the corner of the bar. It came into sight heading for the exit, but then it abruptly turned around and stopped in front of me. The motor shut off as the rider ripped off his helmet.

I steeled my shoulders, ready to deal with whatever this asshole was about to throw at me, but I wasn't prepared to see James Malcolm's furious face.

His eyes narrowed. "The fuck you're drivin'."

I shot him a glare. "Who said I was driving?"

His brow lifted slightly, just enough for me to notice in the white neon light cast by the Scooter's Tavern sign. "Maybe the keys in your hand."

My grip on the keys tightened, the metal edges digging into my flesh. "I'm going to sit in my car until I'm sober, not that it's any of your business."

His back stiffened. "It becomes my business if you get pulled over for a DUI. Or worse, you kill some poor family."

I hadn't planned on driving, but his accusation was like a stab wound to the heart. He thought I was that irresponsible? Then again, he didn't even know me, so why was I taking it personally?

"You have three choices," he said with a challenging gleam in his eyes. "One, you go back inside, hand Misti your keys until

she deems you ready to drive, Two, you call an Uber and leave
your car here. Or three, I call the sheriff and tell him one of my
customers is about to drive home and she needs a breathalyzer
test. Which is it?"

What the actual hell? He was going to call the sheriff on
me?

God, *that* was rich.

It was also embarrassing as hell. "How about you trust me
to judge whether I'm ready to drive or not?"

His eyes hardened. "No offense, but I don't trust *anyone*, let
alone a drunk. Now which is it? Option one, two, or three?"

While it wasn't hard to pick, it *was* hard to spit out, "One."
Because I was broke, had nothing to rush home to, and I had no
idea how I'd get my car in the morning.

"Good choice," he said, pulling his phone out of his back
pocket and tapping something onto the screen. "I let Misti know
you're coming back in. She's gonna take your keys until she says
you're ready."

"I'm not some kid," I snarled.

"Maybe not, but your sense of pacing while drinking is shit.
Now go inside." He pointed to the door.

"Fuck you," I grumbled, flipping him off as I opened the
door.

His response was to start his motorcycle back up and gun
the motor.

I was pissed as hell, but I went back inside and sat at the
bar. Misti walked over to me and held out her hand with a
sympathetic look. "Boss's orders."

I wanted to tell her that her boss was an asshole, but instead
I handed her my keys.

"Would you rather have nachos or fries?" she asked.

"Surprise me," I grumbled, pulling out my phone. In all
honesty, I couldn't be mad at either of them. It was the right

thing to do, which was surprising coming from James Malcolm, especially given his alleged criminal history. If anything, I was embarrassed. This person wasn't me. The real Harper Adams had a couple of drinks a month. She didn't wallow. She sure didn't have bartenders monitoring her consumption of alcohol.

Misti handed me a glass of water, then headed through a door to the back.

My cheeks burned but a quick glance around the room told me that no one had watched my walk of shame back into the bar, or at least they weren't ogling me now, which I found to be a relief. I let my gaze drift to the TV screen over the bar, watching a basketball game as I sipped my water and tried to not think about the way my life had crashed and burned.

"Here you go," Misti said, placing a basket in front of me. "Best damn nachos in southern Arkansas." The basket was piled high with cheese, shredded chicken, sour cream, and guacamole.

I took a bite, then released a soft moan.

"I told you they were good," Misti said with a big smile. "Eat those, down your water, and you'll be right as rain in no time." She wandered down to the end of the counter to take someone else's order before I had a chance to say thank you.

An hour later, Misti declared me ready to go. I'd finished the nachos and two glasses of water, using the forced downtime as an opportunity to study the place. While there were a few rougher looking characters back by the pool tables, most of the patrons looked like people you'd find hanging out at a pub in Little Rock. Louise was right. Malcolm might own the bar, but he didn't seem to have stuffed it full of his cronies.

She handed me back my keys, giving me a sympathetic look. "I don't know what's goin' on in your life, but no man's worth it. The best revenge is to have a life worth living. Show him not only do you not need him, but that you're a hell of a lot better without him."

I took the keys and lifted a brow. "What makes you think a man screwed me over?"

She laughed, placing her hand on the bar and leaning closer. "Aren't men always screwing women over?"

She had a point, and it was damn good advice. Probably the best I'd received since this nightmare began, but it wasn't that easy. And the Little Rock Police Department didn't give a shit how well I lived my life. Neither did Keith.

I pulled out my wallet to hand her some cash, but she waved me off. "Nope. On the house. Believe it or not, I was a lot like you three years ago, and someone helped me. Just paying it forward." A warm smile lit up her eyes. "If you ever need a friend to talk to, I'm a great listener."

Was she a criminal too? Maybe not, but I figured there was no way she didn't know about her boss's past. "Thanks," I said, not adding that I doubted I'd ever be back, at least not alone.

Why would I come here when I had a perfectly good bottle of Jack Daniel's back at my new apartment calling my name?

Chapter Four

I WOKE TO A POUNDING ON THE DOOR.

Prying my eyes open, I winced from my throbbing headache. Soft sunlight poured through the cracks on the sides of the window shades. It was either really early or a thick cloud cover had rolled in.

"Harper, I know you're in there!" my mother shouted. "Open the goddamn door before I'm forced to get the key!"

I sat up in shock, then nearly threw up as my studio apartment started to spin.

My mother never shouted, and she definitely never cursed. Especially *that* word. Growing up, she'd always told me and my sister Andi that good Christian Southern women did neither. She didn't allow cursing in the Adams household, and even my father abided by her rules. Mostly. So to hear her this worked up sent my heart racing.

"Coming!" I shouted despite my dry mouth. A fresh wave of pain washed through my head.

I got up and stumbled the short distance from the daybed to the solid wood door. Last I remembered I'd been on the sofa, drinking directly from my bottle of Jack Daniel's. When had I stumbled to the bed? I blinked to clear my vision as I unlocked the door and opened it.

My mother stood on the porch, fury on her face as her upper lip curled in disgust. She was wearing a velour tracksuit, and her shoulder-length blond hair hadn't been brushed. Even more shocking, she wasn't wearing any makeup. I couldn't remember the last time I'd seen her face bare. Probably when I was nine and vomited all over my bed in the middle of the night.

"Jesus, Mary, and Joseph, Harper Leigh," she said, eyeing me up and down. "Are you wearing the clothes you had on last night?"

A quick glance down confirmed I was indeed wearing the jeans and olive-green sweater I'd worn to meet Louise.

Her nose scrunched, then she waved her hand in front of her face. "You smell like the bottom of a barrel of whiskey."

I wasn't sure how she knew what a whiskey barrel smelled like since she never allowed hard liquor in her house either, but it didn't seem like the best time to ask. Especially since she was right.

"Good morning to you too," I said, my eyelids half-closed. The sky was barely pink at the horizon. "Why are you over here this early?"

She gave me a soft shove back inside, followed me in, then shut the door behind her. I stumbled backward and grabbed onto the short kitchen counter to stay upright.

"Are you *drunk*?" she asked in horror. "*At six-thirty in the morning?*"

No, but I had one hell of a hangover. "I just lost my balance," I said. "Why are you here?"

Her gaze scanned my studio apartment, well, technically, *her* apartment. I just happened to be staying here, rent free.

"Do you never *clean*?" She picked up a half-empty glass and a plate smeared with cream cheese and a half-eaten, now petrified, bagel from the small two-person table by the window and carried them to the sink.

"Mom," I said in exhaustion and a little bit of fear. This wasn't like her. At all. Sure, harping about my filth and cleaning up after me fit her like a kid glove. No, it was her appearance that was startling. I was fairly certain she kept a tube of Estee Lauder lipstick in the nightstand drawer and put it on before she got out of bed, even to pee at three a.m. Something was really wrong, but she couldn't bring herself to tell me yet.

"What happened?"

She eyed the empty Jack Daniel's bottle on the floor next to the sofa opposite the door, and after picking it up between her thumb and forefingers, she dropped it into the trashcan with plenty of pomp and ceremony. "You're going to destroy your liver, Harper Leigh."

"My liver's just fine." Obviously, she wasn't ready to tell me whatever was bothering her. I'd learned from past experience that she couldn't have a difficult discussion before releasing her pent-up anxiety. Cleaning and criticizing were her typical go-tos.

Check and check.

"Is Daddy okay?" I asked, but her lack of hysteria practically assured me that my father wasn't lying on their bedroom floor in the middle of a heart attack. Still, I felt the need to check. He'd had some chest pain recently, but the doctors had determined it to be stress-induced.

To be clear, *I* was the stress.

When I'd permanently moved to Little Rock fourteen years ago, I'd sworn never to return except for short visits, but fate just loved giving me a big F-you.

She grabbed more dishes and glassware from around the small room and started loading them in the dishwasher. "You're father's *fine*. He's currently walking on his treadmill, something you could probably stand to do." She gave me a pointed look and glanced down at my midsection.

I'd gained ten pounds stress eating and drinking, but being accused of murder and losing everything would do that to a woman. Still, I was far from obese. I'd been obsessive about staying in shape for my job.

"I'll go for a run later."

She stopped with a plate mid-air, bent over the open dishwasher. "It might not be safe."

I narrowed my eyes. "Why not?"

My mother started opening cabinets and closing them with a bang.

A fresh wave of pain shot through my head. "Are you looking for something?" I asked.

"Coffee. Surely you haven't gone to a strictly alcoholic diet."

"Bottom cabinet to the right." I headed to the bathroom on the other side of the room. She wasn't ready to talk, so I could at least brush my teeth and get the rancid taste out of my mouth.

"Why would you store coffee in a bottom cabinet?" she asked. "Animals could get into it."

I grabbed my toothbrush and smeared paste across the bristles. "I don't have any pets, so if an animal gets into it, losing my coffee will be the least of my worries." I popped the brush into my mouth and turned it on. The small vibration aggravated my throbbing head.

Why had I thought finishing off that bottle of whiskey after I got home was a good idea last night?

She pulled the package out and opened it, scrunching her nose again. "They're *beans.*"

"Yes, Mother," I said around my toothbrush, heading over to her, mostly because drinking a cup of caffeine wasn't the worst idea in the world. "My Breville grinds the beans."

"Harper Leigh," she said, staring at me as though I'd emerged from the bathroom holding a bloody knife. "We do not brush our teeth outside of the bathroom. Have you become *completely* uncivilized?"

"Good to know the barometer of civilization is where one brushes their teeth." I gave her the side eye as I turned on my espresso machine. The engine hummed to life.

"Your fancy pants coffeemaker," she said in disgust. "There's nothing wrong with a KitchenAid coffee pot."

"It's saved me a fortune from Starbucks," I said around the toothbrush, then leaned over the small kitchen sink and spat toothpaste into the drain. Not that Jackson Creek had a Starbucks. I was pretty sure the closest Starbucks was over fifty miles away.

"Harper Leigh! I raised you better than that! Is that what they taught you in the police academy? To spit like the boys?"

"They're not boys, Mom. They're men."

"That's right," she declared, her fingers clutching the hem of her jacket and twisting. "*Men*. You should never have tried to become one of them. Look what happened!"

My mother had been truly scandalized when I'd announced I'd been hired by the Little Rock Police Department and that I would be attending the police academy instead of attending the University of Arkansas School of Law so I could join my father in his practice. The thought of me wearing a patrol uniform gave her the vapors. Then, after my fall from grace, she was certain she'd become the center of even more gossip in this stupid town.

But the last part was an educated guess since until last night, I'd pretty much stayed in this apartment or their kitchen since I'd come back. Oh, and the liquor store in Wolford, the town to the north of us, but no one gossiped there. They were too busy buying their own booze to be judgmental of anyone else. Liquor stores in southern Arkansas were a great equalizer, especially this close to a dry county.

I turned off the toothbrush, rinsed it under the water at the bathroom sink, and set it upright on the counter. I hadn't done a good job of brushing my teeth, but at least the rancid taste in my mouth was gone.

She was still holding the bag of coffee beans, so I took them from her and dumped some into the hopper. "I'll make you a latte."

"Half and half in my Folgers is just fine," she said in a snippy tone.

This was the version of my mother I was most familiar with. She'd used that snippy tone almost every time she'd spoken to me since I'd moved into this apartment. Then again, she'd used it with me long before that. Ever since I'd come home that afternoon twenty-one years ago…and my sister hadn't.

Strangely, it made me more comfortable, like I was on familiar ground. The zombie woman who'd walked through the door had scared me. Even after Andi had been taken, my mother had fixed her hair and put on her face.

"You never know when a news crew will want an interview," she'd insisted. "I can't be lookin' like a homeless woman on TV."

She hadn't been delusional. There had been plenty of interviews after my sister was taken. Nothing like the kidnapping of a blond, blue-eyed girl to capture the public's attention. My parents had made multiple pleas with the kidnapper to return my sister.

And he *had* returned her, a week later.

I grabbed a container of milk from the mini-fridge under the counter, then poured some into the stainless steel mini-pitcher. "What happened, Mom? Why are you here?"

My mother sat on the edge of the daybed, despite the fact it was unmade, the sheets looking like they had been in the center ring of a wrestling match.

"It's happening again, Harper Leigh," she said so softly I wasn't sure I'd heard her correctly.

I grabbed a mug out of the cabinet—the last clean one—then set it under the portafilter, pressed a button to start making espresso, then turned back to face her. "What's happening again, Mom?"

She stared up at me, suddenly looking older than her fifty-nine years. Her eyes were wide and haunted, her face pale. Her hands shook on her lap.

"There's been another kidnapping."

Chapter Five

IT TOOK ME A FULL TWO SECONDS to process what she'd said, all while the machine behind me was working hard to force water through coffee grinds. When the whirring stopped, I seemed to come to my senses. I shook my head, a spike of pain piercing my temples, then said, "What are you saying?"

A tear slid down her cheek. "Vanessa Peterman's little girl was taken last night."

Gasping, I stepped back, my butt hitting the counter. "*Andi's best friend?*"

She nodded, glancing down at her lap, then back up at me. "Lisa Murphy called me this morning. She lives down the street from Vanessa and TJ. She saw police show up at the Peterman house early this morning, so she called Vanessa's next-door neighbor to see what the commotion was about. The neighbor told her that Ava was missing."

The detective part of me sprang to life. I may have lost my badge, but I was still an investigator at heart. "Ava? That's the name of Vanessa's girl?" I knew from my occasional social media stalking that Vanessa had two little girls, but somehow I'd forgotten their names.

My mother nodded. "She's twelve." More tears pooled in her eyes. "A little younger than Andi."

The *when she was taken* was implied. Andi's kidnapping and murder had become the defining moment in our lives. Before and After. Andi was forever fourteen.

"The neighbor said she was missing. She didn't say that she ran off?"

"Ran off?" my mother said, becoming exasperated.

Some of the tension drained from my body. "Statistically, she's more likely to be a runaway."

Mom's jaw locked, and a hard glint filled her eyes. "Vanessa's daughter would *not* run away. She's only twelve, for heaven's sake."

"Kids younger than her have run away." Although they usually ran from drug dens and hell holes. I'd seen it happen often enough to know. "How well do you know her?"

She lifted her chin and gave me a defiant look. "She's grown up in our church. I've known her since she was a baby."

"So not well."

An indignant look filled her eyes. "I ran vacation bible school for three years in a row, I'll have you know," she spat out in disgust. "I know that child, and she's a good little girl." Her eyes narrowed. "She wouldn't run away."

I held my mother's gaze. "Well, in this instance, running away is the preferable alternative."

She started to say something, then stopped. She couldn't really argue with that.

I turned on the steamer on my machine and started to heat up the milk, my mind racing as best it could with my lingering hangover. I'd be the first to admit that at the beginning of my law enforcement career, my mind had rushed to the worst-case scenario with every missing child case. How could it not when my family had been a member of the less than one percent? But it hadn't taken many years on the force for me to accept what I already intellectually knew—stranger abduction is *extremely* rare. The vast majority of the time, missing kids are either runaways or taken by family or someone they know.

I frothed the milk and poured it into the mug. "Is Vanessa divorced?"

"Good Lord, no," she said as though I'd suggested she was a stripper. "She and TJ have been married since they graduated from college."

That ruled out a custody dispute or parental kidnapping.

I'd been invited to the wedding, but I hadn't gone. I'd sent a gift card instead. Vanessa and I had tried to keep in touch after I'd left Jackson Creek, but after a while it had felt too painful. In some twisted way, it had felt wrong. Like we were betraying Andi by spending time together without her. So we just gave up.

"Do their families all get along?" I asked. "Grandparents? Aunts and uncles?"

"As far as I know. They all go to church together and often go out to lunch afterward."

"Both Vanessa and TJ's parents?"

"Well, Vanessa's parents and TJ's dad. His mother passed on a few years back. Breast cancer."

"So no animosity that you know of? What about TJ's siblings?"

"He has a younger brother, Travis."

"Married?"

"No, single."

"Does he get along with TJ and Vanessa?"

My mother's face shifted from devastation to concern. "Why are you asking so many personal questions?"

"You had a reason for coming over here before the sun rose to tell me that Ava was missing, Mom." She wasn't one to share personal feelings with me or with anyone else that I was aware of, so she wasn't here for me to hold her hand and tell her everything was okay.

Did she want me to investigate Ava's disappearance?

That possibility was shocking. My mother hated my police work, and the only advantage to my "distasteful situation" was that I'd likely be giving it up for good.

"I came over to tell you it's not safe!" she said in exasperation. "That it's happening again!" She took a breath. "I thought you, *of all people*, would understand what I'm feelin' right now!"

She got up from the bed and started for the door, but I stepped in front of her and took her hands in mine, looking her in the eye. "Mom, John Michael Stevens is locked in a cell in the maximum-security prison in Pine Bluff." I knew this for a fact because I'd checked less than a month ago.

But even as I made the declaration, my stomach churned.

"That man isn't the only person capable of perpetrating evil acts on this earth, Harper Leigh," my mother said, fury in her eyes.

"No," I said softly. "He's not. Trust me, I saw plenty of evil things in Little Rock that had nothing to do with him." I resisted the urge to shudder as some of them played in my head like a slide show.

"Why on God's earth did you choose to go into such a dirty, *vile* profession after everything this family has been through?" she demanded, jerking her hands from mine.

"I went into it *because* of what we've been through," I said, forcing myself to keep my voice even. "So I could try to stop some of the evil in this world."

But I'd been young and idealistic back then. Hell, I'd still been idealistic a year ago, although admittedly, jaded. I'd truly thought I could make a difference, but I'd learned evil wasn't just out on the streets. It was lurking in the places we thought were the safest.

How could I keep the world safe when I couldn't even save myself?

"You're a *woman*, Harper Leigh," she said in disgust.

"Thanks for the verification," I said dryly as I took a step back. "But keep your misogynistic comments to yourself."

Anger flashed in her eyes.

It was too damn early to rehash this argument.

"It's a moot point," I said, rubbing my forehead with the back of my hand. "I'm no longer in law enforcement. You got your wish."

"Not like this," she seethed. "Not crawling back home with your tail tucked between your legs. I can barely show my face in public. People whisper about us as I pass."

I nearly called her out for exaggerating, but I knew the town well enough to know she was probably right.

"I'm sorry about that, Mom," I said with a sigh. "Truly I am. If you like, I'll move out and go somewhere else."

She took a deep breath as she stood up straighter. "No. Your father decided you should move back home, and so you did."

She was right. And it had surprised the crap out of me that he'd been so adamant about it. My father didn't blame me for what had happened to Andi—he'd always said he was thankful he'd only lost one daughter that day instead of two. Still, he'd fallen apart when they'd found Andi's body, and he'd never treated me the same since. I knew he still loved me, but it was as though he was terrified of losing me too, and the only way to protect himself was to not love me quite as much.

So I'd been shocked when he'd shown up at my house in Little Rock a month ago without any notice. I'd just sold my century-old craftsman home to pay for my attorney fees and was packing boxes when he rang the doorbell. He'd scanned my living room from the porch, taking in my packed belongings, and asked, "Where are you moving to?"

I hadn't figured out a new plan for my life, so I'd told him the truth. "I don't know."

He'd taken me out to lunch and told me I always had a home back in Jackson Creek and that I shouldn't be too proud to come back.

"At least until you get your sea legs back under you," he'd said kindly. "It doesn't have to be a permanent thing."

So I'd put most of the belongings I hadn't sold off into storage in Little Rock and moved into the furnished apartment, because even if my mother and I could have survived under the same roof for more than twenty-four hours without verbally tearing each other to shreds, the multitude of memories in the house—both good and bad—were too oppressive.

I knew my mother didn't want me around, the constant reminder of the daughter she'd lost and the current pariah bringing down the Adamses' good name, but my father gave few absolute directives, and she knew better than to cross him when he did.

"I won't be here long," I told my mother now. "Just until I figure out what to do with my life."

She shot daggers at me. "Call me naïve, but I doubt you'll be finding it at the bottom of a whiskey bottle." Pushing past me, she walked out the door, leaving it open. "Don't make plans for tonight," she called out as she started to descend the stairs, her angry clomps on the wooden steps. "You will be at dinner promptly at seven, semi-formal attire. I won't take no for an answer." Then she crossed the backyard before heading into my childhood two-story home.

"Sure you don't want to try a latte?" I half-called out, then picked it up and took a sip. A hell of a lot better than Folgers. The woman was crazy.

Required attendance at a semi-formal dinner tonight? I shuddered at the thought. What was she up to? But I tried to shove it out of my mind. That was nearly twelve hours from now.

But I was up, so what did I do right now?

My bed looked enticing, but the sun was beginning to peek over the horizon, and I was feeling more than a little slovenly after being called out by my mother. So I took a couple of ibuprofen tablets, picked up the remaining dishware scattered around, and then started the dishwasher. After stripping the sheets off the bed to wash them later in my parents' house, I decided to clean myself up next.

I took a long shower, my mind racing over what my mother had told me. While I truly believed that the chances of Ava Peterson being kidnapped were slim, the detective in me decided it wouldn't hurt to check on Vanessa to make sure she was okay. We may not have stayed in touch, but Vanessa and I had a bond that transcended most relationships I'd had. We'd shared Andi, and Andi would want me to offer her friend my help.

I knew I should let it go. The police were handling it. But if they were as inept as they had been after my sister's kidnapping, Ava would be in trouble.

She's probably a runaway.

But what if she wasn't?

I couldn't stop thinking about the break-ins at my house several months ago, and how the only thing the perpetrator had taken was a framed photo of me and Andi. They'd found the broken frame tucked in my dresser drawer.

More than creepy.

I couldn't help wondering if both instances were related. There was no denying that Ava Peterman was missing only two weeks after I came back to Jackson Creek.

What if this had something to do with Andi?

My stomach churned, and I realized I wouldn't rest until I knew for sure it was an unrelated incident.

Time to pay a visit to a childhood friend.

Chapter Six

AFTER I BLOW-DRIED my slightly past shoulder-length dark hair, I got dressed in jeans and a blue button-down shirt, stopping just short of putting on a blazer, instead topping it with a long tan cardigan. I felt naked without my badge and my gun, but I'd turned in both when I'd resigned. I had another handgun—most cops had a backup piece—but I left it locked in my small gun box.

I thought about dropping by the house to check on my mother. She was obviously terrified a new kidnapper was on the loose, and despite the fact that we didn't get along, I didn't want her to worry. All the more reason to go talk to Vanessa and get the facts for myself.

I drank another cup of coffee before I left, and between the caffeine and ibuprofen, I was feeling more like myself. Well, more like the version of myself I'd been before the shooting in Little Rock. I wasn't sure I'd ever be the woman I was before again.

I didn't have Vanessa's address. I could have asked my mother, but I doubted she'd give it to me. So instead, I pulled up social media. I glanced at Vanessa's Facebook and Instagram profiles and figured out she lived on the east side of downtown based on the photos she'd posted of her house. All I had to do was drive down a few streets until I recognized it.

Turned out the two police cruisers parked in front of the house were a pretty good tip-off.

I parallel parked across the street and a couple of houses down, then stood on the sidewalk to take in the neighborhood.

It was a mild February for southern Arkansas, with the temperature in the upper forties and sunny. According to the weather app on my phone, it had gotten down to the low forties overnight and was expected to get up to the low sixties by four p.m. A girl could stay outside all day with a jacket, but it would have been harder for her to rest at night. If she'd left the house on her own, she was likely at a friend's place. Even "good girls" got pissed enough to want a break from their parents. Lord knew how many times I'd wished to escape mine.

The Petermans lived on a street of older, stately houses in a varying mix of worn and renovated. Their two-story, white Southern colonial, complete with full front porches on both levels, fell into the renovated category. Their landscaping was manicured, the bushes no taller than the bottom railing of the front porch, which meant a would-be kidnapper wouldn't have much cover, but there were several mature trees with branches close to the railing of the second-floor porch along the north side of the house.

Branches a kid could climb across to get out of the house.

Or potential access for a kidnapper.

A woman was loitering on the sidewalk in front of the house—probably curious about the two police cars and hoping to get more information—but I didn't see any police presence on the outside, nor any signs of the Petermans.

I walked across the street and toward the house. The woman did a double-take when she recognized me, then recoiled.

"What are *you* doing here?" she demanded.

Guess I knew where her opinion about me fell.

I didn't answer her, and instead decided to take my chances by walking right up to the house. As I headed up the sidewalk toward the porch, the woman called out, "You don't belong here! Go back to where you came from!"

It took all my training in dealing with hostile suspects to keep me from turning around and telling her I was born and raised here and had just as much right to be here as she did, but she wasn't worth the wasted breath.

The porch was clean and in good repair. A girl's bicycle was propped against the railing on the far left side. Was it Ava's?

Steeling my back, I knocked on the front door and waited. Several seconds later, a uniformed officer opened the door and gave me a stern look. He looked to be in his mid-twenties, which meant he hadn't been part of the force when they'd handled my sister's kidnapping. I saw that as a positive thing. "The family's not receiving visitors," he announced and started to shut the door.

I wasn't surprised by his response. In fact, I respected it. "I'm a friend of the family."

His gaze narrowed as he scrutinized me, but then recognition filled his eyes, and his jaw hardened. "You're not wanted here."

So much for holding out hope for the next generation of Jackson Creek police. "Maybe you should ask Vanessa before you reach that conclusion," I stated calmly, my hands at my sides.

"Who is it?" a woman called out from inside the house, then she appeared a few feet behind him. A flood of affection stole my breath. While she'd changed since I'd last seen her— her hair was blonder and cut into a sleek above-the-shoulder bob, and she was thinner than I remembered her—she was still unmistakably Andi's best friend, just all grown up.

"*Harper?*" she asked in disbelief.

I leaned to the side to see around the officer and held her gaze. "I came over as soon as I heard."

"Let her in," Vanessa said forcefully, pushing the officer out of the way. She rushed out the door onto the porch and wrapped her arms around me as she began to sob. She was several inches shorter than my five-foot-seven height, and her face burrowed into my shoulder.

I held her tight, tears burning my eyes. I wanted to tell her everything would be okay, but while the chances were high that they would be, I couldn't bring myself to say it. Too much of my police training still clung to me.

We stayed like that for several long seconds until I became aware of the hole being burned into my back by the woman on the sidewalk. "Let's get you back inside," I said.

Vanessa lifted her head, glanced at the woman, and drew in a sharp breath. I gave her a soft push past the stern-faced officer guarding the door and back inside the warmth of the house.

We moved into the middle of the large foyer, with a grand staircase to the left, next to an opening to a very formal dining room with a table long enough to entertain a large dinner party, but it was the living room to the right that held my attention.

Thankfully, Vanessa wasn't alone, but I didn't expect to find a friendlier reception here than I'd gotten from the woman outside.

Several people sat around the room, some I recognized, and others I didn't. Vanessa's mother sat in an overstuffed chair with a small child on her lap, a little blond girl who looked like she was around kindergarten age. Vanessa's father was sitting next to another older man on the sofa, and a much older woman sat by herself in another chair, knitting. TJ or Vanessa's grandmother, maybe? She looked confused as I made my way into the room. The older men were very clearly irritated. A younger man, in his thirties, was walking into the living room from what looked like a sunroom, carrying a cup of coffee in one hand and a newspaper in another. He gave me a blank expression as though he was reserving judgment until he had more information. He might not recognize me, but I knew him. Todd Peterman III, known to his friends as TJ. At least that was how I'd known him back in high school.

In addition to the officer by the front door, an older police officer leaned against the opening between the foyer and the living room.

"What's *she* doing here?" Vanessa's mother demanded, pulling the girl on her lap closer, as though I was there to snatch her away. I suspected her reaction had more to do with her perception that I was a bad luck charm than my recent legal trouble. Mrs. Hogan had treated me like I was cursed after Andi's kidnapping.

"I'm just here to check on Vanessa," I said. "See if I can do anything to help."

"We don't need your help," said the officer next to the living room. He was maybe in his early forties, with a bushy mustache over his upper lip and a heavy Southern accent that suggested he'd been born and raised here and rarely left.

He was old enough to have been part of the band of nitwits who'd bungled my sister's case, and his response made it pretty damn clear he knew who *I* was. I could have been there to ask if the family wanted a casserole, not if they wanted additional investigative assistance.

"Would you like a cup of coffee?" Vanessa asked. Not bothering to wait for a response, she led the way to the dining room. "Let's go get you one."

I followed her through the room with four-foot-tall wainscoting and large pastoral oil paintings, through a butler's pantry then into a kitchen that had been remodeled in the recent past. Massive white cabinets lined the ten-foot walls, with white marble counters and shiny stainless steel appliances. It looked like it was ready for photographers to show up and shoot for a decorating magazine cover. It definitely didn't appear lived in.

Vanessa walked over to an espresso maker on the counter that looked like it was much better quality than mine...and that was saying something.

"We don't have a regular coffee maker," she said, her shaking fingers pressing the on button. "What kind of espresso drink would you like?"

"You don't have to make me a drink, Vanessa," I said. "I'm just here to check on you."

She turned to face me, and it was then I noticed the small baby bump under her pale pink button-down shirt. She was pregnant, four or five months I'd guess.

"It gives me something to do. I need to stay busy."

"Then just a latte," I said, putting the island between us. "Tell me what's happened. Mom told me that your daughter is missing."

Fresh tears filled her bloodshot eyes. "The police say she ran away, but I don't think she'd do that. Not after Andi."

"I know," I said past the lump in my throat. "Trust me, I understand."

A tear slipped down her cheek, and she brushed it away. "I think you're the only one who does."

I tried to ignore the way my gut twisted. "When was the last time you saw her?"

"Last night. At dinner. She was upset because she wanted her cell phone to call her friend, and TJ wouldn't let her have it. She stomped off to her room. Everything was fine when I went in to tell her goodnight around nine, but this morning when I went to get her up for school, her room was empty, and her window was open."

"Where's her room?"

"Upstairs."

"Where is it in regard to the layout of the house? The front? The back? The side?"

Her hand reached up to the base of her neck and she began to play with her necklace. "The front."

"So her window opens to the porch?"

"Yes, but there aren't any stairs to the porch, and no one goes out there. It's just for show."

I nodded, but truth be told, I would have spent a lot of time on that porch when I was twelve. Andi and Vanessa would have too. The three of us would have made it our clubhouse. Was Ava that different? Or had Vanessa thought it didn't matter? Or, more horribly, had she omitted it on purpose?

You're here to offer support, not treat her like a suspect.

But I couldn't help the small amount of doubt. I wanted to believe that Vanessa didn't have anything to do with her daughter's disappearance, but again, stranger abduction was extremely rare. That automatically made both of her parents suspects…whether they realized it or not.

"Do you have a home security system?"

"Yes. TJ turned it on last night around ten and only turned it off when we went outside to look for Ava."

"And what time was that?"

She ran a hand over her head. "Around six."

"What time did you go in to wake her up?"

"About five-fifty. We looked around the house, then we looked outside."

I frowned. "Do you typically wake Ava up before six?"

"Not most days, but she has choir practice before school on Tuesday mornings. She has to be there at seven, and it was our turn to get donuts."

"Does she like singing in the choir?"

She squinted at me. "Why would you ask that?"

"Maybe she didn't want to go to practice, and she snuck out so she wouldn't have to go."

"Oh no," she said insistently, shaking her head. "Ava wouldn't do that. She's too responsible."

"She's also twelve, correct?" I asked. When she nodded, I added, "No matter how responsible she is, she's still twelve, stuck between being a little girl and a more mature one. Twelve-year-olds are allowed moments of irresponsibility."

Her lips thinned. "Not with TJ. He has expectations."

The likelihood of Ava running away just jumped higher on my likely scenario list.

"Did you or TJ look at the alarm system? Any chance it was deactivated and turned back on sometime before he turned it off this morning?"

She twisted her necklace tighter. "He looked. It hadn't been turned off."

She was anxious, but was she anxious because she was worried about her daughter or because I was asking a lot of questions?

"Do the police think she went out the window?" I asked.

Vanessa turned to the coffee machine and opened a cabinet above it, pulling out a white mug. "They're not sure. They say there's an hour gap between the last time I saw her at nine and when TJ turned the alarm on at ten. They think she could have left then."

"Are the windows connected to the security system?"

"No."

"What about cameras?" I asked. "Do you have a Ring doorbell or any other surveillance cameras?"

"We have a doorbell camera, but it hasn't been working for about a month."

"What about the neighbors?" I asked. "Do any of them have cameras?"

She shook her head, starting to get upset. "I don't know. Most are older and don't like technology."

"That's okay," I assured her. "Did the police ask around?"

"No," she said, wiping another tear. "They're having some officers check with her friends."

"You didn't already do that?" I asked in surprise.

"We did, but they said the parents or kids might be more forthcoming with uniformed officers."

It wasn't a bad idea, but in case it was an abduction, they needed to canvass the neighborhood. Time was of the essence.

They'd failed to do that with my sister too.

"Tell me about Ava. Is she a good student?"

She nodded as she set the mug under a nozzle on the machine. "Straight As." She turned her head to face me with a soft smile. "Obviously, she takes after her father, not her mother."

"You were definitely smart enough," I said, with a subdued smile of my own. "You just chose not to apply yourself."

She laughed, then seemed to realize what she'd done and lifted her thin fingers up to her lips, as though trying to push it back in. "Well, TJ doesn't give her the chance to slack off. He expects better."

I doubled back to something she'd said earlier. "You said TJ didn't let Ava have her phone last night. Was she being punished for something?"

"Oh, no," she said, then pushed a button to grind the beans. Once it started, she walked over to the island across from me. "TJ believes teens spend too much time on social media, so we limit the amount of time she spends on her phone."

I didn't disagree with that, in fact, I was pretty certain social media had a detrimental effect on teens, but that was beside the point at the moment.

The runaway theory was becoming more and more likely. So why was my stomach still a ball of nerves?

"What time did you have dinner?"

"At seven. TJ works long hours at the family business, so we often eat late, especially lately, which is why we schedule it. He puts it in his calendar like a meeting."

"What's the family business?"

"Peterman Manufacturing. Right now they manufacture small appliances. They got a new contract a few months ago and it's taking more of TJ and his father's attention than they'd planned."

"TJ's father's the owner?" I asked.

She nodded. "But TJ is a vice president. He helps his father negotiate contracts and finds new business. He's also the one who deals with all the regulations on manufacturing and waste."

"How many people does Peterman Manufacturing employ?"

"One hundred and forty-three people from all over the area."

"Is TJ's brother also a vice president?"

Her face clouded. "No. He doesn't work for his father."

"What does he do?"

A tight smile stretched across her face. "He works for Sunco Inc. They're kind of Peterman's rival."

"In manufacturing?"

She nodded. "Travis just got them a deal with Walmart."

"I would guess a deal with Walmart is something big."

She nodded again. "You have no idea." Her voice lowered. "TJ works on getting contracts like that too, only he's never got a deal as big as Walmart." She grimaced. "Thanksgiving and Christmas were a bit tense last year."

"I bet." Which brought me back to what we'd been discussing. "So y'all sat down to dinner at seven last night. What time did Ava leave the table?"

She ran a hand over her head, frowning. "About seven-twenty. She was angry and took her plate into the kitchen."

"Was there a chance she left the house then?" I asked. "Went out the back door and you just thought you saw her in bed at nine?"

She shook her head. "I talked to her when I told her goodnight. And even if I hadn't, I heard her stomp up the stairs and slam her bedroom door. In fact, TJ was pretty pissed about it and wanted to go up and ground her."

"But he didn't?"

"No," she said with a grimace. "I convinced him that preteen girls need to blow off steam, but I suspected he still planned to ground her. He was just placating me by not going up then."

"I'm guessing TJ's the disciplinarian," I said.

Her eyes widened. "I don't want you to get the wrong idea. I *do* discipline her."

"I'm not suggesting otherwise," I said reassuringly. "It's not unusual for one parent to discipline more than the other. But it doesn't mean the other parent gives up all disciplining."

Her shoulders relaxed. "TJ has stronger beliefs on discipline than I do." She made a face, and her stiff back seemed to soften. "Hell, you know how we grew up, Harper. Or at least until Andi."

She was right. While my mother had stricter rules about grades than Vanessa's parents, she didn't like Andi and me in the house messing up things, so we spent the majority of our time away from it. The same had been true for Vanessa. But everything had changed after Andi was kidnapped. The citizens of Jackson Creek had realized the hard way that the town wasn't protected from the big bad world after all.

"TJ's parents were stricter," Vanessa said. "And he says he turned out just fine, so he believes we should raise our children the same way."

"You disagree?" I asked because something about the way she said it was unsettling.

She made a face and started to answer, but the machine turned off. She spun around, grabbed the cup, and handed it to me. "The best latte you'll find in Jackson Creek." She made a smile that didn't quite reach her eyes. "Not that that's hard to manage."

"I don't know," I said. "Now that I'm back in town, I may give you a run for your money. I make a pretty good latte myself." I took a sip. "Nope. You've got me beat."

"It's the machine," Vanessa said. "TJ believes in having the best of the best."

He sounded like a narcissistic prick, but I kept that to myself.

"Has Ava run away before?" I asked as I lowered the mug and set it on the island.

"Oh, no," she said, shaking her head. "She's a good girl. She follows the rules."

"Do you think she ran away this time?"

Her top teeth scraped over her bottom lip. "I don't know." Terror filled her eyes, and she lowered her voice to a near whisper. "The police think she'll come back home on her own, and the only reason they're out there," she nodded toward the front of the house, "is to placate TJ."

"Why would they feel the need to placate TJ?" I whispered back.

"He's on the city council. He could make things difficult."
Memories slammed into me hard.

Chapter Seven

MY FATHER'S POSITION AS MAYOR had gotten extra attention from the police department too when Andi was kidnapped, but in the end it hadn't made a difference. Vanessa had to be thinking the same thing. I had two choices. I could tell Vanessa she'd be in my thoughts and prayers, take my leave, and stop off at the liquor store in Wolford to replace my now empty bottle of Jack, or I could stick around and keep digging.

Sometimes the investigator in me wouldn't leave well enough alone. Then again, that's why I'd always had a high close rate as a detective. That and a lack of a personal life, other than my relationship with Keith. But in hindsight, our relationship had revolved around work too.

"Is Ava's room sealed off?" I asked.

Her nose scrunched in confusion. "What do you mean?"

"Have the police denied you access to her room? Have they sealed it off with crime scene tape?"

"No," she said slowly. "I don't think so."

Huge mistake number one, right ahead of not canvassing the neighbors, but I had no qualms about exploiting it. "Can I take a look?"

Her face turned hopeful. "Would you?"

"Of course."

She shot a glance toward the front of the house again, then walked around the island and cupped my elbow. Lowering her voice, she said, "We can go up the back staircase."

I was presuming she didn't want her family to know what we were up to. I was okay with that too.

We walked up the narrow wooden staircase that had likely been made for servants when the home was originally built, both of us stepping lightly so we didn't make any noise. When we reached the top, we were in the middle of a short hallway with doors on either end, all shut. The hall turned toward the front of the house, and I couldn't see where it went.

"Ava's room's this way," she said, taking the lead and brushing past me toward a door to the right. It led to a short hallway that ran the side of the house, with two windows on the right overlooking the house next door, and two doors on the left. The hallway bottomed out at another door, also shut. She opened that crystal knob too and pushed the door open, entering the room.

Pink was everywhere. Pale pink walls, a pink comforter on the canopied bed, surrounded by pale pink organza curtains. The bed was made with a stuffed brown dog up against the pillows. Two large windows at the front of the house overlooked the porch. The sills were fairly low, about two feet off the floor.

A large white dollhouse stood on a table in the corner next to a window, and there was a white dresser between the windows. A white desk sat against the far wall to the left.

"No closet?" I asked when I noticed there wasn't another door.

"It's in a short hallway we just passed through," Vanessa said, twisting the necklace at the base of her throat as she scanned the room. "A bathroom too."

So Ava had a suite. "Where's your and TJ's room?"

"On the other side of the front staircase," she said. "It faces the street too."

"The arrangement of rooms is a little unorthodox," I said, choosing my words carefully.

"It was like this when we bought it before Ava was born," Vanessa said, dropping her hand to her side. "Someone used it as a boarding house in the past and completely changed the upstairs layout, which is why we got it so cheap. We finished remodeling the first floor a couple of years ago, but we were planning on starting on the upstairs next month." She put her hand on her stomach. "We wanted it to be done before the baby's born."

"And when's that?" I asked absently, walking around the bed to look over the desk.

"July. I'm four months along. We're finally having a boy."

I didn't have gloves, so I pulled my shirt sleeve down and used my cloth-covered hand to open a notebook in the center of the desk.

"I bet TJ's thrilled," I said, keeping my voice neutral.

The notebook was full of math problems—fractions and decimals.

"He's always wanted a boy, and I've struggled with miscarriages," she said wistfully. "So yes."

I wanted a better look at that notebook, but I'd need gloves to do it justice. "Will the baby be Todd Peterman the fourth?"

She let out a little laugh. "Yes. His father is thrilled about that. We'll call him Todd since TJ is TJ and his father is called Junior."

A corkboard of photos hung over the desk—a little girl with long brunette hair was in many of them in a variety of settings. So this was Ava. In one of them she was with Vanessa, TJ, and the little girl downstairs on the beach. In another, she and Vanessa had on fancy dresses and were sitting at a table with teacups and a tiered cake plate covered with multiple tiny cakes. In three photos, she was with a group of friends. One looked like it had been taken at school, another on some occasion where they were dressed up (probably cotillion), and another with them in swimsuits at an outdoor pool. There were also several photos of the girl in dance costumes by herself and with other dancers.

"This is Ava?" I asked, pointing to one of the dance photos.

"Yeah," she said, choking back a sob. "She didn't run away, Harper. I know it in my gut."

I still wasn't sure. I could see how Ava might have reached her breaking point with her controlling father, but a girl like her would have gone to friends, and the police surely would have contacted all their parents by now and let Vanessa and TJ know.

Then again, I'd learned to never assume anything when it came to the Jackson Creek Police Department.

"You said TJ turned off the alarm to look outside this morning?"

"Yes, we searched the house, backyard, and the detached garage out back. It faces an alley."

I grimaced, hating to ask the next question, but feeling the need to do so anyway. "Did you check everywhere, Nessi? The basement? The attic?" I swallowed, then added, "Any crawl spaces?"

Tears brimmed in her eyes again as her face paled. "Yes," she finally whispered. "Even the crawl space under the pool shed out back."

We held each other's gazes for a few moments as we remembered my sister and where she'd been dumped like a piece of trash.

"Harper, I'm so scared," she whispered, terror filling her eyes.

"I know," I said, walking over to her and wrapping her in a hug.

"I think the police are fucking it up," she said against my shoulder. "Just like they did with Andi."

"Do you want me to find her?" I asked before I could think better of it.

She pulled back and looked up at me with wide eyes. "TJ won't like it."

I gave her a dry look. "Good thing I didn't ask if TJ wanted me to find her then, huh? I'm asking if that's what *you* want, Nessi."

"No one's called me that in years," she said, fresh tears falling down her cheeks. "I think I stopped being Nessi when Andi died."

"I'm sorry," I said. "Habit, but I can stop."

She shook her head. "No. I like remembering who I used to be." She took a breath. "Will you look for her even though TJ will hate it?"

"Unlike when we were kids, I don't give a shit what people think about me," I said sarcastically, then turned serious. "Why aren't you treating me like a pariah?"

Empathy covered her face. "There's no way you'd kill a kid who wasn't armed. And if you did, which would have been a tragic accident, you'd own up to it."

I stared at her in disbelief. "How can you be so sure?"

"Because I know you, Harper Adams. And if there's anyone who can find my Ava, it's you."

"The police won't like it either, so this will have to be a shadow investigation."

She shook her head. "I don't care. Just find my little girl."

I wished I had a pair of gloves, my notebook, and a CSI team. Instead, I'd have to make do with taking notes and photos on my phone.

"I'm going to need names, addresses and phone numbers for all her friends, and anyone else she knows well. Teachers, Sunday school teachers, dance instructors. The sooner the better. I'm also going to need you to alert them that I'll be asking questions so they'll talk to me."

"Okay."

"Show me which window was open when you came up to her room."

"That one," she said, pointing to the window to the right.

"Do you have an unused towel or something else I can use to open it?" I asked, walking closer.

"You can just..." Her voice trailed off. "They didn't fingerprint anything."

"I can see that," I said dryly. "But I don't want to screw anything up in case they decide to later." I kept the *when they get their heads out of their asses* to myself.

Vanessa walked out into the short hall and came back a few minutes later with two fluffy white washcloths.

I took them from her and used both to grab the handles at the bottom of the window. I gave the window a good tug, but the house was probably close to a hundred years old and between the southern Arkansas humidity and the inevitable multiple paint jobs on the wooden frame, it was stubborn to budge.

My heart sank. While I was behind on my workout routine, I had decent upper body strength. If *I* struggled with it, could a twelve-year-old girl have gotten it open?

I gave it a good tug, and it finally moved about six inches before I shoved it high enough so I could fit through it. That done, I poked my head through the opening, scanning the bare porch. "There's no screen."

"None of the windows have screens. We never open the windows. Paisley has a lot of allergies, so we only run the A/C or furnace."

"Paisley?"

"My five-year-old."

I stood upright in the room. "How far was the window open when you found it?"

"All the way open, like that." She gestured to the window.

"And how tall would you say Ava is?"

She lifted her hand to her shoulder. "The top of her head comes to here now. She had a growth spurt last summer." I estimated Vanessa to be five-three, which meant Ava was about four-eight. Her voice broke. "Tell me I'm going to see her again, Harper."

I looked into her tear-filled eyes. I knew better than to make promises, but I held her gaze and said, "I'll do everything in my power to find her."

She continued to study me but must have accepted my answer because she finally nodded and broke our gaze. "Thank you."

I nodded back in acknowledgment then bent down to climb through. "Have you ever seen Ava open the window?"

"No."

I stepped through, then stood upright, taking it all in. The porch was completely empty, not even any furniture positioned for decorative purposes. Then again, it looked like the windows were the only way to access it and they weren't exactly wide enough to fit a rocking chair or wicker settee through. It still looked like the kind of place a kid might go to get away from her domineering father. Other than the open window, though, there were no signs that she'd ever been out here.

So maybe she didn't hang out here. Maybe she'd used it as an exit.

Curious to see how close the branches were to the porch, I walked toward the railing.

"Does Ava like to climb trees?" A large branch from the oak tree was close enough that a twelve-year-old could make the leap, but there was a two-foot gap from the thick branch and the railing, which meant she'd have to be a dare devil to attempt it. "Does she like to take chances? Would she have dared to get up on the porch railing and leap for the tree?"

"Oh, no," she said emphatically. "No way. She's terrified of heights. She won't even climb up a ladder."

"What about any of her friends?"

"Her friends?" she asked in confusion.

"Are any of them climbers or dare devils? Maybe someone convinced her to make the jump."

She was quiet for a moment. "Maybe Casey. She's a bit of a tomboy. I doubt it would be Ainsley."

"Does she like boys? Or girls? Anyone she's interested in romantically?" I asked as I looked over the yard. With the six-foot-deep porch and the massive tree in the front, it would be hard for someone to look through Ava's windows. Hard, but not impossible.

"What?" she said in disbelief. "She's only twelve."

"Nessi, you and Andi were both boy crazy at twelve," I reminded her.

"I suppose," she said thoughtfully. "But Ava's different. More serious. I've never seen any signs of her being interested in boys *or* girls like that."

Parents often didn't know everything going on in their children's lives, especially teenagers, or in this case, a preteen. If Ava had a crush on a boy—or girl—she might keep it from her mother to make sure her overprotective father didn't find out. Especially if her father disapproved of her crush's gender.

"And how would TJ feel if Ava liked girls?"

Her face went slack. "He wouldn't like it." Her gaze lifted to mine, panic on her face. "But surely she wouldn't run away if she liked another girl."

I didn't answer. She seemed a little young to have run away from home for a romantic reason, but I wasn't ruling anything out.

"What grade is she in? Sixth?"

"Yes."

"Is it a big school?"

"It's Jackson Creek Elementary," she said. "It's pretty much the same as when we went there. Mrs. Donahue is her teacher. She changes classrooms for most of her subjects. They're getting them ready for junior high."

"No middle school?"

"No, it's like when we were kids. Kindergarten through sixth here in Jackson Creek. Seventh and eighth at the junior high in Wolford, then the high school."

When we were kids, Jackson Creek had been large enough for its own elementary school, but junior high students were bussed to Wolford which was fifteen miles away.

"Do you have a school directory with everyone's names and phone numbers and addresses?"

"Downstairs in my office off the kitchen. It's the mudroom, but I have a desk there."

"I'd like to grab it before I leave."

"Okay."

"Have you seen any unusual vehicles hanging around the neighborhood? Delivery vans? Cars that don't look familiar?"

"No, but I don't pay much attention either," she said, then gasped. "I should have been paying attention."

I held her gaze. "No, Nessi. You were living your life."

"Is that what you were doing when you became a police officer instead of going to law school?" she said in an accusatory tone.

"Yeah," I said, turning back to look at her. "In my own way."

And that's when I saw the deep dents on the bottom of the window.

"Shit," I mumbled to myself, as I walked over to get a closer look. The gouge marks had to be pretty recent since the exposed wood didn't look weathered.

How did I ask about this without freaking her out? Then again, she had every right to be freaked out. "Has anyone ever had to force the window open from the outside?"

Her face went slack. "No."

I remembered the upcoming remodel. "A construction worker? Maybe the contractor when he was working up the bid. I suspect they evaluated the structural integrity of the porch."

Relief covered her face. "Maybe. I know he was particularly worried about Ava's room. This side is so chopped up from previous renovations, he's worried they might have knocked down something structurally important."

It was a great theory, but it occurred to me that the contractor and his men would likely have opened the window from the inside, not the outside. Then again, maybe they'd come out through another window in the front. Vanessa and TJ's room?

I started to walk down the length of the front of the house, looking at the windows and checking for signs of anyone trying to pry them open. There were five windows total—two in Ava's room, one overlooking the open foyer, which meant the other two were likely in the master bedroom. The other four showed no signs of forced entry. My hair stood on end.

I was about to turn around when something caught my gaze out of the corner of my eye.

A red ribbon was wrapped around the spindle of the porch, fluttering in the wind.

My heart slammed into my chest, but I told myself it was nothing. I was totally overreacting. Or was I?

Another red ribbon from twenty-one years ago was sharp in my mind's eye, fluttering just like this one.

"Vanessa." I slowly turned to face her. "Does Ava have any red ribbons?"

"No," she said, climbing out the window. She must have noticed my change in demeanor. "She hasn't worn ribbons in her hair since she was in second grade."

"What about Paisley?"

She started walking toward me. "Paisley doesn't like red. She wants pink or purple. You know how girls are at that age. Pink and purple everything." But her last word trailed off as the ribbon caught her eye. She stumbled backward, her eyes round with horror.

I caught her about three feet away, holding her back before she touched something that could turn out to be evidence.

It was my resistance that broke her, convincing her this was something to freak out about, and she let out a heart-breaking wail.

This had just become a kidnapping investigation.

Chapter Eight

I FIGURED IT would only be a matter of minutes before one of the police officers rushed upstairs and they'd not only make me leave the porch and bedroom, but also the property.

Based on where the ribbon was tied, I suspected someone had put a ladder up against the house, climbed up, then pried open Ava's window. They'd grabbed her, then taken her over the side of the railing and down the ladder. There would have been a lot of opportunities for things to go wrong, especially navigating the ladder part while trying to restrain a protesting twelve-year-old quietly. But Ava was a petite girl, which meant someone with any upper body strength could probably have carried her. Still, it would have been easier to handle an unconscious child rather than a squirmy one. Had he subdued her with drugs or a blow to the head?

One thing I knew for certain: the first forty-eight hours of an investigation were the most important, and the Jackson Creek Police Department had possibly wasted at least three of them. She might have been gone for as long as twelve hours. I didn't trust them to handle it correctly.

Dammit. I needed more time to look over Ava's room, search for some sign of struggle. Not to mention, I wanted to go downstairs and look for more evidence that a ladder had been propped against the side of the house.

Vanessa was still screaming, so I pulled her into a sideways hug. "Nessi, it might be nothing. We can't read too much into this yet."

She looked up at me with a tear-streaked face. "Do you really believe that?"

I wanted to lie to her, but I'd never once lied during the course of my career, and I wasn't going to start now. Even if I did want to comfort Vanessa. "My gut says no."

She looked up at me and nodded. She was close to collapsing, but I could see she was fighting to hold on. If she was like most mothers I'd dealt with, she was telling herself that her daughter needed her to be strong.

"Vanessa?" a man's voice demanded from Ava's room, then TJ's red face appeared in the window. "What in God's name are you doing out here?" He climbed out and stalked toward us.

"TJ," Vanessa sobbed, turning to him and grabbing the front of his navy three-quarter zip pullover when he reached us. "There's a ribbon."

"What the fuck does that mean?" he asked, annoyed. He turned a glare on me. "What the hell are you doing up here?"

"She's—" Vanessa started, but I interrupted her.

I held her gaze as I said, "I asked Vanessa to let me see the porch." I didn't want TJ to know that I was looking into his daughter's disappearance, because I knew he'd do everything in his power to stop me. He hadn't liked me much in high school, and it seemed like his opinion hadn't changed much, whether it was because of the shooting or something else. I already had enough obstacles going into this. I didn't need him throwing his weight around town. Especially since I hadn't ruled him out as a suspect.

I looked up at him with an innocent expression. "I love old houses like this, and I wanted to check it out. So we came out here. That's when we saw the ribbon."

His eyes narrowed. "Vanessa has no business being out here in her state. What in God's name were you thinking?"

"If we hadn't come out, we wouldn't have found the ribbon," Vanessa said in a meek tone.

The younger officer from front door duty crawled out of the window next, glowering at me. "What's the trouble?"

"Is Chief Larson still running the force?" Based on a few articles I'd read about a bank robbery case in Jackson Creek a few years ago, I knew he'd still been in charge then, but he had to be in his sixties by now.

The front door officer hiked up his pants, copping an attitude. He was close enough for me to read his name tag— Officer Brent Stillman. "Yeah, why?"

"I'm not going to explain this to you, Officer Stillman. I'm going to talk to *him*. Now either get him here or call him and let me talk to him."

A sneer spread across his face. "How about you go down to the station to talk to him like any other ordinary citizen?" Then he added with extra malice, "Or felon."

I hadn't been convicted of a felony, merely indicted, and the charges had been dropped. But fuck him. I wasn't playing his mind games.

"Tell him it has to do with Andrea Adams."

His jaw went slack, but it only took him seconds to come to his senses and start to argue. I held up my hand. "Think twice before you blow this off. That case was a mess and you've got a city council member's daughter involved this time, not just a mayor. Plus, the press is a lot less forgiving of mistakes these days. Better to play it safe than sorry."

He swallowed hard then shot me a dark glare as he slipped out his cell phone and placed a call.

"Why do you think this has something to do with your sister?" TJ asked, his hands clenched at his sides. I noticed he wasn't comforting his crying wife. He was more interested in provoking me.

"I can't tell you," I said. "The information was never made public, and I doubt the chief wants it getting out now."

"What the hell are you talking about?" TJ demanded, then looked down at Vanessa. "Why did you scream?"

She turned watery eyes on me, but I slowly shook my head.

Did TJ really not know?

Vanessa knew about the ribbon because I'd told her before I'd been warned not to, but she'd been sworn to secrecy, and when John Michael Stevens had been convicted, as far as I knew, the information had still been withheld.

But someone knew, and now they were toying with Vanessa.

Or were they toying with *me*?

"Someone tell me what the fuck is going on!" TJ shouted.

The officer walked over to me, holding out the phone with a look of surprise on his face. "He wants to talk to you."

I took the phone. "Chief Larson?"

"This better be important," he grunted.

Turning my back to TJ and the officer, I walked over to the ribbon and squatted. "There's a red ribbon tied to the railing on the porch outside of Ava Peterman's bedroom."

He was silent for several seconds. "They left a doll at your sister's kidnapping."

"The doll was wearing a red ribbon. And a red ribbon was tied in Andi's hair when she was found."

"Could be a coincidence."

"It's the same width," I said. "A half inch and grosgrain. It's the same." I'd seen the China doll with dark human hair and a white ruffled dress. I'd taken note of the red ribbon tied around her head like a headband. Just like the ribbon that had been tied around Andi's head when she was found.

"A copycat?" But he said it more to himself than to me.

"You need to send a CSI team right away. And get the family out of the house."

"You might be from the big city, little girl," he spat, "but don't you try to tell me how to run my investigation. Besides, last time I checked, you were fired for murdering someone on the job."

"My apologies," I said as I stood, trying to sound contrite but seething with anger. "And I wasn't fired, I quit."

"Semantics. You're lucky you're not in prison for killing that boy and tarnishing the image of good cops everywhere."

I nearly laughed because I was pretty sure he placed himself squarely in the good cop category. "That's a discussion for another day. Right now, we need to worry about a little girl who might have been kidnapped."

"Get the hell out of that house, Adams. And I want to question you myself in two hours. Meet me at the station at ten-thirty." He went silent after that, so I handed the phone back to the officer.

"He said to make you leave after he talked to you," Officer Stillman said with a look of disgust. "He doesn't want you messing with the crime scene."

Vanessa let out a fresh sound of anguish. She was too distraught to make eye contact with me, so I headed to the window and climbed back inside, moving to the side and out of sight. No one else had come upstairs, which I found shocking given Vanessa's scream. Then again, maybe they'd attributed her scream to being an over-emotional woman. But Officer Stillman and TJ seemed too busy having a muffled conversation to notice what I was doing in Ava's room. I quickly started taking photos on my phone, hoping to get what I needed before someone realized what I was doing and had me bodily removed. As I covered the room, my frustration grew. I hadn't gotten nearly enough information to conduct a thorough investigation, not to mention I wouldn't have access to all the tools I needed—like an evidence collection team and search warrants. But I'd have to make do with what I had, which at this moment was my iPhone and my hangover-addled brain.

Still, I wasn't totally hamstrung. I could talk to the neighbors and see if they'd noticed anything or, even better, had surveillance footage. I especially wanted to talk to the neighbor to the Petermans' right, where the ladder had likely been used.

I snapped multiple photos of the corkboard, then got daring and grabbed the bottom of a photo of Ava and her mother. Pulling it free from the tack, I then shoved it into my jacket pocket.

I could hear footsteps in the hall outside the room, so I headed for the door, bumping into the older officer—Officer Weinberg, according to his name tag.

"What the hell are you doing here?" he asked in a snide tone.

"Apparently your job," I said with raised brows. Not a smart move. "Did anyone look outside the window?"

"She's a runaway," he said with a sneer. "Why would we waste our time?"

"Don't be so sure," I said. "In fact, I have reason to believe Chief Larson is sending an evidence team, so you might consider setting up a perimeter and starting a log sheet." Then I walked away before he could come back with a not-so-witty retort.

I walked slowly until I was out in the main hallway, then I hurried down the back stairs, stopping halfway down to make sure no one was in the kitchen. Once I'd determined the coast was clear, I finished the rest of my descent and headed through a door at the back of the house and found myself in the mudroom. Where Vanessa had said she kept the school directory.

Thank God.

Partially closing the door behind me, I ran over to the small built-in desk and started rummaging through the neat stacks of bills and pamphlets. I was about to give up, when I found a thin white booklet with the title Jackson Creek Elementary School Directory, Home of the Bear Cubs. I stuffed it into my jacket and headed out the back door.

I suspected no one was watching to make sure I'd left, so I started snooping around the backyard, looking to see if any ladders had been left out. It would have been a lot easier for the perpetrator if he could have used one already on the property, but unless he'd staked out the place, he would have been relying on pure luck.

If they hadn't brought their own ladder, I was betting they'd been on the property before. Especially if they knew which room was Ava's.

But I was getting ahead of myself. I didn't even know if a ladder had been used to access the porch. For all I knew, they'd snuck in through the back door and tied the ribbon as a distraction.

I walked around the house, keeping close to the side as I looked around.

I could hear Vanessa still crying upstairs, and part of me wanted to crumple with grief. This wasn't just some random citizen's child. It was *Vanessa's* little girl. While I'd cared about every case I'd worked, this one struck too close to home.

The only thing I knew to do was find Ava.

Chapter Nine

I STUDIED THE GROUND underneath the porch railing and found what I was looking for—two rectangular indentations spread far enough apart that they appeared to be from the base of a ladder. I slipped my phone out of my pocket and snapped several images of the markings, then took a quarter out of my wallet and placed it on the ground next to one of the marks before taking more photos. They wouldn't do me much good without a crime lab, but it didn't hurt to have as much information as possible.

Worried the officers upstairs would notice what I was doing, I stood as I slipped the quarter back into my pocket and walked over to the house next door. Hopefully, they wouldn't slam the door in my face.

This house was just as old as the Petermans', but it wasn't as well maintained. The porch had some soft spots on the floor, suggesting wood rot. Skirting around them, I walked up to the front door and knocked.

An older woman opened the door, wearing a deep scowl. She had on a pair of jeans and a black cardigan sweater buttoned up to her neck. Eyeing me with a distasteful look, she asked, "Can't you read? No solicitors." And she emphatically pointed to a sign posted next to the door.

"I'm not a solicitor, ma'am." And here's where it got tricky. "I'm looking into Ava Peterman's disappearance. Have the police been by to ask you any questions?"

Her eyes narrowed. "No. I only spoke to Vanessa this morning when she called asking after her."

Idiot police force. "Did you see her last night or this morning?" I asked.

"I'll tell you the same thing I told Vanessa—I haven't seen or heard anything." Her eyes narrowed. "Who are you? Are you a reporter?"

"No. I'm a good friend of Vanessa's." I considered adding a lengthier explanation but left it at that, hoping she wouldn't press. "Have you seen any unusual cars or trucks on the street lately? Maybe someone who parked and watched the house, or drove past it multiple times?"

"I thought Vanessa was overreacting this morning. Are you saying the girl's still missing? Was she kidnapped?"

"We're not sure," I said carefully.

She studied me with pursed lips, and I was sure she was going to slam the door in my face, but to my surprise, she opened it wider and took a step back. "No sense letting the warm air out. Come on in."

I followed her inside, casting a glance over my shoulder at the street, then shut the door behind me.

She walked into a living room with older furniture and plants scattered everywhere. The room was comfortable, unlike the Petermans' living room, which felt more like a showroom than a space to be lived in. Although, to be fair, I hadn't spent any time in it—I was basing it on the chilly reception.

Two sofas faced each other with a long coffee table between them. They ran perpendicular to the fireplace on the opposite wall, which had a small fire burning behind a metal screen.

She took a seat on one sofa, and I sat on the other, opposite her. "I'm sorry," she said, "I didn't offer you anything to drink."

"That's fine," I said with a reassuring smile. "I've had about five cups of coffee today already." I decided to jump right into it. "Do you know Ava?"

She made a face. "Not very well. Those girls don't spend much time playin' outside. Not like kids did when mine were little."

"But you have had interactions with her?"

"From time to time," the woman said. "Mostly in passing."

"You say the girls don't play outside much?" I asked. "I saw a bike on the porch. Do they ever ride bikes?"

Pursing her lips, she seemed to consider it. "I've only seen them out on bikes a time or two, and not recently, but…" She leaned closer, holding my gaze. "It's not like I'm watching out my windows, spying on my neighbors."

I lifted a hand in a conciliatory gesture. "I apologize if I gave that impression."

Her shoulders relaxed. "Sorry. I guess I'm just a bit defensive after TJ accused me of being a busybody last week."

"What prompted that?"

"You asked about strange vehicles… I saw a van parked in front of their house multiple days in a row, but across the street and down a bit. So it wasn't so obvious."

"But it was obvious to you," I said encouragingly.

"Again," she said, her back stiffening. "I wasn't being a busybody. I take Margo for a walk twice a day, and I couldn't help noticing the van parked there."

"Margo?"

"My corgi. She's full of energy and she loves to shit in other people's yards." Then she hastily added, "But I clean up her messes. I'm not one of *those* people, although I am tempted to leave shit in TJ's yard sometimes." Her nose scrunched. "Very rude fellow."

I restrained myself from agreeing with her. If he was rude to his neighbors, who else was he rude to? Had TJ pissed someone off enough that they'd decided to kidnap his daughter? "Did you happen to see anyone inside the van?"

"No. I could only see the front seats, nothing inside, and there wasn't anyone sitting in there. I thought maybe it had been abandoned, since it was there for so long, but then it was gone this weekend. I guess someone was having work done on their house and they were parked there while on the job. But it was strange that it never left. It was parked in the same spot every day."

"Did the van have any writing on it? Anything to make it look like a work van?"

"It was one of those stereotypical white vans, but it did have a logo on the side. B&G Woodworking."

I pulled out my phone and typed it into a note. "Do you know if anyone was having work done?"

"Half the neighborhood's having work done, but I couldn't tell you who's using what company," she grumbled. "The neighborhood's not like it used to be. When my kids were growing up, everyone knew everyone. We hung out on our front porches in the evening while our kids played in the street. I don't know half the people who live here now."

"That's okay," I said. "Do you remember when you first saw the van?"

She nodded. "Last Tuesday. It showed up after our morning walk and was there when we took our evening walk."

"Do you happen to remember what time?"

"We always go right after dinner, so around seven-thirty."

"You walk in the dark?"

"It's not so dark lately, and I bring a flashlight to make sure I don't trip on the cracks in the sidewalk. It's quiet and Margo likes it."

"So last Tuesday, you noticed the van when you were on your evening walk. Did you see it leave that night?"

"No, but I wasn't lookin' either. But I can tell you it was there the next morning when we went on our seven a.m. walk. I thought it was odd, but some of those contractors like to show up early."

"True," I said. "So what about later that day? The van was still there?"

"I don't think it ever left. It was parked there all day and night until Friday. Then it was gone when we went for our evening walk."

"And you never saw anyone in it?"

"Nope."

I sat back as I mulled that over.

A loud bark came from the back of the house, and the older woman smiled. "That's Margo. She's been chasing squirrels in the backyard. I need to let her in."

"Of course."

She headed to the back, and I got up, moving to the front window. Parting the lacy sheers, I looked down the street, past the crowd. I needed to figure out which house the van had been parked in front of.

The clickety-clack of nails on the wood floor approached me from behind. I turned just in time to see a corgi running toward me in excitement. When she reached me, she lifted up on her back legs, her tongue hanging out as her front paws landed on my thighs.

I reached over and scratched behind her ear. "You must be Margo."

"Guilty," the woman said, and I realized I still didn't know her name. When I conducted interviews, I always started by introducing myself and asking the person's name. The need to hide my identity changed things a bit.

"You're a beautiful, girl, Margo," I said, leaning over to give her more attention, then glanced up at her owner. "Can you tell me which house the van was parked in front of?"

She moved over next to me and peered out the window. "About where that black car is parked." Then she pointed for good measure.

She was pointing at my car.

"And you think it was there the whole time?"

"Like I said, I never saw it leave, but it could have driven off and come back."

"Have you happened to see anything strange going on at the house next door?"

"The Petermans?" she asked, her upper lip curled. "As I previously mentioned, TJ's an asshole. His wife is too meek and mild to suit me." Then she grimaced, probably remembering that I'd introduced myself as Vanessa's friend. "But I've only seen her a few times, and on one of those TJ was pissed off about something. If it had been me, I would have given him a good tongue lashing, but she just took it." She shook her head. "I have to say, I feel sorry for the lot of 'em."

"You haven't seen anyone snooping around the house? Adults or kids?"

"I've seen some guys walking around, but they were talking about what needed to be done to the Peterman house and how much it was gonna cost."

"Did they have a van out front?"

"A pickup truck. Munster Construction."

I typed that into my notes. I needed to ask Vanessa about both companies. "Do you happen to have any surveillance footage of the street?"

"Like video?" she asked in disbelief. "No. Don't even have an alarm system. My kids keep harping on me to get one, but that's what Margo's for." She gave the dog an affectionate smile. "She's my alarm system."

"Still, an actual service is never a bad idea," I said, although I hadn't gotten one for my Little Rock house until after I'd been put on administrative leave. "Do you know of any other neighbors who might hold a grudge against the Petermans?" I asked. "Maybe a dispute over the lawn or the kids being too loud or parking on the wrong side of the street?"

"You think someone with a grudge hurt that little girl?" she asked in horror.

"Honestly, Mrs...." I let my voice trail, waiting for her to fill in her name.

"Celia Watts. Call me Celia."

"Celia, I don't know what happened to Ava, but I'm going to do my best to find out. Do you know anything that might help me? Anything at all?"

Regret filled her eyes. "I wish I did, but I told you everything I know. But you might check with Lisa Murphy down the street. *She's* the neighborhood busybody. In fact, she called this morning, wanting to know if I knew what was going on."

Lisa Murphy, the woman who had called my mother.

Celia pointed in the opposite direction of where I'd parked my car. Unless Lisa Murphy was on the opposite side of the street, she wouldn't have a good view of the house. Given that she'd felt comfortable calling my mother at six in the morning, I also had to assume she'd tell her that I'd come around asking questions.

Still, thoroughness mattered, and some things couldn't be helped.

"If you think of anything, would you call me?" I asked. I reached into my jeans pocket and realized I didn't have any cards. All I had was a receipt from my booze run two days ago. I pulled it out of my pocket. "If you have a pen, I'll write my number down."

She eyed the receipt with distaste then turned and headed down the hall to her kitchen, returning with a pad and pen. "It might be better if you write it down here."

"Thanks," I said and started to write my name and cell number. Crap, would she throw it away when she realized who I was?

But when I handed it to her, she glanced over the name and smiled up at me. "Tell your mother I said hello."

"Yeah," I said trying not to grimace. "Will do. Now, if you could point me in the direction of Lisa Murphy's house…"

She walked me to the door and opened it, indicating an orangish stone house across the street, three doors down. "I suspect Lisa's peeking out the front window at us now." Celia gave her a wave.

Two more police cars were parked on the street, and someone had put police tape up around the perimeter of the house.

"Looks like they're taking this more seriously now," she said, glancing over at the Petermans' house.

"Looks like," I agreed, then turned back to her. "Can you let me know when they come talk to you and what they ask?"

She lifted the notepad. "I'll text you."

"You don't think it's strange that I asked that?"

"Nope. Half the town knows they're incompetent. I feel better knowing someone else is looking into it. I'll help however I can, including not telling them you came by asking questions."

When I gave her a stare of disbelief, she rolled her eyes. "What? I watch true crime shows, and I don't plan to lie, so don't you worry about that."

"Thank you."

"Just go find that girl." Then she shut the door in my face.

Chapter Ten

I HURRIED DOWN THE STEPS, then cut across the yard diagonally, heading toward Lisa Murphy's house. As far as I could tell, no officers had noticed.

I stayed on the Petermans' side of the street until I was directly across from Lisa Murphy's place, a solid stone two-story house. The yard was manicured, and I suspected Lisa Murphy judged her neighbors' less polished lawns. Based on the fact she knew that Ava was missing before the sun rose and Celia said she watched everything, she might be a busybody, but she also might be able to help me.

I walked up to the front porch and barely had time to register that she had a doorbell camera before she opened the door. I guessed her to be about my mother's age. She was wearing dark brown slacks and a cream silk blouse. Her makeup was understated, and her dark, shoulder-length hair was perfectly styled.

No wonder she was friends with my mother.

"Mrs. Murphy?" I asked.

She glanced down the street toward the crowd then back at me. "Well, Harper Adams. What are *you* doing at my front door?"

I needed to handle this carefully. "I'd like to ask you a few questions if you're up to it."

"About Ava Peterman?"

"Yes."

She glanced down the street again, then gave me a smug grin. "I just made a fresh pot of coffee. Come in." Without waiting to see if I listened, she turned and headed into the house.

I followed, shutting the door behind me, and trailed her to the back of the house. From the quick glimpses I caught of the living room, dining room, and entryway, the house was tastefully decorated.

She was pulling a coffee cup out of the cabinet when I entered the kitchen. "How do you take your coffee?"

I stood at the entrance, taking in the older kitchen. A breakfast nook full of windows was to the left, overlooking her back and side yards. "I'll take a glass of water if it's not too much trouble."

"Sure thing." She grabbed a glass out of a cabinet and filled it with water from a pitcher in the refrigerator. As she handed it over, she gestured to the small table and chairs. "Have a seat, Harper. I'll pour myself a cup before I join you."

I sat in a chair against the wall, giving me a better view of the yard. With the exception of a few evergreen bushes, all the plants were dormant, but it was easy to see that Lisa Murphy was a member of the garden club.

She opened her fridge and brought the creamer and a spoon to the table. Sitting in a chair opposite me, she held my gaze. "Are you looking into this kidnapping?"

I gave her a weak smile. "Mrs. Murphy, the police haven't made a determination as to what happened to Ava Peterman."

She tipped her head back and snorted. "Please. We both know that child didn't run off."

"Most children run away and aren't—"

"Don't come into my house and bullshit me," she said in a cold tone. "I know why you walked into the Peterman house, came out and looked at the ground, then went to Celia's house and now mine. If that little girl had run away, you'd be asking her friends where she was. Not asking neighbors if they'd seen anything."

I started to say something then stopped. Kudos to Lisa Murphy for not only being observant but also deductive. "I'm not a member of the Jackson Creek PD, Mrs. Murphy."

"And yet you're investigating her *disappearance*."

"I'm merely asking questions."

"For a child you don't even know."

"I know her mother."

Her eyes widened, and she looked almost gleeful. "Oh, I know. She was your sister's best friend."

Even if my mother hadn't been friends with Lisa for years, it wasn't unreasonable for her to know all of that. Still, it made me feel naked and exposed.

"Are you trying to make a point?" But my mind leapt to that photo again, stolen from my house. Then to the ribbon, the end floating in the breeze. I couldn't help thinking there was a connection between the two things—as narcissistic as it seemed.

She sat back. "Merely making an observation."

"You seem like a vigilant neighbor," I said.

She laughed. "That's a nice way of putting it, but yes, I can be very vigilant."

"Did you notice a van parked across the street from the Petermans' home last week?"

"I'd have to be a blind woman not to have noticed it."

I couldn't stop the grin tugging at the corners of my lips. "Mrs. Murphy, you seem like a very direct woman too."

"Then your observation skills are top notch, *Detective*," she said with a wry grin. "But call me Lisa."

I held her gaze. "It's important you know I'm not currently a member of any law enforcement agency."

"Maybe not, but you're still a detective." She motioned to my glass. "You haven't touched your water."

I picked up the glass and took a drink. No need to piss off such a valuable source of information, even if she was having fun playing games.

"You called my mother before the sun even rose. Why?"

Shaking her head, she rolled her eyes. "We already know that I'm an observant, vigilant neighbor, and given what happened to your sister, I figured your mother had a right to know." Her lips pursed in annoyance. "Now ask me something that will actually help you."

"A little girl's life is in danger, Lisa, so let's dispense with the games. Why don't you just tell me what you know."

"I know a great deal about a lot of things," Lisa said smugly. "And I'm good at keeping secrets that don't need to be told."

Was Lisa Murphy just a busybody or did she use the information she gathered to her advantage? I was going with the latter.

Did my mother know what her friend was like? A second's consideration was all that required. Sarah Jane Adams was a lot of things, but a fool wasn't one of them. Of course she knew.

I gave her a stern look. "Do you know anything that can help me find Ava Peterman?"

She tilted her head. "Now that's a loaded question."

"Is it?"

She watched me.

I didn't like the game she was playing, but I had no authority to be here, and she could kick me out whenever she pleased. I had to play along.

"Tell me about the van parked across the street from the Peterman home last week."

A smile lit up her face, but her eyes remained cold. "It was parked in the street on Tuesday afternoon and stayed there until Friday night."

"Did you ever see anyone in the van? Anyone get in or out?"

"No."

"Do you know if any of your neighbors were having any work done?"

"I know the Petermans are getting ready to renovate their second floor, but they're using Munster Construction."

"And *how* do you know that?"

"I thought we'd established I'm an observant woman who likes to ask questions, Detective."

"Once again, I feel it's important that you know I'm not associated with any law enforcement agency."

Her jaw set in irritation. "I'm not an idiot."

I lifted a hand in apology. "I didn't mean to insinuate otherwise. I just want to be clear on that point so you don't think I'm misrepresenting myself."

She settled back in her chair, sniffing as though clearing her nose of the stench of my insult. "No one was using B&G Woodworking for any work in the neighborhood. In fact, there is no B&G Woodworking listed in the entire county."

"I take it you looked."

She rolled her eyes again. "Of course I did."

"Did you call the police and report it as suspicious?"

She gave me a look that suggested I was an idiot. "What were they going to do other than tow it away? It was up to no good, and I was determined to find out what."

"And did you determine what it was up to?"

A scowl crossed her face. "No. I didn't see who finally showed up to drive it off."

"What about the neighbors close to where it was parked? Did they see anything?"

"No." Her answer was curt, but I didn't necessarily believe her. I wasn't sure how any of this information was advantageous to her, but there was still a lot I didn't know.

I decided to move on. "Did you happen to see anyone lurking in front of the Petermans' house last night or very early this morning?"

"You mean her kidnapper? No."

I nearly corrected her assumption, but it wasn't my job to control information. Still, I wasn't convinced she was telling me the truth. She'd insinuated to my mother that Ava had been kidnapped, long before anyone else had leaned in that direction. Didn't that suggest she'd seen something?

"You didn't see anything at all?" I pressed.

"Nope." She picked up her coffee cup and took a sip.

I decided to press her more about my mother. I wasn't satisfied with the explanation she'd given. "Why did you call my mother?"

"I already told you that I thought she had a right to know."

I considered the timing of my mother appearing at my door and Vanessa calling the police. "Had the police even arrived yet?"

She laughed. "I have my sources, Harper, but don't ask me to divulge them."

So she'd known before the police had arrived. I suspected her source was a police dispatcher. Someone like that could prove invaluable to someone like Lisa. But how did she get them to feed her information?

Not my concern. Not right now, anyway.

"Harper," she said with a sigh, setting her cup on the table. "There was another reason I called your mother." She tapped her nose. "Don't you find it strange that this happened only a couple of weeks after you came home?"

Of course I did, but I wasn't about to discuss it with Lisa Murphy.

I could spend the next hour trying to drag information out of her, but I had a neighborhood to canvass and a shit ton of people to talk to. Time was of the essence.

"What do you suppose they're doing in there right now?" Lisa asked, gazing out the window.

I turned to see where she was looking. Another police car had pulled up to the front of the house. "I guess it depends on which they you're referring to."

A knowing smile lit up her eyes. "The Jackson Creek police, of course. Do you think they're spinning their wheels like they did with your sister's case?"

My heart seized, but I tried to hide my roiling emotions. "I'm sure they're following police procedure."

She released a bitter laugh. "That's bullshit and we both know it. If they were trying to follow procedure, don't you think we'd see a sheriff's car or two out there? We both know the Jackson County Police Department's too small to handle a case this big. Just like they were too small to handle your sister's kidnapping and murder twenty-some-odd years ago."

Twenty-one. I never forgot how long Andi had been gone.

"The sheriff's department was involved with Andi's case," I said.

"Not in the beginning. They only brought them in once it became public." She leaned closer. "They'll try to keep this quiet too. Mark my words."

"Why wouldn't they want the sheriff's department involved? They have better resources. They have a crime lab."

"Exactly," she said, picking her cup up again. "Why would they try to keep this under Jackson Creek jurisdiction? Why not bring in all the help they can?"

Dammit. I'd always presumed they were incompetent, but I'd never considered they might be up to something sinister or underhanded.

"What do you think they're hiding, Lisa?"

She shrugged. "I never said they were hiding anything—then *or* now. But it makes you wonder, doesn't it?"

If her goal had been to plant a seed of suspicion, she'd just transplanted a sapling.

I held my breath, trying to refocus. "Do you know of anyone who has an unhealthy interest in Ava?"

"Does her father count?"

"You think he has an unhealthy interest in his daughter?"

"He's a very controlling man, including with his children. He stifles that child. Expects perfect grades, perfect manners and behavior. He pushes her to be the best of the best in everything."

"Which only makes the case stronger for her being a runaway."

Her lips pinched together. "No. Ava's a lot like her mother—scared of her own shadow. She would never run away."

That was twice now that someone had accused Vanessa of being timid, which was funny since she'd never been like that as a kid. Not even immediately after Andi's kidnapping and murder. "So Ava's a timid girl?"

Her head bobbed in an exaggerated nod. "Definitely. She can't even ride a bike. Too scared she'll fall. Much to her father's outrage."

"Outrage?"

"He had her out in the street last weekend, trying to force the issue, and he shouted at her when she didn't get it right. It didn't help that her sister picked it up within a few attempts."

I cringed. All the more reason to think Ava might have run away, despite the evidence that she'd been taken.

"What about her mother?"

"Vanessa?" she asked, then pushed out a breath. "She lets the man do as he sees fit. Perfect little Stepford wife."

"Do you think TJ Peterman physically abuses his daughter?"

"Now that, I don't know, either with corporal punishment or sexual abuse, but let me say I wouldn't be surprised to find out he was guilty of both."

Shit.

What if TJ had set it up to look like his daughter had run away or been abducted by a stranger? Vanessa had last seen her daughter around nine last night and then checked on her right before six this morning. That would have given TJ plenty of opportunities to remove his daughter from the premises.

If he'd removed her. She could be up in the attic or the basement. Vanessa had said *they'd* checked those places, but she hadn't indicated that she'd done so personally.

In an investigation like this, the parents were always the first suspects, and then suspicion spread out like a tightly coiled wheel. Would the Jackson County police follow protocol and question him accordingly? Or would his council member position grant him special privileges?

"Mrs. Murphy—"

"Lisa," she insisted.

"Lisa," I conceded with an apologetic smile. "Did you see TJ Peterman leave his house last night or anytime in the middle of the night?"

"While I like to think I see everything, I do occasionally need sleep," she said.

"So that's a no?"

She nodded. "I didn't see him leave, but…" She paused dramatically. "They have an alley garage. He could have gone out the back."

She was right, and it was actually more likely. Still, that scenario didn't account for the ladder marks on the ground next to the porch. "Do you think I could review your doorbell camera footage from last night?"

Her hand fluttered to her chest. "Oh dear, of course you can. But it doesn't point anywhere near their house. I already looked up the footage, and it didn't record anything suspicious."

"Still," I said carefully. "I'd like to see it for myself."

"I'll see what I can do." She gave me an apologetic look. "I'm not the best at cutting and splicing and emailing." She took another sip of her coffee.

She had no intention of sending it. But why? I definitely couldn't force her to show me.

"Is there anything else you can think of that will help me find Ava Peterman?" I asked.

She turned sober. "Only prayer. I fear that child will meet the same fate your sister did."

So did I.

I CANVASSED THE NEIGHBORHOOD, but half the neighbors weren't home and the other half either refused to talk to me or didn't know anything. From start to finish, I didn't see any police going door to door, questioning neighbors like I was doing.

Did they still believe this wasn't a kidnapping?

My appointment with Chief Larson was fast approaching, so I headed back to my car, surprised to find the door unlocked. I was certain I'd locked it, more out of habit than on purpose, but it only took me half a second to figure out what had happened. On the floorboard by the gas pedal was the photo of me and Andi with the broken frame that had been removed from my dresser in the break-in last October. And written in print on the glass over the photo was a message to me.

HARPER,

IT SHOULD HAVE BEEN YOU.

Chapter Eleven

I STARED AT THE MESSAGE IN SHOCK.

The person who'd broke into my house months ago was here in Jackson Creek. Were they responsible for Ava's kidnapping or had they just followed me?

I considered asking the neighbors if they'd seen anyone get into my car, but they'd already blown me off. I wasn't going to get anything else from them.

Squatting next to the door, I tugged the sleeve of my sweater down and picked it up as I slid into the driver's seat and stared at the message, sunlight reflecting off the glass. What did *It should have been you* mean? That I should have been kidnapped twenty-one years ago, or that I should have been taken instead of Ava? Or did it mean something else entirely?

The frame began to shake, and I realized it was because my hand was violently shaking. I dropped the frame in the passenger seat and gripped the wheel to steady my hands as I stared out the windshield. If this had happened in Little Rock, before the shooting, I would have called my partner Keith. We would have worked through it together. But Keith was a piece of shit, and I never should have trusted him. I had Louise, but I needed to see how my interview with Chief Larson went before I decided whether I wanted to loop her in.

The only time I'd felt this alone was after I'd lost Andi.

Tears burned my eyes, and the beginning of a sob clogged my throat, making it difficult to breathe. I dragged in a gulp of air. I couldn't lose it here. Not across the street from Vanessa's house. I couldn't afford for anyone to see me break down, especially all of those officers inside.

Deep breath in. Slowly push it out.

After a minute, my panic had settled into a slow simmer and I felt more in control. Freaking out wouldn't help anything, and it definitely wasn't professional. I needed to compartmentalize my feelings and treat this like any other case. Letting my emotions lose control would only interfere with the investigation.

I needed to figure out what to do with this new piece of the puzzle. I didn't trust Chief Larson, but I wasn't sure it was smart to withhold this from him either. If he wasn't investigating, this could convince him to do so, and if he was, this could be a piece for his case. Whether I told him about the frame or not depended on how our discussion went.

Still, I needed to tell Louise. I definitely trusted her more than I trusted Larson, and she already knew the photo had been taken. I just needed to get through this interview with the chief.

I started the car and pulled away from the curb, focusing on the drive to the police station. I couldn't look like I was about to fall apart when I met the chief. I needed something to calm my nerves. I knew what I wanted, yet it would be stupid to seriously consider it. Still. My mind had latched onto the idea like a barracuda on fresh meat, so I when I pulled into the parking lot, I made sure to park facing away from the building, apart from the scattered cars in the lot, and turned off the engine.

Don't do it.

My hands were still shaking, and I needed something to settle my nerves, so before I could stop myself, I opened the console between my seats and dug to the bottom. Pulling out an airplane-size bottle of vodka, I uncapped it and tilted my head back, swallowing it down in one gulp. The familiar warmth was already working as it moved down my esophagus. I closed my eyes and focused on the nerves in my body slowly relaxing. My breathing evened, and I felt even more in control even as self-loathing squirmed in my head.

I was okay with the loathing. I deserved it and so much more.

My hands had stopped shaking, but I was about to walk into police station at ten in the morning with alcohol on my breath. I was a pro at this by now, so I reached into my purse and pulled out a couple of mints and popped them into my mouth.

I was as ready as I'd ever be.

Somewhere deep in my brain, I knew I had a problem, but in the scheme of things, did it really matter?

I could fall off the face of the earth tomorrow and it would barely be a blip in the cosmos. Perhaps a couple of paragraphs in the *Arkansas Democratic Gazette*, and depending on how I went, perhaps an embarrassment to my mother, but other than that…no one would give a fuck.

Get your shit together, Harper. A little girl's life is in trouble.

I wasn't prone to drama and now seemed like a bad time to start.

I got out of the car, taking in the motorcycle parked a few spaces away under the shade of a magnolia tree.

The dark clouds filling my head receded slightly as I crossed the parking lot, and by the time I opened the door to the station, I felt the heavy mantle of control slip back into place with a resounding click.

Freakout complete. Time to get to work.

The small police station waiting room smelled of BO and bleach, and I wondered if the latter was from cleaning up vomit or blood.

I hadn't spent any time inside the building around the time of Andi's kidnapping, but based on the grimy floors and stained walls, they hadn't spent much money on updating it over the years. Not that I was surprised. Small town police departments have small budgets, and most of it goes to the low salaries paid to small town cops. Anything left over is used for training and equipment.

I approached the counter at 10:29 exactly and told the receptionist I was Harper Adams and had an appointment with the chief.

Her mouth dropped open as she stared up at me.

So no ally here.

It was clear that she, like most everyone in town, knew that I'd escaped murder charges. Maybe she thought I was here to confess to some other heinous crime. Or maybe she thought I'd had a come-to-Jesus moment and wanted to confess to the first one, not that there was anything to confess. I'd already admitted to killing the boy. It was the why that was in question.

I decided to take pity on her and gave her a tight smile. "Just tell him I'm here."

She started to say something, then swallowed. "I'll let him know." She gestured to several cheap plastic outdoor chairs in the waiting area. "You can take a seat."

I was still too on edge to sit, so I stared at the photos, framed newspaper clippings, and plaques on the wall, stopping at the clipping of a twenty years younger, grim-faced Chief Larson standing by the lake at a press conference. The headline read, "*We protect our own!*"

That had been a lie, of course.

I hadn't read the articles about my sister's kidnapping back then, although I'd read a few of them since. This one was new to me, though, and a quick scan of the first few paragraphs and the date on the byline told me it was published the day after the kidnapping.

The familiar pain in my heart hit, quickly chased by the equally familiar guilt.

Why had John Michael Stevens taken Andi and not me?

Why hadn't I tried to stop him?

I didn't have time to dwell on it because a sudden burst of agitated male voices interrupted my thoughts. I turned just as two men rounded the corner, Chief Larson on their heels.

The chief hadn't changed much over the years, although his salt-and-pepper hair was grayer and his large belly had grown larger. Of course, more wrinkles covered his face. He wasn't a tall man, so I noticed how he shuffled as he walked.

My focus quickly turned to the other two men approaching me. The first one had on dress pants, a button-up shirt and a tie that screamed attorney, paired with an air of confidence and arrogance that guaranteed it. That arrogance came from the knowledge that he could stall a police investigation with merely a few words to his client, telling them not to answer.

The second man took me by surprise.

James Malcolm.

He wore a brown leather jacket and a pair of worn jeans that looked like they'd aged the old-fashioned way. The dark look in his eyes told me he hadn't enjoyed his visit to the station this morning, but he wasn't going to stir up trouble either.

"Thank you for your cooperation, Mr. Malcolm," the chief said amiably, but the vindictive look in his eyes suggested he didn't mean it.

Malcolm continued out the door, casting me a momentary glance as he passed me—so brief I would have missed it if I hadn't been outright staring at him. As he pushed the door open, he lifted his right hand and flipped the chief the bird without a single glance back. His attorney followed close behind.

"And here's shit stirrer number two," the chief said, turning his attention to me. "Harper Adams. Didn't bring an attorney?"

I lifted a brow and gave him a cheesy smile. I had no idea how skilled of an interviewer he was, but if he was even halfway decent, he was sure to notice if I showed any sign of agitation. "Should I have? I got the impression this was a friendly chat."

He gave me a dark glare, then grunted, "Come with me," before turning back down the hall he'd come from.

I followed, taking in the stained ceiling and overall grimy appearance that looked like it needed a thorough cleaning. But I suspected no amount of scrubbing was going to get this place clean. What it needed was a good coat of paint...or a wrecking ball. Given the budget, it wasn't likely to get either.

The chief led me to his office, which I took as a good sign. I'd been fifty/fifty on whether he was leading me to an interrogation room.

He settled behind his desk, the leather office chair creaking. I took a chair in front of the desk, ignoring the large rip in the faux leather that revealed the dirty, stained foam underneath. I needed to focus on looking normal, whatever that meant.

Resting my arms on the arms of the chair, I said, "What can I do for you, Chief?"

"What can you do for *me*?" he demanded, his face flushing. "What the hell were you doing at the Petermans' house this morning?"

"My mother told me that Ava was missing, so I went to check on Vanessa."

"And you started snooping?"

"I asked some questions and looked around the little girl's room." And then because I couldn't help myself, I added dryly, "Unlike your officers."

His face flushed. "You don't have any idea what my officers were doing."

"I know they should have sealed her bedroom until they determined *why* she was missing. They didn't."

A feral look filled his eyes. "You think you know better than my officers? *You're* the one hiding in disgrace."

I couldn't argue with that.

"Who else knows about the ribbon in Andi's case?" I asked.

He drew in a deep breath and sat back in his office chair. "Your sister's case is resolved and closed, which means it's fair game. You of all people should know that anyone who petitions the case files can get them. Hell, you got them yourself. We can stall anyone who requests them, but we ultimately have to release them."

The Freedom of Information Act was both a blessing and a curse. It all depended on which side of the law you stood on.

"When I got the report when I was twenty, the part about the ribbon had been redacted. Has that changed?"

"No."

"Has anyone petitioned to see the case?"

He gave me a hard stare.

I lifted a brow. "Is that a yes or a no?"

"This is *my* department, *Ms.* Adams. You have no right to such information."

"As the sister of the dead girl and the key witness to the kidnapping, I think I have *every* right to know who's asked for the case file."

He stewed for a few moments, then said, "No one has asked to see it."

"How do you know?"

His jaw set. "Because every request that comes in is approved by me."

"Then who knows about the ribbon?"

"What the fuck difference does it make?" he snapped.

"Because someone is trying to copy my sister's kidnapping and murder, and finding out who knows will narrow the suspect list."

Fury filled his eyes, so I wasn't expecting his next question. "How'd your mother find out the girl was missing?"

I knew I should tell him she'd heard it from Lisa Murphy, but I wasn't ready to rat her out yet. "Gossip network."

"Huh," he grunted. "How convenient."

"What's that supposed to mean?"

He gave me a long, hard stare. I stared back. I'd stared down hardened criminals. An incompetent, small town police chief was nothing.

He blinked first.

"Are you suggesting I had something to do with Ava Peterman's disappearance?" I asked.

"Did you?" His gaze locked with mine again.

"Do you know how asinine that question is?" I asked in disbelief.

"There hasn't been a kidnapping in this town since your sister, and you're back two weeks and look at this." He swung his arm out, gesturing to nothing. "We've got a missing girl."

If he expected me to fly off the handle, he was going to be disappointed. "Are you suggesting I kidnapped and murdered my sister too?" I asked wryly.

His scowl deepened. He knew I'd had no part of it. He was just being a tool.

"I'm still not one hundred percent convinced it's a kidnapping," Chief Larson said, sliding his chair back and resting his interlocked fingers over his gut.

"*What?*" I asked, sitting up. "How can you say that? What about the ribbon? What about ladder imprints next to the porch?"

Surprise filled his eyes, but he quickly shut it down. Had he even been out to the house? He shrugged. "The father says it's hers."

TJ Peterman had just become a hell of a lot more suspicious...only, why would he have put that frame in my car? He would have had absolutely no motive to break into my house last October. I'd barely known him in high school.

"Vanessa said Ava doesn't have any red ribbons and neither does her sister," I argued. "Seems to me she'd be in a better position to know."

He made a face. "The mother was hysterical."

"Yes," I said carefully, "she was upset, but she wasn't so upset that she couldn't answer questions. I've interviewed enough people in my career to know when they are cognizant enough to answer questions. Vanessa Peterman knew what she was saying."

He shrugged again. "You may believe that, but this is *my* investigation."

What the hell was this man thinking? I knew he was incompetent, but this was flat out negligence. "So you're back to pursuing the runaway angle? Have you talked to her friends and their parents?"

He clenched his jaw. "As I just pointed out, this is *my* investigation. You aren't any part of it."

"Please tell me you sent a crime scene team out to take prints," I pleaded.

He moved his chair closer to the desk and picked up a ballpoint pen. "There's no need to be spending money on a crime scene investigation when the girl's a runaway."

"You sent a third police car after I talked to you."

His brow lifted. "Keeping tabs on the crime scene? That's not a good look. Are you so desperate for another fifteen minutes in the limelight that you're manufacturing a kidnapping?"

I couldn't believe what I was hearing. Had he lost his mind? I considered telling him about the photo in my car, but there was no official record of it having been taken, and I wouldn't put it past him to accuse me of planting it.

"Have you at least notified the sheriff's department?"

He slammed the pen on the desk. "How many times do I have to tell you that this is *my investigation*?" he shouted. "Ava Peterman ran away, and that's how we're handling it."

"Are you going to ask the public to look for her?" If I wanted to be in the loop, I had to play the game, as much as it killed me, so I added a meek, "So we can put up flyers and get the word out."

He shook his head, sitting back in his seat again. "TJ doesn't want a media circus. We're keepin' it quiet for now." But he at least he had the sense not to look happy about it.

"Why would TJ Peterman *not* want everyone looking for his twelve-year-old daughter?" I asked in disbelief.

Chief Larson shifted in his seat. "He thinks they can find her quietly on their own."

"Wait," I said in confusion. "Was there a ransom note?" That could explain TJ wanting to avoid attention.

His jaw firmed. "No comment."

While I wanted to believe that was a roundabout confirmation, I suspected the chief was just trying to annoy me. "So if TJ wants to handle this on his own, does that mean you're not even looking for her?"

"Of course we're looking for her!" he blustered. "We're just keepin' it quiet. No publicity."

"Sorry to be the bearer of bad news, but that ship has sailed, Chief. News of her disappearance is all over the Jackson Creek Facebook page."

His lips pursed. "Not for long."

"You can control what gets published on that page?" Even if he made it disappear, people would still be talking about it.

He shifted in his seat and took another long look at me. "How long you plannin' on staying in town?"

"I didn't realize I needed to declare my residency."

"I don't know if you noticed, Harper Adams, but you're infamous. You're stirrin' up trouble around town, and we don't like trouble here, if you know what I mean."

"I've pretty much kept to my parents' house," I retorted. "I've barely left."

"Be that as it may, people are still pretty riled up."

"I can't really help that, now, can I?" I said in a smart-ass tone. "And last I checked, I'm allowed to live wherever I want. Free country and all."

"Not if you're a felon. Or a sexual predator."

This man was really pissing me off. "And we both know I'm neither of those things. I was accused of a crime, and the charges were dismissed. What happened to innocent until proven guilty in a court of law?" But even as the words left my mouth, I felt like a hypocrite. I'd presumed plenty of suspects guilty long before they ever entered a courtroom. I also wondered why I was arguing to stay in a town I couldn't wait to get out of.

"My job is to keep peace in this town, and your presence is rilin' it up." He circled a finger in the air. "You can see my dilemma."

"So your solution is to run me out of the place where I was born?"

A sly smile lit up his face. "It's nothin' personal, Harper."

My brows shot up to my hairline. "Really? Because it sure *feels* personal, Chief Larson."

We locked gazes for several seconds before he finally said, "I know what you think of me. You think I bungled your sister's case. You think I'll bungle this one, but you can keep your opinions to yourself, because this is *my* town." His face flushed as he worked himself up. "*My* people. *My* cases. I'll handle them as I see fit, and you'll keep your damn mouth closed and stay out of it!" He'd started shouting again and spittle flew out of his mouth, landing on his desk.

How had he found out that I thought he'd screwed up my sister's case? While I believed it to be true, I'd kept my thoughts mostly to myself. My parents knew. And my ex-partner/ex-boyfriend, Keith, knew. I'd told Kara, my old roommate and best friend in Little Rock, and a handful of other friends from college, because it was in college that I'd really started to tease Andi's case apart. Larson had been slow to bring in bigger agencies with more resources and manpower to find her. He'd also failed to release information to the public that could have led to finding my sister before she was killed. And he hadn't locked down the crime scene or called in the county crime scene team until over twenty-four hours after her abduction. But no one official and definitely no one in town other than my parents knew my disgust at how he'd handled the case.

Someone had told Chief Larson how I really felt about him.

Who?

Then again, half the state thought he'd screwed up—an official state investigation into how he'd handled the case agreed—so maybe he just figured, correctly, that I shared the public opinion of him.

But one thing was crystal clear: this man was a loose cannon who resented the hell out of me, and I could see him pursuing the runaway angle just because he knew I thought she'd been kidnapped. But would he really put her life in danger like that?

Based on the fury on his face, I'd say yes.

Goddammit.

There was absolutely no way I'd tell this man about the photo and message on the glass. I was even more certain he'd try to make it my fault.

"Good chat," I said, getting to my feet and turning toward the door.

"I never said we were done!" he shouted after me.

I turned back to face him, my face a mask of patience. "Am I being detained?"

"What?" He grew flustered. "No—"

"Then have a good day, Chief Larson. I hope you can sleep at night." I opened the door and headed out to the hall, the police chief shouting after me as I walked out of the building.

While I was beyond curious to know who had told Chief Larson my opinion on his investigation of my sister's kidnapping, if someone had indeed tattled, I wondered if it mattered.

There was probably no saving me. But I'd be damned if I'd stop trying to find Ava Peterman before it was too late.

Chapter Twelve

WHEN I GOT BACK IN MY CAR, I needed a moment to collect myself. The bottle of vodka had glued all the pieces of me back together enough to get me through the interview, but I was starting to fall apart again. Even if I hadn't already drunk my last mini-bottle of alcohol, I was smart enough to know that drinking wouldn't help me figure this out.

I suspected I was working two different cases—Ava's kidnapping and whoever was stalking me. It just didn't make sense for the stalker to have kidnapped Ava. In all likelihood, they'd followed me to the Petermans' and taken the opportunity to put the photo in my car. If they'd been watching me for a while, they probably knew that my parents had surveillance cameras on their property. Breaking into my car at their property would be too dangerous, but it had sat unobserved on the Petermans' street for an hour and a half. It had provided them with an opportunity they may have been looking for.

Ava's case took precedence, of course, but what if I was wrong? What if the person who'd left the frame *had* kidnapped Ava? Even if it was unlikely, it wasn't totally inconceivable.

Maybe it didn't matter. I didn't have any leads on the broken frame, but I had something solid in Ava's disappearance: that strange van that had been noticed by a couple of neighbors. For now, I'd focus on that.

I needed to get out of the police parking lot, so I drove downtown and parked in an empty space on Main Street. Pulling up a search engine on my phone, I looked up B&G Woodworking. There weren't any hits in Arkansas, but there was a business with that name in Memphis. I placed a call to them, wondering how to introduce myself and get them to talk since I wasn't Detective Adams anymore.

"B&G Woodworking," a man answered.

"Hi," I said, my mind still scrambling, and then it hit me. "This is going to sound crazy, but I live in Jackson Creek, Arkansas, and all last week a van with your business name was parked on a street near downtown. It showed up last Tuesday and left on Friday. Could that be one of your vans?"

"No shit?" the guy asked, sounding excited. "We had a van stolen two weeks ago. Sounds like it might be ours. Jackson Creek, Arkansas, you say? How far away is that?"

"About three hours from Memphis."

"And you said it's gone?"

"Yeah," I said. "It left last Friday night, but it struck me as odd that it was parked there all day and night for several days and then it was just gone. I guess maybe I should have called sooner, but I thought they were doing work on the neighbor's house. Then I checked with my neighbor today and they said they hadn't hired them."

"Can you call the police there and tell them?" the guy asked.

"I think it would be better coming from you." I was pretty sure the Jackson Creek police wouldn't take anything I reported seriously. "You said it was stolen two weeks ago? Did you happen to catch the thief on any surveillance cameras?"

"Sure did, not that it did much good. He was wearing all black and had a hoodie over his head."

"So it was a guy?"

"Looks like it from the build, and the police thought so too, not that they put much effort into it other than taking a report." His disgust was palpable. "Did you see a guy around the van?"

"No," I said. "I was just wondering if you had a description so I could be on the lookout."

"If you see a tall guy with a black hoodie, ask him what he did with the cabinets in the back. Took me nearly a week to make 'em and now I'm a week behind because I have to remake 'em."

Confronting the thief would be an incredibly stupid thing to do—not that a black hoodie was enough of a lead for me to find the guy—but instead of saying so I said, "I'll see what I can do."

"I'll call the police there," he said, "although I doubt they'll do much more than the Memphis cops did. But if you happen to see the van, can you give me a call? And maybe make a citizen's arrest?"

"I can't promise to make the arrest," I said, "but I'll definitely give you a call." Then another idea hit me. "Say, if I happen to see it, do you want me to open it up and check to see if the cabinets are still inside?"

He was silent long enough that I thought he was going to say no, but then thankfully, he asked, "Shit, would you? If you find them it would save me a ton of work."

"Absolutely." Now I had the owner's permission to search the van, but what were the chances I'd find it?

I told him my name was Harper and that I'd made the call from my cell phone. He gave me his name—Mike Rivera—as well as his cell phone number, which I typed into a notes app on my phone.

When I hung up, I realized I needed a notebook not only for interviews but to keep track of contacts and jot down ideas. I was about to drive to the grocery store when I noticed a bookstore a few businesses down the street. They likely had journals, and while it might cost a few more dollars than I wanted to spend, it would save me some time.

I got out and headed down to Morty's Bookstore, which had two large picture windows on either side of an old wooden door with a window in the center. All I could think about was how easy it would be for someone to smash the single pane glass and break in. The door was as flimsy as I'd expected when I pushed it open, a bell on the inside window jangling. The shop wasn't very big, but it held the usual tableaus of featured books along with a couple of stuffed chairs by the window and a few peeking out behind the bookcases. It looked cozy but deserted.

A man emerged from the back wearing jeans and a black sweater. His dark hair was a little on the long side and his black-framed glasses gave him a studious look. He smiled when he saw me. "Welcome to Morty's. Is there anything I can help you with?"

"Journals?" He looked familiar, yet I couldn't place him. I guessed him to be about my age. Then again, the older I got, the bigger the age span got for "my age."

"I can help you out with that." His brown eyes brightened as he walked around the counter. "Right this way."

I would have preferred if he'd just pointed me in the right direction, but I suspected he was bored. Or maybe he worked on commission.

"We have several different kinds," he said, stopping in front of a shelf in the middle of the store. "Journals with prompts, bible study journals, lined journals. Take your pick."

"Lined. And cheap. To take notes."

If the request for something cheap bothered him, he didn't let on. Instead, he pulled a book from the top of a shelf and handed it to me.

It was covered in textured cheap—or maybe fake—black leather. I opened the thin cover and flipped through the lined pages. "This will work."

"If you want options, I have a few other styles you can choose from."

I held it up with one hand. "Is this the cheapest?"

He grinned. "It is."

"Then this is it." I headed to the cash register, leaving him to follow.

He slipped behind the counter and took the journal from me. He scanned the bar code then told me the total.

There was no doubt it would have been cheaper to buy a two-dollar spiral notebook at the grocery store, but this would make me look more professional. I gave him a twenty-dollar bill and he started pulling out my change.

When he handed it back to me, his gaze held mine. "You don't remember me, do you?"

I tilted my head and studied him. At least he didn't seem to be hostile. "I'm sorry. You look familiar, but I can't make the connection."

"Nate. Nate Davis."

My eyes widened. "Nate? From high school band?"

His grin spread. "Brass section for the win."

I'd played trumpet, although I'd never been very good at it. Nate had been first chair in the trombone section.

"So you work here?"

His grin turned mischievous. "I own it."

"You do? But it's called Morty's Bookstore."

"My dad," he said. "After my wife died, I came back and lived with my dad until he passed a few years ago." He shrugged. "The brooding widow/orphan thing got old, so I decided to get off my ass and do something. I knew I didn't want to go back to corporate America, so I opened a bookstore." He laughed. "I know, maybe not the brightest idea since the town is so small, but I like it and it pays for itself."

I lifted my hands, still holding the journal. "Hey, no judgment. I'm currently living in my parents' garage apartment trying to figure out what to do with the rest of my life."

His smile fell. "I heard you were back." He made a face. "*And* what happened last fall."

"You and everyone else." I hesitated. "I confess, I've barely left the apartment, which I guess is pretty stereotypical for adults who move in with their parents. I haven't gotten out much. If you heard I was back…" I wasn't sure how to finish my question.

His brow lifted. "You're wondering if you're hot Jackson Creek gossip."

Cringing, I shook my head. "Forget I asked."

"You are," he said in a no-nonsense tone, "but the town seems split on whether you're a murderer or you were hung out to dry."

I cringed a little more. "Percentages?"

"I could lie and say it's fifty/fifty, but you deserve to know the truth. Before you came back it was more like seventy/thirty."

"Against me?"

"In favor." He gave me a nod. "Very pro police down here, you know. Thin blue line and all that."

"So what is it now?"

"It's flip-flopped. Now public sentiment seems to be seventy percent against you, although that's not scientific. Just what I'm hearing." Then he laughed. "And not in the shop, which would skew the results. This is stuff I've picked up when I'm out and about in town."

"You've become a social butterfly, then?" I asked. In high school he'd been pretty introverted.

"A little, maybe. I'm told store owners need to get out and socialize. It encourages people to come to the shop." He gave me a direct look. "Public opinion started to change right about when you moved here."

I frowned. "Why?" I wasn't naïve enough to think I was the most likable person alive, but I hadn't interacted enough with the outside world to piss this many people off.

"I don't know. I did ask a few people what changed their minds, and they said they'd talked to so-and-so, who convinced them you were lying last October and were trying to make the Little Rock Police Department look bad."

"That has to be the stupidest thing I've ever heard," I grunted.

He lifted his hands. "Hey, don't shoot the messenger." He quickly lowered his hands with a grimace. "Sorry, bad choice of words. Regardless, no one gave the same answer, so I'm not sure who started it."

"Thanks," I said, dropping my gaze to the counter as I went over what he'd just said. If the tide of popular opinion had changed over the past two weeks, had it been the doing of the person who'd left that photo in my car? Had he or she followed me here from Little Rock? The thought sent a chill down my spine.

Glancing up at Nate, I asked, "Could you keep asking people where they heard the rumors? It would be really helpful if I could find out the source."

"What are *you* planning to do with the information?" he asked warily.

"I'm not planning to shoot them," I deadpanned, then grimaced. "Sorry, couldn't resist."

A grin spread across his face, making his eyes dance. They were warm and inviting, and I felt a draw of attraction that caught me by surprise. I hadn't noticed a man like that since Keith. "I suppose I deserved that."

"Seriously though. Someone has made it known they don't like having me back in town, and I have to wonder if they're the one who started these rumors. If we could find out, I have a sheriff deputy friend who could pay them a visit."

"Sure, although the farther out it gets the less likely to find the original source."

"I know, but Jackson Creek isn't *that* big."

"True."

I took a step backward, intending to leave, surprised by the realization that I didn't really want to, and then a new thought hit me. Nate knew people in this town and seemed to have a feel for what they thought. "Say, do you happen to know TJ Peterman?"

His face went blank. "Know him personally or know of him?"

"Either."

"I know him from high school of course, not that we ran in the same crowd." He pointed to his chest. "Band geeks and football players didn't mix."

"Yeah, I wasn't friends with him either." Hell, I wasn't friends with many people at that point in my life. I kept to myself and most people had been a little scared of me, as though my bad luck might rub off on them.

"What about now?"

"I still don't know him well. More like I know *of* him. He makes sure everyone in Jackson Creek does."

"What do you mean?"

"I've never met a bigger braggart, especially after he was elected to the city council last year. He takes credit for just about everything good that happens in the town and places the blame for all the bad stuff on everyone else. Ever seen *The Music Man*?"

"The musical?" I asked in confusion.

"Yeah. It's about a con man who's as slippery as they come. That's TJ for you, only he's not selling instruments. He's selling promises. And just like Harold in the musical, when it's time to put up, TJ pulls out some song and dance and slips out the door. Sometimes literally at city council meetings."

"But the guy in *The Music Man* only came to town to run his con and then planned to leave, didn't he?"

"And so does TJ," Nate said. "He plans to run for some higher office. The city council position is just a stepping stone."

I leaned against the counter. "What do the townspeople think of him?"

"I'd say about eighty percent of the town loves him."

"And the other twenty percent?"

"Hate his fucking guts."

"Enough to hurt him?"

His eyes narrowed. "Hurt him badly."

Chapter Thirteen

GREAT. JACKSON CREEK had around 3,100 citizens, so that narrowed it down to about 620 suspects. Then again, about a third of *those* people were children, which brought my potential list down to two hundred. Still a large list.

"Anyone *really* hate him?" I asked. "Enough to jeopardize his safety?"

"Like has he ever gotten death threats?" He shook his head. "I have no idea."

"But is there anyone particularly angry with him? Like he's really pissed someone off with his song and dance?"

"A couple of businesses come to mind. He's trying to shut them down."

That could do it. "Why?"

"He considers them potential trouble. He wants to shut them down for prophylactic reasons."

I coughed. "Did you say prophylactic?"

He grinned. "Get your mind out of the gutter. He claims he's cutting off the source of cancers that threaten to harm our town. And that's a direct quote." His mouth twisted to the side. "I'm telling you. It's like he's using *The Music Man* as his literal playbook right down to the pool table." When I gave him a blank look, he said, "You know. When Harold Hill convinces people that the pool table that's just come to town is going to corrupt their youth." When I continued to give him a blank stare, he said, "Trust me. Or read the synopsis on Wikipedia. One of the businesses he's trying to close is Scooter's Tavern. He even cites the pool tables as one of his grievances."

"And I suspect his real problem with it is that James Malcolm is the owner."

He pointed his index finger at me.

"And the other business?"

"A laundromat north of town. Suds and Duds. It just so happens to be *in* the city limits."

"Why's he going after that one?"

"He says it's a front for a drug business. In this instance, I suspect he's right. He has an actual shot at closing that one since it falls under his purview. But Scooter's?" He shook his head. "That one's harder. It's county, not Jackson Creek, and the sheriff has said on numerous occasions that Malcolm's never shown any sign of criminal activity. Not to mention he was granted a liquor license and the state had to thoroughly investigate him for that."

He was right, although from what Louise had said, the sheriff gave him plenty of grief too. That tracked with what I'd seen at the police station earlier.

"Do you know who owns the laundromat?"

"Ricky Morris. A scumbag in his fifties. The only reason I know his name is because TJ has brought it up numerous times."

"What's TJ done so far to shut them down?"

"Nothing during city council meetings. So far it's all talk, and from what I gather he brings it up in casual conversation. The first time I heard any talk about shutting them down was right before Christmas. TJ must think he's drummed up enough support to act, because it's on the agenda for next week's meeting."

I held up a hand. "Wait. He can't just revoke the laundromat's business license for no reason."

His jaw set. "True, but he'll manufacture a reason, mark my words."

"What about Scooter's?"

"Like I said, that one's harder, but if he shuts down the laundromat, I suspect he'll use it as an example and try to get the county commissioner to take on closing Scooter's." He winked. "While claiming credit, of course."

I had to wonder if Malcolm's visit to the police station today meant the police chief was on board with TJ's plan to shut down Scooter's. Then my mind did some mental black flips. Malcolm had been at the station today. Did he have something to do with Ava's kidnapping?

"Have you seen any interactions between TJ and the owners of either establishment?" I asked.

He slowly shook his head. "No, but neither owner is the kind to take part in the town square ice cream socials, if you know what I mean."

Twisting my mouth to the side, I nodded. "Yeah."

"Why the interest?" he asked, cocking his head.

"Did you happen to see the Jackson Creek Facebook page this morning?"

His eyes widened in surprise. "Holy shit. I saw that his daughter was missing, but I figured it was something innocent, like they forgot which friend's house she was staying at. Especially since the post was removed shortly after it went up. I confess I didn't worry about it. It's not like we have kidnappings around here." His cheeks flushed and contrition filled his eyes. "Jesus, Harper. Sorry."

I waved him off. "You're right. That was over twenty years ago, and I bet the most exciting thing that's happened since is the bank getting robbed a few years ago."

"Actually," he said slowly. "There was a body discovered a few miles north of the laundromat last night."

I'd forgotten that Louise was called out to help with a motor vehicle accident because other officers were working a murder. "And those still aren't too common around here, I'm guessing."

"Definitely not," he said, then paused. "Sure, they happen occasionally in the county, but mostly up around Wolford. I can't remember the last time we had a local murder."

"Happen to know anything about it?"

"If Peterman's daughter is missing, why are *you* asking so many questions?"

"The police station hasn't announced that she *is* missing."

His gaze held mine. "That's a bullshit answer if I ever heard one."

He had a point, but I wasn't ready to tell him anything. He seemed to gather information from a lot of sources, and while I found that helpful, I wasn't sure if he'd keep what I knew to himself.

"I can only tell you what Chief Larson told me."

He studied me, obviously catching on that I knew more than I was letting on, but he didn't push it. I liked that he seemed to know when to stop.

"Know anyone else who hates TJ?" I pressed.

"No…wait. Maybe."

"Go on."

"TJ took Betty Campbell's seat on the council. He ran against her and won. She was the favored candidate during the campaign until rumors about her cheating on her husband started to circulate about two weeks before the election. To no one's surprise, TJ won." He crossed his arms over his chest. "Betty had been on the council for sixteen years, and she was pretty bitter."

"Was she having an affair?"

An indignant look crossed his face. "That's irrelevant."

"As to whether she was fit to run for city council? I agree. I'm trying to figure out whether the rumors that get floated are generally true or fabricated."

"Did you try to make the Little Rock Police Department look bad by lying about the shooting?" he asked in a dry tone.

He had me there. "Touché."

"Still," he added. "Some rumors have been based on fact. Betty *was* having an affair with her next-door neighbor."

"Do you think she'd be open to talking to me?" I asked.

"That depends," he said, then added, "on whether you can communicate with dead people. Betty died right after Christmas. Bad case of the flu. Not a surprise given her age."

"How old *was* she?"

"Eighty-seven."

"And she was having an affair with her next-door neighbor?" I asked incredulously.

He laughed. "You think octogenarians don't have sex? Yes, she and Walter had been sleeping together, but Betty's husband died ten years ago, and Walter's wife has been in a nursing home for the past five years after a stroke left her unable to communicate and move." He held my gaze. "They were lonely. Who can judge?"

I held up my hand. "No judgment." I gritted my teeth. "Okay, maybe I had some judgment before you shared the details. But you're right. Loneliness will drive people to do things they ordinarily might not do."

I knew firsthand.

"So is Ava Peterman really missing?" he asked again.

"Chief Larson hasn't made an official statement," I repeated as I held his gaze, hoping he interpreted what I was saying. "And we should probably let him keep this quiet for now."

Realization lit up his eyes. "I see."

"You seem to hear a lot of what goes on in this town," I said. "If you hear something that might be helpful, would you give me a call? Anything at all."

"So you *are* looking for her."

"I never said that," I insisted.

He nodded. "Yeah, of course. I'll need your number though."

"Yeah," I said, opening my notebook to write my number down.

"Don't rip a page out," he said, looking like he was in pain. "Write it down on this." He handed me a business card and a pen.

I wrote down my cell number and handed back the card and pen. "Thanks, Nate. I really appreciate it."

"Anything I can do to help. Seriously."

"One more thing," I added. He seemed like he genuinely intended to keep this quiet, so I figured I might as well make use of him. "If you hear anything about someone seeing a white utility van with the name B&G Woodworking, could you let me know? It was stolen from a cabinet place in Memphis and they're looking for it."

His gaze didn't leave my face. "And they think it's here in Jackson Creek?"

"It was spotted in town last week."

"You doing some PI work, Harper?"

I nearly laughed. "Something like that."

He was staring at me so intently it felt a bit unnerving.

"Do you mind if I take one of your cards?" I asked. "You know, in case I need to get in touch."

He picked up a card and wrote on the back, then handed it to me. "My cell's on the back. Feel free to call me for any reason. It doesn't have to be about TJ. In fact—" a mischievous look filled his eyes, "—I'd like to hang out and get reacquainted. If you're open to it, that is."

I glanced down at the card then back up at him. "Yeah." I hadn't been interested in a man since Keith had screwed me over. Was it a good sign that I was intrigued by Nate?

But this wasn't the time to think about my love life. I had to find that little girl.

Chapter Fourteen

AFTER I LEFT THE BOOKSTORE, I headed back to my car. My phone buzzed with a call, and I saw my mother's name on the screen. I considered ignoring it, but she'd been really upset this morning, so I stopped on the sidewalk next to my car and answered.

"Hello, Mom."

"You've been gone all morning."

"How observant of you," I said in a forced cheery tone.

"I know you talked to Lisa Murphy."

"She sure doesn't let grass grow under *her* feet."

"Why are you looking into this? Chief Larson claims Ava ran away."

"You called the police chief?" I checked for traffic and walked around my car and opened the door. "Besides, this morning you were very insistent that there was no way she would run."

"I called the station because I had to know for myself what was going on, and the chief assured me he has everything under control."

"Like he did with Andi?" I bit out as I got into the car and closed the door.

She was quiet for several seconds before she said more meekly than I'd ever heard her, "That vile man took your sister, and there was nothing Chief Larson could have done any differently to stop it."

A sharp retort about his incompetency was on the tip of my tongue, but I swallowed it. For the first time, I realized that my mother still held to the party line because to think otherwise would mean there'd been a chance to save her. Thinking he had done everything he could helped her sleep at night.

I closed my eyes and leaned back in the seat. "I'm not going to fight with you on this, Mom. Now, was there a reason for you to call other than to establish that you know I'm gallivanting around town, possibly tarnishing the family name?"

"I wanted to remind you of the dinner tonight. Your attendance is mandatory."

"What's with this dinner?"

"Show up at seven o'clock and you'll find out. Dress up."

"Why?" I pressed.

"I'll see you tonight." Then she hung up.

What was she up to? I didn't have the bandwidth to figure it out, and even though I'd rather swim in a shark tank than attend a semiformal dinner at my parents' house, I couldn't *not* go. I was living in their apartment rent-free.

After I took a deep breath to try to clear my head, I told myself to focus on what to do next for Ava's case. If murders were really that rare around here, it seemed like a very strange coincidence that a body had been discovered the night Ava Peterman was kidnapped. I also couldn't ignore that the murder had taken place in the direction of the laundromat.

I searched for murder and Jackson Creek on my phone, but nothing current showed up, so I looked up Ricky Morris, the owner of the laundromat. His name popped up on my first search. While he'd made the news for being linked to some drug cases, as far as I could tell, he hadn't ever gone to trial or been convicted. This was helpful but nowhere near as efficient as running his name through a database would be. Too bad I didn't have access anymore…

But I knew someone who did. Louise.

I hoped to get some information from her about the murder, but how much should I tell her about Ava?

I pulled up her number and called, not surprised when she didn't answer. Somehow, even though she was relatively new to the department, she'd found herself on a daytime shift. I figured it probably had something to do with the sheriff trying to add more women to visible positions in the department. When her voicemail message came up, I asked her to call me back when it was convenient.

What now?

Even though I believed Ava had been kidnapped, it was still procedure to talk to the people closest to her. Her family was obviously out, but I could still talk to her friends and maybe her teacher. Kids' friends often knew things their parents didn't—like if they'd made an adult friend either in person or the internet. The internet seemed doubtful in this case, given TJ's tight control on her internet access, but maybe one of her friends had noticed a man following her home after school or someone who'd paid her more attention than customary at church. Anything would help.

I also needed to find out more about the laundromat. If TJ was messing with criminals, he might have naïvely—or not—jumped into the frying pan. Kidnapping a family member to shut someone up wasn't outside the realm of possibility, especially since TJ planned to bring up shutting down Suds and Duds at next week's city council meeting.

I should also conduct an informal interview with James Malcolm. TJ was going after him too, after all, and he'd been at the station earlier.

No, I wasn't ready to go back to Scooter's.

I considered my other two options for a few seconds, then decided going to the laundromat won out since it sounded like the laundromat was first on TJ's shit list. While I didn't expect to get any real information, I could at least look around and get a feel for the place.

After a fifteen-minute drive up Highway 24, I pulled into the parking lot and took note of the two cars in the lot. I parked next to a beat-up Ford Taurus and headed inside.

The space was gray and dingy and looked like it hadn't been updated since it was built, probably a good forty or fifty years ago based on the look of the washers and dryers lining both sides of the walls. If Ricky Morris was making any money from this place, he wasn't reinvesting it.

An older man sat in a plastic chair next to two tumbling dryers, a laundry basket on wheels parked in front of him. He didn't seem to notice me walk in, his intense gaze on a flat-screen TV that hung on a wall—the only thing inside the building that looked younger than twenty years old.

In the corner was a window to a back room, with a sign overhead offering personal services. I headed that direction, realizing I had to take a different approach than what I would have used if I were wearing a badge.

A man in his late teens to early twenties sat in a chair behind the counter, watching something on his phone with his feet kicked up on the desk in front of him. He was wearing jeans and a T-shirt with the logo of some obscure band. His dark brown hair was long enough to touch his collar. He looked like he was attempting to grow a beard and a mustache but struggling to pull it off.

I rested my hand on the counter and tried my best to make my voice sound inquiring and not authoritative. "I have a few questions."

He glanced up, looking annoyed. "It's a laundromat. What's there to ask?"

"Buster!" a man shouted from the back. "Customer service!"

Buster offered me a weak smile, dropping his feet from the desk and turning to face me. "What would you like to know?" he asked in an overly polite tone that didn't reach his eyes.

I looked for some sign of recognition now that he'd really looked at me, but all I saw was not so thinly veiled annoyance.

"I'm new to the area," I said. "My apartment doesn't have a washer or dryer, so I'm looking for a laundromat. What are your hours?"

He looked at me like I was an imbecile and gestured toward the front. "As it says on the door, we're open from seven a.m. until midnight."

"Wow. You're open pretty late." Suspiciously late given the low population in the area.

"We're a full-service laundromat," he said with a cheesy grin that looked like it was part of the spiel he'd learned when he was hired. "We try to accommodate all manner of customers with a variety of services." He handed me a laminated rectangular flier. The corners were curling inward, and it looked dull from use and oily fingers. I was going to need to coat my hands in multiple layers of sanitizer when I left. The services listed on the menu were all pretty standard for a laundry service with the exception of dry cleaning. I could use that to my advantage.

I handed it back to him and leaned closer. "I hear that you have a few services not listed on the card."

His brow shot up, and he went from looking annoyed to wary. "Nope, that pretty much covers it."

His body language told me all I needed to know. I sat up straight. "Aren't you the only laundromat in Jackson Creek? I would think you'd offer dry cleaning."

His shoulders relaxed. "You have to go to Wolford for that."

"You really should consider adding it to your services," I said with a sigh. "You could save your clients the drive."

"Nobody gets dry cleaning anymore, lady," the guy spat out. "Why would we do that?"

"To continue providing such excellent customer service?" I asked with forced politeness, letting my voice rise at the end.

A door opened behind Buster, and a big burly man walked out, his face red.

I took an involuntary step back even though there was a counter between us.

"Buster," he grunted, his voice confirming he was the one who'd admonished the guy before. "Take a break."

"But—"

"*Now.*"

Buster scurried through the door, shutting it, while the big guy turned his full attention on me. "You don't look like the dry cleaning type."

"Is there a type?"

He ignored my question. "You look like the just crawled out of the gutter after shooting a citizen type."

Shit. So Mountain Man recognized me. And based on what I'd discovered during my hasty investigation, Mountain Man was none other than Ricky Morris himself.

"We both know you no longer have a badge to hide behind and rumor has it you prefer the bottle to pills." He stepped up to the counter, bending over to see me through the window. "So what the fuck are you doing here?"

So all my trips to Wolford's liquor store hadn't gone unnoticed. Had it become part of the rumor mill gossip, or was Ricky Morris watching me?

I wasn't about to tell this guy why I was really here, but I could tell him a partially true reason. "Honestly? I heard about the council meeting next week and TJ's attempt to shut you down. I wanted to see the place for myself before deciding whether to agree with him or not."

"You're not even a citizen of Jackson Creek," he grunted. "You have no say one way or the other. So try again. Why. Are. You. Here?" The last four words sounded like they were ground out through his teeth.

I held his intense gaze. "The laundry part is true. I'm scoping out options, so I figured I'd kill two birds with one stone."

He crossed his arms over his chest. "Get out."

"What?"

He slowly unfolded his arms and pointed to the door with a big beefy finger. "Leave the premises now or I'll throw you out."

I had no doubts that he would.

"Good to see where Buster got his great customer service skills," I said wryly, then took several steps backward before heading to the door. I didn't like turning my back on this guy, but I couldn't back up the entire way to the door.

Once I got outside, I got in my car and started it up, immediately locking the door.

My hands shook on the steering wheel, and I told myself it was from my rattled nerves and not my sudden need for a drink.

What had I learned here? That TJ was likely right about Suds and Duds being a hub for drug distribution, but I suspected that was only the tip of the iceberg. You couldn't use a storefront to move all your product. It just wasn't realistic.

Unless the police chief turned a blind eye to what you were doing.

Shit. Had that been happening? While I thought Chief Larson was a babbling, arrogant idiot, I didn't know him well enough to determine whether he'd turn a blind eye to illegal activity.

My phone rang and I pulled it out of my pocket, relieved to see Louise's name on the screen. I pulled out of my parking space and answered using my car's Bluetooth as I headed back to town.

"Sorry about last night," Louise said when I answered. "I've never been called in while off duty before, but the sheriff's department is spread a little thin and well…"

"Don't worry about it," I assured her. "That's not why I called."

"Okay."

"I have a huge favor to ask."

"What is it?" she asked without hesitation.

Start with the small favor and work my way up.

"Last week there was a van parked in a neighborhood close to Jackson Creek's downtown. It was there for multiple days, day and night, and then it disappeared. The logo on the side said B&G Woodworking. Turns out that van was stolen from a business in Memphis two weeks ago. Could you maybe spread the word that the van's in the area and ask the other deputies to keep an eye out for it?" I hastily added, "The owner had some custom cabinets in the back and he's hoping to get them back."

She was silent for several seconds, long enough for me to make sure our call hadn't been disconnected.

"Do I want to know how you got involved in this?"

"It depends on if you want to know officially or unofficially."

"Crap. What are you messed up in?"

"I haven't done anything wrong," I protested defensively.

"Harper, I never said you did, but you have to admit it's an unusual request for a civilian. Especially since your parents don't live near downtown."

It was my turn to pause. I still hadn't decided whether to tell her what I was really up to, but if there was anyone I could trust, it was Louise. She'd stood beside me in Little Rock when no one else would. "Have you heard of TJ Peterman?"

"Who hasn't?" she scoffed. "The asshole's trying to make a name for himself. All bluster and ego."

"His twelve-year-old daughter has been kidnapped."

"*What?* When? I'm on duty and haven't heard anything about it."

"And you won't, because Chief Larson and TJ Peterman are declaring her a runaway and have agreed not to announce it to the public."

"Wait. Back up a few steps." She paused. "I'm about to take a lunch break. Can you meet me somewhere so we can discuss it in person?"

"As long as it's not anywhere in Jackson Creek," I said. "I can't afford for anyone to overhear us. How about in Wolford?"

"I'm not anywhere near there," she said. "I know we were there just last night, but how about Scooter's Tavern? They have a good food menu, and it never hurts for a uniformed officer to hang out inside to let them know we're watching."

I didn't really want to go back yet, not after my humiliating confrontation with Malcolm, but I'd already decided I needed to try and talk with him. It wouldn't hurt to go back and check the place out with a new intention. And the place also had booths, which would help make our conversation more discreet.

"Sure, but I'm a good twenty minutes away."

"I'll be there in ten and order for you. What would you like?"

"A burger sounds good." Along with an icy cold beer.

Chapter Fifteen

THE PARKING LOT AT SCOOTER'S had more cars than I'd expected. A good half of them were work trucks and vans. It was no surprise Malcolm catered to the blue-collar working crowd. Then again, most of Lone County fit that description. Louise's Lone County Sheriff's cruiser stuck out like a sore thumb.

Louise was in the same booth as the night before, only her long, dark hair was pulled back into a low bun, and she was wearing her light brown uniform. A plate with a half-eaten sandwich and the remnants of fries sat on the table in front of her, along with a half-empty glass of what looked like iced tea.

She gave me an apologetic look. "Sorry I started without you, but I never know if I'll get a call."

"Understood. I remember all too well," I said as I slid into the seat opposite her, then glanced down at the plate of burger and fries in front of me. "This looks good."

"Best in the county, everyone says so."

I lifted a brow. "It's Lone County. Is it really that hard to be the best here?"

She shook her head, her dark brown eyes dancing. "Just try the damn thing."

I picked up the burger took a bite, unable to stop my moan. My life might have been in the shitter, but I appreciated good food when I tasted it.

"See?" Her eyes lit up with vindication. "Told you."

"So you come here a lot?" I asked despite the fact my mouth was half full.

"Often enough for the daytime waitresses to know me." Her eyes were locked on something past me, and I turned to see a waitress heading over to our table.

The waitress stopped next to us, her hand on her hip. She looked like she couldn't be a day over twenty. Her bright blond hair hung to her shoulders in bouncy curls and her blue eyes shone with friendliness. "How's that club sandwich, Deputy Martin?" she asked in a sweet voice.

"Delicious as always, Kylie. My compliments to Petey."

Kylie beamed. She'd been pretty before, but now she was radiant. I wouldn't be surprised if she was part of the reason all the men spread around the dining room were here for lunch.

She turned to me. "Deputy Martin ordered your food for you, but we didn't know what you wanted to drink."

Everything in me screamed to order a beer, because it would be the perfect accompaniment to a juicy burger and fries, but I was working a case. And Louise was here. And—

"Iced tea would be great," I said. "Unsweet."

"Coming right up," she said as she turned and flounced away.

"She's cute," I said as I picked up a fry.

Louise flashed me a grin. "The patrons love her, but Malcolm's *very* protective of her. If any of them try anything inappropriate, he's on them like a tick to a coon dog."

"They're in a relationship?" I asked in surprise. She was young enough to be his daughter.

"I don't know. He's protective of all of his staff—he doesn't allow any bullshit—but especially so with her."

"There has to be a story there," I said, my gaze following her as she walked behind the bar to fill a glass with ice. I let my gaze linger behind the bar, looking for Malcolm. I found him, pulling a beer, and his gaze was directly on me. Shame burned into me from our interaction last night, but I was still curious about his visit to the police station earlier. Our eyes locked for a second before my shame won out. I jerked my gaze away and stuffed a fry in my mouth.

"I'm sure there is," Louise said, "but one mystery at a time. Starting with your sudden fascination with a stolen van," she leaned closer and lowered her voice, "and your statement that TJ Peterman's daughter was kidnapped."

I swallowed the fry in my mouth.

She held my gaze. "I double checked, and we haven't heard anything about a kidnapping."

My heart slammed into my throat as I practically vaulted across the table in panic. "You didn't directly ask anyone, did you?"

I needed to stay under the radar. Sure, I wanted the sheriff's department to be working Ava's kidnapping—hell, I wanted the FBI to be working her case—but they weren't. So I was. If Chief Larson caught wind, he could try to make me stop.

"No, I just checked what cases were open, but even if I hadn't, I would have heard about it if there was an investigation. Kidnappings aren't all that common around here. Especially ones involving kids." Her face blanched. "Shit, Harper. Sorry."

I waved her off, relief flooding through me. "The girl's mother was my sister's best friend."

Louise's face paled.

"A neighbor called my mother early this morning, and I went over to check on Vanessa—the missing girl's mother. She told me the police were acting like Ava was a runaway, but when I went upstairs to check over her room, which hadn't been sealed off, I found a red ribbon tied to the upstairs porch railing."

Confusion clouded her eyes.

"A red ribbon was significant to my sister's case," I said, dropping my gaze to my plate and picking up a fry. "And it wasn't made public."

Louise gasped, then quickly recovered. "Shit, Harper."

I glanced back up. "I made sure Chief Larson knew, but he told me they were treating it as a runaway and to butt out."

"How do they explain the ribbon?"

"TJ says it belongs to Ava, that's the girl's name, but Vanessa insisted neither Ava nor her sister have red ribbons."

Louise made a face that suggested she might not be totally on board with my theory. "I can see how it looks like a kidnapping, but—"

"You know the photo that was stolen from my house in Little Rock? I found it in my car this morning after I talked to some neighbors on the Petermans' street."

She dropped her sandwich onto her plate, a piece of lettuce falling onto the table. "*What?*"

"A note was handwritten in marker on the glass saying *It should have been you.* And I know it's the same photo. Same broken frame and everything."

She planted both hands on the table, palms against the surface. "What does that mean?"

"I'm guessing they were referring to my sister or Ava." A new thought hit me. "Or maybe they meant I should be dead and not the kid I killed." I shook my head, the little food in my stomach churning. "It's too vague to know for sure."

She brushed off her hands with her napkin, concern wrinkling her brow. "Do you want to file a report?"

"Are you serious?" I scoffed. "After what happened in Little Rock? Hard pass." While Louise believed my home in Little Rock had been broken into multiple times, everyone else had insinuated I was making it up. Poor, crazy Harper Adams. She

cracked one day, and look what's become of her. No, I wasn't
going down that path again.

"This isn't Little Rock," she insisted.

"Maybe, but Chief Larson isn't my biggest fan. In fact, he
sort of tried to run me out of town." I picked up a fry and took
a bite off the end.

Her eyes flew wide. "He did *what?*"

"He said my presence was riling up the good citizens of
Jackson Creek and hinted that the sooner I left town, the better."
I popped the fry into my mouth and watched her reaction.

Her cheeks flushed as her eyes narrowed. "You've got to be
kidding me."

I shrugged my shoulders with a wry grin. "I'm infamous."

"But—"

I cut her off. "So you see my dilemma. The chief wouldn't
exactly be open to my report. Not entirely unlike what happened
in Little Rock."

She sat back in her seat, some of the fight bleeding out of
her.

"I think it's safe to presume the person who broke into my
house in Little Rock is the same person who planted the framed
photo and note in my car. The real question is if they're tied to
Ava's disappearance or if they stalked me here and took
advantage of my car being parked for an hour on the Petermans'
street."

"Has this person tried to contact you before?"

I shook my head. "No. And the break-ins stopped after the
photo was stolen from my dresser drawer. That was last October.
Nearly four months ago."

"Was there anyone in Jackson Creek who was obsessed
with your sister's case?" Louise asked.

"*Everyone* was obsessed with her case. But if you're asking
if one of the people in town has the potential to stalk me…" I

pushed out a sigh. "I have no idea. I spoke to a guy I went to high school with, and he told me that right about the time I came back into town, the tide of public opinion about me started to change."

"How so?" she asked, tilting her head.

"He said that most people approved of the way I'd handled the situation in Little Rock, but when I came back to town, rumors started to spread that I'd lied about the gun and was trying to make the Little Rock Police Department look bad."

Her nose scrunched. "That's nearly the stupidest thing I've ever heard."

"I asked Nate if he knew who'd started spreading the rumors. He didn't, but he said he'd try to find out."

"Do you think the person who left the framed photo was just trying to run you out of town?"

I shook my head. "I don't see how that could be the master plan. Last October, I had no intention of coming back to Jackson Creek. They'd have to be playing some crazy long game to steal the photo on the presumption that I might come back and they'd need to run me off. Besides, if someone wants me out, there are far easier ways."

"I don't know," she said with a laugh. "You're pretty stubborn."

I picked up another fry. "True, but still…"

"That's not why they stole the photo," Louise said. "I'm worried you're in danger."

I shook my head. While I could admit to myself that the stalker's behavior worried me, I wasn't going back to hiding in my parents' garage apartment. After four months, I finally had a job to do, and it felt good to be doing something other than wallowing in guilt and shame. This was a chance to atone for my sins. I'd killed one kid, but maybe I could save another. "I'm not so sure. They had plenty of time and opportunity in Little Rock.

The real question is if they're responsible for Ava's disappearance. It's pretty coincidental that it's *Vanessa's* daughter. Especially since Vanessa was supposed to be with Andi the day she was kidnapped. Not me."

"Shit. I didn't know that."

"Most people don't."

It should have been you.

Chapter Sixteen

KYLIE RETURNED WITH MY GLASS OF TEA and set it on the table. "Everything okay here, ladies? It's as silent as a tomb."

Louise flashed her a smile. "Great. We're just talking work stuff."

"Sorry to interrupt," Kylie said with a cringe.

Louise smiled at her. "Don't worry, Kylie. You didn't. Thanks for bringing Harper's drink."

Kylie started to walk away, then turned back and put a hand on the table. "Say, Deputy Martin. Have you heard anything about that murder last night?"

"I've told you a million times, it's Louise," she said with a smile, then turned sober. "But I'm sorry to say that I can't really talk about it."

Kylie's face fell. "It's just that my cousin didn't come home last night."

"Oh," Louise said with a frown. "Have you notified the sheriff's department?"

"It ain't been long enough," Kylie said, her eyes misting over. "My other cousin saw him late yesterday afternoon, so it ain't even been twenty-four hours."

"What's his name?"

"Chuck Cunningham, but he mostly goes by Chowder."

The corner of Louise's mouth quirked up. "I suspect there's a story there."

Kylie made a face, then released a short laugh. "A disgusting one involving vomit."

Laughing, Louise held up her hands. "Enough said, but you know you can still contact the non-emergency number and make sure we're aware he's missing." When Kylie remained silent, Louise reached into the front pocket of her shirt and pulled out a business card. "I hope he shows up soon, but if you haven't heard from him by tonight, call me on my cell and I'll come take the report myself."

Kylie took the card and looked it over before sliding it into her back jeans pocket. "Thank you, Deputy Martin."

"*Louise*. And no problem, but for your family's sake, I hope I don't hear from you."

"Me too."

Kylie walked over to a group of patrons a couple of booths down, asking if they needed anything. Louise watched her for several seconds before turning back to me, a guilty look in her eyes.

"You know more than you told her."

She pushed out a sigh. "True, but not much. The sheriff's keeping a tight rein on this case."

"Was her cousin involved?"

"I know he's not the victim, but I don't know about his involvement. I'll ask a few questions."

"Do you know if it had anything to do with the laundromat north of Jackson Creek? Suds and Duds? I heard the body was found a few miles from it."

Her brows lifted. "How do you know that?"

I told her what I'd learned from Nate about TJ Peterman going after the laundromat and Scooter's. "I don't know," I said, "it seems a bit suspicious that TJ wants to keep his daughter's disappearance a secret after he's publicly and aggressively trying to shut down the laundromat, an alleged site of drug distribution."

Her mouth pressed into a firm line. "Agreed. From what I've learned, the sheriff's department has long suspected that Suds and Duds is a hub for drugs, but while they've arrested a few low-level dealers, the perps have never ratted out the Morris brothers."

"That's weird," I said with a frown. "You can usually get at least one of them to break. Are the Morris brothers making threats or promises to buy their silence?"

"Maybe both?" Louise suggested. "I haven't been around long enough to make an educated guess. But you're right. This all feels related." She glanced around, then leaned forward and lowered her voice. "The victim was an alleged off the books employee of the Morrises, but no one's proven it yet."

"And he was killed the night Ava Peterman was either kidnapped or ran away."

"She," Louise whispered across the table. "The victim was a she, which is how I know for certain it's not Chowder Cunningham." She cringed. "But I'm pretty sure he has ties to the Morrises."

"You think he had something to do with the murder?"

She shook her head. "I couldn't say. It's not my case. I'm just telling you what I've heard around the proverbial water cooler."

"Shit." Poor Kylie. She seemed too sweet to be involved with drug kingpins, but then again, you never knew.

"She's not part of it," Louise said, reading my mind. "Besides, the Morrises *hate* Malcolm. If she was messed up with them, they'd never allow her to work here."

"Why do they hate Malcolm?"

"Who knows? Maybe they think he's encroaching on their turf, but like I said last night, Malcolm seems to be on the up and up. No sign of criminal activity."

It occurred to me that he'd taken off on his motorcycle mere minutes after Louise had learned about the murder. What if Malcolm had just heard of it too?

Louise glanced at her watch and reached for her wallet. "I've only got a couple of minutes before I have to leave. Tell me about the van."

I told her everything I knew about it, including that I had the owner's permission to check inside if we found it.

"You think it was part of the kidnapping?" she asked, flagging Kylie down with some cash in her hand. "Did anyone see it last night?"

"Not that I know of, but then, most people weren't exactly forthcoming when I knocked on their doors. Still, it's suspicious."

"Agreed. I'll spread the word to keep an eye out for it. I'll let you know what I find out."

"Thanks."

Kylie stopped at the table with a ticket in her hand. Louise handed her the cash without looking at the bill. "Keep the change," she said, "and call me if your cousin hasn't turned up tonight."

"I will, and thank you, Deputy—" She cringed. "Louise." Pocketing the money in her apron, she headed off to another table.

"I covered your lunch too," Louise said, grabbing her jacket from the seat.

I felt like a freeloader. I was going to need to find a job sooner rather than later. "You're gonna start thinking I only hang out with you for the free meals."

Louise winked. "We both know you hang out with me for my charming personality and witty humor."

She wasn't wrong. I would have been friends with her regardless of my circumstances.

She left, and I stared at my half-eaten meal. I'd lost my appetite and all I could think about was an ice cold beer. So when Kylie passed the table, I flagged her down and ordered one.

I opened my notebook and made a few notes while I waited. I really wanted to talk to Ava's friends and wondered if it was safe to call Vanessa to ask her to set something up.

"Our paths keep crossing," a deep male voice said, as I noticed movement across from me. James Malcolm was placing a glass of beer in front of me as he took Louise's seat.

My brow shot up.

"The burger not to your likin'?"

I glanced down at the barely touched hamburger on my plate. "I haven't had a chance to dig in."

His gaze dipped to my notebook, and I covered the pages with my arm.

"I didn't realize you'd been employed by a law enforcement agency, Detective Adams," he said in his even tone.

"Not a detective anymore," I said, holding his gaze as I shut the notebook. "How do you know anything about me?"

A wry grin twisted his mouth, but it didn't look friendly. "Sometimes I can't help overhearing the patrons talking."

While I believed he knew my history, I didn't for a minute believe that he'd gotten all his information from eavesdropping on his customers. As the head of a crime organization, he would have kept track of things like that. I found it hard to believe he'd lost the habit.

I took a sip of my beer. He had a reason for coming over here. I was going to wait him out to see what it was.

"You were at the police station this morning," he said dryly. "And I keep finding you in my bar. What am I supposed to make of that?"

"You were at the police station this morning too," I said, matching his tone. "Are *you* working with the Jackson Creek PD?"

To my surprise, he laughed. "Has hell frozen over?"

"I'm not working for them either," I said, not sure why I'd told him other than I didn't want to be associated with a lazy, incompetent department. "Just as I presume you were, I was *invited*—I used air quotes—"in for a visit."

He sat back in the seat and crossed his arms over his chest, his presence seeming to fill the entire booth. I was pretty sure he could pour on the charm, but right now he was downright intimidating. "You're obviously working on *something*."

My back stiffened. "What I'm working on or not working on is none of your damn business."

"TJ Peterman is *very much* my business," he said, his voice dark with anger.

"What makes you think I'm working on anything to do with TJ?"

"Kylie heard you mention his name."

I took another sip of my beer to stall. I thought we'd been careful, but it was good to know that Kylie had been listening in. The real question was why she'd reported that Peterman's name had come up. "How is TJ Peterman your business?"

He snorted. "He's trying to get me shut down."

I already had this information, but I decided to play it out. "And why would he be doing that?"

"Peterman's trying to use me as an example for when he runs for the state senate."

Nate had mentioned TJ's political career aspirations, but this was the first I'd heard any details. "TJ Peterman's running for state senate?"

"He plans to announce his candidacy in another month. He came to me asking for a large donation, and said if I refused, he'd use me as an example of his plans to be tough on crime."

There was no hiding my shock. "TJ Peterman tried to extort you?" I didn't have much respect for the guy, but I would never have expected that from him.

"Call it whatever you want, but if he's some kind of suspect, I'll help you in any way I can to bring him down."

The last thing I planned to do was team up with this guy, but I wasn't opposed to getting information out of him. "Do you know if Peterman has a vendetta against anyone else?"

"He's trying to shut down the laundromat north of town. He's bringing it up at the city council meeting next week."

"Anyone else?"

"That's not enough?" he asked with plenty of snark. "Besides, how would I know?"

I tilted my head. "Seems like you might have heard your patrons talking about it."

A slow grin spread across his face, but his eyes remained hard. "Haven't heard any rumors floatin' around."

That wasn't an answer, not that I could have trusted him if he'd told me no. I decided to move on. "Why were you at the police station this morning?"

He grimaced. "A bullshit excuse. There was a robbery last night and the chief wanted to know if I was part of it. Not that I was surprised to be called in again. I get hauled in for bogus questioning when someone so much as jaywalks downtown."

Was the chief really questioning him about a robbery or had it been about the murder north of town? Then again, the murder was county business, so why would the chief get involved?

"That's harassment." When he shrugged, I asked, "How many times has it happened?"

"Over a dozen in the last few weeks."

If it was anyone but Chief Larson, I'd presume they had a case against Malcolm and were trying to find something to make it stick. But even then, a dozen times was ridiculous. They weren't looking for something, they were trying to make a point. If Peterman had threatened to shut him down, it seemed like it could be the next phase of that plan.

"You think Chief Larson is working with Peterman?"

"Obviously. I just don't know what's in it for Larson."

That was a very good question, but their harassment brought forth another possibility—if Malcolm had beef with Peterman, he might have kidnapped his daughter to get him to back off. And if Peterman suspected it was Malcolm, he'd want to deal with it quietly. He'd declare his daughter a runaway, keep the information private, and deal with Malcolm himself.

His gaze dropped to the basket at my side, then back up. The corners of his lips lifted, but his eyes remained dark. "Petey's the best damn fry cook in the whole damn state, and he's gonna be offended you didn't eat his masterpiece."

I couldn't stop my snort. "Masterpiece?" It was good, but I wouldn't go that far.

His arms dropped and he placed his hands on the table, leaning closer. "TJ Peterman wants to put him out of a job. The rest of my crew too. I'll be damned if I'm going to let that happen."

Which only made him more of a suspect.

"Where were you last night between the hours of nine p.m. and six a.m. this morning? Where did you go when I saw you leave?"

His left eye twitched. "You were sober enough to remember me leavin'?"

My anger flared. "I was barely at the legal limit, possibly under, and I *never* would have driven drunk. I planned to sit in my car." I took a breath. "So where were you?"

"Why're you askin'?"

"I have my reasons. Good ones. So humor me."

He shook his head in disgust. "I don't answer to you or anyone else."

He started slide out of the booth. I doubted he'd talk to me again after he left, so I decided to play part of my hand.

"It's about a missing girl."

He stopped at the edge of his seat, his jaw clenching. "What missing girl?"

This wasn't the kind of guy who'd do his own kidnapping. He'd have someone else do it. So it didn't matter if he could prove where he'd been last night. Still. I could watch his body language for clues as I picked and chose what to tell him.

"A twelve-year-old girl. The police chief thinks she ran away, but I believe she was kidnapped."

His eyes darkened. "I don't mess with kids. Never have. Never will. You're barkin' up the wrong tree if you think I have anything to do with that, Detective." Then something in his eyes shifted. "Why were you asking about TJ Peterman? You think he had something to do with it? He's a fucking asshole, but he never struck me as a pedophile."

"You never know who the monsters really are, Mr. Malcolm," I said, my voice cold. "Many of them like to hide in plain sight."

He seemed to appraise me, then gave a slight nod. "True, but a lot of the monsters I've met didn't hide who they really are, not if you looked close enough, so I suppose it goes both ways. Why do you think TJ Peterman kidnapped a kid?"

I rested my forearm on the table. "The man blackmailed you. You tell me why he might kidnap a kid."

"Revenge. Money." He paused, and his voice hardened. "Nefarious reasons."

"What nefarious reasons can you think of?"

"Could be wrong about the pedophilia. Trafficking. The kid saw something she shouldn't have."

Holy shit. Was he onto something with that last one? Had TJ done something to keep Ava quiet because she'd seen or heard something she shouldn't have? It seemed like a stretch. If he was involved, it seemed more likely that he'd accidentally killed her and was covering it up. But if that were true, as calm as he was this morning, he had to be a sociopath.

Malcolm shook his head. "So why are you asking for my alibi other than the usual harassment? Why would I kidnap a kid? To get back at Peterman for his threats?" His eyes widened. "Fuck. It's *his* kid."

I saw no reason to deny it, especially after seeing his reaction, what had looked to be genuine shock. "Yeah. But keep it to yourself for now. They're not making it public."

"So why tell me?"

That was a question I was currently asking myself. This was James Malcolm, who had supposedly made a deal with the FBI to hand over an international drug cartel, which meant he'd dealt with some high rolling crime bosses. And that was after he'd allegedly run his own crime syndicate. What was a man like that doing running a bar in Lone County, Arkansas? And why did I think I could trust him?

I didn't, but that didn't mean he couldn't provide me with useful information. It was obvious he knew a lot more about TJ Peterman than I did, and he knew things I wouldn't find out from Peterman's neighbors and friends.

"What did Chief Larson ask you this morning?"

He scowled. "Where I was and what I was doing last night." His jaw clenched, and he seemed to be considering something before he added, "If I had a thing for kids."

"He thinks you took her?"

His jaw ticked as his gaze shot to the bar. "Fuck. They're gonna try to pin this on me."

"Did you do it?"

His eyes turned murderous as he shifted his attention back to me. "I already told you. I don't fucking hurt kids. They have nothing to do with the evil of the world, and it should stay that way."

Call me crazy, but the intensity of his anger convinced me he wasn't lying.

"I'm trying to find Ava," I said. "But my notoriety and my lack of a badge are working against me. Have you heard anything about a kidnapping?"

"What makes you think I would have?" he grunted, pissed.

"If I remember correctly, you supposedly hear things from your patrons."

"If I ever heard of one of 'em hurting a kid, you'd be looking for them, and I can guarantee you'd never find 'em."

I grimaced. "I'm not sure you should be telling me that."

He shrugged, looking indifferent.

"Do you know anyone else who might have issues with TJ Peterman?" I asked.

"No, but I'll look into it."

I gave him a questioning look.

One side of his mouth lifted. "People tell me things."

"Because you're a bartender?"

He didn't answer, but the look in his eyes told me it wasn't the only reason.

Shit. Trusting this man to get me information wasn't a good idea, but I needed all the help I could get.

He glanced over at the bar, scowling. "I've gotta get back to work. Get out your phone."

"Why?"

The look he shot me made it clear he considered me an imbecile. "I'm gonna need your number."

Chapter Seventeen

"WHY?" I DEMANDED. The last thing I wanted to do was give my personal number to a crime boss.

"So we can stay in contact. Share information."

My jaw locked. "We're not working together."

"You're trying to find a kid, and I plan on proving I had nothing to do with her disappearance. We need to share our information."

"Forgive me for not giving a shit about your personal problems while I try to find a missing child."

His eyes narrowed, and I wouldn't have been surprised if his hand had jerked out and snatched me by the throat. "I'm gonna help you find her," he grunted, "if for nothing else than to prove I had nothing to do with it."

"How selfless of you."

But something in his eyes told me he was doing this for other reasons. The fact he'd sworn to make anyone who hurt a kid disappear forever backed it up. Of course, it could have all been a ploy to get me to trust him—which meant it was working—but my instincts told me he was on the up and up. That didn't mean I had to share anything with him. Still, it wouldn't hurt to have his number.

I pulled out my phone and opened the text app. "Shoot."

He made a face. "Is that a word you should be throwin' around, Detective Adams?"

My anger reignited. While I'd joked about it with Nate, Malcolm's cavalier attitude plucked a raw nerve. "Fuck you."

"You wish, but sadly, I can't accommodate."

He said it with so much arrogance, I was tempted to throw my nearly full glass of beer in his face.

The corner of his mouth ticked up, and he rattled off a number. I typed it in with angry stabs, which pissed me off. I was used to being the epitome of control. While I'd lost that part of myself months ago, this man made me feel like I was toppling into an abyss.

After I entered his number, I texted.

In your dreams, asshole

He removed his phone from his jeans pocket and studied the screen with a sardonic grin, typed something, and then put his phone down.

"Pleasure doing business with you, Detective." Then he slid out of his seat and headed back to the bar, checking on customers at their tables as he went.

I glanced at my phone and scowled.

Maybe in yours

Asshole.

I picked up my glass and drank a good quarter of my beer in one gulp. I was feeling pretty slimy after exchanging numbers with a criminal, but finishing the beer at one in the afternoon would only make me feel worse.

Fuck me.

Resting my elbow on the table, I ran my hand over my eyes. I needed to get my shit together. I had to find Ava, and I couldn't let that asshole think I was weak. Men like James Malcolm ate weak-willed people for breakfast.

I'd lost my appetite, but I took a couple of bites of my burger before grabbing some cash out of my purse and setting it on the table to cover the beer and an additional tip.

When I got outside, I dragged in a low, slow breath. It was still early in my unofficial investigation, and I'd gotten some valuable information, but I felt like I hadn't gotten anywhere.

I'd been to the laundromat and talked to Malcolm, so it was time to see if I could get anything from Ava's friends. That meant I needed Vanessa's help.

I looked up her number in the school directory and sent her a text. I would have preferred to call her, but since she was keeping my investigation a secret, a text seemed more discreet.

Hey Nessi. Just checking in on you. I have a few questions, so when you get a chance, call me back on this number.

I had the school directory and Vanessa had given me a couple of names. I could just cold call the friends' homes, but I doubted the parents would talk to me unless Vanessa made the request. Besides, Ava's friends would still be at school.

My phone vibrated seconds later with a text. I expected to see a reply from Vanessa, but it was from a unknown number.

Harper, this is Nate. When I walked down to the Sparrow for lunch, I ran into Drew Sylvester. He's on the police force, and he told me a few things you might be interested in.

While I was eager to get any information, I was worried about how Nate had gotten it. Had he been discreet?

I called the number, and Nate answered on the first ring.

"That was fast," he said.

"I just finished my own lunch and was about to head back into town. Tell me how this conversation with the officer came about."

He chuckled. "He doesn't suspect anything, so don't freak out. I just asked him what the commotion on the Petermans' street was all about, and he volunteered that the girl was missing."

"I thought the police were keeping that quiet."

"They are, but we're kind of buddies. He asked me to keep it to myself."

"Yet you're telling me." It made me wonder if I could trust him with my own secrets.

He huffed in frustration. "You already know, so I'm not breaking his confidence."

He had a point.

"Do you want to know what he told me or not?" he continued.

"Yeah. I do."

"He said the mother is out of her mind with anguish, but TJ is calm and collected."

"And that doesn't look suspicious to the police?"

"It looks suspicious to *him*. He disagrees with how they're handling the case, but he's fairly new to the force. Says he can't make waves."

"So he's young and fresh out of the academy?"

"Hardly. He's our age. We went to school with him. He was a year older than us. You don't remember him?"

"Drew?" I asked, searching my brain.

"Drew Sylvester. He played football. He was in the popular crowd."

The name and information sounded familiar, but I couldn't place him. "It's like we were saying earlier, I didn't exactly hang with those kids. Did he start out as law enforcement somewhere else?"

"I'm not sure about that, but I think his last job was selling office equipment in Jonesboro. He said he's in training here, whatever that might mean."

It didn't mean much. As lax as the Jackson Creek department was, I would hope they'd have an orientation program for all of their new officers. Every department ran things differently. I had a million questions about why he'd come back to Jackson Creek, let alone to work as a low-paying police officer, but now wasn't the time. "Did he say anything else?"

"Not much, but I invited him out to Scooter's for a beer tonight. I thought maybe you'd want to drop by and talk, casually, of course."

"Of course," I repeated, my head spinning. It would be great to have someone on the inside giving me information about the case, but I doubted that was what would happen. Drew was more likely to talk to Nate without me, and I told him so.

And I had my mother's required dinner to attend. There was no way I was getting out of that if I wanted to keep living in the apartment over the garage.

"He might not talk tonight," Nate continued, "but after he gets to know you, he might be more forthcoming tomorrow or the next day."

I wanted to tell him that I couldn't wait for information, but I needed whatever I could get.

"What time are you meeting?" I asked.

"Seven." I heard the smile in his voice. "We'll be there a few hours. Burger and beers, maybe catch whatever game's on TV."

"I thought it was just beers," I countered.

"Then show up around seven-thirty for just beers," he said. "I've set the groundwork. The rest is up to you."

"I have a dinner at seven with my parents. The soonest I can be there is around eight."

"Don't worry. We'll still be there."

I resisted the urge to sigh. The thought of going to Scooter's tonight raised the hairs on the back of my neck, and if I were honest, I knew why.

James Malcolm.

But I couldn't let him stop me from doing what needed to be done. "I'll be there. I'll see if my friend Louise wants to join us there so it doesn't look too awkward."

He laughed. "Sounds like a plan. See you tonight."

After we hung up, I checked my phone screen and saw I'd missed a text from Vanessa.

Call me ASAP. I'm in the bathroom and can't stay in here long.

I quickly called her back, and she answered on the first ring, her voice a half whisper.

"I don't have long. Every time I try to get a moment to myself, my mother hunts me down."

"I'm sorry," I said as I opened my notebook to jot down whatever she had to tell me.

"Casey LaRue and Ainsley Sumpter are Ava's best friends. Millie is Casey's mother. She's agreed to let you speak to Casey at four, after she comes home from school. Millie is eager to help any way she can." Her voice turned bitter. "Ainsley's mother is another story. She won't let you speak to Ainsley, but she did agree to talk to you before she leaves to pick her daughter up from school."

"Did she say why?" I asked. "Is it because she doesn't want to speak to *me*?"

"No, it's more that the girls had a falling out a week or so ago, and Lori has always taken her daughter's battles personally."

Now I really wanted to talk to Lori Sumpter. "Do you know why they had a falling out?"

"Ava said it was over something stupid. Like who sat by who at recess. It's hard when there's a triangle of best friends."

"So Casey, Ainsley, and Ava are all best friends?"

"It's more like Ava is the anchor, and she's best friends with both girls, but if I'm honest, I feel like Ava started growing apart from Ainsley before their fight. She and Casey have more in common."

"Like what?"

Vanessa hesitated. "Well…Casey has an easier time at school than Ainsley. And Casey's family goes to our church."

There was something she wasn't telling me, but hopefully I'd figure it out from my interviews. "Anything else I should know?"

"Like what?"

"Any new information? I hear the police are still treating this as a runaway case."

"TJ insists," she spat out. "I nearly ripped his head off, but he told me he has things under control. He's spent most of the day in his office downstairs with the door closed."

"I heard he's trying to shut down two businesses and one of them is on the agenda for next week's city council meeting. Suds and Duds." I had questions, but I wanted to see what she'd volunteer first.

"Yes." Her voice was tight.

"I take you don't agree."

"I told him it was dangerous to take on someone like Ricky Morris, but once again, he insisted he knows what he's doing."

"Vanessa, has Ricky Morris made any threats against you or your family?"

"What?" She paused and I heard her heavy breaths. "Oh my God. Do you think he took my daughter?"

"I don't know, but I'm considering it as a possibility. Do you know if TJ has gotten any ransom notes or secret calls?"

"He's taken several calls," she said, her voice shaky. "I have no idea what they were about." She let out a sob. "I'm such a fool.

Why didn't I consider that Ricky could have stolen my daughter?"

"What did you mean when you said he was dangerous?"

"He threatened TJ's business. He said if TJ took his business, he'd retaliate by taking TJ's."

"And how would he go about doing that?"

"He said he'd burn it to the ground."

"And you believe he'd make good on his threat?"

"He's done it before."

My head popped up from my notebook. "Ricky Morris has burned businesses down before?"

"Businesses. Homes. No one could ever prove it was him, but we all know. You do *not* want to cross Ricky Morris, and now he's taken my daughter," she wailed softly.

"I don't know that he took your daughter," I said. "But I plan to look into it. Anything else I should know about what's happening over there?"

"No," she choked out, sounding close to a breakdown.

"I'm going to find Ava," I said, knowing I was an idiot for promising that, but I had to give her some hope. I realized I was probably giving some to myself too. "You have to trust me."

"I do."

"Thank you. I'm going to talk to Lori and Millie, and if you hear anything else that you think could be helpful, let me know, okay?"

"Do you think my daughter is still alive?"

My stomach clenched. If she'd been kidnapped and raped, then statistically, no. But if someone like Morris had taken her, then he'd want to keep her alive so he could use her as leverage. "Yes," I said firmly. "We have to believe that she is. *You* have to believe that she is, Nessi."

Vanessa started to cry. "Oh, Harper…"

"Don't give up hope. Let me do my job. I'll bring her back. I promise."

There was banging on her end and a faint voice calling out, "Vanessa?"

"My mother," Vanessa whispered. "I've got to go." She hung up before I had a chance to said goodbye.

I lowered the phone to my lap, cursing myself for promising to bring Ava home. There were no guarantees I could do any such thing, let alone alive, but I couldn't bear to hear her anguish.

Or maybe I couldn't live with my own.

Chapter Eighteen

I WANTED TO DO MORE DIGGING into Ricky Morris, but I wanted to talk to Lori Sumpter first. Using the directory, I plugged Ainsley's address into my GPS and pulled up to the house twenty minutes later.

The Sumpters lived on the opposite side of Jackson Creek, not that the town was all that big. The neighborhood consisted of small homes built in the 1940s and '50s. One-level homes with few architectural features. The Sumpter home was a pale yellow with black shutters and looked fairly well kept. An older minivan was parked in the narrow driveway that led to a detached garage behind the house.

I parked at the curb and scratched my name and number on a page in the back of my journal, tore it out, and got out of the car. The front door opened after I'd only taken a few steps toward the house. A woman wearing black yoga pants and a long-sleeved gray T-shirt with several stains stood in the opening with a toddler on her hip. Her dark hair was pulled back into a ponytail, but multiple strands hung loose. She barely looked twenty-five, but dark circles underscored her eyes, making her look exhausted.

"Are you Harper?" she called out.

I stopped about fifteen feet away. "Yes. Lori Sumpter?"

She grimaced and didn't answer the question. "Vanessa said she was having someone come talk to me, but she didn't say she was sending *you.*"

I shouldn't have been surprised that she both recognized me and had an opinion about what I'd done. The thin blue line sticker on the back of her minivan next to the stick figure family suggested she'd heard those rumors Nate had told me about. There was a good chance she wouldn't talk to me, but I had to try. "I'm sure you've heard that Ava Peterman is missing. I only want to ask a few questions that might help Vanessa find her."

"I heard she ran away."

"The more we know, the likelier we are to find her." When she didn't seem swayed, I took a step forward. "Please. Anything you tell me can help. How would you feel if your daughter went missing? Wouldn't you want Vanessa to help you?"

She looked stricken, then glanced at my car before her gaze landed on me. She shifted the toddler on her hip. He wore a pair of overalls over a long-sleeve T-shirt and no socks. "If Jimmy finds out I let you in the house…"

"Is Jimmy your husband?"

She nodded.

"How about I ask you a few questions from out here?" I suggested. "Then you don't have to let me in." It wasn't ideal, but it was better than nothing.

She tugged the little boy closer to her body. "Maybe…"

It wasn't a no. "When was the last time you saw Ava?"

Frowning, she said, "Last Sunday at church. She and Ainsley were sitting together at Sunday school."

"Wait," I said in confusion. "You go to the same church as the Petermans?" Vanessa had said Casey and Ava had more in common because they went to the same church, implying that the Sumpters didn't.

Her brow wrinkled. "Just about everyone in town goes there."

I remembered that had been true twenty years ago. My parents went to Jackson Creek Baptist, and my mother said she knew Ava from Vacation Bible School. "Are Ava and Ainsley close?"

She nodded, but a dark look filled her eyes. "Ainsley would like to be closer, but TJ won't let 'em."

"Why do you say that?"

"He won't let her come over for playdates," she said with a sniff. "And they sure don't invite her over there much."

"Why won't he let her come over?" I asked.

Her brow lowered. "Look at this place. It's a dump compared to the Petermans' or the LaRues'. TJ Peterman wants only the best for his little princess, and Ainsley's not the best."

A sick feeling washed over me. Maybe it wasn't just TJ Peterman who believed that. I took a few steps closer. "Has he told you that?"

"No, but it don't take a rocket scientist to figure *that* out."

Based on what I was learning about TJ, I suspected she was right, but I really wanted to believe Vanessa didn't feel the same way. "So the girls hang out together at school and church?"

"And dance class. They go to the same dance school."

Funny that Vanessa hadn't mentioned that. "And where is that?"

"Miss Deedee's School of Dance." She made a face. "TJ don't like it much that my Ainsley not only goes there, but is better than his precious Ava, but my family's been going to Miss Deedee's for three generations now." She lifted her chin. "My momma went, and I went, and now my Ainsley and Becca." The toddler on her hip squirmed, wanting down, but she shifted his weight and gave an aggrieved sniff. "Hell, TJ ain't even from Jackson Creek. He's from Wolford. He ain't got no right to be trying to run off the people who have been born and raised in this town for generations."

"Do you think that's what he's doing?" I asked. "Running people off?"

"Now that he's on the city council he says he's trying to class up Jackson Creek. Like we were shitty before."

"Like shutting down the Suds and Duds?"

"Among other things."

"What else does he want to do?"

"He calls it beautifyin' downtown. He wants to make us a tourist place. Bed and breakfasts and such."

"That sounds like it would bring money to the town," I said. "Why are people against it?" I suspected because it meant change and a lot of the people in this town resisted change. Or at least they had when I'd been raised here. Sounded like Lori might be on that bandwagon too.

"He wants to make all kinds of rules about how the fronts of the businesses look. He says he wants downtown to be *picture perfect*. He ain't from Jackson Creek, so he needs to stick his nose out of our business." Her eyes narrowed. "Why are you askin' so many questions about TJ if you're lookin' for Ava?"

"Sorry," I said with an apologetic smile. "I guess I got sidetracked." She believed Ava had run away, so I decided to stick with that angle. "Do you have any idea where Ava might be?"

"Why are *you* asking instead of the police?"

"They haven't talked to you?" I asked, not that I was surprised.

"Nope. Vanessa called me before school, then about an hour ago sayin' someone was comin' by to ask me some questions, but that's it. So why are you here?"

"Vanessa and I have been friends since she and my sister were toddlers," I said. "She knows I understand what it's like when someone you love goes missing."

She looked a little chagrined. She obviously knew about Andi if she'd lived here her entire life.

"If Ava were hiding, do you know where she might go?" I asked.

She shook her head. "She'd likely go to Millie's house, but I'm sure you talked to her already." There was an air of hostility in the last part of her statement.

"I haven't had a chance," I said, then added, hoping to win her over, "I wanted to talk to you first."

Her eyes widened, and she looked pleased.

"Do you know if Ava has an adult she'd go to if she were in trouble? Someone she really trusts?"

"Just Millie," she said, a cat streaking past her leg and darting outside.

"No one from school or church?"

"Not that I know of."

"Does Ainsley hang out with Ava during recess or any free time?"

"She did, but over the last few months, Ainsley says that Ava and Casey haven't been playing outside as much during recess."

"Does she know where they go?"

She shook her head. "No, but she asked to be included and they told her she wouldn't understand."

"Understand what?"

She shrugged. "Understand what they were doing? I don't know."

"Did she report them to the teacher?"

A fierceness filled her eyes. "She ain't no snitch."

"Aren't you worried the girls could be up to something dangerous?"

"What could be dangerous at the school?" She shook her head in disgust. "Damn helicopter parenting is gonna be the end of us." She pointed a finger at me. "Now if it was Ainsley hiding during recess, I know for a fact Millie or Vanessa would be running off to the principal, talking about how children need to be monitored every step of the way." Her brow lifted. "But girls that age like their secrets."

"Even when they keep them from their friends?"

"Those two ain't really Ainsley's friends, and I told her so. They'll always be lookin' down on her on account of we ain't got a fancy house and cars like they do, but we got something better. We've got *heritage*. So I told her let 'em hang themselves, although knowing that TJ Peterman, they'll get out of it." She glanced over her shoulder. "I gotta get back to my kitchen. It's Becca's birthday, and I'm makin' her favorite Oreo cake."

My heart sank. I was pretty sure that was the reason Vanessa thought Casey had more in common with her daughter.

Lori started to close the door, but I held up a hand and pulled the piece of paper out of my pocket and approached her, my hand extended. "This is my number. If you think of anything else that might help Vanessa find Ava, could you give me a call?"

Defiance filled her eyes. "Why wouldn't I just call Vanessa?"

She had a good point, but to my surprise, she descended the two steps to her porch and snatched it out of my hand. Without saying a word, she hurried up the steps and started to walk through the door.

"Just one more question," I said before she shut the door. "What is your impression of Ava?"

She turned, surprise in her eyes.

"She's a spoiled brat, if you ask me. She gets anything and everything she wants. The lead role in the dance recital. The spelling bee title, you name it."

I shook my head. "I thought the spelling bee was won by knowing how to spell the most words correctly. How could the school have just given that to her?"

"They gave her easy words," she said in disgust, rolling her eyes. "I don't know where Ava Peterman is, but I wouldn't be surprised if she's hiding just to get even more attention." Then she slammed the door shut.

I headed back to my car and wrote down notes while the conversation was still fresh in my mind. Lori Sumpter painted a very different picture of Ava than I'd expected, but then again, I suspected Lori's perspective was colored by jealousy. Both of the examples she'd given of Ava's privilege were things the girl had likely earned based on merit. Nevertheless, it wouldn't matter if Ava was a stone-cold bitch. She was too young to take care of herself on her own if she'd run away, and no one deserved to be kidnapped.

Chapter Nineteen

I HAD NEARLY TWO HOURS before I was scheduled to meet with Millie LaRue. I needed to make use of it, so I decided to look into Vanessa's allegation that Ricky Morris had set fire to the businesses and houses of people he had issues with.

But first I had to ask Louise about going back to Scooter's tonight. I sent her a text telling her about Nate's invitation and explained that I wouldn't be able to be there until closer to eight because of my parents' dinner.

She responded a few minutes later saying she'd be there.

I released a sigh of relief and sent Nate a text letting him know. Then, because I'd already asked Louise for several favors, I decided to risk asking for another, even though it made me feel like pond scum.

Me: *One more thing. Do you know anything about Ricky Morris burning the businesses and homes of people he doesn't get along with?*

She sent a text back right away.

Louise: *I haven't heard anything about it, but I'm still new, so that doesn't mean it hasn't happened. I'll ask around when I get a chance.*

No sense in sitting around and waiting, so I decided to do an internet search of my own. I didn't want to do it on my phone, so I considered my options—heading up to Wolford and using the computers at the public library or heading back to my apartment and using my laptop on my parents' wifi. I quickly nixed my apartment. I found the place utterly depressing. Besides, Wolford was the county seat, so if I came across any useful information, I might have time to go to the courthouse and request records.

And it happened to be near my liquor store.

But the library first.

The Wolford library wasn't crowded, but I had to apply for a library card to access the computers, which chewed up about ten minutes. Since I'd already done a search for Ricky Morris and hadn't seen anything about any fires, I looked up house fires in Lone County. There had been multiple house fires over the past few years, but only three had been labeled as arson. There weren't any follow-up articles on the arson cases, but I wrote down the information, planning to ask Louise to pull the sheriff's reports.

No question about it, she was going to hate me before this case was done.

Next, I looked up business fires in the county, surprised to see quite a few of them. Over the past two years, eight of them had been arson. A few had been solved, but five of them had not. I printed off the articles, making note that two of them were mechanic shops, one was an auto body shop, and two were salvage yards—all within an eight-month period.

That seemed suspicious as hell.

A quick glance at my phone told me I had forty minutes before I needed to be at the LaRue house, so I paid for the print job and headed out to my car. I had just enough down time to stop by the liquor store and get back to Jackson Creek.

The sales clerk nodded to me as I walked in. I was familiar enough with the store to know where the whiskey was shelved, so I headed right over, grabbed two bottles and brought them to the counter.

The older gentleman rang me up and told me the total as he started placing them in paper bags.

"No mini-bottles today?" he asked matter-of-factly.

Holding back a cringe as I placed my debit card on the counter, I said, "Not today."

Admitting you had a problem was the first step to getting help, and while I knew drinking tiny bottles of vodka to deal with difficult things wasn't right, I was giving myself some grace. I was going through a lot. How was alcohol any different than Xanax?

Deep down, I knew there was a difference. I just didn't want to admit it.

I needed to find Ava first, and then I'd sort through this drinking situation and figure out my life.

I entered my PIN, relieved when the sale went through. I needed to check my bank account, but it was too depressing to look up the figure now.

I'd put that off until later too.

I carried the bottles out to my car and put them in the trunk so I wouldn't be tempted to open one and take a few sips.

I didn't need it. Interviewing people was like riding a bicycle.

But as I drove back to Jackson Creek, a slew of doubts began to slither into my head, and I worked myself up into enough of an anxious state that I considered stopping on the side of the road and opening one of my whiskey bottles. I could only imagine what my mother would say if she knew what I wanted to do.

"Your problem is your lack ambition, Harper," she'd told me more times than I could count. "You never live up to your full potential."

Not like Andi was a given, understood by everyone in our now family of three.

And I'd lived with the guilt ever since, alternating between wanting to prove my mother wrong and not giving a shit what she thought. Every failure fed her voice in my head, telling me I'd never be enough. Every victory had her telling me it still wasn't enough.

No matter what I did, it would never be enough to replace the life snuffed out twenty-one years ago.

I would never be enough.

By the time I was back in town, I wasn't sure I could work any case, let alone find Ava. But I was the only person looking for her, and I couldn't quit now.

The LaRues lived a few miles outside of downtown, closer to my parents' house, in a neighborhood that had been developed in the nineties. Andi and I had made a few friends who lived in the neighborhood, but I hadn't been back here since I was in high school. The trees were taller and the landscape around the houses was more developed. Memories of Andi came rushing back, stealing my breath. Riding bikes. Talking late at night when we were supposed to be asleep.

That day.

She'd been gone longer than she'd been alive, but I still missed her, sometimes so much it hurt straight to the depths of my soul. Sometimes it didn't feel right that she was gone and I'd been left behind. Of the two of us, she was the better person. The sweet one. The one who tried to make our mother happy. I was the one with a mouth. I was the one who pushed all the wrong buttons.

Parking at the curb in front of the LaRues' house—a two-story standard stucco house from the nineties—I sucked in a breath and held it, trying to become more focused.

Grabbing my notebook and pen, I got out of the car and walked up to the front door. The curtains in the one of the front ground floor windows fluttered, and the door opened before I could ring the doorbell.

A woman in her early thirties hung to the side of the door as though trying to hide herself. Her blond hair brushed her shoulders, and even though she wore full makeup, dark circles underscored her blue eyes. "Harper?"

I offered a warm smile. This woman was either weighed down by guilt or she was truly grieving Ava and fearing for her daughter's safety. I was betting on the latter. "Yes. Millie?"

She nodded and opened the door wider, still staying behind it. I walked inside, and she quickly shut the door behind me. I was face to face with her now, and my belief that she was reeling from the news of Ava's disappearance increased.

"Vanessa said you'd probably want to talk to Casey, but I wanted to talk to you first," she said, her hands clasped in front of her. "If that's okay. I'll do whatever you need me to do to find Ava."

"That sounds like a good plan," I said softly, hoping I was reassuring her. "Where is Casey now?"

"Upstairs. In her room with her brother. I told her to get started on her homework."

I nodded and gave her a smile. "That's good. I was going to suggest we chat first anyway."

"Okay." Her voice was shaky as she gestured to the living room. "I don't know where you want to do this. I've never been interviewed by a police officer before."

"First, you need to know I'm not currently an officer. I was a detective with the Little Rock Police Department for six years and before that a patrol officer. So while I'm not currently employed by any law enforcement agency, I *do* have experience that I think will be beneficial to helping Vanessa find her daughter."

Tears flooded Millie's already bloodshot eyes. "Okay."

"And we can do this wherever is more comfortable for you. The living room? Some people like to sit in the kitchen."

"I was making cookies." She grimaced. "Nervous baking."

"Then let's go in the kitchen and you can keep making them if you like."

"Okay."

She led me to the back of the house, an open concept space that took up the full width of the house with a family room, kitchen, and breakfast nook. A cookie sheet was on the counter along with a mixing bowl containing what looked like chocolate chip cookie dough.

Millie started to scoop dough into the miniature scoop then looked up at me. "Vanessa said your sister was kidnapped when you were teens."

I was surprised this seemed like fresh news to her. "I take it you aren't from here?"

"No, my husband transferred here for a job about ten years ago. I've heard rumors about a girl getting kidnapped twenty years ago, but sometimes it's hard to tell what's rumor and what's fact." Fear filled her eyes. "*Was* Ava kidnapped?"

"The police think she's a runaway."

Her eyes darkened as she dumped the ball of dough on a parchment-lined cookie sheet. "That's what Vanessa said. She's *furious* with TJ because he thinks she's overreacting and Ava will walk in the door any minute."

"Do *you* think Ava will walk in the door at any minute?" I asked gently.

Tears fell down her cheeks, and she swiped at them with the back of her hand. "I don't know."

I let her cry for a few moments and then catch her breath before I opened my notebook and asked, "How well do you know Ava?"

Millie sniffed and resumed her task of making cookie dough balls and dumping them onto the sheet. "She's over at our house a couple of times a week, so pretty well."

"Do you know if Ava is happy at home?"

She froze. "What does that mean?"

"Does she get along with her parents? When she was with you, has she ever expressed a desire to run away?"

Her teeth caught her bottom lip. "I know she and TJ don't see eye to eye. TJ's too hard on her, if you ask me. He expects too much of her. She's a good girl, and she wants to make him happy, but he's much too controlling. He's stifling her."

I leaned forward. This could change everything. "So you think Ava could have run away?"

She considered it a moment, then shook her head. "She might run away from home, but she wouldn't just *leave*. She'd call Casey or me. She knows I'm a safe place. Like I said, she spends the night with us all the time. She's comfortable here." Millie hesitated, then added, "She's told me before that she wishes she could live with us." Tears filled her eyes again. "But it would kill Vanessa to know she said that."

Vanessa loved her daughter, but at the same time, she had to know that TJ was making Ava miserable. The sentiment couldn't have surprised her that much.

"Did Ava call you anytime last night or this morning?" I asked.

She shook her head. "No. I told Vanessa I don't know where she is."

"But you feel badly for Ava," I said, "so I'd understand if Ava *did* call you and you agreed to let her hang out with Casey for a while to decompress."

Her eyes flew wide. "She's not here. I swear."

I held her gaze. "Millie, I know you care about Ava."

"Like she's a second daughter." She swiped a fresh tear from her cheek. "If she called and asked me to come get her, I'd do it in a heartbeat, TJ be damned. But I wouldn't keep it from Vanessa. I wouldn't do that to her. Ava's not here, and I haven't heard from her. I swear."

I rested my palm on my notebook, staring into her tear-filled eyes. "I believe you."

She pushed out a breath and sagged a hip into the edge of the counter. "Thank you."

"I think we all want the same thing, Millie. We want Ava to be safe. But it *does* sound like she's unhappy at home. Do you know of anyone else she might have gone to if she decided she couldn't take it anymore and needed to get out of the house?"

"But..." Confusion clouded her eyes. "Vanessa seems so certain she was kidnapped."

"I need to explore all the possibilities." When she didn't protest, I asked, "Other than you, is there anyone else she might call or go to? Her grandparents? A teacher? Another friend?"

"Definitely not her grandparents. Vanessa's parents are much too strict—no wonder they love TJ so much—and TJ's mother died a few years back. His father barely pays any attention to the kids, and TJ's grandmother is too old and halfway senile to care. If Ava was going to call anyone other than us, she might call Ainsley, but probably not. She's not as close with Lori—that's Ainsley's mom—as she is with me."

After speaking with Lori Sumpter, I believed that. "Does Ava like school?"

Millie made a face. "Yes and no. She likes her friends and teachers—she has several since they move around to different classrooms to get them ready for junior high, but she feels a lot of pressure from TJ to not only get straight As, but A pluses."

TJ was a real asshole. "Do you know if she has a favorite teacher?"

Her mouth twisted to the side as she considered it. "Mrs. Marshall. Her math teacher."

"Does Ava have any male teachers?"

Her eyes flew wide. "You think one of *her teachers* has something to do with her going missing?"

"I don't know anything right now," I said patiently. "That's why I'm asking questions."

Contrition filled her eyes as she grimaced. "I'm sorry. I'm just so nervous and jumpy." Her gaze lifted to the ceiling, then dropped again to lock eyes with me. "I have two children, Harper. If anything happened to them..." Her voice broke and she started to cry again.

"Millie, everything you're feeling right now is perfectly normal and understandable." I gave her a soft smile. "It's not selfish to be worried about your kids. You're their mother. Of course you're worried."

Her mouth twisted into a tight smile. "Thank you."

"Does Ava have any male teachers?" I asked, repeating my earlier question.

She shook her head. "No. In fact, Vanessa was just saying last week that she wishes there were more male teachers. The only man in the whole building is the janitor. Mr. Eddie."

"Do you know Mr. Eddie's last name?"

"Johnson."

"What do you know about Mr. Eddie?"

She pursed her lips and studied the counter. "He's not your typical janitor. He's young. He's very energetic. The kids love him. *Everyone* loves him."

"How long has Mr. Eddie worked at the school?"

"He's fairly new, I guess. He started working there last year."

I wrote down his name. "Do you know if he's from the area?"

She shook her head and made a face. "I think so, but I'm not sure. I know a lot of people make a big deal about whether they were born and bred here, but the principal, Mrs. Deaver, she won't allow any of that. She's only been at the school for a few years, but she made it so I can be a room mother. I couldn't before."

"They had rules about that?" I asked in surprise.

"Not actual rules," Millie said. "But definitely unwritten ones. The legacies controlled everything. I was always rebuffed when I signed up to be a room mother or volunteered for the PTA. Kids were treated that way too. Even if they were born here and their parents weren't."

I frowned as I made more notes. "What do you mean?"

Millie reached up and rubbed a strand of her hair between her thumb and forefinger. "Well, when Ava and Casey were in second grade, they had a school play and they both wanted the lead role." She made a face. "It was just a stupid kids' program. You know, one of those all-class musical presentations, but this one had a speaking part throughout. Kind of like a narrator. Ava and Casey were the only ones to try out and Ava got the part. I didn't think much of it until the music teacher told me months later over margaritas that she wanted to give it to Casey, but TJ threw his weight around and insisted she give it to Ava since it was *owed* to her." A quiet fury washed over her face. "Can you believe that? *Owed* to her."

"Because he was born here?" I asked. "He isn't from Jackson Creek either. He's from Wolford."

She shrugged. "But it beats Jackson, Mississippi. I was furious, of course, but Austin—that's my husband—said to let it go. We'll probably be here for a while with his job at the plant, and he didn't want me making waves we couldn't ride out in the long run."

"That had to make things uncomfortable," I sympathized. It also gave Millie a reason to resent Ava, even subconsciously. "Have there been other instances of that kind of favoritism?"

"Not since Mrs. Deaver started at the school."

"So no more preference given to native-born children and families?"

"There's still a little, but she squashes it pretty hard when she hears about it."

"But TJ," I said, letting his name linger for a second before I continued, "he's a force to be reckoned with, I'm sure."

She made a face.

"A guy like him," I continued. "I bet he's not happy with the new way of things. He thinks he and his kid are entitled to the perks of being legacies."

She nodded.

"Is Ava well-liked by her classmates?"

"She is, but I think some of them see the favoritism and hold it against her."

"Is she bullied?"

"Oh, no," she said, waving her hand in dismissal. "Nothing like that. More like when Ava is picked for something, the other students aren't surprised and are a bit resentful."

"I'm sure some of what she's achieving is merit based," I said. "It sounds like she's an excellent student."

"And an excellent singer and dancer," Millie said with a sigh. "Yeah. Sometimes the girls especially resent her a little. But no one hates her. She's definitely not bullied." She snorted. "TJ would never allow it."

Of course he wouldn't.

"Is there anyone in particular who sees Ava as a threat? Either another child or maybe a parent?"

Her eyes flew wide again. "You mean someone who would kidnap Ava because of their kid?"

"Not necessarily," I said. "I'm still just asking questions."

She looked horrified as she considered it. "No," she finally said. "I don't think so."

"How do the other parents and teachers see TJ's relationship with his daughter?"

She squinted in confusion. "What do you mean?"

I hesitated, trying to figure out how to word it without leading her. "Obviously, TJ intervenes when he thinks his daughter is being treated unfairly. So they must think she's special to him."

She rolled her eyes. "Yeah. They call her his precious angel, stuff like that."

Kidnapping Ava would be a good way to get back at TJ, which led me back to Ricky Morris or James Malcolm, especially given the covert way TJ was handling the entire thing.

Unless TJ himself was the one who took her.

Still, that didn't explain the red ribbon. Surely it wasn't a coincidence. But I couldn't center my entire investigation around it. Not when there were multiple other leads to explore.

But what if TJ knew about the ribbon and it was his way of trying to throw me and the police off the correct scent?

"I know TJ's hard on Ava," I said, "but has he ever been physical?"

"Do you mean, does he hurt her?" She shook her head. "I don't think so. He has other ways of punishing her. Just his presence can be terrifying to her. I've seen her shrink under his glare."

I hated bullies, especially when they were parents. I wanted to drive over to the Peterman home and personally punch him in the mouth. "But you never saw any questionable bruises?"

"No."

I paused before shifting my line of questioning. "You attend the same church as the Petermans?"

She scoffed. "Practically everyone in Jackson Creek goes to the Baptist church."

"How active are the Petermans at church?"

"TJ's a deacon if that tells you anything."

It certainly did. It was surprising, however, since the church had always been full of congregants who ascribed to the born and bred philosophy. Wolford was ten miles away but might as well have been on the other side of the ocean. "How do the Petermans get along with people at church?"

"Everyone loves Vanessa, of course. She's such a sweetheart and helps out with Vacation Bible School. Everyone loves the girls too. They're little angels. Especially Paisley, the youngest. TJ doesn't seem to put as much pressure to succeed on her, so she's much more light-hearted."

"Isn't she only five?"

"Yeah, but TJ started on Ava when she was pretty young. I've known her since three-year-old preschool, and he was on her, even back then."

"Sounds like a lot of pressure for a little girl."

"It is. But as for what people think of TJ...I think it depends on who you ask. The church leaders love him, but he could be a little condescending to the nursery workers back when Paisley was in the nursery. I used to work there and witnessed it firsthand."

"How does he treat everyone else?"

She inhaled deeply, then blew it out. "TJ can be a charmer. He knows how to butter people up and get them to do what he wants."

"Like a politician," I suggested.

"Yeah," she said, her face brightening as though she'd mentally connected some dots. "*Exactly* like a politician."

"Has TJ or Vanessa mentioned TJ possibly going into politics?"

"Neither one of them have said anything, but last week Ava said something about her daddy running for office. She said they might be moving to Little Rock if he wins. She wasn't happy about that."

I folded my hands on top of one another on the table as I looked into her eyes. "Millie, do you know anyone who hated TJ? Or held a grudge against him?"

She lifted her knuckles to her lips. "TJ's not the most liked man in town, but I don't know anyone who hates him enough to hurt his daughter." Tears filled her eyes again. "Do you think Ava's okay?"

"I don't know, but I want to believe she is," I said truthfully. "I'm going to do everything in my power to find her."

Her chin quivered. "I'm just so worried about her. I want to *do* something."

"I understand that feeling, but trust me, answering my questions *is* doing something. In fact, if you think of anything else could you give me a call?"

"Of course."

I flipped to the back of my notebook and wrote down my name and phone number on the corner and tore it out. "You can reach me here," I said, handing her the paper.

She looked it over and stuck it in her jeans pocket.

"Do you think it would be okay if I talk to Casey?" I asked. "I promise to tread lightly."

"Okay." She looked worried but also slightly relieved. "She mentioned that Ava wasn't at school, but she doesn't know anything about what's going on. I didn't want to worry her."

"I understand."

"I'll go get her," Millie said, then got up and walked toward the front of the house. I heard footsteps on the staircase, and Millie called out, "Casey? Can you come down for a minute?"

I heard footfalls on the hardwood floor and looked up to see Millie coming toward me, her hand on the shoulder of a preteen girl in front of her. Casey was nearly as tall as her mother and had the same shoulder-length cornsilk blond hair and blue eyes. She was wearing jeans and a pale pink sweater. She didn't have on shoes, but her feet were covered in pink fuzzy socks. Her face was pale, and she looked confused.

I stood and offered her a friendly smile. "Hi, Casey. I'm Harper, and I'm a friend of Ava's mom."

She stared at me with wide eyes but didn't speak.

"Where are your manners?" Millie chastised softly, lightly squeezing Casey's shoulder.

Casey forced a smile. "Hello."

"I understand that you might be a little nervous to talk to me," I said, still smiling.

Casey glanced down at the floor and wouldn't meet my gaze. Her hands were clasped tightly in front of her and her shoulders hunched forward.

Casey LaRue wasn't just nervous. She was hiding something.

Chapter Twenty

I KNEW BETTER THAN to get my hopes up. Casey was a twelve-year-old girl who looked like she was scared to get in trouble. I had no idea what her mother had told her about me, but if she thought I was a cop, she might be scared I was here to bust her for shoplifting gum from a convenience store or throwing a rock in a neighbor's window. (Both had happened over the course of my career.) I knew better than to expect too much.

Yet I hoped anyway.

Whatever she was hiding, I'd bet the title of my Ford Taurus that she didn't want her mother to know.

But I doubted Millie would let me question her daughter without her present, not that I blamed her. If I had a kid, I'd probably advise them to not talk to police in an investigation without an attorney present. I hated attorneys, but I also knew a few stupid kids who'd admitted to shit they shouldn't have. But I wasn't a cop anymore, so Millie might be more lenient.

For now, I'd play it by ear.

"Why don't we sit down somewhere to talk," I said, keeping my voice breezy. "Where would you be most comfortable?"

"The sofa," the girl said, her voice just above a whisper as she pointed to the family room.

"Great idea," I said, picking up my notebook and phone and heading over to a love seat.

Casey and her mother sat on the sofa perpendicular to me. Once they got settled, I looked Casey in the eye. "Did your mother tell you why I want to talk to you?"

She glanced down at her lap and nodded. "Ava wasn't at school today, and Mom says her mom and dad can't find her."

I suspected Casey was shy, which explained her lack of eye contact, but I was feeling more confident that she was hiding a secret.

"Miss Vanessa asked me to help her find Ava. You might know something really important that can help me do that." Her fingers twined together, and she kept her gaze down. "When was the last time you talked to Ava?"

She looked up at me. "Yesterday at school. She was supposed to call me last night about our social studies project, but she never did."

"TJ monitors Ava's phone activity," Millie interjected. "So for her not to call wasn't all that unusual. Sometimes Vanessa would intervene, or if it was really important, I'd call Vanessa to arrange for them to talk or meet the next day."

"I'm sure that's difficult," I empathized.

Casey nodded. "A lot of kids don't want to be her partner on projects because we never really know if she can do her part."

"That must upset Ava."

A frown creased her brow. "She's embarrassed about it. *He* embarrasses her."

"Does that make her angry?" I asked.

A fire filled her eyes. "She hates him."

"Casey!" her mother protested.

Casey looked up at her. "Well, she does!"

Millie started to say something, then pressed her lips together and folded her hands on her lap, obviously restraining herself.

I made a few notes in my notebook to give them a moment, then looked up. "Does Ava ever sneak phone calls to you when her father has banned her from using her phone?"

Casey made a face. "I don't want to get Ava in trouble."

I leaned closer and tried to look reassuring. "You won't. I won't tell her parents."

She still didn't look certain she was making the right decision, but she said, "Sometimes she uses her mom's phone. She's pretty sure her mom knows she's using it. Sometimes Miss Vanessa leaves it out where Ava can get it and take it to her room."

"Has Ava ever talked about running away?"

Casey's eyes widened slightly, but then she shook her head. "No."

"She's not in trouble if she did, but anything you tell me can help me find her, okay?"

She studied my face then nodded.

"Thank you," I said sincerely, then waited a beat before I said, "Everyone needs to take a break from stressful situations, and it sounds like maybe Ava was in a state of constant stress."

The girl nodded and a tear streaked down her cheek. "She talks about leaving home but not running away. She's excited for camp this summer, mostly because she can get away from her dad. She also talks about going away to college and never coming home, but she's never, *ever* talked about running away. I swear."

Maybe so, but I was pretty sure Casey was still hiding something. What?

"That's okay," I said. "But for the sake of argument, let's say she *did* decide to run away. Where do you think she would go?"

Casey looked like a deer caught in headlights, then she glanced up at her mother before answering, "I think she'd come here, but she's *not* here. I *promise.*"

"I believe you," I said, offering a warm smile. "So if she didn't come here, is there someplace else she might go?"

She looked nervous. "Maybe Ainsley. But she doesn't like her house much." She wrinkled her nose. "It smells."

"Casey!" Millie protested.

"But it does!" Casey insisted, then turned to look at me. "She has a lot of cats, and it stinks. Plus, it's tiny. They only have one bathroom."

Millie's face flushed with embarrassment.

"Cats can be pretty stinky," I said, trying to ease the tension. "Especially if their litter boxes aren't changed enough."

"Or they pee all over the place," Casey said belligerently.

"That too," I conceded. "Anyone or any place other than Ainsley's house that Ava might have gone?"

She shook her head but refused to make eye contact.

"Does she have a grown-up she talks to when she's upset? Someone she trusts?"

Her gaze lifted, but her forehead was wrinkled. "You mean like Ms. Donahue?"

Millie saw my questioning look and volunteered, "Ms. Donahue is their homeroom teacher."

"Ava trusts Ms. Donahue?"

Casey nodded. "Everyone does. She's really nice, and she's really understanding about Mr. TJ."

"What do you mean she's understanding?"

Her mouth twisted to the side. "Well, you know…she gets why Ava can't always meet to do group projects and stuff."

"Do you have a lot of group projects that require outside-of-class time?" I asked in surprise. I didn't remember doing many group projects in elementary school.

"It's something new they're trying this year," Millie said. "We've had one or two in the past, but this year, they've had one just about every month."

"If TJ wants Ava to get perfect grades, why isn't he more supportive of the projects?" I asked.

Millie rolled her eyes. "Because he always thinks Ava is carrying the group. He's not a believer in the group project idea. He thinks everyone should carry their own weight."

"And her grades aren't affected by it?"

"Oh, they are," Millie conceded. "It's been a source of tension between him, Ms. Donahue, and Ms. Snyder, the principal."

I jotted that in my notebook before I asked, "Is Ava close to any of the other adults at school? One of the teachers, maybe?"

Casey started to say something, then pressed her lips together.

"You thought of someone," I said with a warm smile.

Casey hesitated before adding in a small voice, "She talks to Mr. Eddie a lot."

"She does?" Millie asked in surprise. I could see the worry dawning in her eyes.

"What do they talk about?" I asked, making sure my tone was light.

She shrugged. "School. Ava's dance classes."

"Does anyone else in your class talk to Mr. Eddie like Ava does?" I asked.

She looked down at her lap. "A couple of people, I guess."

"Can you give me their names?"

She started to say something, then stopped and lifted her gaze to mine. "I don't want to get anyone in trouble."

"You're not getting anyone in trouble," I assured her, although Mr. Eddie might be in trouble if he was being inappropriate with the kids.

"How is this going to help Ava?" she asked, suspicion filling her eyes.

"I need you to trust me, Casey. I know you don't know me, but I've found missing girls before. I know what to look for and who to talk to. So I need you to answer honestly. The more I know, the better my chances of finding Ava."

She swiped at her face as tears began to fall down her face.

I locked eyes with Millie and tried to warn her to be calm before I turned my attention back to Casey. "Do you talk to Mr. Eddie a lot too?" I asked, then quickly added, "I mean, if he's talking to Ava and the two of you are best friends, I would think you'd be with her when they're talking."

Thankfully, Millie didn't say anything, although I could see the growing panic on her face.

Casey nodded.

"And when you talk, are there other grown-ups around?"

Her forehead wrinkled as she frowned. "Sometimes, yeah, I guess."

"But sometimes not?"

She bowed her head and nodded.

"When do you usually talk to him?"

"After lunch," she said, her voice barely above a whisper. "We get to go outside for recess after lunch, but they don't take roll or anything, so sometimes Ava and me stop by his office and we talk."

"Mr. Eddie has an office?" I asked.

She shrugged. "It's kinda more like a closet, but we hang out in there."

"Talking about school and Ava's dance classes?" I asked. "Anything else?"

She refused to meet my gaze, lifting one shoulder into a small shrug. "Mr. TJ, I guess."

"Did *you* ever talk?" I asked gently.

"Sometimes," she said in a whisper.

"Do you remember what you talked about?" I purposely gave her the option for an out. Obviously, she didn't want her mother to know about her and Ava's meetings with Mr. Eddie, and only her worry for her best friend had pushed her to confess. I wasn't surprised when she shook her head no.

When Millie started to say something, I held up my hand a few inches. She stopped, but she looked like she was on the verge of tears.

"How often do you girls meet with Mr. Eddie?" I asked. "Once a week? Every day?"

She shrugged again, keeping her head bowed.

"I'm sure Mr. Eddie is a good friend to you and Ava," I said gently. "And I'm sure that he helps Ava feel safe."

Her head jerked up. "Yes! He makes her feel better."

Millie flinched but didn't interrupt.

"When you're in Mr. Eddie's office, does he ever close the door?"

She nodded. "Sometimes Ava cries, and she doesn't want people to see her."

"Does Mr. Eddie ever give either of you hugs?"

She glanced back at her mother, then looked at me and nodded.

"Does Mr. Eddie ever touch either one of you in a way that makes you feel uncomfortable?"

She shook her head adamantly. "No. Never. He's not like that, but he said people wouldn't understand and we needed to keep it a secret."

Relief flooded Millie's face as a tear slid down her cheek.

"Do Ava or you ever hang out with Mr. Eddie alone?"

"I don't," Casey said. "But I think Ava did when I was sick with the flu."

"That was just a few weeks ago," Millie said tightly. "Casey was home all week."

I nodded in acknowledgment.

"Casey," I said, trying to catch her gaze, which proved difficult since her head was still bowed. "Do you know if Ava talked to Mr. Eddie outside of school?"

"I don't know," she said in a whisper. "But I think maybe she talked to him last week, because I saw them whispering about something in the hall, and they stopped when I got closer. I heard them say something about 'tonight.'"

"Like they were going to meet somewhere?" I asked, keeping my voice even.

"Maybe," she said, then hastily added, "But I don't know for sure. I just know that they were talking about something that night."

"Do you know what night that was?"

"Last Thursday."

"Can you think of anything else about Mr. Eddie that you think will be helpful?"

"Not really," Casey said, worry etched on her face. "Is Mr. Eddie in trouble? He said he could get in trouble if anyone found out."

"You don't need to worry about Mr. Eddie," I said. "He's a grown-up and can take care of himself." I gave her a warm smile. "Do you know anything else that might help me find Ava?"

She sniffed, swiping at her cheeks again. "No. Do you think she's okay?"

"I'm trying to figure that out, and you've helped me get closer to finding her. Thank you."

Casey lifted her face to her mother. "Can I go now?"

I nodded, so Millie dismissed her daughter.

Casey didn't waste any time bolting from the sofa for the staircase, leaving her horrified mother behind.

"I had no idea," Millie said. "I had no…" Her voice broke off into tears.

I leaned closer and lowered my voice. "Millie, it's important to remember that Mr. Eddie may have only offered Ava what felt like a safe place to talk. He may not have done anything inappropriate in the way you're thinking."

"He shut the door, Harper! With two twelve-year-old girls in a closet!" she whisper-shouted in outrage.

"Yes," I agreed calmly. "That was *extremely* inappropriate. But again, it may not have been *sexually* inappropriate. We need more answers before that can be determined."

"I'm calling the school!" she exclaimed, getting to her feet. "I'm putting a stop to this right now!"

"I agree," I said carefully, looking up at her. "You need to notify the school, but I'm asking you to wait until tomorrow morning. Let me have a chance to talk to him first. If you call the school, the police will be involved—as they should—but I won't get that chance. Will you wait until tomorrow?"

"I don't know," she said. "What if..." Then she took a big breath, her hands shaking as she said, "I have to tell Austin before I talk to the school, and I don't want to call him about this at work. He had a big meeting today." Her shoulders squared and a determined look hardened her eyes. "You'll have until this evening before we do something."

"Thank you," I said. "I'll let you know what I find out after talking to him. It probably won't be admissible in court, but at least you'll know what you're dealing with."

Chapter Twenty-One

KNOWING I'D STIRRED UP A HORNET'S NEST, I quickly left. Still, if the janitor had been molesting children, at least it was coming to light.

I still needed to talk to Eddie Johnson to get more details, but he had just become a person of interest.

When I stopped by the school, I found the doors locked and only one car in the parking lot, an older white Jeep Cherokee. I didn't know who it belonged to, and I didn't think it was a good idea to go around the school, knocking on windows to get someone's attention, so I sucked it up and headed to my apartment. I needed to find a way to talk to Eddie Johnson, so I could do an internet search on him then possibly pay him a visit after the meetup at Scooter's.

I parked in the driveway and kept an eye on the back of the house as I walked around to the trunk and grabbed my bag from the liquor store. I didn't see my mother peering out the back windows, but that didn't mean she wasn't watching.

I'd forgotten about the pile of sheets on the floor. I considered taking them to the house to start them in the washing machine but didn't feel like seeing my mother just yet.

Instead, I sat on the sofa and opened my laptop, starting a search for Eddie Johnson. His name wasn't all that unique, which would make things harder, but I combined it with "Jackson Creek," and a post on someone's blog about gardening popped up. It was from three years ago and said Eddie had been helping with her massive gardening plots. There were a few photos of a sweating man in his mid-twenties with a wide, infectious grin.

I stared at the photo, wanting to believe the wholesome image but knowing far too well that monsters masqueraded as great guys all the time. How many times had I heard friends and neighbors say, "I never would have expected him to do…" whatever evil thing the person had done.

"What about you, Eddie?" I murmured out loud to the screen. "Are you a wolf in sheep's clothing?"

After more searching, I found a post on the school website stating that Eddie had started as the school janitor, along with a photo of a more cleaned-up version of the man in the blog photos. He was blond and blue-eyed, with full cheeks. A swoop of bangs covered one side of his forehead. He was smiling, looking happy to now be employed by Jackson Creek Elementary.

Was that because he was pleased to have a job or because his job had put him closer to kids?

I shut my laptop screen. I'd been hanging around evil too long. It skewed my view of the world and everyone in it. Then again, that was my job.

Or at least it used to be. And I was no closer to finding Eddie Johnson.

I glanced at my phone and realized I had only a half-hour before I needed to be at the house for dinner. A good daughter would already be there, setting the table, helping finish the dinner. But we'd established long ago that the good daughter was gone, and my parents were left with the bad one.

I needed a drink.

I knew I'd get a drink at the bar, but the thought of sitting through an entire dinner with my parents was nerve-wracking.

A quick one wouldn't be a bad thing.

I opened a bottle, poured a finger of whiskey into a juice glass and drank it like a shot, relishing the burn as it slid to my belly.

I closed my eyes and let the feeling settle over me. It wouldn't solve all my problems, but it was a decent interim solution.

I brushed my teeth and reapplied my makeup with a heavier hand to appease my mother, then lightly curled my shoulder-length hair with a curling iron. I searched through my clothes and put on a simple rust-colored sweater dress and a pair of brown boots, then stuffed my sheets into a laundry basket, grabbed my coat and purse, and headed out the door.

My mother was in the kitchen when I walked in through the back door. She gave me a cursory head-to-toe glance, then turned her attention back to the roasting pan she was removing from the oven.

"Your laundry, Harper?" she asked in a dry tone. "Really?"

"Laundry still needs to be done, Mother, regardless of semi-formal dinners."

She set the pan on top of the stove. The smell of roasted chicken hit my nose, making my stomach growl. "At least you dressed appropriately."

"Getting dressed was one of the many life skills you taught me, so kudos."

Her eyes shot daggers at me, but she bit her tongue.

After I dumped my purse and coat on the breakfast table by the back door, I brushed past her into the laundry room off the kitchen and started my load of sheets. I could move them to the dryer after dinner before I left for Scooter's, but I'd have to come back and get them before going to bed. I took solace in the fact that my mother was usually in bed by ten. My dad was usually up until eleven, so I'd have time to get them before he turned on the alarm system for the night.

My mother insisted I didn't need to know the security code. I think she expected me to sneak in and steal her grandmother's silver. Little did she know, most people didn't want silver these days. Who had time for all that polishing?

When I reentered the kitchen, my mother shoved a dish of roasted potatoes toward me. "Take this out to the dining room."

I looked down at the generous amount of food. "For someone who thinks I've put on too much weight, you sure made a lot of food."

Her gaze darkened. "We have guests, Harper, and I expect you to be on your best behavior."

"Guests?"

"You didn't think we dressed up for just the three of us, did you?"

I had. I mean, our weekly Sunday lunch had always been semi-formal, held after church while we were still in our fancy clothes. Andi hadn't minded the dinners, but I'd hated them, wanting out of my stiff, starched dresses and often too-tight shoes. I'd thought my mother would let go of the tradition after Andi's death, but we'd continued to have those lunches until I left for college. We kept a lot of things up after Andi's death, possibly out of habit, but they'd all felt meaningless and hollow without my sister—an echo of the life we'd had.

I'd presumed this dinner was my mother's attempt to start those dinners up again. The revelation that there were guests was completely unexpected. She was embarrassed by me. Why would she be parading me in front of her friends?

I was still confused when I walked into the dining room and set the platter on the elegantly dressed dining table. In the living room across the entryway, my father was entertaining two of his law partners. They reclined on opposite facing sofas in front of the fireplace, sipping drinks from highball glasses.

My father glanced up and saw me and a warm smile lit up his face. "Harper, come over and say hello to Mitch and John David."

I crossed the entryway and clasped my hands in front of me, wondering why my father's law partners were here for dinner on a weeknight without John David's wife and Mitch's flavor of the month. Especially since I'd been informed my attendance was mandatory. Was I in some kind of new legal trouble my father somehow knew about, and I didn't?

Both men stood up and offered me warm smiles.

"Hello, Mr. Morgan and Mr. Hightower," I said, extending my hand to Mitch first.

He shook it firmly, saying, "Now, now. I was Mr. Morgan when you were a girl. We're all adults here. Call me Mitch."

"Okay, Mitch." I dropped his hand and shook John David's.

"Same with me," he said. "Although I remember a time you used to call me Mr. John David."

I smiled at the memories. When Andi and I were elementary school students, our mother would take us to visit our father at the office, sometimes bringing him lunch while we were on summer break. We'd gotten to know the staff and my father's partners and had called everyone Mr. or Miss along with their first names.

"How's Frieda doing?" I asked John David as I released his hand. He and Frieda had been married longer than my parents, but I'd always remembered them being distant with each other.

"She's doing well," John David said. "She's started quilting."

"That sounds fun."

"She's only just begun and complains about her pieces not lining up or some such issue." He shook his head with a frown.

"I don't even begin to understand. I just let her chatter to get it out of her system."

I smiled, biting my tongue to keep from saying maybe if he tried to understand they'd both be happier.

None of my business.

"Dinner's ready," my mother said from the dining room, carrying a platter of chicken.

"Smells delicious, Sarah Jane," Mitch said as he set his nearly empty glass on a coaster on the coffee table, then headed toward the dining room. "As always."

"You're just happy to eat a homemade meal," she said with a laugh. "You could get remarried, you know."

"No one will ever live up to the memory of my beloved Trina," he said with a sigh. "So I don't even try."

Maybe he wasn't looking for a wife, but he'd had plenty of mistresses before Trina had died, soon after I graduated from college, and I knew he'd had plenty since. Since he'd likely used up the available pool in the county, I was sure he was working on the unsuspecting women in El Dorado, an hour away.

We all took a seat at the elegant table, my parents on either end, me on one side and my father's partners on the other. My father took some of the roasted chicken and passed it to Mitch. "How's that case about the Wilsons' property dispute going?"

Mitch responded, but I tuned them out, my mind drifting to Ava. She was missing, and I was sitting here sipping water from a crystal glass. But I reminded myself that my investigation was far from official. In fact, if the police caught wind I was looking into it, they could arrest me for interfering in an investigation.

My mother would surely convince my father to kick me out then.

Everyone made small talk while I picked at my food, still wondering why I'd been invited to this dinner, let alone why it was taking place. I finally figured it out when my mother began serving her classic tiramisu for dessert.

"So, Harper," Mitch said, holding my gaze. "We hear you're currently without a job."

I gave him a tight smile. "You've heard right."

Mitch glanced at John David, then back at me. "We have an opening at the law firm if you're interested. It's not much, mostly filing and such, but it's a start and something to do until you figure out what comes next." He glanced at my father, then back to me. "And if you change your mind about law school, well, John David and I want you to know we'd welcome you into the firm once you pass the bar."

My brow lifted. "You want me to work at the firm?" I glanced to my father for confirmation.

He gave a slight nod.

While part of me was grateful to my dad, nepotism had never really been my thing. Maybe that was one of the reasons I'd balked at law school. Not just because I'd been *expected* to come home and work with my father.

"That's a generous offer."

John David placed his hand on the table and gave me a direct look. "We like to take care of our own, Harper, and your family is our family."

"I've heard that rumors are being spread about me in Jackson Creek," I said carefully. "Ugly things. Are you sure you want to be associated with that?"

Mitch laughed. "We're attorneys, Harper. People already think badly of us, but you can bet your ass—" he gave my mother an apologetic look "—excuse my language, Sarah Jane." He turned back to me. "You can be assured that when those judgmental people have problems, we're the first people they'll seek out, and the more of a reputation we have, the more they want us."

"In certain matters," my mother added, her lips pressed thin. "Criminal cases. Not real estate like my Paul." She gave my father a tight smile.

"Yes and no," Mitch said. "True, the meaner we appear, the more they want me for a criminal case, but Paul has a reputation for getting his clients what they want, so while he may not have his character questioned, his expertise at winning cases keeps gaining him clients."

"Paul rarely goes to court," my mother said dryly.

"Because he knows how to settle disputes without going to court," John David said.

Mitch nodded in agreement.

"Are you suggesting my reputation might actually be an asset to the firm?" I asked in disbelief.

"We're not exactly planning on making an announcement you're there," Mitch conceded, "but we don't see it as a detriment."

"This is not what I agreed to," my mother snapped, her eyes dancing with anger as she stared at my father.

"We both agreed she needs a job," my father said firmly.

"Yes, but not to parade her misdeeds around like they're something to be celebrated."

"That's not our intent, Sarah Jane," Mitch said. "Our intent is to take care of our own. Just like you took care of my sweet Trina when she was ill."

"That's different," my mother shot back, her cheeks flushed. "I held her hand during chemo."

"And we're metaphorically holding your daughter's hand while she gets back on her feet."

"She was supposed to stay in the background," my mother spat.

"She will," John David said. "She'll be filing."

"What would you have me do, Mom?" I asked quietly as I turned to face her. "Would you rather I work at the Gas and Go in Wolford?"

"Of course not!"

"That's because you'd rather not have me here at all, right? You'd rather I be anywhere but here."

"I never once said that," she countered.

She became blurry through my unshed tears. "I think you just did." I turned to face my father's partners. "Thank you for your generous offer, but I think I should pass."

"Now, don't be hasty," Mitch said, patting his hands toward me. "Emotions are high right now, so why don't you take some time to think it over?"

I placed my napkin on the table. "While it's been a lovely evening, I have another appointment I need to get to. It was wonderful seeing you both." Pushing my chair back, I got to my feet.

"Where do you think you're going?" my mother demanded.

"I'm not seventeen anymore," I said in a firm tone. "I'm a grown woman, capable of making my own decisions."

"Obviously not wise ones."

I sucked in a breath. I already knew she felt that way, but it still hurt. Maybe because the woman who had raised me would never have said such a thing in front of an audience. That was the sort of thing that was only said in the deep privacy of one's home.

"Wise or not, I'm leaving anyway." I headed into the kitchen, not surprised when my mother followed me. I grabbed my purse from the breakfast room table as I headed for the back door.

"Why are you still looking for Ava?"

"Because Chief Larson won't!" I practically shouted.

"You think the police failed your sister," she called after me. "But did you ever consider that the blame may fall at your feet?"

My heart stuttered as I turned to face her, words escaping me.

Her face was crimson and her eyes wild. "If you hadn't disobeyed me, if you hadn't gone to that creek, your sister wouldn't be dead."

I sucked in a breath, her words like a knife to the heart. "And then you'd have the good one, right?" I pushed past the ball of emotion burning in my throat. "You wouldn't be stuck with me."

I didn't give her a chance to respond, because while I'd always believed it, I was too fragile to have it confirmed.

I fled.

Chapter Twenty-Two

THE PARKING LOT WAS FULL at Scooter's when I pulled in a few minutes after eight. I saw Louise's car in the back, so I knew she'd beat me here.

When I walked in, I let my eyes adjust to the light before I found Louise at a table with Nate and a man I didn't recognize. Empty baskets had been shoved to the side of the table, and the three were deep in conversation when I approached them.

Louise glanced up at me as I pulled out a chair. She was wearing a cream-colored cable-knit sweater over jeans, her dark hair spilling over her shoulders.

"I see you've met Nate," I said as I slipped my coat over the back of the chair.

"They found *me*," she said with a laugh. "They realized who I was and invited me to their table."

The man next to Nate glanced up at me, his face expressionless.

Nate saw where my gaze had landed and said, "I'm sorry. Harper, this is Drew Sylvester. Drew, this is Harper."

I wasn't sure if Nate had purposely left off my last name, but I was guessing Drew knew exactly who I was.

"Nice to meet you," I said with a nod, not sure if he was up for a handshake.

"Likewise," he said with a slight dip of his chin.

"I'm going to get a drink," I said, thumbing toward the bar. "Can I get anyone anything?"

They glanced down at their fresh-looking drinks. "I'm good," Louise said.

"Same," the men said in unison.

I headed over to the bar, not surprised when James Malcolm walked over to me with an expectant look.

"Your usual, Detective?" he asked in a sly tone.

"How would you know my usual?" I asked flippantly. "I've been in here twice and ordered different things both times."

His eyes shifted to the side toward Nate's table, then back to me. "Jack and Coke."

I lifted a brow. That was what I'd planned to order, but I wasn't about to give this man the satisfaction of thinking he was right. "Wrong. I'll take a beer."

Releasing a short laugh, he shook his head. "Right. The draft you had this afternoon?"

"You don't remember what I got this afternoon."

"Try me," he scoffed, then headed down to the draft taps.

Asshole. I could read the labels on the taps, and sure enough, he was getting my order from hours before.

I didn't see a point in making him bring it all the way down to me, so I walked over to that section and sat on an empty stool.

He lifted his gaze, still filling the glass. "Make any progress on our mutual interest after you left?"

"Maybe," I said, glancing around the room. A rough-looking crowd was gathered around the pool tables again, but there were a fair number of more upstanding citizen types hanging around too.

Leaning closer, I whispered, "Know anything about a janitor at the elementary school? Eddie Johnson?"

His face went rigid. "He's a regular here. What about him?"

That was an interesting reaction. I doubted he'd be so concerned about any old regular. Did Eddie Johnson have ties to James Malcolm? "I was hoping to talk to him this afternoon, but by the time I got to the school, it was locked up tight."

He placed the glass on the bar in front of him. "Why do you want to talk to him?"

I sure as hell wasn't telling him everything. "His name came up in an interview I had today. I need to ask him what he knows about Ava Peterman."

His jaw ticked. "He doesn't know anything. Leave him alone."

Now my interest was fully piqued. Seemed to me, Malcolm would only care if this Eddie worked for him in some way. Maybe Malcolm had Eddie keeping tabs on Ava, getting information and feeding it back to him.

Which would put him high up on the suspect list.

There was obviously no way in hell I was leaving it alone now, and the way his face tensed told me he knew it.

I tilted my head. "Why would I leave him alone when he possibly has information?"

"Because he didn't have anything to do with it," he grunted, fury building in his eyes.

"Forgive me if I'm not going to just take your word for it."

He leaned closer, radiating ominous energy. "If you make trouble for that boy, I'll…"

I arched a brow. "You'll what, Mr. Malcolm?"

He took a breath, regaining control, and his shoulders relaxed slightly. "The boy's had a hard life and things have finally turned around for 'im. Don't you fuck it up."

That was the last thing I'd expected him to say. "I only want to ask him questions."

"About a missin' kid. How many other people have you told about your interest in Eddie?"

"None," I said with plenty of self-righteousness, but I felt a niggle of guilt for not telling him that Millie LaRue planned to go to the principal about him first thing in the morning.

Malcolm released a grunt and shook his head. He didn't believe me, but there wasn't anything he could do about it.

"You want it on a tab?" he asked, sliding the glass toward me.

"Please."

I picked up the glass and headed back to the table. All three of my party watched me as I made my way back. After I sat down, their gazes were still on me, expectant.

"What?" I asked, then took a long drag of my beer. Damn Malcolm. I'd really needed that Jack and Coke.

"What do you mean, what?" Louise said, incredulous. "We saw you having a conversation with Malcolm."

I shrugged. "Oh that."

"Yeah, that," Nate said, leaning closer.

Drew looked interested but didn't say anything.

Great. I was a lot less likely to get information from him if he thought I'd formed some sort of relationship with Malcolm.

"He recognized me," I said with a wave of my hand. "You know. Same old shit."

Louise cringed. "Sorry, Harper."

"We can go somewhere else," Nate said.

I released a half laugh. "If I avoided every place that gave me shit, I'd live in my car. I even get it at home with my mother." Remembering how I'd left things with my mother had me lifting my beer back up to my lips.

"Still, it's not right." Louise patted my arm. "I'm sorry you have to deal with it."

"Did that kid have a gun?" Drew asked bluntly, his neutral gaze on me.

"Jesus, Drew," Nate protested.

"What the hell?" Louise demanded.

"It's okay," I said, glancing over at Louise. "I'll answer." I turned back to Drew and held his gaze with my cold detective stare. "He had a gun. I saw it with my own two eyes. I even recognized the make—a Glock. He fired the gun at me, but his aim was off, and he missed. I'd already drawn my weapon, so I fired in self-defense. It hit him in the chest, and he fell. I tried to contain the scene while the store owner called 911. I checked for a pulse, but the kid was dead, a bullet straight to the heart. The gun was still at his side. I. Saw. It."

"But the responding officers didn't."

I shrugged and picked up my beer again, taking another long drink. There was no defending that. I'd spent the past four months trying. Someone took that gun, but I had no idea who they were or why they did it. And now that I was on the outside, I had no way of figuring it out.

Jesus. I needed something stronger.

"She's gotten enough shit," Louise said in a cold tone, glaring at Drew. "So if you're going to give her more of it, you can get the hell out of here."

"*They* invited us," I reminded her dryly.

"I don't give a shit," she shot back, still locked in a staring contest with Drew.

Drew broke the stare and released a shaky laugh as he looked over at Nate. He flicked a finger toward Louise. "This one's got balls, huh?"

"That's ovaries, thank you very much," she said with a huff. "And my ultimatum stands. You're either her friend or you can take your shady ass somewhere else." She picked up her beer bottle and looked down at him. "It's a wonder I'm sitting with a Jackson Creek PD member anyway."

He laughed. "And I can't believe I'm slumming with a Lone County deputy, but when your options are limited, you'll even hang out in the bar of an organized crime boss."

Her eyebrows lifted slightly in acknowledgment.

"It's not up to me to say what happened or didn't," Drew said evenly, then his body seemed to release some tension. "It's a tough job and you have to make tough calls. Even if you *thought* you saw a gun and shot, it's understandable. You can get killed in the blink of an eye."

"You're taking her side now?" Louise asked skeptically.

"I'm not taking anyone's side," Drew said, leaning back in his chair and picking up his beer bottle. "I just wanted to hear her version."

"The Jackson Creek PD hates me," I said, giving him the side-eye. "I think you're required to hate me out of solidarity."

He grinned. "Chief Larson may be able to tell me what to do when I'm on the clock, but he sure as hell can't tell me what to think." He shrugged. "And trust me, I don't always agree with his calls. Especially on a case from today." He tipped up his bottle and finished it.

Was this my opening? It couldn't be this easy, could it?

No, I needed to earn his trust more. Small talk. "How long have you been on the force?"

Releasing a chuckle, he rolled the bottle around on its base on the table, keeping his gaze on it. "I joined last fall. My mom's not in the best health, so I moved back here from Jonesboro. Sold office equipment up there." He shrugged again. "I needed a job, and I heard they needed an officer. I'd never worked in law enforcement before, but the chief and my mom are friends and he knew how much she wanted me here, so…" He grimaced and looked up at me. "The rest is history."

"Do you like working for the Jackson Creek PD?" I asked.

"It's a job. A relatively safe one here, so you know." He shrugged, sounding defeated. "I make some money, and I'm around to make sure my mom's okay." A grin tugged at the corners of his lips. "I don't plan to do this forever, but it's okay for now." His smile faded. "Until I saw something I disagreed with so strongly, I considered quitting."

I shot a quick glance at Louise, who was watching Drew intently.

"The case from today?" I prompted.

He forced a smile. "I'm gonna get another. Anyone want anything?"

I glanced down at my near empty beer, feeling the pull for more, but I needed to pace myself. "I'm good for now."

Nate and Louise said the same thing, and Drew headed toward the bar.

"Do you think he's talking about Ava Peterman?" Louise asked.

"Has to be," Nate said. "Trust me, they don't get that many interesting cases. He was right when he said the job was relatively safe."

"You need to ask him, Harper," Louise said. "It can't be me because I'm not supposed to know anything about it."

Maybe I could ask him about Eddie Johnson while I was at it?

Nodding, I finished my beer. Damn. I wished I'd asked for another. Or something stronger.

Drew came back with a new beer bottle, and I studied him. He was a good-looking guy and in decent physical shape. He seemed confident in his own skin, so he probably hadn't taken his position on the force as a way to boost a sensitive ego. But could I trust him?

"So how do you like living back in Jackson Creek?" I asked before he'd barely slid into his seat.

"How do *you* like it?" he countered with a grin.

"It's too soon to tell," I said. "I really need to get a job somewhere, although I got an offer right before I came here tonight."

"Oh?" Louise asked in surprise.

"My mother ambushed me with my father's partners at dinner. They offered me a job at the law firm. It's just doing scut work, but I'm sure they'd pay me well." I made a face. "Nepotism at its finest."

"You don't have to stay there," Louise said. "You can just work there until you figure out what you want to do."

My frustration bubbled over. "I want to work in law enforcement, but that's no longer an option."

"You could find a job in security," Drew said. "A lot of those bigger places would consider you an asset."

"Because I shot that kid?" I asked dryly.

"Because you didn't hesitate."

I bit my tongue to keep from blasting him for condoning what I'd done. What the hell was wrong with me? I hated it when people judged me for what happened without knowing the facts, but I also wanted to jump down the throats of anyone who accepted me.

Maybe part of me thought I deserve their judgment.

"We'll see. I'm not sure working for my father's firm is a good idea. My parents expected me to go to law school and join the firm. It was a huge disappointment to my mother when I entered the police academy. I can't help thinking this is her way of finally getting what she wants."

"Even if you take the job, doesn't mean you're stuck there," Louise said matter-of-factly.

"But it feels like she's winning." I inwardly groaned, cursing myself for saying that out loud.

"Maybe she just wants what's best for you," Nate said. "You might be taking it the wrong way."

I considered it for a moment, but then her parting words hit me square in the chest. "No, this is more about making sure I don't embarrass her any more than I already have."

"It looks like you need another drink," Nate said, trying to sound cheerful, but it came out flat. He got up from the table, leaving me and Louise with Drew.

"Chief Larson really hates you," Drew said.

His statement caught me by surprise. "Yeah, he made that pretty clear when he asked me to stop by his office this morning."

"Why?"

"Are you asking why he asked me to his office or why he hates me?"

"Maybe both."

Chuckling, I shook my head. "He invited me to his office to harass me. As for the hating me…I have no idea. He must have caught word that I think he bungled my sister's case."

Drew took a sip of his beer and leaned back in his chair. "Did he?"

"Yeah, and he's making the same mistakes with Ava Peterman that he made with Andi."

"Way to subtly jump in there about the kid," Louise said under her breath.

Drew didn't look surprised or thrown, though.

"You think he's handling it correctly?" I asked him. I didn't bother asking if he'd been assigned to the case. The Jackson Creek police staff was small. Everyone would know about it.

He lifted one shoulder into a lazy shrug, his hand still wrapped around the bottle. "He says she's a runaway."

"Even if she's a runaway, he should still notify the sheriff's department," Louise said. "She's the daughter of a city council member who's stirred up a bit of controversy. He needs to cover his bases."

He turned to her in surprise. "You know about this?"

She gave him a smug grin. "She told me this morning, asking if I knew anything about it."

Drew's face went expressionless. "Chief Larson says he has it under control."

The old stand by your supervisor gimmick. I knew it well. I'd done it a hundred times or more myself.

"He told us the same thing after my sister was kidnapped. And look how well that turned out."

Drew shifted in his seat, grimacing. He pulled in a deep breath as he cast an unfocused gaze across the room, then he turned to me, his eyes intense. "I remember how helpless we all felt when your sister was taken. I don't know much about how things were handled on the force—still don't, to be honest—but even a rookie like me can tell things are getting screwed up on this one."

Louise leaned closer to the table. "Like what?"

It was clear this conversation was making Drew uncomfortable, but I could see a war waging in his eyes. Finally, he scraped his teeth over his bottom lip and said, "He should have treated the room as a crime scene. Canvassed the neighborhood to see if anyone saw anything. Looked around the house for evidence. How did she get out if the alarm wasn't triggered?"

"The balcony," I said. "I found imprints from what looked like a ladder next to the balcony where the red ribbon was tied. Ava's window was found wide open. Whoever took her snatched her and carried her over the railing and down the ladder."

"Ava is small, but she'd likely still be thrashing around," Drew said, interest filling his eyes. "They could have both fallen over the edge."

"Not if the kidnapper drugged her," I said.

"Chloroform?" Louise asked.

"Maybe?" I said, uncertain.

"Unless he got her to go with him," Louise said.

"She's right," Drew said. "But it would have to be someone she'd trust."

Like Eddie Johnson.

Chapter Twenty-Three

"WHAT?" LOUISE ASKED, narrowing her eyes as she watched me. "You know something."

"Maybe, maybe not. But I need to ask more questions before I can be certain."

"Don't hold out on us," she exclaimed.

"Ava's best friend says the girls were spending their recess after lunch with the school janitor, Eddie Johnson. He's a young guy in his mid-to-late twenties. The friend swears nothing inappropriate happened, but it was inappropriate for him to spend time alone with a couple of twelve-year-old girls in the first place, and she seems to realize that. I'm guessing she's worried about getting in trouble. Besides, there were a few opportunities for the janitor to spend time alone with Ava when Casey was sick." I turned to Drew. "Have you heard anything about him?"

He gave it a moment then said, "No, but I'm new enough to the force and Jackson Creek that I might have missed something."

Nate rejoined us, placing my glass and his on the table as he sat down. "I forgot to ask what you preferred, but Malcolm seemed to remember which beer you'd ordered before."

Louise gave me a concerned look.

"Don't make too big of a deal out of it," I said as I reached for the glass.

"So what did I miss?" Nate asked, looking relaxed as he took a sip.

"Do you know anything about Eddie Johnson, the elementary school janitor?"

Nate frowned and was silent for a moment. "Nope, don't think I've heard of him. Why?" His brow lifted. "Shit. Is he important to your case?"

"Your case?" Drew asked, lifting his eyebrows.

"Surely you've figured out that Harper is looking into Ava's disappearance," Louise said.

"No," Drew said carefully. "I hadn't." He turned to look at me. "You could get in trouble for that."

I gave him a sly look. "Only if I'm caught."

Who had I become? Miss By-the-Books was turning into a liar and a sneak. But I'd also been a social drinker and workaholic. That was me then.

This was who I was now.

Drew made a face, glancing down at his beer bottle.

I still needed to talk to Eddie Johnson before Casey LaRue's parents went to the principal or possibly the police tomorrow, but I didn't know where he lived. It wasn't in the school directory, and I hadn't found it on the internet.

I lowered my voice. "Can one of you get his home address?"

Both of them remained silent. Finally, Louise asked, "Why?"

"Isn't it obvious?"

She flicked her gaze to Drew, who sat motionless. Her eyes drifted back to me. "I don't think that's a good idea."

I understood her concern. If it got back to her boss or Chief Larson that one of them had used their department resources to give me a citizen's home address, they could get in trouble, and possibly be fired. There was also a chance that he was the kidnapper, in which case I might screw up evidence that could convict him. But I'd been trained as an officer. I'd keep that in mind.

"I might be able to get it," Nate said.

We all turned to him in surprise.

"I dated the school secretary last year. Things ended on a good note, so she might be willing to help."

"How can you break up with someone on a good note? I always leave them weeping for more," Louise said flippantly, reminding me she was younger and less jaded than I was about romance.

Drew watched her, the corners of his lips tipping up, making it obvious he was intrigued.

"She went back to her previous boyfriend, and I wasn't feeling much chemistry," Nate said with a slight grin. "Satisfied?"

Louise shot him a curious glance. "I still think there's a bigger story there, but I'll let it go for now."

"Don't get distracted," I said. "Nate, do you think you can find out his address tonight?"

"Tonight?" Louise asked. "Why not tomorrow?"

"So I can go visit him bright and early before he goes to work," I said. "I'm sure he wouldn't want to have this conversation at the school."

Nate groaned, but he pulled his phone out of his jeans pocket and tapped on the screen. "You're gonna owe me for this, Harper."

"Sure," I said. I'd probably agree to anything if it meant saving Ava.

He sent a text, then set his phone on the table. "We'll see if she answers."

Drew finished the last of his beer and put the bottle on the table. "Ladies, it's been great meeting you, but I need to head home. I've got an early start tomorrow."

"Yeah," Louise said. "Nice meeting you too."

Drew held out his hand to me. "Sorry about being a hard-ass when you first showed up."

I shook his hand and looked him in the eye. "Thanks for giving me a chance."

He dropped my hand and nodded. "Back at ya."

Louise watched him walk toward the exit. "He's kind of cute if you can ignore the fact that he's with the Jackson Creek PD."

Nate laughed. "Funny, he lamented about you being his sworn enemy when you went to the restroom before Harper showed up."

"He's a little old for you, don't you think?" I asked. There had to be an age difference of at least a good decade.

She shot me a look. "Okay, *Mom.*"

"She has a point," Nate said.

"Which one of us?" Louise narrowed her gaze.

He lifted his hands in surrender and laughed. "Both of you."

"Seriously, Louise," I said. "Are you really interested in him? I mean, he's with the Jackson Creek PD."

She laughed. "We all have our faults. There's no way I'd date a deputy I work with, which means my options are pretty limited."

"Trust me," I grumbled, picking up my beer. "I learned it was a bad idea to date your coworker the hard way. Stay away from dating fellow employees."

"Now, I know there's a story *there*," Nate prompted.

I shook my head. I wasn't about to get into my relationship with Keith. Not tonight. I was already feeling pretty shitty about myself. No point in tossing another log or two onto the fire. "Another time."

We chatted for about fifteen minutes before Nate's phone vibrated with a text. He glanced down at his phone, then lifted his gaze to mine. "She sent the address."

My heart beat faster. "Send it to me."

"Be careful, Harper," Louise said. "You're not in law enforcement. If you press him too hard, he could report you for harassment."

"I'll be careful." In fact, I had a plan. It was probably crazy, but it just might work.

We called it a night soon afterward, and as Nate and Louise left, I made an excuse about needing to go to the bathroom. After I finished in the restroom, I headed straight for the bar and sat on a stool in front of James Malcolm.

He glanced at me with a smirk. "You ready to order that Jack and Coke now?"

Little did he know how badly I wanted it, but this wasn't the time. "No. I want you to run an errand with me."

He laughed, but it quickly faded. "You're serious."

"As a heart attack." I leaned closer. "Here's the deal. Your boy Eddie is looking really good as a suspect right now. You believe he's innocent, and you don't want me talking to him, but trust me, the Jackson Creek PD will be talking to him tomorrow, and he has a better shot at proving his innocence with me than with them."

There was a reason for my madness. I had a strong suspicion that Eddie was working for Malcolm. If Malcolm was with me, I could watch their interactions and get a better handle on the situation.

He rested the palm of his hand on the counter and leaned toward me. "I thought a court of law was supposed to prove his guilt, not the other way around."

"Come now, Mr. Malcolm," I said, syrupy sweet. "You of all people know you're guilty until proven innocent. Why else would the police be harassing you?"

His eyebrow quirked. "You mean like they're harassing *you?*"

I shrugged. I could concede he had a point.

"I'm not gonna go with you to watch you interrogate an innocent man," he spat out, fire burning in his eyes.

"No, you're gonna come along so I can prove to you that I'm not going to try to hang this on him if he didn't do it."

He shook his head in disgust. "You've got no authority to do *anything* to him."

"No, but I might be able to convince the authorities that he's not guilty."

"How are you gonna convince them of anything when you can't even convince them that *you're* not a threat?"

He had another good point, but I hoped he'd come with me anyway.

His jaw worked, and he looked furious, but he ground out through his clenched jaw, "I still don't get why you want me along."

I really hoped this plan didn't backfire. There were whispers that Malcolm had killed people before and gotten away with it. I hadn't brought my gun, so he would have every chance to kill me and hide my body somewhere no one could find it. But I believed he really did want to work with me. And Louise, Nate, and Drew had all seen me at Scooter's tonight. Malcolm would be taking a real risk if he hurt me.

Then again, maybe all the alcohol I'd consumed over the past few months had killed a lot of brain cells.

"Look," I said, trying to sound perfectly reasonable. "This afternoon, you said you wanted to work with me on this, so here's your chance. You sit with Eddie while I ask him some questions, and I can prove I'm not trying to railroad him. I only want answers. He might have another lead for me to pursue. Ava's best friend says Eddie had a special bond with Ava. He might be able to tell us something no one else can."

When he cursed under his breath, I knew I had him, but it still took him nearly another minute to agree.

"We need to meet with him tonight," I said.

He shot me a gaze that suggested I'd lost my mind. "In case you haven't noticed, I'm working."

"Yeah, and so am I, only my job seems a bit more important than helping people get drunk."

Anger burned in his eyes. "You didn't seem to mind when I was serving you."

I held his gaze, trying to keep my temper in check.

"You realize it's after ten o'clock," he said dryly.

I shot him a look of disbelief. "You about to turn into a pumpkin?"

"No, but the kid has work tomorrow. He might be in bed."

Why was he stalling so hard? It only made me more suspicious. "He's in his fucking twenties. Why would he be in bed?"

A vein in his temple throbbed. "Fine. We'll go tonight. Go outside and wait for me by your car," he grunted, looking pissed that he'd agreed to my terms. "I need to tie up some loose ends before I leave."

Like call Eddie and warn him we were coming? "I'll head over there now. Meet you when you get there."

He shook his head. "No fucking way. We go together or not at all."

Was it worth the risk of Eddie running to get Malcolm to come? In this case, yeah. "Fine." I slapped some cash on the bar top to cover my two beers and a tip. I was quickly running out of money. The job at my father's firm was starting to look more appealing.

When I went outside, the cool night air felt good on my flushed cheeks. I still wasn't sure I'd made the right call, but it was too late to change course now.

About ten minutes later, Malcolm finally emerged from around the back. He was wearing his leather jacket and looked pissed as he strode toward me. "This is inconvenient as hell," he grunted at he walked up to me and held out his hand expectantly.

"What?" I barked, glancing down at his open palm.

"You've had two beers and there's no telling how much you had to drink before you walked into my bar. I'm driving."

"There's no way you're driving my car. I'm perfectly sober!"

"You want me to join you on this expedition? Then I'm driving."

I could argue, but this might be another stall tactic. We'd wasted enough time.

"Fine." I dug my keys out of my purse and dropped them into his hand before I stomped to the passenger side and opened the door. There were papers on the seat, and I reached to pick them up, my fingers wrapping around the photo frame. Malcolm was still outside, grumbling under his breath, which thankfully meant he hadn't seen my horrified reaction. I tossed the frame onto the floorboard, the papers covering it.

Malcolm got into the driver's seat, filling my car with his presence. His knees hit the steering wheel, and he cursed under his breath as he groped around the side of the seat, presumably to push the seat back.

"It's a bar to push it back in the front, underneath."

He grunted in disgust, "Of course it is, cheap ass car."

I shot back. "I was a Little Rock police detective. I sure wasn't in it to get rich."

The driver's seat shot backward, and his knees fit under the steering wheel. "Unless you were on the take."

My anger flared. "Already attacking my character?"

"I never said you *were* on the take," he said with a smirk as he turned the key in the ignition. "I merely stated it was possible."

"That's a myth. Detectives in the Little Rock department aren't on the take." But even as I said it, I didn't believe it. Something was going on in the department, and I'd been swept up in it as collateral damage.

A bitter sound emerged from his throat. "Don't be so sure about that."

I crossed my arms over my chest. "I take it you know this from personal experience? Maybe you've offered a few bribes of your own?"

He shot the car in reverse, and when he stopped, he turned to me with a wolfish look in his eyes. "I could answer that, but I plead the fifth in case I incriminate myself."

"Your fancy lawyer teach you that?"

He punched the gas, throwing me back in my seat. "Yep."

He made a running stop at the edge of the parking lot and headed toward town.

"How do you know where to go?" I asked.

"Because Eddie told me where he lives, or at least the general area, and it's south of Jackson Creek." He shot me a glance. "I take it you have the address?"

"Yep."

"You get it from one of your dates?" he asked in a snide tone.

"What makes you think I got it from one of the two *gentlemen* I was with?"

"Because one of them is a Jackson Creek officer and the other runs the bookstore and is known for sticking his nose into places it doesn't belong. Stands to reason you got it from one of them."

My heart skipped a beat. "How many people feel that way about Nate?"

"That he's a busybody? Most people like him, but some of the nefarious ones think he's up to no good."

"Like yourself?"

He grinned like a Cheshire cat as he shot a look at me. "What makes you think I'm nefarious?"

"Call it a hunch."

His grin spread, but it didn't reach his eyes. "People often have reputations for a reason."

"Who are you trying to warn me about, Mr. Malcolm?"

He shot me another quick glance before turning to the road. "No one in particular. It's a good life lesson in general."

"Ah..." I said with a smirk. "You hand out idioms and platitudes while serving your drinks? We're not in your bar, so why give me one on the house?"

He kept his gaze on the road. "Makes you wonder, doesn't it?"

What *was* he warning me about?

"Why did you open a bar out in the middle of nowhere?" I asked, deciding to just go for it. "With no apparent ties to anyone or anything?"

"Seems you like it well enough to have shown up three times within about twenty-four hours." One side of his mouth quirked. "And who says I don't have any ties?"

"Then what are they?"

"Didn't say that I did either," he said good-naturedly.

"What brought you to Lone County?" I asked, my tone short.

"Everyone loves a good mystery, Detective. You of all people should know that."

"I love solving mysteries, Mr. Malcolm."

"Then you won't find this one very interesting. I found a good deal on a piece of land with little competition and a strong demographic market." He tilted his head toward me. "Bet they weren't teaching that in detective school."

"Bullshit answers?" I countered. "Actually, they did."

His grin spread, but he didn't respond and neither did I. When we got to the edge of town, I told him to turn south on a country road, then gave him directions until he pulled up in front of an older ranch house that was a good hundred yards from its nearest neighbors. The driveway was empty, and no lights were on in the house.

I had a very bad feeling about this.

The house was faded red brick with a white single-car garage. The bushes in front of it were overgrown, and the yard looked like Eddie had skipped the last mow job of the season last fall.

I opened the car door and got out, my gaze on the front door. Malcolm emerged from the driver's side and moved to the front of the car.

"What's Eddie drive?" I asked. "Where's his car?"

"Hell if I know," Malcolm muttered and headed to the front door. "He might not be home. Or maybe it's in the garage?"

Or maybe Malcolm had warned him we were coming and to leave.

I glanced up at the eaves of the house. No cameras and the front door had a small, illuminated button next to it. No camera there either.

I followed, surprised when Malcolm pounded on the solid front door with the meaty flesh of his fist. When there was no response after a few seconds, he pounded again.

I wandered over to the driveway, regretting my decision to involve Malcolm.

He pounded again, this time shouting, "Eddie. Open the door."

The single-car garage door didn't have any windows, but I turned the corner and saw a door on the side of the house. Nine panes filled the top half of the door. I pulled out my phone, turned on the flashlight, then shone it through the glass. The light revealed an empty garage.

Fuming, I went back to the front and found an impatient Malcolm on the front porch.

"He's not here," I said in a flat tone, giving him a dark look. "But then, you already knew that, didn't you?"

"What the fuck are you talking about?" he demanded, his eyes blazing. "Why would I leave the bar if I knew he wasn't here? Why would I waste nearly an hour of my time?"

"To throw me off?" I asked, moving closer. "You had plenty of time to warn him."

"Warn him about *what?*" he shouted, descending the steps toward me. "That you're going to interrogate him about God knows what?"

"Does Eddie Johnson work for you?" I asked, a few feet from him.

He shook his head as though to clear it. "You're the one who told me he works at the school, which means you *know* where he works. What the hell do you think he does for me?"

"Get you information."

"About *what?*"

Shit. I'd already told him too much. I took a step back and ran my hand over my head.

"What did you plan to ask him?" Malcolm asked in an ominous tone.

I shook my head.

"You're not conducting an official investigation, so there's no reason you can't share it with me," he said, his voice tight. "You think you have something on him. What?"

"He was spending time alone with Ava at school," I shot back. "Maybe he was grooming her."

He released a short laugh. "Eddie? No fucking way." He marched up to the door and pounded again. "Eddie, it's Malcolm. Open the fucking door." He waited a few seconds, then lifted his right foot and kicked the door next to the handle.

Cracking wood filled the night air, but the door remained closed.

"What the hell are you doing?" I shouted.

Ignoring me, he kicked it again, and this time a large crack appeared where he'd kicked it. One more kick had the door swinging inward. He pulled a small pen-sized flashlight out of his jacket pocket and flicked it on, shining it into the open doorway before he took a step inside.

"You can't just go in there! That's breaking and entering!"

"You gonna call the cops on me?" he asked from inside. A few seconds later, he grumbled a few curse words. "Get in here."

An inner battle waged inside me. Sure, I was breaking rules by looking into Ava's disappearance, but I hadn't broken the law. This would be crossing the line.

Did I really want to do that? Wouldn't that make me the bad person everyone thought I was? Then again, they already thought it, so what was stopping me?

I stood on the step and stared through the open door. I could see a light in the back of the small house, and I knew Malcolm had found something.

We had to be careful. Depending on what we found, we could be implicated. Chief Larson would be happy to toss us both into jail. But I hadn't come this far to turn back now.

"What did you find?" I asked, stepping inside.

Malcolm stood in a small galley kitchen, shooting a pissed expression at me, then flicked his light to the back door. The glass was broken in a small pane on the door, just above and to the right of the doorknob.

"Shit," I moaned.

The light dropped to the floor, pieces of broken glass spread out along with a few drops of blood.

"Double shit."

"Someone beat us here," Malcolm said, then squatted next to the blood. "And not long ago. This blood looks fresh. It's still wet."

"You're suggesting someone kidnapped Eddie Johnson?" I asked in disbelief.

His sarcastic gaze lifted to mine. "What do you *think* happened here?"

Okay, he was right. Stupid question. But the better question was who had taken him and why?

Chapter Twenty-Four

"DID YOU DO THIS?" I asked, really wishing I had my gun.

"Why the fuck would I kidnap the guy I was trying to protect from you?" he asked, sounding like I'd asked the stupidest question he'd ever heard.

I motioned toward him. "Why would you be this involved in protecting a regular in your bar unless you had some kind of investment?"

He stood and narrowed his gaze. "What are you suggesting?"

"I'm not suggesting anything," I countered. "Answer the question."

"I'm here because the kid has no one else to look after him. His mother died and his father remarried. The old witch treats him like a literal version of the proverbial stepchild. He's a good kid. He just needs a break."

"A break like kidnapping a twelve-year-old girl?"

"What? Fuck no," he grunted.

"How well do you know him?"

"Well enough to know he didn't do that," he spat out, and spun to look around the room. "They were in a hurry, and this was recent." He looked up at me. "Who else knew you were planning to pay a visit?"

"You," I countered, my brow lifted. "You had a good ten minutes inside your bar to arrange for someone to take him."

"If he worked for me, why wouldn't I just tell him to go into hiding?"

"Maybe you did," I said, not wanting to consider the alternative suspects. "Maybe he cut himself while he was fleeing."

His gaze was dubious.

Even I knew that sounded far-fetched.

"Who else knew you were interested in him?" he asked. "Tweedle Dum and Tweedle Dee?"

"Nate and Drew?" I asked in disbelief. "One's a Jackson Creek police officer and the other is a mild-mannered bookstore owner."

"And, as we've established, the bookstore owner's awfully nosy."

I shook my head. "I don't see him doing it."

"Sometimes it's the ones you least suspect," he said, then a grin lifted the corners of his mouth, even though his eyes still looked deadly. "Ever watched that Netflix show, *You*?"

"Have *you*?" I asked in shock.

He snorted with a look that made it clear he hadn't. But he had a point. Ruling someone out based on outward appearances was bad practice. Still, would Nate or Drew have had time to pull something like this together? Whoever had taken Eddie had also stolen his car.

"Who else knew?" Malcolm asked.

I rubbed my forehead, my hand shaking. Dammit, I needed a drink. "The school secretary. She gave Nate the address when Louise and Drew refused to get it."

"She got any skin in this game?"

"Not that I know of, but I don't even know her name. I know absolutely nothing about her."

"Who else?"

"I didn't exactly go broadcasting that I was headed over here," I said in exasperation. "And I doubt anyone overheard us at the bar." Dread washed through me as another suspect popped into my head. "Casey LaRue's parents. They planned to go to the principal tomorrow morning to tell her about Eddie taking Casey and Ava to the janitor's closet."

His eyes narrowed. "What?"

"Instead of going to recess after lunch, the two girls were hanging out with him in the janitor's closet. Casey swears nothing inappropriate happened, but she was home sick with the flu a couple of weeks ago, giving Eddie time to form a closer bond with Ava. Then last Thursday, Casey caught them being secretive and heard the word *tonight*."

"Fuck," he muttered under his breath. "Her father's not gonna want to wait for the police. He'd want to take things into his own hands."

"But why take Eddie's car?" That part didn't make sense.

"To make it look like he fled on his own."

"With the broken window?" I asked. "And the blood? It looks like a home invasion."

"Because they were damn sloppy about it," he said, gesturing to the door.

"I doubt either one of them are criminal masterminds. She's a stay-at-home mom and he runs a manufacturing plant."

His lips pressed together as he considered it. "Sure, and they might be into those murder podcasts. Plenty of people consider themselves experts after listening to those."

"I'm searching the rest of the house," I said, pulling a pair of leather gloves out of my coat pocket and tugging them on.

"You think he left a note that says, 'I molested little girls'?"

"You never know what he might have left."

He grunted. He knew I was right.

I started looking around the room for anything that might help. Malcolm used the bottom of his coat to tug open a couple of drawers until he pulled out a small dishrag and used it to look around. There was a stack of mail on the edge of the counter. A quick glance through it ruled out anything important. A couple of bills and a parking ticket from Jackson Creek from a few weeks ago.

One dirty plate, glass, and set of silverware sat in the sink, and a half-empty cup of coffee sat on the kitchen table.

"Fresh?" I asked when I realized Malcolm was looking at it too.

He stuck his finger in the liquid, then flung off the drops from his finger. "Cold. Probably from this morning."

The coffee pot on the counter by the refrigerator was empty and off, so I suspected he was right.

I walked past Malcolm to the door and looked through the panes to study the back patio. There wasn't much out there, just a rusted outdoor loveseat with no cushions and a couple of terra cotta pots filled with weeds. But when I shined my phone's flashlight out the window, I noticed a couple of dark spots on the concrete.

Blood.

"I think whoever broke in cut themselves. There's blood on the glass and outside."

"Amateurs," Malcolm sneered in disgust.

"All the more reason to suspect the LaRues."

He glanced over at me. "Wanna pay them a visit?"

"On what grounds?" I asked. "I don't have a badge, and I don't have a ready excuse to show up around midnight asking them if they know where the guy who took their daughter into a janitor's closet on the daily might be."

He grunted.

"I'm going to keep looking." I headed into the living room and poked around. For a bachelor in his twenties, he had a pretty picked-up home. Besides a large TV, he had two game systems and one of the consoles was in the coffee table.

Malcolm joined me, using the dishrag to look under cushions and pull furniture away from walls.

I moved down the hall toward a bedroom empty of everything except for a few boxes. I opened them and found family photos that included a blond boy at various ages and his parents. I found one of the boy as an older teen and handed it to Malcolm. "This Eddie?"

He took it and frowned. "Yep."

I opened the other box and found more of the same along with old report cards and children's artwork. The closet had a few coats, including a camouflage jacket. I checked all the pockets and only found a couple of gas station receipts and a gum wrapper.

I turned around and saw Malcolm's frame filling the doorway, watching me.

"Not off searching on your own?" I asked in a snotty tone.

"No. If I found anything, you'd probably claim I planted it."

He had a point.

We headed into the bathroom next, which also seemed relatively clean for a twenty-something guy living on his own, but then again, he was a school janitor. Maybe he was a neat freak. Malcolm stood in the doorway watching me as I searched. I only found the usual toiletries and cleaners. I brushed past Malcolm to move into and through the last door.

The door was partially closed. I pushed it open, not surprised to see a full-sized bed with no headboard and a small nightstand on the far side. From the doorway, I shined my flashlight around the room. The bed was rumpled and unmade, but everything else looked neat and clean. The closet had two track doors that were closed.

"He was in bed when they broke in," Malcolm said behind me.

"Yeah," I said. "As neat as the rest of the house is, I suspect he makes his bed, or at least tossed the ends of the sheet and blanket up to the pillows."

I pointed the light at the bedside table, where an iPhone was charging.

"Idiots," Malcolm grunted. "Who runs off and leaves their phone? They could have at least tried to make it look like he really took off."

"Or maybe your goons had short notice and didn't have time to clean their tracks."

He exhaled in disgust. "If anyone working for me had been this sloppy, they would have found themselves out of a job."

I was glad my back was to him, so he didn't see my shock at his admission to criminal activity.

I might not know all the details, but it was clear that Eddie Johnson wasn't here.

Dammit.

I pushed out a sigh. "I need to find out what Mr. LaRue drives and ask the neighbors if they saw anything within the last hour."

"How do you plan to do that?"

I felt like I'd exhausted my favors from Louise, but I really needed to know. I ran a hand over my head, trying to make myself focus. "I'll call Louise. She can look it up."

"Don't bother," he said. I looked over my shoulder to see him tapping on his phone. "I have someone looking into it."

"Do I want to know who you're asking?"

He glanced up, a sly look on his face. "Probably not."

Great.

I searched the bedside table drawers and found underwear and socks, neatly folded. Nothing underneath.

I lifted the edge of the bed to look underneath, surprised when the weight suddenly lessened. Malcolm was lifting the corner of the mattress.

I didn't find anything underneath on either side, nor under the pillows or covers. I got down on my knees to search under the bed, and Malcolm handed me his much better flashlight.

"Thanks," I mumbled as I took it and searched the floor, only finding a few dust bunnies. "Nothing."

"The closet," he said as I got to my feet. He walked over and slid a wooden door on tracks to the side. After handing back his flashlight, I searched between the hanging clothes and pockets, inside shoes and on top of the shelf.

"Nothing," I said, my mouth twisted to the side. If Eddie was a pedophile, I would have expected to see something hinting at that, especially since he lived alone. "Did you see a computer or tablet anywhere?"

"Nope."

"Me either. Did you see any place where he might have kept one? An empty spot surrounded by dust?"

"As clean as this place is, not likely. But I've seen him with a tablet at the tavern, though, so I know he has one."

I looked up at him. "What if whoever took Eddie took the tablet too?"

"To see if he has photos of little kids?"

I grimaced. "Yeah."

"Sounds logical to me, except they left his phone, but we've already established that they're sloppy. Or it could have just been in his car."

"Which is missing too."

He shrugged, looking pissed, but I suspected he wasn't angry about me or my questions.

I stepped back into the hall. "Did you see a door to a basement?"

"Nope. Pretty sure the house is built on a concrete slab."

"Let's check the attic." I headed toward the kitchen. "The access is probably in the garage."

The garage smelled faintly of gas and had shelves on one side covered in paint cans and various odds and ends. A quick search didn't reveal anything useful, so I turned my attention to the nine-foot ceiling. A cord hung from a rectangular door, just out of reach over my head. Malcolm walked over and easily grabbed it and tugged it down. A fold-up ladder descended onto the concrete floor.

"You goin' up?" he asked in a mischievous tone.

"Yep." I started up, and he handed the flashlight back to me. It was skinny enough to hold while I climbed up. It occurred to me that I was wearing a dress and he was directly beneath me, holding the sides of the ladder. But it was dark, the skirt hung to just over my knees, and I was wearing underwear. More power to him if he got his thrills checking out my blue cotton panties covered in tiny flowers.

I shifted the flashlight when I started to emerge from the hole, shining it around the space and resisting the urge to sneeze. Pulling down the stairs must have disturbed dust in the unfinished attic space. Insulation was stuffed between the rafters, and from what I could tell, there wasn't anything else.

"Nothing," I said as I climbed down and handed the flashlight back to him.

His phone vibrated in his pocket, and he slipped it out and read the screen. "Eddie drives a ten-year-old white Jeep Cherokee." He snuck me a dark look. "Easy enough to stash someone in the back."

"Don't you think the LaRues would have had a plan for carrying him away if they did this?" I asked dubiously.

"The LaRues have two luxury sedans. The trunks are large enough to stash a body, but it would be easier to use the back of the SUV."

I still hoped Casey's parents weren't involved, but they seemed more likely than Nate or Drew. "How would they know about his Jeep?"

"They would have seen his car in the parking lot after school," Malcolm said.

Shit. I'd seen the SUV there, which meant Eddie had been there when I'd gone by the school earlier. I should have tried to go in and talk to him.

But something else caught my attention.

I narrowed my eyes. "How do you know they would have seen it?"

A lazy grin lifted his mouth. "They go to the school to pick up their kid."

Or he'd looked up their residence. Not exactly giving me the warm fuzzies. That and the fact that he'd managed to find out so much private information within minutes by texting someone.

"We can drive by the LaRues' house, but other than peeking in their garage windows—presuming they have any—we won't know if they took Eddie's Jeep."

His eyes darkened, his face looking even more intimidating swathed in shadows. "Leave that to me."

I put a hand on my hip. "You think I'm going to let you go rogue on this unsuspecting family?"

"Who the hell said I was going rogue?" he demanded. "I'll make some calls. Do a little snooping."

"I don't like the sound of this."

"Do you want to go over to the LaRues', who I'm sure live in a nice, respectable neighborhood, and skulk around the house peeking in windows?" He gave me look of pity. "I'm sure Chief Larson would love any reason to stick you behind bars."

"Um...I could say the same about you."

He laughed. "Just leave it to me. Let's go."

My heart sunk as we headed out the front door. Eddie was my best possible source of a lead, and if he was truly missing or dead...

Malcolm made a half-hearted attempt to close the front door. As I descended the front steps, tugging off my gloves, I realized I needed to do a more thorough investigation of the break-in.

"I'm checking the back," I called out as I walked across the driveway and turned on my phone's flashlight again, stuffing the gloves into my left pocket. Since the grass was about eight inches tall, I could see where I'd trampled it to get to the side door of the garage, but I could see another set of footprints swinging wide of the house. Why hadn't I thought to look?

Damn, I was getting sloppy.

I didn't want to add more prints, and the light from my phone wasn't cutting it, so I called out to Malcolm to bring his flashlight.

"What did you find?" he asked, holding it out as he joined me.

"Footprints." I flicked the light back on and pointed out the ones close to the house. "These are mine." I swung the beam over several feet. "Those are someone else's." Some of the imprints were pointed toward the house but others were smashed. Sections of the grass looked trampled by something that had been dragged.

"I think they wrapped him up in something," I said, my heart sinking, I spun around and headed back inside the house.

I started searching the hardwood floor in the living room. "Dammit," I exclaimed in frustration. "He was such a neat freak I don't see any signs of a rug."

His voice was hard. "You think they rolled him up in a rug?"

"Maybe." I headed to the back door and started to pull a fresh glove out of my pocket.

Malcolm reached around me with the cloth he'd stuffed into his own pocket and grabbed the doorknob and turned it.

"Unlocked," I muttered under my breath.

"Fucking amateurs."

"Could be a good thing in this instance." Trying not to crunch the glass on the floor, I headed out the doorway and down the two concrete steps onto the patio. The yard was small, about twenty feet deep before it shifted into woods. I swung the flashlight to the right of the patio, looking for the footprints.

A clear set of prints could be seen running close to the house from the corner, heading toward the patio. Based on the size, I guessed them to belong to a man wearing dress shoes.

"Bingo."

"What?" he asked behind me.

"Male dress shoes or loafers." I pointed to the prints.

"How can you tell?"

"The size tells me they belong to a man. You can tell the type by checking out the print in the mud next to the concrete." I shifted the beam to the muddy section next to the house. "It's only a partial print, the middle section and the heel, but there's no tread. It's smooth and look at the shape of the heel. No boot's going to leave an imprint like that." I pointed to the square shape of the heel.

Malcolm glanced over at me, and a predatory gleam filled his eyes. "LaRue."

"Maybe, maybe not," I said. "Do factory directors wear dress shoes? Or do they wear work boots?"

He frowned. "Then who?" His eyes darkened again. "Peterman."

Chapter Twenty-Five

"THERE'S A WHOLE LOT of speculating going on with little evidence to back it up," I said. "Besides, why would Peterman kidnap Eddie?"

"Maybe the LaRues told him about his daughter and the janitor's closet," Malcolm said.

That was a possibility, but it was close to eleven, much too late for us to be calling the LaRues. Or the Petermans.

I ran my hand over my head. A throbbing pain was stabbing my temple.

"No drag marks in the back here like on the side of the house," Malcolm said, taking the flashlight out of my hand and pointing to the grass. "They entered through the back and likely left through the door in the garage."

He was right.

I pushed past him, going back into the house and through the garage door. I opened the side door and looked outside, confirming what Malcolm suggested.

How had I missed it before?

I swallowed bile that rose in my throat.

What else had I missed? I wasn't at the top of my game, and the alcohol and lack of sleep weren't helping.

"You were right. They dragged him out the side door," I said.

"Why not just stuff him in the back of the Jeep in the garage?"

Why indeed? Then it hit me. "Maybe whoever it was came over on their own and dragged him out to their car before coming came back to get the Jeep."

"The blood couldn't be more than an hour old," Malcolm said.

"Unless whoever took him lives close by, there had to be two of them. Otherwise, how would they manage dropping off their car and coming back to get Eddie's Jeep?"

"Or they stashed his Jeep somewhere close by," Malcolm said, his gaze scanning the yard.

"True, but with all these trees, they could have stashed it anywhere. Finding it in the dark could be impossible."

I opened the door and pointed my phone's flashlight on the doorway, squatting when I noticed something stuck to the threshold. "Looks like carpet fibers."

"If they rolled him up, then he's likely dead," Malcolm said in a flat tone.

"Maybe," I said. "Maybe not. Maybe they knocked him out and carried him out in the rug because it was easier."

"For one person to carry him out alone?" He sounded skeptical.

Pushing out a long sigh, I said, "I have no idea. I'd love to get a forensics team in here, but we both know that's not going to happen. Or at least I wouldn't have access to the results."

"You want to call this in to Jackson Creek PD?" he asked in surprise.

My brow shot up. "You don't? They have better resources than we do to find him."

He snorted. "Like they're going to look."

"There was an obvious break-in. His car's gone."

"Exactly. They'll think he took off. If those girls' parents push it, they'll be looking for him, but not as a victim. They won't pay any attention to anything here."

Knowing Chief Larson, he was probably right.

We stood in silence for several long seconds before he said, "We're spinning our wheels. Let's go."

"Yeah," I said, feeling defeated.

We headed back through the front door and got in my car. I insisted on driving this time. Malcolm didn't protest.

He sat in the passenger seat, his feet hitting the pile on the floorboard.

My heart leapt into my throat. I didn't want him to see the photo. I wasn't ready to share the message with anyone yet.

To my relief, he ignored it and buckled his seat belt.

He also didn't protest when I didn't drive toward the tavern, instead taking a diversion to downtown.

"The Petermans' house," I said as we turned the corner onto their street. The house was lit up inside, even at this late hour, but there weren't any police cars parked out front. I parked across the street, one house down from the Petermans'.

"Which one is the girl's window?" Malcolm asked, pointing to the second story porch.

"The two on the left." The only ones not lit up. "Vanessa found the window wide open this morning and I found the imprint of a ladder in the dirt down below."

"You think whoever took her carried her down the ladder?"

"Yeah, but I suspect he either drugged her or she went willingly. Otherwise, it would have been precarious for them to descend the ladder."

"You think she might have gone willingly?" he asked.

"If she trusted Eddie, maybe," I said. "Her father is awful to her, and according to Casey, Eddie's kind to her. She needed an escape and maybe he provided it."

"Okay," he said slowly. "Let's say Eddie decided to save her and came for her last night. Where is she now?"

I shook my head. "I don't know. I saw an older Jeep Cherokee outside the school this afternoon, so I know he was at work."

He was quiet for a moment. "What if she was at Eddie's house when whoever took him showed up?"

"If she was there, why didn't we see any evidence of it? One coffee cup. One plate and set of silverware in the sink."

"All the more proof that he didn't take her."

I was starting to agree with him.

I rubbed my temple, trying to ease the pain. "Maybe you're right and Eddie didn't take her. Maybe someone is trying to pin this on him."

"Who? The girl's friend?"

I considered it a moment. "No, not Casey, but I'm not entirely sure TJ Peterman is clear on all of this. He insists his daughter ran away and refuses to let the police make it public. I think you're right and there's a chance the LaRues told the Petermans about Eddie, especially knowing that Ava is missing. Maybe TJ saw this as an opportunity to throw any possible trail off him and pin it on Eddie? If Eddie's missing, that turns out to be pretty convenient."

"You saw that back door. TJ Peterman is a fucking asshole, but he's not an idiot. Besides, do you really think he could kill his daughter?"

I turned to look him in the eyes. "Do you have any reason to believe he wouldn't?"

Pain flashed on his face. Something I said hit close to home, but then his face hardened. "No. Peterman is capable of being a monster."

"Yeah," I said, barely above a whisper. Then I decided to lay it all out. I didn't believe Malcolm was responsible for her disappearance, although maybe that was wishful thinking. I couldn't really tell what was instinct or what I wanted to believe anymore. This case was personal, and any detective with experience knew you didn't work personal cases for a reason. But I couldn't just leave it. *Someone* had to try to save Ava.

"My working theory was Ricky Morris took her, and TJ either knew or suspected it. It makes sense that he wouldn't want to involve the police. He's trying to work it out on his own." I glanced over at him. "Do you know anything about the murder last night north of the laundromat?"

His mouth pressed into a thin line, his gaze still on the house. "Drug deal gone bad."

"Did Kylie's cousin have anything to do with it?"

He gave me a sharp look.

"She was asking Louise at lunch, but Louise didn't have any information."

"No, although I know he's mixed up with the Morrises. That boy's gonna break her heart."

"Is that why you're so protective of her?" I asked quietly.

"Who the fuck says I'm protective of her?" he grunted.

"Louise says it's common knowledge."

"I'm protective of everyone in my establishment," he growled.

"But Kylie's young and pretty—"

"*Drop it.*"

I did, but I couldn't help wondering if they were sleeping together. Malcolm said he liked to keep tabs on things. Sleeping with a naïve young woman whose cousin worked for a potential nemesis might be a way to do it.

"Let's go down the alley behind the Petermans' house," he said, rubbing his chin. "See what's behind there."

"I doubt TJ would park Eddie's Jeep in the alley or his garage."

"If he was stupid enough to pull off that kidnapping, then who knows?"

"But you don't think he did it," I said. I agreed, if only because TJ wasn't stupid enough to leave behind such a messy crime scene.

"Indulge me anyway."

I drove down the street, then turned into the alley. A few streetlamps were scattered down the one-car lane, but most of it was dark. I drove slowly, trying to figure out which garage belonged to the Petermans. Once I found the white clapboard, two-car garage with newer doors, I pulled to a stop and put the car in park.

I turned to him. "Wanna peek in the windows?"

He grinned. "I thought you'd never ask."

We got out at the same time and walked over to the window on the side of the structure.

Malcolm flicked on his flashlight and pointed the beam inside. Two cars were inside, neither a Jeep Cherokee.

"Well, neither of us thought he'd be that stupid," Malcolm whispered. "But to keep things interesting, what do you say we drop by the LaRues'?"

An hour ago, I would have said no. Hell, I *did* say no, but now I was too committed to let him do it on his own.

Turned out their garage was locked up tight with no windows. Malcolm said that wouldn't necessarily stop him, but I refused to let him break in to check. Possible Peeping Tom charges were one thing; B&E charges were another.

"Take me back to the tavern," he said. "We'll start fresh in the morning."

I gaped at him. "You think we're going to work on this together?"

He released a short bark. "Hate to break it to you, Detective Adams, but we already are."

"I can only imagine what my mother would say if she found out we've teamed up," I murmured to myself.

"You don't strike me as the type to give a shit what your mother thinks."

I threw a dark look at him, then turned back to the road. "Former rule follower here."

We rode in silence for a few minutes before he said, "You're still holding out on me."

"Excuse me?" I shot back.

"There's something about this investigation that has you panicked."

My thoughts went immediately to the photo at his feet, but I ignored the compulsion to look down there. "Couldn't it be my concern for a missing girl?"

"It could," he conceded, "but it's more than that." He paused, then said quietly, "Your sister was kidnapped. You were there."

Bitterness bled into my words. "Someone's been doing his homework."

"I have to know who I'm working with."

"Well, forgive me if I haven't had time to research you all that extensively, seeing how I'm trying to find a missing child. So while I'm flattered you've decided to trust me, I'm still on the fence about you."

He released a dark chuckle. "What do you want to know?"

My mouth dropped open, and I looked over to see if he was being an asshole, but he seemed amused.

"Go ahead," he said. "I might not answer all your questions, but I might answer some."

"I'm too tired for fucking guessing games."

"Fine," he said, stretching out his legs and leaning back. "Yes, I've worked in organized crime—local, statewide and internationally." He grinned and swung his head to face me.

"And when I say local, I don't mean here. My previous residences."

"Why would you just admit that to me?" I asked in disbelief. "I used to be a cop."

"Used to be is key there, and I never admitted to anything specific. Plus, I can deny it later, claim I was bullshitting you."

"But you're not."

His mouth twisted into a dark smile.

Hell, why not try to appease my curiosity. "Why did you move here?"

"Needed a change of scenery."

"Too many bad influences where you were before?" I asked in a snide tone.

He was quiet for a moment, then said, "Something like that."

"Care to expand on that?"

"No."

"I know about your arrest, obviously. Why did you screw up your deal with the feds?"

He grinned. "Who says I did?"

"The press."

He snorted. "They don't always get things right. *You* of all people should know that."

"But you did help bring down an international drug cartel," I continued. "Why? Especially when you knew it would blow up your life?"

"No comment."

I was tired enough to be ballsy. "Have you ever killed anyone?"

"Have you?"

"You know I have," I said past the lump in my throat.

"Other than the kid?"

"Once. Early in my career. A rapist who had kidnapped a woman. I responded to a domestic situation, called in by a neighbor. Found out later that the guy had kidnapped his coworker and was holding her against her will. I showed up, and it felt like things were fishy. I made up a bullshit excuse to come in and he let me, probably thinking he could subdue me too, but when he pulled a gun, I shot him. Then I found the woman chained to a bed in the bedroom."

"I'm guessing they didn't lose the gun on that one."

"Yeah," I choked out. That had been hard, but the guy was scum, and I'd been commended for trusting my instincts and saving a woman's life. Funny how I'd lost everything when I'd trusted my instincts years later.

"Why'd they lie and say the kid didn't have a gun?" Malcolm asked as the lights of the tavern parking lot came into view.

"Why do you think he had one?"

"Because if you fucked up, you'd admit it."

Maybe I'd been like that then, but I'd been fucking up right and left lately and not copping to it. "Maybe I'm not that woman anymore." I slowed down to turn into the parking lot.

"Maybe not, but maybe that's not a bad thing."

"You think I should be more like you?" I asked bitterly.

"No, but maybe you should live your life outside the shadow of your sister's death."

I pulled in front of the tavern and threw the car into park. I turned to him, my fury building. "You don't know anything about me, James Malcolm, and you sure as hell don't know anything about my sister."

His dark brown eyes held mine. "Maybe not, but I know a shitload about regret, and you, Harper Adams, are fucking drowning in it." He opened the door, then turned back to me. "The answer is yes."

I squinted in confusion.

"Yes, I've killed someone. I've killed more than one someone." Then he got out, walking into the tavern without a backward glance.

Once I got over the shock of his admission to murder, I focused on his other shocking statement.

I told myself he was wrong about me living in my sister's shadow, but he wasn't wrong about the regret. I'd been drowning in it for years. I'd been pummeled by waves more times than I could count, and right now I was covered by a giant one, only this time I wasn't sure I'd surface soon enough to survive.

Chapter Twenty-Six

THE NEXT MORNING, I woke up with a hell of a hangover, made worse by the chiming of the alarm on my phone. Groaning, I blindly reached for the button to turn it off.

Why had I set an alarm for six-thirty?

I'd gotten home around eleven-thirty the night before, James Malcolm's words pounding in my head. As soon as I opened the apartment door, I realized my sheets were still in the washing machine at my parents' house. If my mother had moved them to the dryer (likely), she hadn't brought them up to my apartment, and I wasn't about to go through the back door to check. The lights in the house were off, which meant my father was probably in bed.

Instead, I grabbed the open bottle of whiskey, poured some into a glass and sat on the sofa, trying to drown out the memories that had flooded my head.

I'd done my best to put Andi's kidnapping behind me, but tonight my head was flooded with snapshots of her kidnapping—and also of the shooting that had ended my career.

The terror on Andi's face when John Michael Stevens appeared out of the woods, his gun trained on me as he told her to come with him or he'd kill us both.

My mother's shock and fear when I'd burst through the front door sobbing.

The endless questioning by Chief Larson, and then the sheriff, and finally FBI agents.

My mother's cry of anguish when the police chief came to inform my parents that Andi's body had been found.

Staring at my sister's casket.

Dylan Carpenter as he ran in the alley, pulling the gun out of the waistband of his jeans and turning to shoot at me. The shock on his face when he realized I'd shot him.

Watching his body crumple to the ground. The sound of his gun clacking on the cement.

The blood seeping into his shirt as he bled out.

Keith showing up within the half-hour, leading me away as he tried to convince me that I'd been seeing things and there hadn't been a gun.

Everyone in the department turning on me.

Being charged with second degree murder and becoming a public pariah.

Losing my friends, my home, my entire life and ending up back here, the one place I'd never wanted to return.

My imagination had also run wild with what happened to Ava and Eddie Johnson.

I continued to drink until the thoughts became more distorted and made little sense. I must have finally passed out around two or three, only to now find myself nauseous and with a throbbing head.

What good was I to Ava this way?

I released a bitter laugh, then nearly threw up. What good had I been to her yesterday?

Leaning my head against the back of the sofa, I closed my eyes and took a breath through my mouth. I just needed coffee and something greasy to settle my stomach. Or at least coffee and a shower.

But first, the room needed to stop spinning.

I fell asleep again, then woke up to another alarm. The room was brighter, and I felt less dizzy. I got up and walked into the bathroom, where I threw up everything I'd had the night before, which wasn't much.

Kneeling on the tile floor, my head resting against the rim of the toilet, I knew I couldn't keep doing this. I needed to get my shit together, but alcohol was the only way I could make it through the day without guilt eating me alive. I knew I saw a gun. I knew if I hadn't taken a shot, I might be the one dead. But I still struggled knowing I'd ended the life of a teen before his life had really started.

When the nausea passed a few minutes later, I got up and brushed my teeth, walking out into the living room to find my phone.

It was a few minutes after nine, and I had several missed calls. One from Louise. One from Nate, and one from James Malcolm.

The first two had left voicemail messages, but Malcolm hadn't.

I listened to Louise's first.

"I'm not sure if you've heard, but the LaRues went to the elementary school this morning and reported Eddie Johnson. Your visit to him this morning must have scared him because he didn't show up for work. Now there's an APB out for him. I don't think they knew you were planning to see him this morning, but Drew might tell them, so be prepared." She took a breath. "Call me."

Shit.

Groaning, I hung up and listened to Nate's message.

"I'm sure you've heard by now that Eddie Johnson is missing. Natalie, the school secretary, has called me twice, asking why I needed his address. I've let her calls go to voicemail, but I have to tell her something, Harper. Call me."

Great. I should have thought of that last night. I was used to working under the shield of the law. Now I was in freefall. One more reason this investigation had turned to shit.

I called Louise back first and she answered right away.

"Jesus, girl," she said as soon as she answered. "What did you say to Eddie Johnson, and did you know he was gonna run?"

"I never spoke to him," I said. "How long has the APB been out?"

"An hour? Long enough for them to realize he hadn't shown up for work and to send a squad car out to his house. His Jeep was missing, so they're saying he took off."

"What a bunch of idiots," I grunted, making my way to my espresso machine.

"Why are they a bunch of idiots?" she asked. "I mean, it's a given that they are, but it sounds like you have specific information."

Could I admit that I went to his house, realized he'd been kidnapped and not reported it to the police?

"I never talked to him," I repeated truthfully.

"I thought you were going to go over this morning."

"I'd planned to, but I overslept. I just got up about ten minutes ago."

"So who tipped him off?" she asked.

"Maybe the LaRues. Millie said they'd wait and tell the school about Eddie's behavior this morning, but her husband didn't agree to anything. He had to be furious. Maybe he showed up at Eddie's house and scared him off."

"Maybe." She didn't seem convinced.

"Not to change the subject, but last night I forgot to ask you if you knew anything more about that murder."

"I still don't know much," she said with a sigh. "They're keeping it pretty tight-lipped, need to know information only."

"We need to tell Kylie it wasn't her cousin."

"Already texted her yesterday." She paused, then said, "If you knew where Eddie Johnson was, you'd let me know, right?"

"I swear I don't know where he is, Louise."

"That didn't really answer my question, did it?" She didn't wait for a response and hung up.

I already felt like horse shit, and now I felt even worse. I called Nate next.

"Hey, Harper, what am I supposed to tell Natalie?"

"Tell her the truth, that you gave me his address."

"Won't you get in trouble?" He sounded worried.

"No, because I never saw him. I overslept until about fifteen minutes ago, when I saw I had messages from you and Louise. When I called her back, she said Eddie didn't show up to work, so the Jackson Creek police had put an all-points bulletin out for him. Millie LaRue knew I planned to talk to him, and I'm sure she told the police. So I don't care if Chief Larson finds out. I've got nothing to hide."

Liar.

Maybe so, but I wasn't about to tell Nate the truth.

"Well, keep me posted," he said, not sounding happy with my answer.

I was disappointing people left and right today, and I hadn't even had a cup of coffee yet.

"Will do."

I hung up and called Malcolm next.

"Malcolm."

"This seems a bit early for you to be up," I said in a falsely cheery tone.

"That's what happens when your lawyer calls to tell you you've been summoned to the police station for questioning."

"Dammit. Is this about Eddie?"

"Probably, but they don't know shit. I told you yesterday, if someone jaywalks in this town, they haul me in. I'll plead the fifth for everything, Carter will spout his legalese, and we'll leave."

"I'm sure they'll haul me in too."

"Why?" he asked, his tone menacing.

"Calm down. It has nothing to do with our adventure last night. Nate got Eddie's address from the school secretary for me, and she wants to know why. I told him to be honest with her. He and Louise both thought I was going over bright and early this morning, but I told them I never made it over this morning because I overslept. Both of which are true."

"Let me guess," he said in a dry tone. "You've got a hell of a hangover."

I snorted. "It's like you're a damn psychic. In any case, I'm sure I'll be called in too. I might even see you there."

"You got an attorney?"

"Why would I need an attorney?"

It was his turn to snort. "Don't be so naive. I'm guessing that's a no. You've got one now. I'll text you his name and number. Let us both know when you're supposed to go in. He'll cover your ass."

"Why would you give me your attorney?"

"I'm not giving him to you. I'm loaning him, and like it or not, we're tied together now. I need to make sure you don't implicate me in anything."

"I'm not going to do that."

"Damn right you're not. Nevertheless, having Hale sit in on your interview is my insurance to make sure you don't."

"I can't afford an attorney."

"I'll cover it. Let me know when you get your summons."

I wasn't thrilled with that, but I'd dwell on it later. "The LaRues showed up at the school this morning to report Eddie. I'm finding it hard to believe they'd do that if Mr. LaRue had something to do with his disappearance."

"The wife told you she was going to the school today. Maybe they thought it would look suspicious if they didn't."

"Yeah, true." But most people didn't have the acting chops to pull that off without suspicion. Then again, I suspected the Jackson Creek PD were incompetent enough that a murderer could walk into the police station to pay a parking ticket, drenched in blood, and leave without arousing suspicion.

"You must be really fuckin' hung over. Get your shit together, Detective."

He hung up that time. Seconds later, the name and number of Malcolm's attorney showed up on my screen, along with a link to his slick website.

Carter Hale, attorney at law.

I was pretty damn sure sharing an attorney with Malcolm was a terrible idea, but having one present wasn't, and God knew I couldn't afford another attorney on my own.

It was merely a matter of time before I was called to the station, so I took a shower and washed away the alcohol oozing from my pores. I was drying my hair when I finally got the call, Chief Larson's number appearing on the screen.

I answered cheerfully, "What can I do for you, Chief Larson?"

"I've heard a few things about you today, Harper Adams."

"Really? All good, I hope."

"Don't be a smartass. I need you to come to the station within the hour."

"Sure thing," I said. "Anything I can do to help." I hung up before he could respond and sent a text to Malcolm and his attorney.

Me: *I've been ordered to come to the station within the hour*

Malcolm responded.

Malcolm: *I just pulled into the parking lot. I'll probably see you when I get out*

Malcolm's attorney sent a message moments after Malcolm's.

Hale: *Don't tell them I'm representing you. Let that be my little surprise.*

Something told me this was going to be a shitshow.

———

THIRTY MINUTES LATER, I walked into the station after finishing my third cup of coffee for the day in the car. My headache was better, yet I still felt two steps behind.

The waiting room was empty, but Malcolm's motorcycle was in the parking lot, so I knew he was in the building somewhere. I told the receptionist I was there to see the chief, then took a seat in one of the rickety chairs in the waiting area.

Ten minutes later, I heard voices in the hall, namely the chief's and the voice of the man Malcolm had been with the previous day.

"You better watch yourself, Malcolm," the chief growled as they rounded the corner to the waiting room. "One day you're gonna slip up, and I'm gonna be there to get you."

Malcolm ignored me as he headed for the door, once again giving the chief the bird as he exited the building.

Chief Larson's face turned beet red, so when he turned to me, he looked ready to tar and feather me in the public square.

"Get your ass in my interrogation room," the chief shouted at me. "Now."

"I don't like how you're talking to my client," my new attorney told the chief. "She's shown up on her own accord, eager to help with whatever you need from her. Perhaps show her a little respect."

Chief Larson's mouth dropped open, and he gaped at me and then the attorney. "What the fuck?"

Yep, bad idea.

I stood and walked toward him. "I figured if you were going to keep calling me in for groundless reasons, perhaps I should cover all my bases." I turned to my new attorney and held out my hand. "Mr. Hale. Thank you for coming on such short notice."

He shook my hand, a mischievous grin lighting up his face. "I just happened to be in the neighborhood, so it was really no trouble at all." He turned to the chief. "Shall we? My client has a busy day, so we need to wrap this up."

"A busy day doing what?" the chief barked.

"Now, now," Mr. Hale chided. "You haven't read my client her rights yet, so no questioning until you do."

Chief Larson fumed as he stomped down the hall into a typical, inhospitable interrogation room with a table in the middle and bare walls. The prerequisite glass window filled up a good portion of the wall across from me.

Mr. Hale and I sat on one side of the table, while the chief dropped his large frame onto the chair on the opposite. The chief didn't have a notebook, nor did he start any kind of recording before he launched into questioning. He didn't read me my rights either.

"What's your interest in Eddie Johnson?" he barked before his ass even hit his seat.

I opened my mouth to answer, but Mr. Hale held up a hand to stop me. "You'll need to be more specific, Chief Larson."

The chief released a low growl. "Why did you want Eddie Johnson's address?"

I glanced over at Mr. Hale, and he leaned into my ear and whispered, "Tell him but keep Malcolm out of it."

I wasn't stupid. I had no intention of letting his name fall out of my mouth a single time during this questioning, but I supposed that was why Malcolm was paying Hale to sit with me. I had no delusions it was an altruistic attempt to save my skin.

I turned to the chief. "I talked to Ava's best friend yesterday afternoon, and she told me that she and Ava had been meeting with Mr. Johnson after lunch. Apparently, the girls were close to him, so I thought he might have some insight on where Ava might have *run away* to." My tone made it clear what I thought about his official take on her disappearance.

His eyes narrowed into slits. "When did you confront Eddie?"

"I didn't. I meant to talk to him this morning before he left for work, but I overslept until around nine. When I woke up, I learned that he was already missing."

"You got an alibi to prove that?" he bit out.

"My mother has security cameras all around her house. They can prove I came home right before midnight and didn't leave until I left this morning, eager to see your bright and shiny face." I gave him a cheesy smile to punctuate it.

I found it hard to respect the asshole, and apparently, I was having a hard time hiding it. Not that I'd bothered trying yesterday. I'd just been less obnoxious about it. I knew it was a bad idea to antagonize him, but he was wasting valuable time and resources to find a missing girl. Maybe if he'd done his job, Eddie Johnson wouldn't be missing and possibly dead.

His eyes narrowed. "What were you doing that kept you out until midnight?"

"My client doesn't have to answer that," Mr. Hale interjected in a congenial tone. "Your questioning has to do with her whereabouts this morning. I'm sure we can get the video feed from the Adamses' residence to prove what she said is true."

Chief Larson clenched his jaw so hard I was surprised I didn't hear his teeth shatter. He took a deep breath. "Why were you talking to Millie and Casey LaRue yesterday afternoon?"

"I like making new friends."

"With Ava Peterman's best friend and her mother?"

"Vanessa arranged it," I said. "She asked me to speak to Millie."

"Why?"

"You'll have to ask her."

"What did you discuss?"

Mr. Hale held up his hand again. "That's not really pertinent."

"I'll say when something's pertinent," the chief ground out. "Now what did you discuss?"

My attorney leaned into my ear and whispered, "Tell him you made small talk."

I found this annoying. I used to be on the other side of the table, on the receiving end of such bullshit. I didn't want to follow Mr. Hale's instruction. It made me feel like a hypocrite, but I also didn't trust Larson not to take anything I said and use it against me. Sure, he hadn't read me my rights, thus making anything I said inadmissible in court, but he'd find another way to go about it. While he might not be sharp, he obviously held grudges.

"We talked about Ava," I said with a forced smile. "My friend is upset, and I wanted to find out more about her daughter."

"Have you ever met Ava?"

"No."

"So then why the interest?"

"Because Vanessa's been through this with my sister. This whole situation has to be a nightmare for her." I decided to go on the offensive. "I take you haven't found Ava yet?"

He squirmed in his seat and drew in a sharp breath as he looked away.

"Still calling her a runaway?"

His gaze jerked up to mine. "We've seen nothing to convince us otherwise."

"What about Eddie Johnson? He was taking two twelve-year-old girls into his janitor closet for weeks, possibly months, and then he disappears the day after Ava goes missing? You don't find that suspicious?"

"You're the one being questioned here!" he shouted, pounding his fist on the table. "Not me!"

"Someone needs to hold you accountable," I said in disgust.

Mr. Hale put his hand on my arm, his fingers pinching tight, but he said in his good-natured tone, "Things seem to be getting a little heated here. Maybe we should all take a beat."

But Chief Larson didn't seem interested in backing down. "If you're gonna accuse Eddie Johnson of taking that girl, maybe I should be lookin' at you as a suspect. You seem mighty interested in a runaway you never met before."

"You know that her mother was my sister's best friend. And you'd be stupid not to realize she's plagued with survivor's guilt."

His face perked up. "And maybe you're full of survivor's guilt too. Maybe you thought it should have been Vanessa Peterman who was kidnapped that day instead of your sister. So you took her daughter as revenge."

My mouth dropped open. "Are you *insane?*"

"My client is not commenting on your accusation," Mr. Hale interjected, sounding a bit panicked. His fingers pinched harder.

"Vanessa Peterman says she hasn't heard from you in years, and suddenly you're showing up on her doorstep less than two hours after she reported her daughter as missing." He cocked his head. "Pretty suspicious, don't you think?"

Mr. Hale pinched even harder. "My client will not dignify that ludicrous question with an answer."

"And then you're talking to Ava's friends. You're getting the address of her school janitor? They say criminals like to visit the scenes of their crimes to watch for reactions from their loved ones. They eat them up. You're just takin' it to a whole new level."

"Do not say one word, Harper," my attorney growled, then jumped to his feet, pulling me up with him. "We're done here, Chief Larson."

"But I'm just getting started," he said with a laugh.

Mr. Hale gave me a push toward the door, and I let him, shocked into a stupor.

Was Chief Larson serious? Or was he just messing with me?

Mr. Hale opened the door and not so gently shoved me into the hall.

But Chief Larson stood in the doorway, calling after us as we turned the corner to the exit. "If I'm investigating anyone for kidnapping Ava Peterman, it's going to be you, Harper Adams. It's going to be *you.*"

Chapter Twenty-Seven

As soon as we exited the building, Mr. Hale turned me toward him, his face taut. "Follow me to my office."

I stared at him, still in shock at how quickly things had turned. "What?"

His jaw clenched. "We have things to discuss, and it can't wait."

I had to swallow the urge to tell him he couldn't order me to go. Going to his office was a smart idea, necessary, but my belligerence with the chief had put me in fight mode.

Don't screw yourself, Harper.

I nodded. "Yeah. Okay."

"It's only a few blocks from here, on the other side of downtown." He headed toward a black BMW a few spaces from my car, and I headed toward mine. It took me two tries to get the door open. I sat in the seat, wondering how the hell I'd gotten here.

I grabbed my phone out of my jacket pocket and was about to send a text to Vanessa before I thought better of it. I needed to talk to Hale first. I tossed my phone in the passenger seat, then backed up to follow Hale's car.

His office was in the end unit of a two-story building that ran the length of the block. I followed him to the back of the building and parked in a space marked For Clients of Hale Law, and he parked in a spot marked with a sign that read Carter

Hale, Attorney at Law. A motorcycle I recognized as Malcolm's was parked next to a dumpster.

This was going to be a meeting for three. Not that I was surprised.

I started to get out of the car, then remembered my phone. I glanced over at the seat to pick it up and noticed a 5 x 7 manila envelope in the seat with *Harper* written in black marker in block letters.

My stomach dropped and I went light-headed. Was this from the person who'd left the photo yesterday?

A loud rap sounded on the driver's window, and I jumped, turning to see Hale peering in with an impatient expression.

I held up a finger. "I'll be inside in a minute."

I turned back to the seat and told myself to get it together. Jesus. It was an envelope. My heart started racing, but I knew freaking out wasn't going to accomplish anything. I picked it up, unsealed the flap, and peered in the opening to see a folded piece of paper.

Reaching inside, I pulled it out, carefully unfolding the sheet of what appeared to be white copy paper. A three-word sentence was written in black marker in the middle of the top part. The same handwriting as on the glass of the photo.

YOU'RE SO COLD

At the bottom of the page, in smaller letters, was another message.

AND POOR EDDIE JOHNSON PAID THE PRICE.

(LOOK UNDER YOUR SEAT.)

Oh, Jesus. Had Eddie been kidnapped because of me?

This changed everything. The person who'd broken into my house four months ago was not only in Jackson Creek, tormenting me—he'd escalated.

What the hell was happening?

I heard a pounding on the window again and saw Malcolm's expressionless face peering down at me. He reached for the door handle and tugged, but the door was locked.

"Open the door," he called out.

Shit. I didn't want Malcolm knowing about this, and I didn't have time for this meeting. I needed to go somewhere private and find out what the fuck was under my seat.

Malcolm pounded again. "Open the goddamned door!"

I stuffed the paper into my purse and opened the door with a shaky hand. "Impatient much?" He may have covered my attorney fees, but I'd never asked him to. I didn't owe him anything. But I did need to talk to Hale, which meant Malcom would be involved. I'd make this meeting go quickly, then I'd deal with my own shit.

"What was in that note?" Malcolm demanded, staring down at me.

So he'd seen it. Of course he had. I suspected not much got past James Malcolm. "None of your fucking business," I snarled as I got out and stood in front of him, shutting the door behind me.

"If it pertains to Eddie Johnson," he ground out through gritted teeth, "then it pertains to me."

He had a point, but this note made it personal to *me*, not him, and while he'd provided an attorney for me, he'd been quick to assure me that it was to cover his own ass, not mine.

I couldn't trust him.

"Tell you what, James Malcolm," I said in a snide tone, getting closer as I looked up into his angry face, "when you're ready to share all your dirty little secrets, then I'll consider sharing mine. So let's get this meeting over with so we can both get on with our day."

"I saw Eddie's name on that note," he spat out, fury in his eyes.

His interest in Eddie didn't make sense. "Why do you care so much about some guy who was just a customer in your bar?" I glanced over at Hale, who looked more tense than after we'd left the interview room, then back at Malcolm. "What is going on and why are you dragging me into it?"

"Let's go inside and discuss it," Hale said in his amicable tone that I recognized as placating.

I took a step back from Malcolm, for the first time realizing I was alone with two men, both larger than me, one significantly so, in a back alley. "*Orrr*...we could discuss it out here."

Hale released a heavy sigh. "I've got too much to do to deal with this bullshit. I'm going inside."

He headed for the back door while Malcolm continued to stare me down. Perhaps he thought I'd fold if he glared at me long enough, but unless he brandished a gun, I wasn't backing down. Sure, he could probably beat the shit out of me, but I knew enough self-defense that while he'd likely win, it would cost him. Besides, I was so full of rage that I was spoiling for a fight.

The door into the building banged shut, and Malcolm and I continued our staring contest for several more seconds before he said, "You know I could just take the note and read it for myself."

"You could," I conceded in a dark tone, "but I can assure you that our partnership on this will be done. And something tells me that it's more important to you that it continue."

A muscle on the side of his jaw ticked but he remained silent.

"What's your connection to Eddie Johnson?" I demanded.

His brow rose slightly. "What's up with that note?"

This was going nowhere fast.

After several more seconds, his eyes narrowed. "I'm not discussing it in the parking lot."

"You want to go inside?" I challenged.

"That was the original plan."

"*Your* original plan. I was ordered to come."

"Consider it your payment for your attorney's fees."

"I *knew* you'd expect something out of it. How much does he charge? I'll be happy to write him a check."

"I suspect it would bounce." He hesitated, then took a step back. "If you want to know more, then come inside. If not, then feel free to go." With that, he turned on his heels and walked inside the building.

I waited several seconds for him to come back out, then turned back and opened my car door. I knew I should wait to find out what was under my seat, but there was no way I could pay attention in whatever meeting they had planned when I knew there was something terrible waiting for me.

I pulled out my phone and turned on the flashlight as I squatted between the open door and the car. I wasn't stupid enough to blindly reach under the seat. For all I knew, there was a spring-loaded animal trap under there. But there wasn't a trap, just another manila envelope that was fatter than the other. Dread washed through me as I pulled it out and saw a lump in the middle section.

I got in the car and shut the door before I broke the seal and carefully opened the flap, revealing a quart-sized Ziploc bag inside. I turned the envelope upside down and dumped the contents onto my lap, releasing a shriek when I saw a bloody thumb inside the bag that was sitting on my legs.

What the *fuck*?

I took several deep breaths to calm down. Was that *Eddie's* thumb? Thankfully, it was too big to be Ava's.

The passenger door opened, and Malcolm got inside. "What did you find?"

Closing my eyes, I internally berated myself. I wasn't entirely stupid. Deep down I knew there was a good chance he'd come out to see what I was doing or watch me on surveillance cameras. It was hard to admit that maybe I actually *wanted* him to know, but right now, he had the upper hand and knowledge was currency in this strange dynamic. If I shared this with him, I'd be deeply in debt.

Covering the bag with the envelope, I gave him a sharp look. "How much is it worth to you?"

He continued to stare at me.

"Last night, you accused me of hiding something from you. Something big. You weren't wrong, but up until a few minutes ago, I wasn't sure if it had anything to do with Ava."

His voice rumbled, deep and low. "Now you think it does?"

"Yes, but I'm not going to tell you until you come clean with your connection to Eddie Johnson. Are you willing to do that?"

"Are you sure you want to know?" he countered. "Because once I tell you, you can't unknow it."

"How profound," I sneered.

His eyes narrowed. "I'll swear you to secrecy, and there will be consequences if you break my trust."

Was he going to admit he was up to something illegal?

"You can't tell your deputy friend," he continued. "Or the Jackson Creek PD one either. *No. One.* Have I made myself clear?"

"What's to stop me from telling on you and then having the authorities hide me?"

He leaned over the console, invading my personal space and looking more menacing than he had in the two days I'd known him. "Try it, and I promise you won't like the consequences."

A chill ran down my spine. "Are you threatening me, Malcolm?"

His gaze turned deadly. "Take it as you will."

I needed to kick him out of my car and head to my parents' house to regroup. But he'd practically admitted that there was more to his interest in Eddie Johnson than being a stellar customer. It wasn't like I was an officer obligated to report his illegal activity. I was a civilian now. And if what he told me was truly heinous, I'd report him anyway.

I shifted in my seat and lifted my chin. "Fine, but you first." My movement made the envelope fall to the floor, though, revealing the bloody bag in my lap.

So much for having the upper hand.

He reached over and snatched it before I could stop him. Holding it between his thumb and forefinger, he stared at it in disgust. "What the fuck is *this*?"

"I think it belongs to Eddie." I pulled the note out of my purse and held it up so he could read it. I'd lost all leverage now, but there was no way to stop this steaming locomotive.

"Why did they leave it for you?" he asked.

"It's not the first note."

His gaze jerked up to mine. "What was the first one?"

I pointed to his feet. "Under the papers."

Still holding the bag, he reached down with his other hand and grabbed the picture frame and brought it up to his lap. The image of me and my sister was clearly visible, along with the handwritten message. "What the fuck?" His gaze lifted to mine, looking furious.

I had no delusion it was out of concern for my welfare.

"Is this a photo of Peterman's daughter?"

"No. It's a photo of me when I was a kid. It showed up in my car yesterday morning." Then I added, "But it was stolen from my house last October."

His face jerked up to mine. "And you didn't think to tell me about it?"

"I don't owe you shit, Malcolm," I snarled. "And I wasn't sure it had anything to do with Ava's kidnapping."

"I think the goddamned thumb in the bag proves that it did."

Unfortunately, I was pretty certain he was right.

He set the bag on the dashboard and studied the frame. "Why would someone steal this from your home in Little Rock?"

"The hell if I know. I figured it was someone obsessed with my sister's case."

"That's your sister with you?" he asked, lifting it closer.

"Taken a few days before she was kidnapped."

"So why would someone suddenly take a photo from your home then wait four months to do anything with it?"

I sagged back in my seat, exhaustion washing over me. God, I needed a drink to help ease the throbbing in my head. "I don't know. It's not like they knew I was coming back here. I returned to Jackson Creek as a last resort. And only because my father came to see me in Little Rock and offered to let me stay in my parents' garage apartment until I figured out what to do."

"So why would someone steal a photo?"

I shrugged. "The only thing I can figure is that he saw my name in the news. The shooting was two weeks before, but it wasn't the first break-in I'd had. There were a couple of others before—both of them after the shooting. The break-ins stopped after he stole the photo, which had been hidden in a drawer in my bedroom. I wasn't sure if he stopped because he got what he was looking for or because I almost caught him."

"A man?"

"Based on the build and height? Yeah. But I only saw his back as he fled."

"So this guy sees your name in the paper and steals a photo of you and your sister. Why?"

I pointed to the message on the frame. "Good question. He thinks it should have been me, except I wasn't sure whether he meant Ava or my sister Andi. Some people blamed me for her kidnapping. My mother included."

He lowered the photo to his lap, confusion in his eyes. "Why would your mother blame you? How could that be your fault?"

"Andi and I weren't supposed to be at the creek. Or at least *I* wasn't. My mother wanted me home to help with chores. Vanessa was supposed to go with Andi to check on a nest of baby birds, but she couldn't go and Andi didn't want to go alone, so after some begging, I agreed to come with her."

"So how is that your fault?"

I scraped my teeth over my bottom lip as I stared at the building through the windshield. "Any *reasonable* person would know it's not my fault, but that's the thing about losing a child: it tends to make you act unreasonably."

He didn't say anything for a few seconds. "So maybe this isn't about TJ Peterman." He turned to face me. "Maybe this is about *you.*"

I felt like I'd been dunked in an ice bath. "Maybe."

"So when exactly did you find this photo?"

"After I met with Vanessa and canvassed the neighborhood yesterday. It was on the driver's floorboard when I went back to my car. I was away from my car for an hour, maybe an hour and a half. It was locked when I left it. Unlocked when I opened the car door."

"Plenty of time to break into your car. No one saw anything?"

"I didn't ask. They barely talked to me before I discovered the photo. They sure weren't going to talk to me after."

His jaw tightened. "So the stalker followed you to the Petermans' house."

I flinched when he said stalker, wanting to deny it, but I think I was past the point of plausible deniability. "Or they were already waiting in Ava's neighborhood, and I missed them."

"And the envelope?"

I closed my eyes to center myself, then opened them. "It wasn't in my car when I left my parents' house to head to the police station."

"So someone broke into your car in the police station parking lot." He shook his head. "Ballsy."

We sat in silence for a few moments, my heart beating fast as everything hit me at once.

I had a stalker, and maybe the chief was right that I was responsible for Ava's kidnapping, just not how he'd inferred. Eddie Johnson was possibly kidnapped and murdered because of me. And now James Malcolm knew my secrets, which meant he had no incentive to tell me *any* of his.

"They knew you were showing up at the station," Malcolm finally said. "Who did you tell?"

"I didn't tell anyone other than you and Hale." I shot him a snide glare as a new thought hit me. "Maybe *you* arranged this."

"Why would I bother stealing a photo from your house in Little Rock last fall?" he asked in disgust. "I didn't even know who you were."

"You said there were officers on the take in Little Rock," I said, turning in my seat to hold his gaze. "And Louise thinks I was set up. Maybe you had something to do with it."

He released a bitter laugh. "Someone has an imagination. I didn't have a fucking clue who you were then."

"You're telling me you didn't see my name in the news?" I countered.

"Of course I did, but it never would have occurred to me to hunt you down and steal a photo."

He had a point. Whoever took it had some kind of connection to my sister's kidnapping.

Malcolm must have been thinking the same thing. "Did they catch the guy who murdered your sister?"

"He wasn't very careful. I got a good look at him and gave them a description of his face, hair, and what he was wearing. They found him a week after she was found."

"Where is the pervert now?" he ground out.

His tone surprised me. "In prison. He pled guilty."

"You're sure he's still there?"

"I checked after the break-in. And then again a couple of weeks ago." I shook my head. "Someone would have notified me if he'd escaped or been released, which would be impossible since he received life in prison with no parole."

"He got any family?"

"You mean to seek revenge? I don't think so. He wasn't married and didn't have any kids. Last I heard, his family wrote him off. When he confessed, they were horrified. They publicly apologized for what he did."

"Who else would be interested in your sister's kidnapping?"

"Half the town," I said with a sigh, then squared my shoulders and lifted my brow. "Now your turn to share. Why the interest in Eddie Johnson?"

His jaw clenched and his eyes shuttered. "I told you he's a customer."

"Fuck off," I snapped. "You either tell me why or I'll do this on my own." I had to admit I didn't want to do it on my own. I suspected he had resources that could help—like his ability to find out the makes and models of both Eddie's and the LaRues' vehicles within minutes—but I refused to be Malcolm's bitch, in any sense of the word.

His jaw worked and I thought he was about to tell me to fuck off myself, but then he surprised me. "Hale's waiting for us. Come in if you want. Or not, but if you leave, you're on your own."

I pointed to the thumb. "What do we do with that? It's not like I plan to take it to Chief Larson. He seems to think I might have kidnapped Ava and that I'm going around getting off on people's grief like an emotional vampire."

"Larson's an idiot." He grabbed the bag and held onto the frame as he opened the door and got out.

I followed him inside, realizing I was sinking myself deeper and deeper into a mess, but I had no idea how to get out.

Chapter Twenty-Eight

MALCOLM LED ME THROUGH the back door and down a short hall to an open door. We walked into an opulent office with wall-to-wall bookcases and a large, elaborately carved wooden desk. The chairs were leather, and the wool carpet was plush under my feet.

"Someone's overcompensating," I said under my breath, but Malcolm cracked a grin.

Hale was behind his desk, and he didn't look very happy to see us. Or maybe it was me he was unhappy with. Fair enough.

He gestured to the chairs in front of his desk. "Take a seat."

I started to follow but spotted a dry bar against the far wall. It was only late morning, but I headed straight for it and poured a finger of amber liquid from a crystal decanter into a crystal glass, then drank it like a shot. I poured another two fingers then turned toward the desk. Hale stared at me with a mixture of surprise and disgust. Malcolm watched me with that damn expressionless stare, his arms crossed over his chest.

"By all means," Hale said dryly, "help yourself."

"I've had a shit day," I said, walking over to the two leather chairs in front of his desk. I took a seat as Malcolm sat in the chair closest to the door, dropping the bag onto Hale's desk. He stretched his long arms over the arms of the chair, looking bored.

"What the hell is that?" Hale asked, cringing as he lowered his head to examine it.

"Eddie Johnson's thumb," Malcolm said.

"What? Where the hell did you get that?"

Malcolm shot me a dark look, then slid his gaze to his attorney. "They left it in the detective's car. Along with a note."

I took a generous sip of whiskey, thankful the warmth seemed to be loosening the bands around my head.

Hale shook his head. "*What?*"

Malcolm gave me an expectant look, so I took the note out of my purse and dropped it on the desk.

Hale picked it up at the edge and looked it over. "*You're so cold.*" His gaze lifted to me. "Is this about Ava Peterman's disappearance?"

"Looks that way," Malcolm said in his same bored tone.

"And because you were looking into Johnson as a suspect, he kidnapped and dismembered him?" Hale asked in the same tone I imagined he used when asking about the lunch special at the local café. Then again, he worked for James Malcolm. Murder, kidnapping, and dismemberment might happen every other Tuesday for all I knew. "He's trying to steer you in the right direction?"

"We think there's a personal component to this," Malcolm said. "A photo that was stolen from her house two weeks after the shooting in Little Rock last fall. It showed up in her car yesterday morning outside the Petermans' home with a message written on the glass that said *it should have been you.* She wasn't sure if they were referring to her sister or the Peterman kid. Now I think it's both."

I'd been thinking either-or, but he was probably right.

I told Hale about the break-ins and chasing the intruder. Then, against my better judgment, I told them about the red ribbon.

"The number of people who know about the ribbon is pretty small. They never publicly released it."

"Maybe not as small as you think," Hale said. "There were multiple law enforcement agencies involved in your sister's case. Then prosecutor's office and Stevens' attorney and his staff." He shrugged. "Not to mention all the inmates housed with Stevens. Inmates love to brag about their exploits. It not only makes them look tough and hopefully less of a target, but they need to feel important somehow. If I remember right, he was sentenced to life with no parole." He gave me a questioning look.

I blinked in shock, then quickly released my anger. "You've been investigating me?"

Releasing a derisive laugh, he said, "Someone's full of themselves. No. I remember your sister's kidnapping. I just didn't make the association to you." He tapped his temple with his pen. "Memory's not as great as it used to be, but in my defense, I was in college and merely fascinated with the legalities. It's highly unusual for someone to plead guilty at a bench trial. Makes me question his legal team. You sure he did it?"

"I saw him," I said flatly. "I was there when he took her. It was him."

He sighed, then twisted his mouth. "That's a shame. Otherwise, I would entertain the idea of him taking the fall and the real murderer going loose. Then, once you made the limelight with the shooting, it triggered something in him."

"It's a solid theory," I said. "Except for the fact that I know John Michael Stevens took my sister. I agree that seeing my name in the news might have triggered the new kidnapper, but I think it has to be someone who was obsessed with my sister's murder."

Hale shook his head. "This has grudge written all over it." He lifted his brow to Malcolm. "Thoughts?"

He turned to face me. "Are you one hundred percent sure you identified the right guy?"

Irritation burrowed under my collar. "He pled guilty."

He snorted. "And we both know people never make false confessions."

"I saw him in a lineup."

"Again, we both know that memories are tricky things," Malcolm said, not an ounce of softness on his face.

"False identifications make up seventy percent of false convictions overturned by DNA evidence," Hale added, at least trying to sound sympathetic. "Did they do DNA testing on your sister?"

I stared at him in shock. "No."

Jesus. Was it possible that I'd helped put an innocent man in prison? "But he confessed," I pled with Hale. "Why would he confess with no chance of parole if he didn't do it?" But even as I asked the question, I knew there could be a wide host of reasons.

"It's not unheard of," Hale said, then made a face. "Payoffs to family. Promises not to harm someone they love. All sorts of things."

How much of that did he know from firsthand experience?

"No," I said, pissed that they were making me question everything I'd held true for the past twenty-one years. "He did it."

"We need to see him," Malcolm said. "Ask some questions."

"Are you insane?" I demanded.

"Have you ever seen him since you picked him out of the lineup?" Hale asked softly.

"No."

"Okay," Hale said, forcing a bit of cheerfulness into his voice. "Let's presume the man sitting in prison actually killed your sister. Then we need to figure out who is acting out now." His eyes were trained on me. "We've established this is personal to him, but I think he's taunting you. It's a game. He's the cat and you're the mouse."

I wanted to argue with him, but he had a point.

"And he's mad that you're not making connections sooner." He gestured to the bag at the corner of his desk. "Hence taking Eddie and sending you the thumb. He's trying to get you back on track. Any clue where to turn now?"

Shame made the pounding in my head more intense. "No." I took another generous sip of the whiskey.

Hale clasped his hands on his desk. "We'll table that for now and discuss another pressing issue." He gave Malcolm a pointed look. "We have a problem with Larson."

"No shit we have a problem with Larson," Malcolm grunted. "Tell me something useful."

"He has a history of harassing people," Hale said to me. "Malcolm was his most recent target, but I suspect you're his current flavor of the week. He brings people in for questioning so many times they eventually wear down and confess to something."

"Well good-fucking-luck," Malcolm said, stretching out his legs, "because I'm clean as a baby's ass."

Hale gave him a dry look.

I snorted. "As clean as a baby's ass in a shitty diaper."

Malcolm's glare turned to me.

What the hell was I doing here? I needed an attorney to deal with Larson, but there were other attorneys out there, and Carter Hale was practically married to James Malcolm.

Malcolm had made national news as being a key part in an international drug cartel. You didn't get into that position by playing hopscotch. He was dirty. He'd admitted to killing people. Now I was working with him…and possibly risking my life by getting mouthy.

At the same time, I doubted he'd kill me. We needed each other to accomplish our goals. Me to find Ava; Malcolm to do who knew what.

I was playing a dangerous game, yet I was still here. The me I'd been last year before the shooting would have driven out of the parking lot before ever walking in the door. Somewhere between yesterday at lunch and this morning, I'd crossed a line. The old Harper would be horrified.

Good thing for me the old Harper was dead.

Leaning back in my seat, I glanced between Malcolm and Hale. "Larson has a one-track mind. He was like that with Andi's investigation two decades ago. Standard procedure for a small department is to call in the sheriff and possibly the FBI right away. Manpower and time are key to finding a kid. You've got to cover lots of ground in an extremely short time. Most kids abducted by a stranger are killed within a few hours of being taken. After John Michael Stevens kidnapped my sister, I wasted ten minutes running home instead of stopping at the first house I came across."

Neither man said anything.

"The chief's got a grudge against me," I continued matter-of-factly, "although I have no idea why. It might be clouding his investigation, or at least getting in the way of it. He knows I'm watching him, and he doesn't like it, so he'd prefer to hide what he's doing rather than let me scrutinize it."

"Do you think he was serious when he accused you of kidnapping her?" Hale asked. "Or was he blowing smoke up your ass?"

I pursed my lips. "Honestly, I don't know. It could go either way."

Hale scowled. "Do you have an alibi for the night and morning Ava Peterman went missing?"

"My parents' security cameras. I came home at about eight p.m. and was in my apartment until about eight to eight-thirty the next morning. My mother dropped by for a chat around six-thirty. It would all have been captured by the cameras."

Hale reached for a legal pad on the side of his desk and began to take notes. "And before eight?"

"I was running an errand."

He glanced up, his eyebrow quirked. "Where to?"

I resisted the urge to squirm. "Vanessa saw her daughter at nine. I was home before she went missing."

"Ten bucks she was buying booze," Malcolm grunted, giving me the side-eye.

Hale's brow furrowed. "Why the big secret? Even if you were buying moonshine, this is a wet county."

"It doesn't matter," I said, shame washing over me, quickly followed by an inferno of anger. How dare James Malcolm judge me? He owned a damn bar. He was responsible for boozing up half the county.

"You were at a bar?" Hale asked, writing again.

Why hide it now? "No, a liquor store in Wolford."

"Would they be able to confirm that?" Hale asked. "I suspect they have cameras and I'm guessing you used a debit or credit card to make the purchase."

"Yes to both." I turned to Malcolm. "I have a solid alibi. I didn't kidnap her."

He looked bored. "Never claimed you did."

"Let's get back on track," Hale suggested sarcastically.

"Agreed." I turned back to face him. "Larson can't make anything stick to me, so we need to focus on who took Ava and Eddie." Then I added, "And sent me his thumb."

"Presuming it's Eddie's," Hale said.

"My suspect list is short, but far from conclusive," I said. "Before the note and the thumb today, I thought the photo issue was separate from Ava's case, so I didn't take it into consideration, which had TJ Peterman and Ricky Morris vying for my number one suspect spot. Statistically, it's usually a close family member or friend. Additionally, Peterman doesn't want to make a spectacle of his daughter's disappearance. Wouldn't an upset father want the word spread far and wide that his daughter is missing? The more people looking, the more likely they are to find her."

"Rumor has it Peterman treated his daughter like she was the Aphrodite incarnate," Hale said. "Which makes it hard for me to believe he'd hurt her."

"You never know what goes on behind closed doors," I said. "From what I've heard, TJ expected perfection out of his daughter, and while she tried very hard to please him, I think there was a bit of rebelliousness brewing. Maybe she pissed him off, and he accidently killed her. Or maybe she heard something she shouldn't have, and he put her into hiding or killed her to keep her quiet. Still, I don't think he killed her. He's too calm. Too unmoved by her disappearance. He may have treated her like a possession, but she's a possession he loves. He'd show signs of distress."

"So not him?" Hale said.

"No, I think it's more likely he's keeping this on the down low because he received a ransom note and is trying to handle the situation himself."

Hale gave Malcolm a questioning look. "Stands to reason."

Malcolm nodded.

"Any other guesses as to who took her?" Hale asked. He tapped his pen on the notebook as though considering it, but I noticed he wasn't taking notes.

"Ricky Morris. TJ's trying to shut down his operation, and from what little I've dug up on Morris, he's got a history of stopping people who get in his way. The only complication is that his method of choice is usually arson, not kidnapping."

Surprise filled Hale's eyes and he gave a slight nod.

"So I'm struggling to reconcile why he'd switch tactics so abruptly. Why not burn down the family business? Or their home? Has he gotten a new associate who might use different tactics? Like a new enforcer?"

The two men exchanged looks, then Malcolm said, "No."

I wasn't sure I believed him. I finished off my drink and set the glass on Hale's fancy desk. "I'm not ready to drop him as a suspect. People can change, and there's something else that caught my attention. A body was found close to the laundromat the night Ava was kidnapped. Someone with ties to Morris. That seems too coincidental."

Hale picked up the glass with a distasteful look and set it aside, next to the thumb. "So why take Johnson?"

"That's just it. I don't see a connection between Eddie and Morris, so I don't know. Maybe the person writing the notes didn't take her. What if he's following me, reacting to what I find out about the case?"

"No, it makes more sense that it wasn't Morris," Malcolm said, keeping his gaze on the bookcase behind Hale's desk. "This has to do with you." His head swiveled to face me. "Someone's following *you*. The only people who knew we were at the station were the three of us and none of us put the note or thumb in your car. And I didn't even know you yesterday, so why would I write a note saying it should have been you?"

He had a point.

"And even if I had put the photo in the car, along with today's present, why would I be robbing a family photo from your house?" He tipped his head down, still holding my gaze. "It wasn't me. Admit it."

"I never said it was you."

"But you never said it wasn't."

"Fine, I know it wasn't you." I shot a glance to Hale. "Or your attorney."

He dipped his head in acknowledgment.

"We have other matters to discuss," I said. "Like your interest in Eddie Johnson."

"Eddie didn't take that girl," Malcolm said.

"I'm not so sure," I countered. "But if we discount the notes, and focus on what we know, we know that Eddie befriended her. Maybe he won her trust for Morris."

Both men sat in their seats with a brooding look.

"Look," I said. "It fits. What if he befriended her at Morris's request? Vanessa admitted that Ava had a bad night with her dad. What if she somehow contacted Eddie and he helped her escape? Or they happened to plan it for Monday night, and fighting with her father was a coincidence. It's not that far-fetched. I take it TJ was hard on her most nights. But after Eddie got her out of the house, maybe he took her to Morris, which would explain why he was at work the next day."

Neither man said anything, but Hale could have bored holes into Malcolm with his laser focus.

"What?" I said, my back tensing. "What are you keeping from me?"

"You've got to tell her," Hale said.

"Fuck," Malcolm grumbled under his breath, then turned to me, looking pissed as hell that he was having to tell me anything at all. "Eddie wouldn't have kidnapped Ava for Morris, because he was working for me."

Chapter Twenty-Nine

I STARED AT HIM, DUMBFOUNDED. "*Eddie Johnson* was working for *you*?"

"Isn't that what I just said?"

My temper flared. "But I asked you if he was working for you and you denied it!"

He released a snort of disgust. "You think I was really going to tell you?"

"Yes."

He lifted a shoulder in a half, unapologetic shrug. "I don't tell people about my shit. I'm only telling you now because you need to know."

"What did he do for you?"

When Malcolm didn't answer, Hale said quietly, "He kept an eye on Ava Peterman."

I jumped out of my chair and took a step backward. "You kidnapped her?" How had I gotten it so wrong?

"Fuck, no," Malcolm said in disgust. "I was having him watch her."

"For what purpose?"

He gave me a challenging glare.

"To kidnap her," I repeated flatly.

"We didn't trust Peterman," Hale interjected. "We never had any intention of touching or harming her in any way. We were only trying to find out what he was up to, and she had a surprising amount of information."

"You used a little girl." I knew James Malcolm had a reputation for being high level on the criminal syndicate list, and you didn't get there by playing with puppies and kittens, but for some godforsaken reason, I'd believed him when he'd said he would never hurt a child.

I started to dart for the door, but Malcolm got up and blocked my path.

"Get the fuck out of my way, Malcolm," I said through gritted teeth.

How had I been so utterly stupid?

"I didn't kidnap her. I didn't use her. She needed a friend, and Eddie befriended her before I had anything to do with it."

I shook my head in disgust. "But since he was already talking to her, Eddie might as well pump her for information about her daddy."

He didn't answer, but he didn't look apologetic either.

"You used that little girl. And you let a pedophile do it."

His face flushed with anger. "Eddie never laid a hand on her. He let her talk when no one else in her life did."

"It was wrong! He took her into a closet!"

"I know it looks that way," Hale said, still seated at his desk and holding up his hands, palms out. "And to be fair, we never knew they were going into his closet. We thought he was talking to her in the hall or outside at recess. When he told Skeeter last week that they'd been in the closet, he told him that had to stop immediately."

I scrunched my face. "Skeeter?"

Hale gave Malcolm an apologetic look. "Sorry, an old nickname he's trying to break."

I considered pursuing it but didn't see the point. I had more important issues to address. "What if I don't believe you?"

Unlike his boss, Hale's eyes were full of regret. "I can't make you believe one way or the other, but neither one of us would ever condone him meeting with her in private, and if Malcolm had thought Johnson was molesting her, he would have killed the guy himself." He pointed to the thumb on his desk. "And you sure as hell wouldn't be finding any pieces of him."

"So where's Ava Peterman?" I asked.

"You're the key to that question," Malcolm said, still blocking the door. "Your little love note said you were not only cold, but *so* cold. Which means the Eddie/Ricky Morris angle is a dead end."

"Or he could be trying to throw us off track," I said.

"Do you really believe that?" Malcolm asked.

I considered it for a moment, then admitted in defeat, "No."

The problem was I had no idea where to start looking. The police had never taken fingerprints after the break-ins to my house, and a million people had a grudge against me.

"We need to pay a visit to the pervert in prison," Malcolm said.

"Excuse me?" I choked out.

Malcolm turned to his attorney. "Can you set that up? Today?"

Sitting back in his seat, Hale's face contorted into an agonized look. "It'll be tough, but I think I can manage it."

"Hate to be the bearer of bad news," I said, "but the prison doesn't allow visitors on weekdays."

A smirk lit up Malcolm's eyes. "Then you obviously don't know Carter Hale. He's capable of just about anything."

I curled my upper lip. "I suppose so if he's kept *you* out of prison all these years."

Hale laughed. "Stop. All of these compliments are going to my head."

"I'm not going to visit that monster," I said, my stomach churning. "But I give you my blessing to talk to him yourself."

Malcolm's eye twitched. "Not worried that I'll withhold information from you?"

I was certain he would. But the thought of sitting mere feet from the man who'd brutalized my sister made me want to vomit. I wasn't sure I'd be able to restrain myself from killing him with my bare hands.

Hale drew in a deep breath and shifted in his seat. "Here's the thing, Detective Adams. You have to go. You'll be the excuse I use to get the special permission."

My back stiffened. "First of all, I'm not a detective anymore, so let's get that clear, but second, we don't even know if he'll agree to see me. In fact, I bet he says no."

"We won't know until we ask," Hale said, sounding far too chipper considering the odds were against him. "But you know that going straight to the source is the best way to get answers."

I rubbed my hand over my forehead. I was horrified at the thought of seeing him, but I had to admit there was a part of me that needed to know if he was sorry.

"Fine," I said with more force than I'd intended. "I'll do it, but I'm not sitting around waiting for you to make the arrangements. The police station will have surveillance but there's no way I can ask them for footage of my car this morning, so I'm going back to the Peterman neighborhood to see if anyone is more willing to talk to me today."

"That's fine with me," Hale said, then looked up at Malcolm. "You good with it?"

Malcolm stepped to the side. "Fine with me, but answer our call or text when it comes in."

I had a snotty retort on the tip of my tongue, but instead I shook my head and walked out. Once I was in the parking lot, I realized I'd left the thumb, but I didn't want it. The sender had made his point. Let Malcolm and Hale figure out what to do with it.

Grabbing the door handle of my car, I peered in the window to see if I'd gotten any new messages or gifts, but it looked untouched.

As I drove toward the Peterman house, I got the creeps thinking about someone breaking into my car, going through my things. What if they didn't stop at leaving me messages? What if they decided to cut my brake line or plant a bomb?

Crap. Would they break into my parents' house or my apartment next? As soon as I parked on the street across from the Petermans' house, I sent my father a text.

Is it okay if I stop by your office for a chat?

I wanted to make sure he and my mother were safe, but it occurred to me that I could also ask some questions about Andi's kidnapping. I was sure there were things they'd kept from me. Maybe I could convince him to share them with me now.

While I waited for a response, I studied the houses on the street. When I'd canvassed two days ago, there hadn't been many neighbors home. I decided I'd pay a visit to the houses on either side of the Petermans. The one directly across from the Petermans, and one three houses down on the corner on the same side of the street. Then I'd try the other houses too. There was a chance they'd been home and hadn't answered the door. I'd press them harder to see if they'd noticed anything unusual at the Peterman house and/or someone tampering with my car.

I got out and headed for the house on the corner when my phone buzzed with a text from my father.

Dad: *Sounds good. How about we have lunch? Just you and me?*

Me: *I'd like that. 1:00? Is that too late?*

Dad: *Nope. Perfect. Meet me at Roots.*

I couldn't help smiling. He knew I'd loved that restaurant growing up. Andi and I both had loved it. Now I had a couple of hours to talk the neighbors and possibly work on something else before lunch.

But to be safe, I sent my mother a text next.

There's some dangerous stuff going on right now. Maybe keep your alarm on all the time, even during the day to be safe.

I knew the fear aspect would get to her, and I bet she'd already set her alarm.

I could see she'd read my text, but she didn't respond. I wasn't surprised.

The next forty-five minutes were a case study of frustration. Most of the neighbors spoke to me this time, although grudgingly. No one had seen the driver of the van, and they all claimed not to have noticed my car, let alone who might have broken into it. Of course, they could be lying, but I had no way of knowing or proving that.

I was heading up Lisa Murphy's front walk when my phone vibrated with a call. Stopping to pull it out, I saw Louise's name on the screen and answered.

"You know that van you were asking about?" she said without preamble. "We found it about a half-hour ago."

Hope sprang up. "Really? Where?"

"Behind Scooter's Tavern. And that's not all." Her voice had an ominous tone.

I knew that was too good to be true. "What?"

"Eddie Johnson's body is inside, and you're never gonna believe this."

"What?"

"He's missing a thumb."

My stomach fell. "Are you looking at Malcolm as a suspect?"

"They kind of have to, don't they? But I can't believe Malcolm would be that stupid. I mean...*really.*"

"Do you think Chief Larson would care about that?"

"No," she said, "And he's already fighting with the sheriff over jurisdiction."

Shit. I had to warn Malcolm. "I need to go. I'm about to have lunch with my dad."

"Oh, that's nice," she said. "Are you discussing the job interview?"

"Among other things."

We hung up and I called Malcolm's number. Of course, he was too cool to answer, or maybe too busy dealing with the fallout of a dead body popping up behind his business. I called Hale next and told his receptionist who I was and that it was important.

"I don't have anything scheduled yet," Hale said when he answered. "I'm still working on it. I'm good but not *that* good."

"That's why I'm calling. They found Eddie Johnson behind Scooter's Tavern."

"Yeah," he said with an exaggerated sigh. "I know. Malcolm's lying low, but it adds more pressure to our timeline."

"Where is he?"

"Not at the tavern, if that's what you're asking. He'll be staying away from there for the unforeseeable future."

"Whoever kidnapped Eddie is framing Malcolm," I said. "Makes me re-question Ricky Morris's involvement."

"Nope. Not going down that path," Hale said with a short laugh. "You're the golden girl, the center of the spotlight. Everything from here on out is for your attention and amusement."

"Amusement?" I asked in disgust.

"Or maybe *his* amusement. But he's escalating. Be waiting for my call."

I suspected he was right. Making an enemy of Malcolm was either stupid or ballsy, probably both.

"Has anyone tried to bring Malcolm in for questioning?"

"Not yet," Hale said, sounding exhausted, "but we know it's coming sooner rather than later." Then he hung up.

I had forty minutes before I needed to meet my father, and since Morty's Bookstore was one block down from Roots, I decided to drop by and make sure I hadn't blown up my budding friendship with Nate.

I parked my car in the lot behind the restaurant, then headed down to the bookstore, stopping in a bakery to get an assortment of cupcakes as a thank you/apology offering.

When I walked in, Nate was behind the counter helping a woman and two small children. With a broad smile, he handed the little girl a brown shopping bag with handles. "Thanks for coming in today, Molly and Micah."

"We always love Storytime with Nate," the woman said as her daughter took the bag. "Although we also always buy the books you read, so it's hard on my credit card."

He leaned closer with a mischievous grin. "It's all part of my master plan."

"Well, it's working," she said, tossing her hair over her shoulder and giving him a warm smile before she walked past me to exit.

Another mother with a toddler approached the counter, holding two picture books.

I stood to the side by the door while he checked them out, noticing how friendly she was to him, and how Nate doted on the little boy when his mother picked him up so he could watch Nate check them out.

"See you next Wednesday," the woman called out as she walked out of the store.

"Bye, Nate," the boy said, waving his pudgy hand.

"Bye, Preston," he called after him.

I waited until the door closed behind them before I approached the counter, holding out the white bakery box. "I brought you a peace offering."

His head tilted to the side, and he gave me an awkward smile. "That wasn't necessary, Harper. I wasn't upset with you."

"It's okay if you were," I said, setting the box on the counter. "I put you in a weird position, and I'm *really* sorry."

He opened the lid and laughed. "So you bought me half a dozen cupcakes?"

"I didn't know what kind you like."

He picked one out of the box. "I'd recognize Ida's Chocolate Carmel Surprise cupcakes in my sleep."

"So it's your favorite?"

Peeling the wrapper down, he merely grinned. "I can't make it *that* easy for you." He took a bite and groaned with pleasure. "But it's pretty damn good even if it isn't."

"Well, again, I want to thank you for going out of your way to help me, and well…thanks for being my friend."

"Hey, us brass knuckleheads need to stick together," he said before taking another bite.

I laughed. "God. How did I forget that's what you named our section in band? I should walk out the door and never speak to you again on principle."

Chuckling, he finished off the cupcake, and said through his mouthful, "You like me too much to do that."

I shook my head and laughed. Nate had been fun when we were in high school. A nerd with a nerdy sense of humor. I'd been a nerd too, just about other things.

"Looks like you have a fan club with the mothers of Jackson Creek," I said with a sly grin.

He grimaced, his cheeks flushing. "Nah, they're just grateful I'm giving them about twenty minutes of entertainment once a week for their kids."

"From what I saw, you seem to like it too."

"I do. It builds community, and I like kids." He shrugged. "I may not have any of my own, so next best thing."

"Unlike us women, you don't have a biological clock ticking. There's still plenty of time."

He turned the open box toward me. "Want one?"

I lifted a hand, even though I was tempted. "I'm about to have lunch with my dad, so I'll refrain."

"To talk about your potential job?"

"That, and I want to ask him questions about John Michael Stevens."

His jaw went slack. "The man who killed your sister?" Fear filled his eyes. "Oh, my God. Do you think Ava's disappearance has anything to do with your sister's?"

I was about to answer when the bell on the door chimed and Drew walked in, wearing his Jackson Creek PD uniform. "Sorry to interrupt," he said, glancing from me to Nate. "I'm gonna have to get a raincheck on lunch today. I need to head out to Scooter's Tavern."

"That's out of your jurisdiction, isn't it?" Nate asked in confusion.

"Yeah, but the chief is trying to get the case moved to us and he wants me to start a log sheet."

"What the hell's going on out there that they need a log sheet?" Nate asked.

"Oh," Drew said, then laughed. "I figured you'd know before me. They found Eddie Johnson in a stolen van behind Scooter's. Looks like James Malcolm took him." He turned his attention to me. "Did you get a chance to talk to him before Malcolm offed him?"

I cringed at his crassness. "A little respect for the dead, Officer," I said before I thought better of it. It's exactly what I would have done if any officer had spoken like that in front of me in Little Rock, but I had no authority to say anything here. Still…

An apologetic look washed over Drew's face. "You're right. Sorry."

"It's easy to turn hard doing that job," I said. "Just try to keep your humanity, okay?"

Irritation filled his eyes. "Yeah, sure." He waved to Nate. "Maybe tomorrow?"

"Okay," Nate said, and we watched him let the door close behind him and head down the street.

"I think I pissed him off."

"He needed to hear it," Nate said with a sigh. "He's kind of lonely here, and the guys on the force haven't exactly welcomed him with open arms."

"Why not?"

"They don't take to newcomers and word has it Drew got the job because the chief is sleeping with his mother."

"Yikes."

"Exactly. But I think he's maybe mimicking what they're saying, trying to break into their cool club, you know? I've heard a few of the other officers say some pretty jaded things."

"He should talk to Louise," I said. "She's having the same issue with the sheriff's department."

"That sucks," Nate said, "but I think it's a good idea." He grinned again. "Have I told you I'm a bit of a matchmaker?"

"No, but I doubt you'll get any complaints out of Louise. You heard her last night. She thinks he's cute."

Nate rubbed his hands together and released a mock evil laugh. "Well, then. My plan is already working."

My phone vibrated in my purse, and I saw a text from my father, telling me he was already at the restaurant but to take my time.

"My dad's early," I said, thumbing toward the door. "I'm glad you're not upset with me."

I started to turn around, but he cleared his throat. I turned back, surprised to see he looked nervous.

"If you'd *really* like to make it up to me," he said, resting his hand on the counter, "maybe we could go out to dinner together."

My face flushed. "Are you asking me out on a date, Nate?"

"Good rhyme." His face lit up. Then, as though remembering the topic of the conversation, he grimaced. "And yes, I am."

"I'd like that. A lot." Nate was nice and obviously attractive. The idea of doing something normal like going out on a date with a man who wasn't a narcissistic asshole was appealing. Then reality washed over me like hot acid. "But not until I finish this case."

"Of *course*," he said enthusiastically, then cringed. "I think I'm losing my cool points here."

"That's presuming you had them to begin with," I said with a laugh. "But I always thought you did." I opened the door and gave him a backward glance. "Bye, Nate."

Chapter Thirty

ROOTS WASN'T A VERY BIG RESTAURANT, but it bordered on fancy with its plush carpet and white tablecloths. People came from all over to eat here. It was fairly easy to get a table for lunch, but a reservation was usually required for nights and weekends.

The dining room was half-full, but I had no trouble spotting my father toward the back of the room. He looked up and saw me heading toward him, and to my surprise, he got up and stood next to his chair, waiting for me.

When I reached him, he pulled me into a warm embrace, holding me tight, then he grabbed my arms and held me back as he searched my face, although I had no idea what he was looking for. "Thanks for meeting with me."

"Of course." Worry niggled at the base of my head. This was unusual behavior for my father. He'd never been demonstrative. Not even before Andi's abduction. "Is everything okay?"

"Yeah, have a seat." He motioned to the chair across from his. "I'm glad you asked to meet with me. I was actually going to come over to your apartment after I got home from work."

"Oh?"

His lips stretched into a thin smile, then he gestured to the two glasses in front of me. "They brought you water, but I also ordered you some lemonade. You always used to love their lemonade when you were a girl."

Andi had been the one who loved their lemonade, but I refrained from telling him so. "Thanks." I picked it up and took a sip, trying not to cringe at the overly sweet drink. "I haven't been here since I graduated from high school."

"Not much has changed," he said, wiping his thumb along the side of his water glass, brushing the condensation onto the table. "Kind of like your mother."

I'd rarely heard him criticize my mother, so I stared at him in shock.

He looked up, tears filling his eyes. "Sarah Jane isn't an easy woman to live with, and I apologize for not doing more to make your life easier. Especially after…" His voice trailed off.

I reached over the table and covered his hand with mine. "Dad, no…" It sounded strangled as I pushed the words past the lump in my throat.

His shoulders rose as he took in a deep breath, and a look of determination filled his eyes. "Yes. The truth is, I haven't been a good father. At first, I was too busy building my career to spend time with you girls, and after Andi was taken, I was too grief-stricken to really consider how hard it was for you." His chin trembled. "And your mother sure never did."

Tears burned my eyes. This was all coming out of nowhere and I was completely caught off guard. The wall protecting my emotions was falling fast.

The waitress approached with a cheerful smile. "Are you two ready to order?"

I hadn't even looked at the menu, but my father had just said nothing had changed so I ordered my old favorite, a Caesar salad. My father ordered pot roast, and the waitress scooped up the menus and carried them away.

I waited for him to continue, but when he didn't, I said, "I've always loved you, Dad."

He held my gaze. "But you felt abandoned by me."

I couldn't bring myself to deny it. Instead, I said, "I'm sure you did the best you could. Especially after Andi. We were all drowning in grief and guilt. We dealt with it in our own, weird ways."

"I should have been—"

I shook my head and gave him a sad smile. "No, Dad. No should haves. There's no changing the past. We can only go forward from here."

He swiped a tear starting to fall and drew another deep breath. "I know you think your mother instigated the job offer, but it was Mitch's idea."

"Are you sure you want me there? I mean, I understand if you don't. It screams nepotism." Not to mention I had a reputation his firm would have to deal with, no matter what Mitch had claimed.

"Yes," he said eagerly. "I would love the chance to work with you. Spend time with you." His eyes turned glassy again. "I've wasted so much time, Harper. I'm sorry."

I choked back a sob. "Dad."

"I'm going to make this right, Harper. I swear," he said earnestly, then his eyes turned serious. "I'm leaving your mother."

My mouth fell open.

"As I said, she's a hard woman to live with, and she's treated you terribly. Honestly, we both did. You needed love and support and all you received from your mother was condemnation, and ambivalence from me. But that display last night…" He shook his head. "I confronted her after Mitch and John David left."

"Dad…" I wasn't sure what to say. Thank you for finally being a parent? After all this time, you don't have to stand up for me anymore?

"I'll be moving out. My secretary is in the process of finding me an apartment or a rental house, but I suspect your mother will kick you out."

My heart sank. "Oh."

"I've asked Donna to look for a two-bedroom if you want to crash with me."

The waitress brought out our food and we fell silent as we picked up our forks and started to eat.

"You won't be homeless, Harper," he said insistently. "You can stay with me."

"Will she kick me out today?"

He made a face. "Well, legally, she can't. There are laws about eviction, all of which take time. But I figured we should have a place lined up before she exhausts her legal options."

Evicted by my mother. I wasn't surprised, but it still hurt. I nodded.

"If you're agreeable to it, we were thinking you could start at the firm next week," he said, trying to sound cheerful. "As Mitch said, we'll have you start with filing and such, but maybe once you get started, you'll like it enough to want to be a paralegal, or even go to law school." He held up a hand. "No pressure from me. You can do whatever you want. I just want you to know you have options."

"Thanks."

We continued to eat, but it was difficult making small talk. I still wanted to ask him about Andi's kidnapping, but it would have felt like kicking him while he was down. He'd just decided to divorce his wife of thirty-nine years. Still, I needed answers, and the only way to get them was to ask questions. I just needed to figure out when to do it.

God love him, he must have sensed there was something else I wanted to discuss because he looked up at me with worry in his eyes. "Now that my news is out in the open, why don't you tell me why you wanted to talk."

I picked at a piece of lettuce in my bowl with my fork. "I have questions about Andi's kidnapping. About John Michael Stevens, to be more precise."

The color faded from his face, and he picked up his iced tea and took a long sip. When he set it down, his gaze met mine. "Sorry. I wasn't expecting that."

"*I'm* sorry."

He patted his hand in the air toward me. "No, no. I'm sure you have questions. It was very much a taboo subject in our house." He sliced off a piece of his pot roast with his knife, then stabbed it with his fork. "I'm not sure what I can tell you about him, but I'll tell you what I can."

"Did they have any other suspects?"

He blinked, caught off guard again. "No. I don't think so." He nodded toward me. "You gave the chief a really good description, and they found him within a week of finding Andi." He set down his fork and knife. "He'd already started stalking another girl and they think he was planning to kidnap her soon. So you saved her life, Harper."

I hadn't known any of that. "So he really did do it? I didn't pick the wrong guy out of the lineup?"

Confusion clouded his eyes. "Have you questioned that you did?"

"Not until recently. But someone pointed out to me that seventy percent of false convictions are based on eyewitness testimony."

"Well, in this instance you were correct. He had photos of Andi in his house. Of while he stalked her and of her…after…" His voice trailed off, and the area around his mouth turned white.

"Oh, Dad." I knew about the photos, but it still hurt hearing about them.

He gave me a tight smile. "It was him, Harper. No doubt about it, Besides, he confessed."

"Yeah, but still…" Why was I questioning his guilt? He'd confessed. He had photos of my sister. *Damn* Malcolm and Hale for making me doubt myself.

He inhaled deeply and tilted his head. "Now, the chief *did* catch some flak for how he handled arresting the guy."

"Oh?"

"Stevens's residence was technically in the sheriff's jurisdiction, but the chief decided to raid the house without their help or notifying them. People claimed he wanted to hog the glory, but he said he didn't want to waste time organizing the task force. He was worried Stevens would catch word and flee. So he and the entire police force—all seven of them—raided Stevens's house. But the guy didn't go willingly, and a few of the officers were shot."

I hadn't known any of this. None of it was in the file. "Killed?"

"No, no," he said, shaking his head. "Just injured. There was an investigation into it all, but the chief came out all right. It was hard to fault him when he was considered a hero." He made a face. "Of course, times were different then."

"Yeah."

"There was a shakeup and restructuring of the department after that. The state thought the chief had too much power, and I think there was some other stuff going on, but it all worked out in the end."

We continued to eat, and then my father's face scrunched up. "Is Ava Peterman still missing? Is that why you're asking all these questions? I'm sure it's dredging up a lot of emotions. I know it has been for Sarah Jane." He gave me a direct look. "And before you think I'm leaving because of that, I'm not. It's so much more than her reaction to Ava Peterman."

I nodded.

"That man who took your sister has nothing to do with Ava. Your mother says she ran away."

"I don't think that's true, Dad," I said softly.

"He's still locked up behind bars, Harper," he said in a soothing tone. "He can't hurt anyone ever again."

Maybe *he* couldn't, but someone else sure was.

"When Andi was taken, were there people who…" I took a breath. "People who blamed me for what happened? I mean, other than Mom."

He started to protest, then stopped. There was no point in him trying to deny it. "No," he said. "There were the typical armchair judges who thought we and the police force should have handled things differently, but I refused to entertain their comments."

"So some people *did* blame me?"

He made a face, clearly uncomfortable. "I suppose."

"Anyone in particular who comes to mind?"

He stared down at his half-empty plate as he considered it. "It's been so long, Harper. I don't remember anyone in particular. It was just the general stuff like you should have fought him. You should have stopped at the first house." He hesitated. "You should have run after her."

Guilt was like a knife to my gut.

"That's all utter bull crap, Harper," he said insistently. "You were fifteen. He outweighed you by a hundred pounds. There's absolutely no way you or your sister could have fought him off. And as for stopping at the nearest house, it was nearly ten minutes from where Andi was taken. It was another five minutes home. It wouldn't have made any difference. By the time you reached the first house, he had already put Andi in his car and taken off." When I gave him a questioning look, he added in a soft voice, "He said so in his confession."

The food in my belly felt like a lump of goo.

"Thanks."

"We've run away from this for too long," my father said. "We thought pretending it didn't happen was the way to get over it, but obviously it hasn't worked. None of us are over it."

I didn't think any of us ever would be.

Chapter Thirty-One

I LEFT THE RESTAURANT a little later, unable to finish my food. My father gave me a long hug when we left, then asked if I'd changed my mind about working for the firm. I still wasn't convinced it was a great idea, but there was no doubt I was desperate, so I said yes. He asked if I wanted to get a head start on looking for a place for us, but I told him my day was pretty full.

His eyes narrowed. "What are you up to?"

"No good," I teased. "If Donna doesn't find anything, I'll start in a few days."

He gave me a worried look but didn't press, leaving me there on the sidewalk.

I headed back to my car and approached the driver's door carefully, terrified I'd find another note, but there was nothing.

I wasn't sure what to do next. I didn't have any other leads, and I was still waiting for Hale's call. A trip to see Stevens was probably pointless given what my father had told me, but I doubted I'd be able to convince Hale or Malcolm of that.

With nothing else to do, I headed home. I still needed to make my bed, and I could get a head start on looking for somewhere for my father to move. While he'd offered to let me move in with him, I still hadn't made up my mind. It might be awkward since we didn't know each other very well. Besides, I'd be making some money as of next week. And although I didn't know how much I'd be earning, I hoped it would be enough to rent a small apartment. It might not be up to the standards I was used to, but I'd make do.

A pile of my sheets was on my bed when I walked into my apartment, and I couldn't help feeling relieved that I wouldn't have to face my mother. The non-response to my text was enough to tell me she was giving me the silent treatment.

I made the bed, then started an internet search for two-bedroom places for my dad. Even if I didn't move in, he needed a spare room for an office or guest room. I'd made a list when my phone rang with Hale's number.

"Hey," I answered, nerves getting the best of me. His call probably meant the meeting was all set up.

"You and Skeeter have an appointment at six. Don't be late."

"Six? Visitors' hours don't go that late."

"You're a special kind of visitor."

I glanced at the time on my laptop. It was three-thirty, and it would take us an hour to get there. "Am I picking up Malcolm?"

"He'll meet you there."

"Won't he have trouble getting in if he's a suspect in Eddie Johnson's murder?"

"You let me worry about that."

He hung up, and I took a deep breath, trying to calm down. I probably should have told him about my conversation with my father, but I knew it would have been wasted breath. Besides, now that I'd accepted that I was about to see my sister's murderer, I wanted to do it. I needed to confront the bastard who'd killed my sister and destroyed our lives.

I poured myself a drink and nursed it, congratulating myself for not getting a drink as soon as I'd come home and for taking my time with it. I needed to figure out what to say to

Stevens. I tried to come up with a list of questions, but it was pointless. The only way I could prepare for this was to figure out a way to keep from crying. Bottom line, there was no possible way to prepare, and it was time to leave.

My anxiety ratcheted the closer I got to the prison. When I pulled into the visitors' parking lot at five forty-five, I wasn't surprised to see Malcolm standing next to his motorcycle.

I parked next to him.

"Wondered if you'd flake out," he said as I got out of the car.

"I should warn you that I don't back down from challenges very easily, Malcolm," I said as I started toward the entrance, leaving him to follow.

"Good to know," he said as he fell into step beside me.

A man in a suit met us at the entrance once we were inside.

"Mr. Malcolm and friend? If you'll follow me."

And *friend?* Carter Hale had made it sound like Malcolm needed me to get in.

Malcolm nodded, and I stared at the man's back in disbelief as he led us through security without us signing in. He didn't appear to know my name. Had Hale done that on purpose?

How many violations were we breaking here? How had Hale pulled this off? A new worry burrowed into my gut. What had I gotten myself into?

Ten minutes later, after going through multiple security checkpoints, Malcolm and I were left in a small, dingy room with a table and four chairs. Neither of us sat. I stood next to the door we'd used to enter, but Malcolm was pacing, his face paler than usual.

"Hard being back behind bars?" I asked without any snipe.

He didn't answer, just rubbed his chin.

"Is this room bugged?" I didn't like the idea of any exchange between Stevens and me being recorded.

He shook his head. "No. I've been assured it's not."

Which meant we could talk freely.

"Can you produce an alibi for the rest of the night after I dropped you off at Scooter's?" I asked. When he gave me a blank look, I added, "Because of Eddie's body turning up behind your bar?"

He shook his head. "Just the usual video surveillance."

"Did any of the cameras in your lot get footage of who left the van?"

"No, they shot out a light in the lot so it was too dark for the camera to pick up any facial features."

"But it's a man?"

"Yep. He drove in about four a.m., parked, then walked to the highway."

"He must have an accomplice," I said. "How else would he maneuver all that?"

He shook his head. "Maybe we'll get some answers when this pervert shows up."

I doubted we'd get anything useful, but it seemed pointless to disagree.

A few minutes later, the door on the opposite side of the room opened, and a guard brought in a tall man with broad shoulders and a dark, bushy beard.

He was older and heavier, but I had no doubt he was the man who'd stolen my sister. A wave of fear washed through me as memories of the day he took my sister bombarded me.

The guard led him to the table and waited for him to sit before he handcuffed Stevens to the table. Then he left.

I took an involuntary step back, my back pressed to the wall next to the door, while Malcolm surged forward, dragging a chair from the table. He sat down and gave Stevens a dark glare.

"Why am I here?" Stevens asked in a gruff voice. "Who the fuck are you?"

"I," Malcolm said in tone that carried plenty of malice, "am your potential worst nightmare. I suggest you answer anything I ask you and don't waste our time by lying."

Stevens looked up at me. "Who's she?"

"She is none of your concern. In fact, ignore that she's even there."

A smirk lit up Stevens's eyes. "Hard to do when she's standing right there."

Malcolm slapped him across the cheek, drawing a startled gasp from Stevens. He held his cheek with his free hand as he stared up at Malcolm in disbelief.

I started to protest, but Stevens beat me to it.

"You can't do that!"

"Looks like I just did," Malcolm growled. "Every time I catch you looking up at her, you'll get more of the same, which means I shouldn't have any trouble holding your attention. Have I made myself clear?"

Stevens shot daggers of hate at him. "Guard!"

"I promise you that he's not coming until I call him, and I'm only getting started. Now tell me what Andrea Adams was wearing the day you kidnapped her."

"Andrea Adams?" Surprise filled Stevens's eyes, quickly replaced by glee. "She had on this little pink dress and sneakers." He gestured to his chest, then toward his feet. A wide grin spread across his face, a devilish look in his eyes. "And her panties had these cute little cherries on them. Fitting, you know?"

Malcolm punched Stevens's face, and blood gushed from his nose.

"Hey! That was the truth!" Stevens said as he covered his face with his free hand.

"You're lucky that's all I've done so far, you sick fuck," Malcolm seethed. "You'll speak about Andrea Adams with respect, or I'll rip your tongue out."

I stared at him in shock. He'd never met my sister. He had no idea who she was, yet here he was defending her. I wasn't sure about Stevens, but *I* believed that Malcolm would actually maim him. Was it wrong that some primal part of me wanted him to?

Malcolm glanced back at me, a vein throbbing in his forehead. He gave me a questioning look, as though asking if Stevens was correct. I nodded.

Malcolm turned back to him. "Who helped you with her kidnapping?"

His question surprised me. Everyone had said Stevens had worked alone. He'd never implicated anyone else in his confession.

Stevens looked surprised too, but I caught a brief glimpse of worry. "No one."

A crack filled the room after Malcolm slapped his other cheek. "Wrong answer."

"What the hell, man?" Stevens cried out. "*Guard!*"

"I told you, he's not coming," Malcolm snarled. "Who helped you?"

"I didn't—"

Crack.

He asked several more times with the accompanying slaps, before Stevens finally cried out, "He didn't help me kidnap her, but he let me know the police were coming. Is that what you want to know?"

I gasped. He'd had help?

"What's his name?"

"Barry Sylvester. He was with the Jackson Creek police."

The police department? I knew they were inept but *corrupt?* I hadn't seen that one coming.

"Why would he help you?" Malcolm asked.

"I don't know, man."

"I don't believe you."

"I *don't. Know.*" Stevens spat out a wad of blood onto the table. "He called and told me the police were on the way and to get out. I asked him why he was helping, and he said to quit wasting time asking questions. With the police coming, it wasn't like I had a lot of time to chat. They showed up less than five minutes later."

Malcolm glanced back at me with a questioning look.

I shook my head. The name Sylvester sounded familiar, but I couldn't figure out why.

Malcolm loomed over him, cupping his bright red cheek. "Good boy. Who else helped you?"

"No one," Stevens earnestly.

"Why don't I believe you?" Malcolm's voice rumbled.

Panic filled Stevens's eyes. "There was no one else! I swear!"

Malcolm lowered his face close to Stevens, and when he tried to look away, Malcolm held both sides of his head. "Not so fucking tough now, are you?"

Stevens started to cry. "What do you want from me?"

"I want for you to not destroy lives with your selfish actions, but it's too damn late for that. So I'll have to settle for this instead." He lightly slapped his left cheek, then stood upright. "Why'd you pick Andrea?"

"I don't know," Stevens said, keeping his gaze on the table.

"That's bullshit and we both know it," Malcolm said. "Try again."

Stevens sniffled, then he adjusted himself. "She was cute, in those little dresses and with her long blond hair." He squirmed in his seat.

Malcolm punched him so hard his chair started to fall backward, but the handcuff attached to the table held him upright. Stevens released an agonized scream, and I was certain he'd dislocated his shoulder or torn tendons. Maybe both.

Malcolm went around the table and grabbed the hair on the back of his head, tilting his head back so his neck was exposed, and he was staring up into Malcolm's furious face. "Don't you even *think* about that child like that. *Do you hear me?*"

Stevens nodded, his face crimson. Blood still dripped from his nose, and his left eye was starting to swell shut.

"Why'd you pick her?" Malcolm asked again in his scary neutral voice that carried an undercurrent of violence. "And think carefully about what you say."

Stevens reached for his shoulder, still crying. "I saw her walking home from school with her friend. I knew she was mine."

I swallowed the bile in my throat. It made me sick to think about him following Andi, yet it made sense that he had.

"Why'd you leave the red ribbon?"

"With the doll?" he asked in confusion, squinting up at Malcolm.

Malcolm glanced over at me, and I nodded.

"Yeah."

"I don't know, I guess because I knew she wouldn't be coming back, so I left a doll there instead."

"Fucking sicko," Malcolm snarled under his breath.

Stevens didn't reply.

"Why'd you put the ribbon in her hair?" I asked from my place by the door, my question coming out less forceful than I'd intended.

Stevens turned his attention to me, looking like he was trying to place me. "It looked pretty." A soft smile tweaked the corners of his mouth as though he was reliving a memory.

My stomach twisted in disgust. I was reliving memories too, but we viewed them in two very different ways.

Malcolm released his hold on Stevens with a shove.

"Who did you tell about the ribbon?" Malcolm asked.

The man looked up at him through his good eye. "What do you mean?"

"It's redacted in the police reports, so who did you tell?"

"No one."

"You expect me to believe you didn't brag about raping that little girl?" Malcolm asked, his voice taking a dark tone. "You didn't brag about wrapping a ribbon in her hair?"

I felt like I was going to vomit. I started breathing through my nose.

"I didn't, dude. Guys in here don't think banging a fourteen-year-old is cool."

"That's because it's *not* cool, Stevens. It's *disgusting*," Malcolm punched him again, and this time Stevens's head sagged.

"I think you knocked him out," I murmured in shock. This entire situation was surreal.

"Fuck," he said in disgust. "I wasn't done beating the shit out of him yet."

Chapter Thirty-Two

MALCOLM POUNDED ON THE DOOR we'd come through and the suited man opened it seconds later.

"All done?" he asked, casting a glance at the man passed out in his chair.

"Unfortunately, yes," Malcolm said as he took a cloth out of his back pocket and started to wipe his bloody knuckles.

We walked in silence as the man led us back out to the visitors' entrance. Once we were out of the prison and in the relative safety of the cold evening, I stopped next to my car, staring at him in disbelief. "What the hell was *that*?"

His eyes hardened. "That was me getting information."

"You *beat* him. A man handcuffed to a table!"

He gave me a cold stare. "You have your way of getting information, and I have mine. Which one was more effective in this instance?"

"Fuck you," I spat out. "That was…"

"Effective. Stevens had help from a Jackson Creek police officer. Recognize the name?"

I shook my head, then grimaced. "No, but yes. For some reason the name Sylvester is stuck in my head, but I can't figure out why."

He pulled out his phone and called Hale.

"I need you to look up a name. Barry Sylvester. He was a Jackson Creek police officer. See if he's still on the force." He paused. "Okay, then see what he's doin' now. He gave Stevens a heads-up that the police were coming to arrest him. See if you can find out anything on him to figure out why. Was he dirty? Did someone pay him to do it? We need answers."

He hung up and stared down at me. "Did you get any closure?"

Did I? I was still overwhelmed by everything that had happened. "I don't know. I mean, I got some answers, but other than finding out someone warned him…" I shook my head. "Seeing him again…" Seeing him again had ripped the scab open all over again, which pissed me off. "Why did you insist that I come? You obviously didn't need me to get in."

He gave me an unapologetic stare. "To see if he was telling the truth."

"Like what she was wearing?"

"Yep."

I wrapped my arms across my chest and stared toward the parking lot exit. "I can still see him coming through the woods. He looked happy, excited…" I shuddered. "He had a hard-on when he approached us."

Malcolm watched me but didn't make any sympathetic sounds. I preferred it that way.

"He told Andi to come with him. We both said no, of course, although *my* words were coarser than that." I shot him a sideways look. "Even back then, I used what my mother called unladylike language, which I'm sure was part of the reason she liked Andi better than me."

He watched without commentary, but I didn't get the feeling he was annoyed. It didn't matter if he was. Seeing Stevens had stirred a pot of simmering emotions, and I needed to get this out.

I rubbed my arms. "We were next to the creek, checking out a stupid bird's nest. The baby birds were close to flying off and she wanted to see them before they left. So we walked there after school. Andi had just climbed down from the tree when he appeared. There was a path that led to the creek bank and dead ended there"—I drew the path in the air with my hand—"and we happened to be at the dead end, so it was either run through the brush in the woods or try to get past him. I knew we'd never make it through the brush. He'd catch us in no time, but if I incapacitated him, then we might have a chance. He approached us, and I bent down and grabbed a handful of dirt and threw it in his face. He couldn't see and we got past him, but he quickly caught up. He wrapped an arm around Andi's waist and pulled out a gun and told me to stay there or he'd kill her. So I stayed there, frozen like a statue. I can still see him running through the woods, my sister flung over his shoulder and screaming at the top of her lungs."

"No one heard her?"

"No one ever said they did. We were in the woods, but her voice carried. Until it didn't." I swallowed hard. "I think he knocked her out."

I stole a glance toward Malcolm, but he still had that expressionless face, the one I'd come to know so well over the past few days. I'd mostly found it aggravating, but right now, I was thankful for it.

"I ran home as fast as I could, and my mother called the police."

"Did you know about the photos?" he asked gruffly.

"Yeah." I swallowed. "I got his file. But I didn't read the evidence log of the photos." I couldn't bear the thought of what he'd photographed, and I felt like I owed her the dignity of not knowing.

"Just the photos? You read what else they found?"

"Yeah."

"Do you remember anything else from that day? Anything at all?"

"I don't know, Malcolm," I said in frustration. "It was twenty-one years ago, and I was traumatized!"

"Well, too damn bad," he spat. "We need to know why Sylvester was protecting him. What if he had someone else working with him from the very beginning?"

"It was just him that day," I snapped angrily. "I remember that much!"

"But what if she stopped screaming because someone else knocked her out?"

I vigorously shook my head. "There was nothing to ever suggest that."

"Well, something shady was going down. Why else would a police officer risk his career to protect a kidnapper and murderer?"

Shit. He was right.

"But he didn't admit to anyone else helping him," I protested. "Either back then or today."

"That's because I got too pissed off and knocked him out," he said in disgust. "I planned to switch topics, then go back to it." He ran a hand over his head. "I know you didn't see the photos, but maybe you heard about them. Was Stevens ever in any of them, or were they just of her?"

I closed my eyes, trying to burn out the images my imagination created. I didn't need to see the actual photos because my mind's eye was probably worse. "Both. Just her and him...with her." I choked out the last words.

"What if Barry Sylvester was actually part of Andi's kidnapping and murder?" Malcolm asked, his voice deep and threatening.

I turned to him in disbelief. "Do you know what you're saying?"

"I know exactly what I'm saying. But I also know a police officer isn't gonna just call and warn a child molester they're coming to get him. He had a reason, either professional or personal. We need to find out which one drove him to make that call."

If he was right, then a police officer helped—or condoned—Stevens repeatedly raping my sister for days and then strangling her.

Had Barry Sylvester molested my sister too? And if so, was he the one who had taken Ava Peterson?

Having just seen the monster who had violated my sister sent panic flooding through my veins. If Morris had taken Ava, I would have presumed he was using her for leverage. But if Sylvester had taken her...

I walked over to the edge of the parking lot and vomited.

"If you've got that out of your system," Malcolm sneered, "we need to get going."

I wiped my mouth with the back of my hand as I stood. "Fuck you."

"Already told you that you're not my type."

"Then double fuck you."

"We have work to do. We don't have time for your hangover vomiting."

I kept my back to him. "I'm not hung over."

"I suspect you live in a perpetual state of either drunkenness or hangover. You need to get your shit together."

I turned to face him. "In case you haven't noticed, my life is a literal shitshow."

"Boohoo," he sneered. "You had something bad happen to you. Two something bads. It fucking sucks. But you didn't let the first one ruin your life, so why let the second?"

"People hate my guts!" I shouted at him. "I've gotten death threats!"

316 Denise Grover Swank

His brow lifted, but his eyes were dull. "News flash. People hate *my* guts and people have *tried to kill me*, multiple times. You don't see me throwing my life into the shitter."

"But you chose that life! I didn't!"

He shook his head in disgust. "Seems to me that you should have learned by now that life isn't fair. I guaran-damn-tee you that someone has it worse than you. *Many* people have it worse than you, and I bet at least half of them aren't soaking their livers in alcohol every damn day."

"Fuck you!" I shouted. Everything he was saying was true, but dammit, why was it that he of all people was saying it?

He leaned close, his face inches from mine. "You have two choices, Harper Adams. Either get your shit together and get off the booze, or as soon as we find Ava Peterman, you go drink yourself into oblivion. But for now, I need you to choose door number one. Are you capable of that?"

I didn't dignify him with a response. I marched over to my car door and got inside and drove back to Jackson Creek.

Chapter Thirty-Three

I NEEDED TO CONFIRM that a Jackson Creek PD officer had alerted Stevens. Unfortunately, I suspected there was only one person other than Barry Sylvester who could give me the answer, and I didn't hold out much hope that he'd share the information. Nevertheless, I had to try.

It was nearly eight, so I doubted Chief Larson was at the station, which meant if I wanted to see him tonight, I would have to drop by his home.

Finding it wasn't an issue. Everyone in Jackson Creek knew where Chief Larson lived. Most law enforcement officials didn't want the public knowing how to find them in case a disgruntled person decided to seek revenge. Chief Larson encouraged them to drop by his house, where he'd meet them at the front door with a shotgun. Any teenager caught vandalizing his property soon regretted it after a stint in juvie and a load of community service. Any adult who tried to show up to intimidate him left with an ass full of buckshot and a sentence in the county jail or a state prison. Sometimes a combination of all three. But it had only happened a few times while I'd been living here. I had no idea how many times it had happened since.

No, finding his house wasn't the problem. Getting him to talk to me without filling me full of shotgun pellets or arresting me was a whole other issue.

His red brick ranch house was on a corner lot with floodlights illuminating the property. Rumor had it that neighbors had complained about the lights over the years, but he was the one in charge of enforcing things like that, so obviously, nothing had been done.

I pulled up to the curb and took in the manicured lawn and the three flag poles with an American, Arkansas, and Marines flag flying. His police cruiser was parked in the driveway.

At least I knew he was home.

I took a moment to calm down, desperately wishing I had a drink, but Malcolm's words were ringing in my head. I hated him for having the audacity to think he was better than me. Deep down, though, I knew he was right. I hated pity, but self-pity was especially egregious. I needed to get my shit together. But I couldn't deal with that right now. I needed to talk to the chief and somehow convince him to confirm Stevens's story.

I got out of the car and headed up to the front porch. It was no surprise when the front door opened before I reached the porch. Chief Larson stepped outside, keeping the door open with his body.

The fact that he wasn't pointing a shotgun at me meant things were off to a good start.

"What the hell are you doing at my personal home, Harper Adams?" he demanded, fire in his eyes. "You tryin' to get yourself thrown in jail?"

I lifted my chin and held his gaze. "No. I'm here to find out why it wasn't in my sister's file that Barry Sylvester warned John Michael Stevens you were coming to arrest him."

Shock filled his eyes, and some of his bluster faded. "Where'd you hear that?"

I steeled my shoulders. "From the source himself—Stevens."

Fury filled his eyes. "When did you go see him?"

"It doesn't matter, Chief," I said, feeling exhausted by it all. "Because we both know it's true."

He opened his mouth as though to say something, then held his front door open. "I'm not having this discussion outside. Come in."

I had so much paranoia about all the lies and the cover-ups that part of me was afraid to go inside his house. But I told myself I was being ridiculous. While the chief was narcissistic and inept, I'd never once thought him capable of cold-blooded murder.

I followed him inside. A baking show was on the television, and his wife was tucked up on their sofa with a blanket over her lap, two knitting needles in her hand, and something deep purple hanging from them.

"We're goin' into my study," Chief Larson said as he passed through the room, sounding nothing like the man I'd encountered in the station.

"Okay, dear," she said, then glanced over me. Her eyes widened in surprise. "Harper Adams?"

I refrained from cringing. Was I about to get a tongue lashing? "Yes, ma'am."

She nodded with a soft smile. "Tell your mother I said hello."

"Thank you," I said in surprise. "I will."

I followed the chief down a hall to a rec room that had a large screen TV and a pool table. Green shag carpet covered the floor. He gestured toward a faded brown sofa. I took a seat while he lowered into a cracked leather recliner that looked older than I was.

Chief Larson's study was a total man cave.

"What do you know?" he asked with a sigh.

"I know Barry Sylvester called John Michael Stevens and told him you were on your way to arrest him."

He pressed his lips together and directed a far-off stare at the wall. Finally, he said, "He nearly got a couple of my men killed."

"Why'd he do it?"

"Never got a straight answer out of him. He damn near got himself arrested, but we smoothed things over. I fired him on the spot, of course, but we saved his family the embarrassment of his actions."

"Which is why it's not in any report."

He didn't answer. He didn't need to.

"So what happened after you fired him?"

"After the investigation died down, he left town, but his wife stayed behind with the kids."

"Where'd he go?"

He shrugged. "Little Rock, last I heard. Got a job on the police force there."

My heart stuttered. "Is he still there?" Was he working for the LRPD when I'd shot Dylan Carpenter? Was he the one who'd stolen the photo from my house?

"Don't know. Maybe. I'm friendly with his ex-wife, but she doesn't talk about him much."

"Was Sylvester a good cop?"

The chief rubbed his face and leaned forward, resting his forearms on his thighs. "Yeah. One of my better investigators. No one was more surprised by what he did than me."

"Do you think there was any way he was working with Stevens?"

He jerked upright, his eyes flying wide. "You're asking if he was part of kidnapping your sister?" He shook his head. "No. No way."

"He had to have *some* reason for warning Stevens," I insisted. "It's too random otherwise. Was there anything off with Sylvester? Had he been acting erratically?"

"Barry was having some financial issues." He grimaced. "I mean, we don't pay much, and his wife wasn't working. His son had some medical bills and I know he felt overwhelmed by that."

"So could Sylvester have tried to extort Stevens? Based on everything I've read, Stevens didn't have any money."

The chief shook his head again. "You're right. He didn't. Stevens lived in a shithole rental house and worked for the gas station on the edge of Jackson Creek. We figured that's how he spotted your sister. She liked to hang out in the park, and he saw her with you and Vanessa." He cleared his throat. "The guy was broke, and Barry knew it. There was no way he'd ever get money out of him."

"It doesn't make sense," I said. "We're missing something."

"I know, but Barry never told me, and I questioned him multiple times. The only thing he ever said was that he didn't think Stevens got a fair shake, which never made any sense. Sure, we went in planning to arrest him, but if the search warrant hadn't yielded the evidence we needed to make the arrest, we would have been forced let him go."

"What happened to the son with the medical bills?"

"I know that Jackie applied for Medicaid, but I think Barry ended up stuck with most of them. Jackie refused to let the boys spend much time with him. Barry lost everything because of what he did."

So maybe he blamed Stevens for the loss of his job and his family. But if he was responsible for what was happening now, why kidnap Ava? Was the shooting last October the trigger that made him set all this in motion, starting with stealing my photo?

"Do you know where his sons are now?"

"One of them is living in Wolford. The other just moved back to town last fall and joined the police department. Drew Sylvester."

My mouth dropped open. "Drew?"

He nodded. "Good kid. He showed up last November asking for a job. I told him it wouldn't pay much, but he said he didn't care."

I took a second to let that sink in. "I actually met him through my friend Nate," I said. "He said he moved back to help his mother."

He scrunched up his face. "Jackie's had some health issues in the past, but she's doin' better now."

"And the other son's name?"

He pressed his lips together. "Danny. Got into a bit of trouble after his father left town. Did a short stint in prison for manslaughter." He made a face. "Bar fight down in Memphis. Drunk off his ass. But it wasn't his first run-in with the law. He had some minor drug possession charges. When he got out, he moved back to the area."

I studied the chief for a moment. "Why are you telling me all of this? This morning you were ready to arrest me for kidnapping Ava Peterman."

"I'm getting too old for this shit. Besides, maybe I felt like you deserved to know." He hesitated. "Despite what you think, I tried my best to find and save your sister. I never wanted it to end the way it did."

Maybe so, but his ego got in the way of saving her. She'd been alive for nearly a week, a week of pure hell. If he'd called in other agencies sooner, I couldn't help but think she might be alive today. Obviously, he didn't feel the same way. I could call him on it, but I didn't see the point. It wouldn't bring my sister back, and Stevens was rotting in jail.

Since he was talking to me civilly, I decided to push my luck. "Do you really think Ava Peterman ran away?"

His face instantly hardened. "Her father says she did."

Tilting my head, I held his gaze. "And we both know that parents are the number one suspects until proven innocent."

"He didn't do it," he said. "He says he's got someone on it."

"What do you mean he's got someone on it? A private investigator? Does he have any leads?"

He looked away. "I have no idea."

"You're not *checking*?" I asked in disbelief. "Why not?"

His cheeks flushed. "I have my reasons."

"And what reasons could trump the life of a child?" And what would entice this power-hungry man to willingly give up power?

"He assures me that he's got it under control," he snapped, anger filling his eyes, but I saw guilt there too. "Running a police department is a hell of lot more expensive than it used to be."

Of course. Money. "And he promised you money from the city budget."

"Peterman's all about growing the town, which means more revenue. He's promised me a chunk of it."

"If you let him handle it," I said dully. Jesus. He'd potentially traded the life of a child for an increased police budget.

"He's about to announce his run for state senate and he's running on making the state safe. He can't very well do that if his daughter was taken from his own home."

"Seems to me he could run on the premise that his daughter *was* taken, and he needs to clean things up."

He shook his head, suddenly looking older than I'd ever seen him. "He's running on the position that he's already cleaned things up. Shutting down the Morris brothers, then Malcolm."

"How inconvenient for his campaign that his daughter was kidnapped and possibly murdered," I said in disgust.

He got to his feet. "I think it's time for you to go."

I stood and held his gaze. "And what if I told you that I had evidence suggesting she was taken, and I have a lead on who did it?"

His jaw clenched, and he looked away before he turned back to me, his face hard. "I'd say turn it over to Peterman."

"You can't be serious."

"We both know Malcolm's behind it. That dead body behind his bar can't be a coincidence."

I stared at him in disbelief. "You can't seriously believe that Malcolm would be stupid enough to leave a man he murdered behind his own bar. The man has evaded charges for years. He's not dumb."

His arrogant attitude came rushing back. "They all slip up sometime."

"He has an alibi."

His eyes narrowed. "And how would you know that?"

"By asking the right questions," I snapped. "Maybe you should try it sometime."

So much for our truce.

He shook his head, defeat filling his eyes. "It's so easy for you to judge me when you haven't been in my shoes."

I leaned closer. "I can assure you that I wouldn't do *this*."

"You seem to be standing pretty tall on that moral ledge of yours, but what's it built on, little girl?" he asked bitterly. "The death of an unarmed teenager and a murdered sister."

His words felt like a slap in the face, but I refused to address the last statement and focus on the first. No matter what I did, I'd always be that hysterical girl, trying to tell him what had happened to her sister. "In case you hadn't noticed, Chief, I'm not a little girl anymore."

I marched past him out of the room and through the living room. When I walked out the door, he followed me onto the porch.

"I'd appreciate it if you didn't spread this around," he called after me.

I didn't dignify that with a response.

I need to find out more about Barry Sylvester and his son Danny. I also needed to talk to Drew. Did he know more about his father's past? It felt a little to on point that he'd come back to Jackson Creek about a month after my shooting incident. And after my break-ins.

I'd bet money that Hale had already gotten the information about Barry by now, and if his investigator was worth their salt, they would have discovered Barry's son had a criminal history. But I didn't trust Malcolm and Hale. Hale must have pulled some serious shit to arrange that visit to the prison. I was trying to clear my mud-covered name, not sink in the depths of a swamp. Besides, I was still pissed at Malcolm for not only making me face Stevens, but also accusing me of being an alcoholic. I knew someone else who could find the information I needed. Even if I hated asking her.

Louise answered with chipper tone. "Please tell me you're just calling for a chat. I've had a day."

The chief stood on the porch, watching me with a scowl as I pulled away from the curb.

I cringed, hating that I was probably about to make it worse. "Sorry. I need you to look into a couple of people. The first is a former Jackson Creek Police Department officer. He was on the force when my sister was murdered."

"Okay…" she said with a sigh. "Any particular reason?"

"Sorry." I shook my head, feeling even more like shit, which was saying something. "It's been a weird day. I saw the man who murdered my sister and just had an interesting conversation with Chief Larson in his personal man cave."

There was a pause before she said, "There's so much to unpack there. You went to the *prison to see the guy who killed your sister?*"

"Yeah, long story, but bottom line, Stevens says the day he was arrested, an officer in the police department called to warn

him that the police were on the way. Chief Larson admitted that
it happened."

"Whoa…"

"The officer's name was Barry Sylvester, and last the chief
heard, he was a police officer in Little Rock."

"Oh shit!"

"I really, really hate to ask this, but can you do a search on
him? I can look up a birthdate if you like, but I don't have
anything else to go on."

"That's insane! Why would a cop warn a murderer?
Especially a *child* murderer?"

"Stevens claims he didn't know why Sylvester warned him.
Chief Larson said he could never get a straight answer out of
Sylvester when he questioned him multiple times. He said
something about Stevens not getting a fair shake."

"Like he thought he was being framed?" she asked in
disbelief.

"I don't know, but he wasn't framed. When I saw Stevens
today, he seemed pretty pleased with what he'd done to my sister.
But I can't help wondering if someone else was involved."

"And that person got off scot-free? If so, then was Barry
Sylvester protecting himself or someone else?"

"I don't know. But there's something else. Sylvester has two
sons. One of them, Danny, acted out after his father was fired
from the department. Larson said he had some minor drug
convictions and was imprisoned for manslaughter after a
drunken bar fight in Memphis. He recently got out of prison
and lives up in Wolford."

"What about the other son?"

I paused. "He's a new officer with the Jackson Creek PD."

"*Drew?*"

"Yep."

"Shit," she murmured. "What's your gut on this?"

"I think two people are involved in what's going on now. Whoever drove that van out to Scooter's likely had help. Someone to pick them up."

"You think this is related to your sister's murder?"

"Yeah. I do." Part of me wanted to tell her about the messages, but something was holding me back. Was it because James Malcolm felt too tied to them now? I had a feeling she wouldn't approve if she knew I'd teamed up with him.

"How'd you end up talking to Chief Larson?"

"I just dropped by his house to confront him about Sylvester. Honestly, I thought he'd try to deny it, but once I told him I knew about Barry Sylvester, he invited me inside and shared plenty of things I didn't expect."

"So where does Eddie fit in?"

While I didn't want to tell her about teaming up with Malcolm, I didn't want to keep any more secrets from her than necessary, so I decided to confess at least part of it. "I went to see him last night."

"You said you didn't see him!" she protested angrily.

"That's because I *didn't*. He was already gone, and I'm pretty sure he'd been kidnapped from his house by the time I got there. The back door was broken into and there were drag marks in the grass, like someone had dragged a body."

"*And you didn't report it?*" she demanded.

"Eddie Johnson lived in Jackson Creek city limits, which means Larson was in charge of the investigation. Do you really think he was going to take investigating advice or suggestions from me? No. The signs were so obvious, it should have been staring him in the face, but this morning everyone was positive he ran off. They weren't treating it like a kidnapping."

"You have to do something, Harper!" she shouted over the phone. "That man was murdered, and you could help find who did it!"

"That's what I'm doing, Louise," I said in frustration. "This is all tied to Ava, which is tied to me. I got another note."

"Oh, Jesus. What did this one say?"

"*You're so cold.*"

"What does that mean?"

"He was telling me I was looking in the wrong direction with Eddie Johnson and Ricky Morris." I glanced down at the passenger seat, remembering finding the note—and saw a new envelope with my name. "Oh, God. There's another one."

"Another note?"

I pulled over to the side of the road, then quickly snatched it up and opened the seal. A photo was inside, and my skin felt like it was on fire when I saw what was in the photograph.

"What is it, Harper?" she demanded.

"A photo."

"Of what?"

"My sister," I said in a desperate push of air.

"*What?*"

I closed my eyes, trying to keep from crying. "It's a photo of my sister tied to a bed."

"Jesus, Harper!"

I tossed it down on the seat and it flipped over, revealing a handwritten message on the back.

MUCH WARMER.

Chapter Thirty-Four

"THERE'S A NOTE WRITTEN ON THE BACK," I said, my voice shaking. "It says *much warmer.*"

"What does that mean?"

I shook my head even though she couldn't see me. "He told me I was cold and said Eddie Johnson paid the price. Maybe going to see John Michael Stevens made me warmer."

"Especially if he had an accomplice."

I closed my eyes, trying to clear my head. "At least this one didn't come with a body part."

"*A body part?*" She paused. "Shit! Are you saying *you* have Eddie Johnson's thumb?"

"They left it with the note."

"Okay," she said, her voice steady, but I could tell she was spooked. "Let's think this through. Barry Sylvester tried to protect Stevens, but we don't know why. Maybe the person doing this is trying to point you toward Stevens's accomplice."

The dull pounding in my head began to throb. "But why would Stevens take the fall and not bring Sylvester down with him?"

"A bribe or a threat?"

"Stevens went to prison for life without parole, and his family disowned him. What good would a bribe do?" I asked.

"So maybe not a bribe. Maybe a threat? Surely there was someone Stevens cared about."

"Maybe I need to look more into Stevens's personal life." Until I'd seen the man a few hours ago, he'd been a two-dimensional character who'd ruined our lives. It had never occurred to me to delve into what his life had been like prior to kidnapping my sister.

Louise said, "You have to tell the sheriff, Harper. You have to tell them what's happening."

"Like they're going to believe me," I scoffed. "They didn't believe me about the break-ins in Little Rock."

"You have proof this time."

"Which they can say I made up. Toss in Eddie Johnson's thumb and the fact I was at his house last night, and they'll be charging me with murder."

"You still have to report this, Harper."

Four months ago, she wouldn't have had to tell me that. I would have already done it. "Give me until tomorrow."

"What do you think's going to happen between now and tomorrow?"

"Just give me until tomorrow. Please. And if I don't have this figured out, you can personally escort me to the sheriff's office."

She released a groan. "Tomorrow morning. Ten a.m."

I'd been hoping for tomorrow night, but I didn't feel like I was in a position to negotiate. "Thank you."

"So do you still want me to get you information about Barry Sylvester and his son Danny?"

I knew someone who probably already had the information. It would fucking kill me to ask him. But, given the deadline, I suspected I was going to need his help. "No. I'll take care of it."

"What about Drew?"

"I'm gonna talk to Drew."

"Be careful, Harper."

"I plan to meet him in public. I'll let you know what I discover."

I hung up and stared out the windshield, refusing to look at the photo on the seat next to me.

It was obviously a photo from the crime scene, so where had it come from? Was Barry Sylvester stalking me? Had Drew suspected and that's why he was back?

There was one way to possibly find out. I texted Nate and asked if he had Drew's number.

He called me back within a seconds.

"Why do you need to talk to Drew? Is everything okay?"

"Everything's fine," I lied. "I have some questions about the Jackson Creek Police Department and thought he might be willing to answer some of them."

"I'm sure he'd be willing to talk. I'll text the number to you."

"Thanks."

I texted Drew a request to meet and then called Carter Hale. I wasn't ready to jump back into the deep end with Malcolm just yet. Better to dip my toes in with his attorney.

"I hear you got some information from John Michael Stevens," Hale drawled when he answered.

"And now I'm calling to find out what you found out about Barry Sylvester and his son."

He chuckled.

"Chief Larson confirmed that Sylvester warned Stevens. What did you find out about Sylvester?" I pressed.

He hesitated. "I'm afraid I can't give you that information."

"Why the hell not?"

"I'm sure Malcolm will tell you what he knows."

He was setting boundaries. While Malcolm and I shared our attorney, he was footing the bill, and he'd requested the information. Not me. Still, it *did* confirm he was getting the info from Hale.

"I need to talk to him then."

"I'm not his receptionist."

"Do you know where he went after we left the prison?"

"Again," he said with an exaggerated sigh, "I'm not his—"

"Got it," I grumped. "I know he's staying away from the tavern."

"Not anymore. I turned over all surveillance footage, and he's been cleared of Eddie Johnson's murder by the sheriff. In fact, they moved the van and reopened the tavern late this afternoon."

"Then someone needs to clue Chief Larson in, because he still thinks Malcolm's Suspect Number One."

Hale chuckled again then hung up. I had no idea what was so funny about that. Maybe it was crime syndicate humor.

I called Malcolm next, surprised when he answered.

"Done with your temper tantrum yet?"

I chose to be the bigger person and ignore his prodding. "I just spoke with Chief Larson." I told him what I'd learned, then said bitterly, "But then, you already knew all of that."

"Yep."

"We need to meet and share information."

"Seems like I have most of it," he said in a slow, easy tone.

"Fuck you," I snapped. "I'm about to meet Sylvester's son."

That seemed to get his attention. "What? *Where?*"

"I'm surprised you didn't ask which brother."

"Which one?" he asked grudgingly.

"The police officer. I was hoping you had some information on the other one. Danny."

"Danny worked for the woodworking mill that owned the van parked behind my establishment."

"Danny worked for B&G Woodworking?" I asked in disbelief.

We'd just found our smoking gun.

"It was parked in front of the Petermans' house all last week," I said. "It was stolen two weeks ago."

"Right about the time you got back into town." He paused. "I'm taking care of some business. When I'm done, I'll meet you out at Scooter's."

I nearly told him I'd pick the location, but I was anxious as hell and a drink would take the edge off. Besides, I could ask Drew to meet me there. "Fine."

"Don't get drunk," he barked, then hung up.

When I hung up, I had a text from Drew.

Drew: *When and where?*

Me: *Scooter's Tavern. I'm headed there now*

Drew: *I'm on my way*

Chapter Thirty-Five

THE PLACE WAS PRETTY CROWDED for a Thursday night, but some people had probably been drawn in out of curiosity and it seemed to be crowded most nights. I could only imagine what the weekends looked like.

Misti was working behind the bar when I slid onto a stool and stared at all the bottles of liquor on the back wall, my mouth salivating at the sight.

I knew deep in my gut that Malcolm was right about my drinking, as hard as it was to admit, but quitting cold turkey was more than my willpower could achieve right now. Every cell in my brain craved the sweet relief that alcohol gave me, washing away the guilt and self-loathing, even if it was fleeting.

"Hey, girl," she said as she sidled up to me. "What's it gonna be tonight?"

"Two fingers of whiskey. Neat." I told myself it was medicinal.

Her mouth twisted to the side as she reached for a glass. "Goin' straight for it. I respect that."

"It's been a shit day, so no judgment," I said, exhaustion in my voice. "I want a burger and fries too."

"No judgment unless you plan on gulpin' it down and heading out the door."

I lifted a brow. "Is your boss here?"

She grinned as she poured whiskey into the glass. "Do you see him anywhere? He hasn't shown his face since that body showed up this morning."

I picked up the glass and took a long sip. "What's your gut on Malcolm?"

She turned sideways and leaned a hip against the counter behind the bar. "Depends on why you're askin'."

Glancing down at the amber liquid, I realized how stupid I was to think she'd be anything but loyal. "Never mind." I took another sip.

She started to walk away then came back, leaning over the bar. "I'm not sure what you're lookin' for, but he's a damn good boss. He's a hard-ass, but when he gives his word, he doesn't take it back." She held my gaze. "That means something when you're surrounded by people who lie through their teeth. You know what I mean?"

I gripped the glass with my fingertips. "So an honorable thief?"

She made a face. "I don't know shit about who he used to be before he came here, but he's been more than fair to me. He gave me a chance when no one else would. So call him a thief if you want, but you're never gonna change my opinion of him."

She walked away, annoyance on her face. I knew I'd pushed too hard, but then again, getting answers from people who didn't want to give them meant pushing hard, tricking them into giving up their secrets. How ironic that James Malcolm sounded more honorable than I felt.

An image of Stevens's bloody face popped into my head. There'd been no self-serving motivation for Malcolm to beat the shit out of him. He hadn't done it for me. I could only guess he'd done it because he found Stevens revolting.

Who was this man who I'd pegged to be a low-life manipulator? Then again, you didn't become the head of a crime syndicate by being a nice guy, and you didn't easily leave that life behind. James Malcolm might treat his employees well, but that didn't mean I was ready to accept him at face value.

I finished off my drink, wondering why Drew hadn't shown up yet. Then again, I'd been on my way. It was late enough that he was probably in for the night. Still, I was keyed up. There was more to Andi's murder than anyone had suspected. Someone had helped John Michael Stevens, and that someone was killing and kidnapping innocent people to get to me.

Guilt and panic washed through my veins.

Misti placed the basket of food in front of me and I tapped the side of my empty glass. Malcolm's admonition not to get drunk rang through my head, but I wasn't some lightweight. I could hold my liquor. I needed it to settle my nerves so I could think straight.

She filled it with two fingers, then studied me. "What's your interest in my boss?"

"No interest," I said with a deprecating laugh. "Just curious."

"Guess you have to be curious to be a police detective," she said. "Gotta ask lots of questions."

I quirked a brow, relishing the way the warmth of the alcohol made my muscles relax and spread a hazy calmness throughout my head. "True."

"You know what they say about cats and curiosity," a voice to my right said, and I turned to see Drew perching on the stool next to me. He was wearing a T-shirt, jeans, and a brown jacket. Dark circles underscored his eyes.

"I hear it never goes well," I said, "but I've still got a few lives left. I thought maybe you weren't coming."

"I'm here," he said, with a scowl, then shot Misti a dark look. "I'll take a beer."

Misti gave Drew the side-eye, then walked down to the end of the bar to fill a mug, not even bothering to ask him which kind.

"You're pretty surly for someone who readily agreed to meet with me," I said as I picked up a fry and stuffed it in my mouth.

"Rumor has it you're stirrin' up shit with the police chief."

So he'd heard about my visit to Larson. "News travels fast around here."

"The chief has nosy neighbors," he said unapologetically.

I decided to take the offensive and not bother easing my way into this. I didn't have time for pleasantries. "Why'd you move back to Jackson Creek?"

His eyes widened slightly. "I thought I answered that last night." His gaze drifted to my drink, then back up to my face. "Or were you too drunk to remember?"

I nearly snapped at him then held back. "I think there's more to it," I said in a low, conspiratorial tone. "According to Chief Larson, your mother's doing better."

He shrugged. "Maybe she's doin' better because I'm back."

"Maybe."

Misti placed his beer in front of him, then moved down to the end of the bar.

"I know about your father."

He froze for a second before taking a long swig of his drink and setting it down. "You'll have to be more specific." He kept his gaze on the back wall.

"I know he warned my sister's murderer when Chief Larson was headed out to arrest him."

He took another drink but held his tongue.

"Do you know why he warned him?"

He pressed his lips together, then finally said, "No. We were kids then. You were a sophomore, but I was a junior. There were rumors he screwed up the arrest somehow, but he never said and the chief was hush-hush about it. We figured he just did something to get the other officers hurt."

"So when did you find out?"

"When I joined the force. The chief insisted he didn't have any problem hiring me, but he thought I should know."

"Did you ever confront your father about it?"

"I haven't spoken to my father in nearly twenty years."

My mouth dropped open.

"Don't look so surprised," he said with a bitter laugh. "He abandoned us."

"He didn't try to make *any* contact?"

"Sure," he said with a shrug then took another sip. "In the beginning, but I was so pissed at him that I refused to visit him or even talk to him. Finally, he got the message and gave up."

"What about your brother?"

"Danny?" He turned to me, his eyes wide. "What about him?"

"Did he stay in contact with your dad?"

"He went to live with him for a while," Drew said, his forehead furrowed. "It only screwed him up more."

"He was screwed up?"

"Drugs. Shoplifting." He took a long breath and pushed it out. "Mom couldn't handle him, so my dad took him until he graduated, then he moved around, kept getting into trouble in new places until he killed someone a few years ago. Manslaughter." He shrugged again. "Maybe part of me wanted to be a cop here to make up for what he and my father had done."

"I heard your dad became a Little Rock police officer?"

"Yeah." He hunched over his drink, looking resigned. "Still is, although I got word that he took a leave of absence a week ago."

My chest tightened. "Do you know where he is?"

"Not a clue."

"What about your brother?"

He turned to look at me, realization and horror filling his eyes. "Last I heard, he's living in Wolford. He's got a girlfriend. But I've only seen him once since I moved back. When he dropped by to visit Mom."

"Did your brother live in Memphis?"

"That's where he got into the bar fight that landed him in prison."

"Was he employed there?"

His face scrunched in concentration. "I think he worked for a woodworking shop."

"B&G Woodworking?"

His face paled as he connected the dots. "Do you think…?"

"Why do you think your father warned John Michael Stevens that the police were on the way?"

He shook his head, staring at the back wall again.

"Do you think your father had anything to do with my sister's kidnapping or murder?"

He turned to me and swallowed. "No." He started to say something, then stopped.

"What?" I prodded.

"We didn't live far from Stevens house. Like a block away."

"So your father could have known him."

"Maybe, but also my brother."

"You think Danny knew him?"

He turned grim, then waved to Misti. "I need another beer."

She got him a new drink, and after she left, Drew said, "Danny was kind of mess back then. He shot birds with BB guns. Picked the wings off butterflies. Typical bully/creep shit."

"Did he ever molest anyone?"

"Not that I know about, but that stuff started right around…" He paused and cringed. "Around the time your sister was taken."

"So you think her kidnapping triggered his behavior?"

"I'm not victim blaming," he said in a rush. "More like I always wondered if he saw something, but he was only fourteen, so there's no way he could have been part of it, right?"

"I don't know," I murmured. My phone vibrated in my jeans pocket. I dug it out and glanced at the screen. Louise was sending me multiple texts.

Louise: *I know you said you'd look into it, but I still know people on the LRPD, so I asked a few of them about BS. They say he's a quiet guy. Seems intent on doing his job. Doesn't socialize with his co-workers. They didn't know anything about his sons. They say he doesn't talk about them or himself. Kind of secretive*

Huh.

Louise: *I also looked up Drew. No prior arrests or record of any kind*

So squeaky clean. Good to know.

Louise: *Daniel Sylvester has a long history with law enforcement, including juvie arrests*

Which confirmed what Drew told me.

Me: *Thanks Louise. I'm meeting with Drew now. I'll call you when I'm done.*

Louise: *Oh, one more thing. The body out by the laundromat was Phoebe Whelan.*

Louise: *She was Danny Sylvester's girlfriend.*

Chapter Thirty-Six

"EVERYTHING OKAY?" Drew asked with a worried look.

How much did I tell him?

I glanced up as I tucked my phone away. "So you said your brother has a girlfriend?"

He made a face. "Yeah. I think she works for Ricky Morris, not that it surprises me given the company my brother keeps. Why?"

"Does your brother have a job?"

"He works at a convenience store in Wolford. *Why?*"

"When was the last time you saw him?"

He became agitated. "What's the deal with the interrogation? I told you; I've only seen him once."

"But when?"

"I don't know," he said, running his hand over his head. "Right after I moved back home. He'd just moved to Wolford. He'd been living with my father after he got out of prison."

"When did he get out?"

"Last August."

"And when did he move to Wolford?"

"Maybe the end of October."

After my break-ins. What if Barry wasn't the one who'd broken into my house? What if it had been Danny? But how did Danny's dead girlfriend play into this?

Drew finished off his beer. "I've got an early shift tomorrow and talking about this shit depresses the hell out of me. I know you want answers about your sister, but I'm not sure I have anything else to add. Can we maybe do it some other time?"

I wanted to tell him no, we needed to discuss this now, but I wasn't sure what else he could tell me, and I wasn't willing to share my inside information.

"Sure," I said with an apologetic smile. "I'll cover your beers if you want to take off."

"Thanks," he said and slid off his stool. "And for what it's worth…I'm sorry about your sister."

He started to go, then turned back to face me. "Why'd you really shoot that kid?"

The blood drained from my face. "What?"

"You said he had a gun, but I hear there are some crooked cops up in Little Rock."

"I'm not crooked."

He glanced at my empty glass and gave me a dry look. "Maybe not, but we both know you have no business being a cop. Not like this."

The buzzing in my head was so overpowering I couldn't find the words to answer him. Not that he stuck around for my answer. He'd already headed out the exit.

What the fuck was that?

I needed to talk to Malcolm, but he still hadn't shown up and Misti was nowhere to be found. I headed to the bathroom and used the facilities. After I washed my hands, I tried calling Malcolm again. No answer.

Was he hanging out in the back? It was worth a shot.

I headed to a door I presumed opened to the kitchen. The knob didn't turn, so I pounded on the door until a fresh-faced kid with red hair and freckles answered looking pissed.

"This isn't the bathroom. It's over there." He pointed to the door a few feet down the hall.

"I'm not looking for the bathroom. I'm looking for Malcolm."

"He's not here."

"He's supposed to meet me here, but he's not out front," I said, getting frustrated. "Which is why I'm at this door. I need you to get him for me."

He rolled his eyes. "If I got Mr. Malcolm for every drunk woman who pounded on this door askin' about him, I'd be the bouncer, not the fry cook." He waved in a shooing motion. "Go on. Get out of here."

He started to shut the door, but I put my foot in the crack. "If you know what's good for you, then you'll get him. *Now.*"

Surprise filled his eyes, then anger. "That's it. You're out of here." Then, to my surprise, he pulled me into a short hallway toward a door in the back.

A metal exit door.

"I told you I need to talk to Malcolm!" I protested.

"And I told you it ain't happenin', lady. He don't sleep with the customers, and we have permission to kick out the ones who won't take no for an answer."

"I don't want to sleep with him! Gross!" I dug in my heels, trying to keep him from moving me toward the door, but my coordination was off, and he was bigger. Before I knew it, the back door was open and I was in the back parking lot.

Fuck me.

I almost pounded on the door again but considering that was what had gotten me into this situation, I doubted it would do any good.

I really shouldn't be out here alone with a kidnapper/murderer who was stalking me, but I'd take that up with Malcolm later. Right now, I needed to get the hell out of here, blood alcohol level be damned.

But when I got to my car, I realized my purse and coat were still inside…yet the driver's door was unlocked, and an envelope sat in the driver's seat with my name written on it in marker.

Shit.

I glanced around the lot, looking to see if anyone was watching me, then opened the door. Without getting in the car, I picked up the envelope and pulled out the handwritten note.

IF YOU WANT AVA, MEET ME AT THE OLD PETERMAN

MANUFACTURING WAREHOUSE. ALONE.

Oh, God. The stalker must have followed me here.

I closed my eyes and my body swayed. I was in no condition to be saving anyone, let alone a child. But I also couldn't *not* go. Nevertheless, I wasn't going anywhere without my keys.

I walked up to the front door and started to walk in, but a big burly guy with a bald head blocked my entrance. "Petey said you'd be trying to come back in."

"Well, Petey can go fuck himself," I said bluntly. "And unless you give me my purse and coat, I'll be filing theft charges."

"No need for that," he said with a smirk, then reached behind the door and held up my things.

"Does Misti know you're kicking me out?" I demanded, trying to see past him to the bar.

"Misti don't give a shit about you," he said with a laugh, then tossed my things at me and shut the door. I grabbed the coat, but my phone fell out of my hand as I reached for the purse and missed. Both fell to the ground, and when I picked up my phone, the screen was white and cracked with lots of horizontal lines.

Dammit! I couldn't afford a new phone, not to mention I needed one immediately.

Okay. Deep breaths. Get your shit together.

I wasn't stupid enough to think I could do this alone, but I couldn't get help until I found a phone to call someone, not that I had any numbers memorized.

Where was Malcolm?

I walked back to my car, got inside, and waited.

Who was I going to call? Louise and the sheriff's department? The old warehouse was outside of Jackson Creek's jurisdiction. Malcolm had no vested interest in this anymore if he'd been cleared of Eddie Johnson's murder. Which meant maybe he wasn't coming after all.

Was it wrong that I wanted him to show up anyway?

I didn't get a chance to decide because seconds later a motorcycle roared its way into the parking lot. Malcolm parked behind my car, blocking me in. He turned off the engine and got off, then stalked over and opened my car door. "Get out."

"Fuck off," I snapped. "You can't tell me what to do, Malcolm."

"Only slightly more mature than you're not the boss of me," he said, reaching in and snatching my key fob out of the cup holder. "You can't drive after four drinks in less than a half hour."

"Maybe tell that to Petey the bodyguard and baldy at the door."

"Ajax?"

"You can't be serious," I said with a bitter laugh. "His name is Ajax?" I shook my head. "Never mind, they kicked me out and I dropped my phone and broke it. I was trying to figure out what to do next."

A deep scowl covered his face, but he didn't call me a liar.

I got out and tossed the paper and the photo at him. "I got another love note. Two, actually. The photo after I talked to the chief. The instructions after I left the bar."

He grabbed the note as it started to fall to the ground, then studied the photo. His gaze jerked up. "Have you told anyone about this?"

"You mean like the sheriff or the police?" I asked sarcastically. "I told Louise about the photo because I was talking to her when I found it. But the note about the showdown? No. And for what it's worth, you were one of only two people on my call list, although in hindsight, I should have probably considered adding Hale."

"So what was your plan?" he asked, holding out the paper.

I snatched it from him. "I may be drunk, but I'm not drunk enough to think I can really show up there on my own."

He grunted.

"So let me guess," I said. "*You* already have a plan."

"No," he said with a frown. "But I'll come up with one." He motioned to the other side of the car. "Get in."

"What about your bike?" I asked, but he was already making a call.

"Ajax, get your ass out here in the parking lot," he growled, then hung up before Ajax had a chance to respond.

Seconds later, the big bald man stalked toward us, glancing between me and Malcolm.

"First," Malcolm said in a deadly calm voice. "You will apologize to Detective Adams. You compromised her safety by kicking her out into a dark parking lot with a dead phone and blood alcohol over the legal limit."

Fear and anger vacillated over his face. "Petey said he kicked her out. He told me not to let her back in."

"Why?"

Ajax swallowed. "He said she was lookin' for you."

Malcolm was quiet so long even I was becoming anxious. Finally, he said, "If Detective Adams is looking for me, you let me know. Is that clear?"

His eyes widened. "Yes, sir."

"And you sure as hell better not be kicking any other women out into the parking lot by themselves, especially after a body was found out back less than twenty-four hours ago. The last thing we need is a rape, murder, or assault to occur out here. We have a reputation to maintain."

And just when I was starting to think he was a decent human being.

Ajax's Adam's apple bobbed as he swallowed. "Yes sir."

"Now move my bike to the back of the lot." He tossed the key to him. "I'm leaving and I don't know when I'll be back."

Ajax didn't respond, just caught the keys and started rolling the bike.

"What are you staring at?" Malcolm growled, glaring at me with narrowed eyes. "Get your ass in the car so we can go save a kid."

Chapter Thirty-Seven

"WHY ARE YOU DOING THIS?" I asked as he zipped the car into reverse, then pulled forward to the exit.

Talk about déjà vu.

"Driving? Because you're drunk off your ass. Again," he spat in disgust.

"Gee," I snarled, "I know it must be surprising after your sweet pep talk earlier." But I was also together enough to know I was practically useless. "I need some coffee."

"You need water. Lots of it. Got any in this car?"

"No."

He grumbled to himself, his hand slung over the steering wheel.

"I never asked you to help me with this," I said, sitting back in my seat and closing my eyes. "Not once. You pushed yourself on me at every step."

He didn't respond.

"What are you?" I asked, sitting up and turning to face him. "The strong silent type?"

A slow grin lifted the corner of his mouth. "Something like that."

"Bullshit."

"Excuse me?"

"You've just trained yourself to say as little as possible so you don't incriminate yourself."

His shoulders rose as he took a breath. "Maybe you're right. Or maybe it's a combination of the two. But it's served me well over the years." He turned to me and winked. "And Carter prefers me that way."

"I still don't get why you're helping me."

"Neither do I, so quit askin'."

He stopped at a convenience store and pulled up to a pump and started to put gas in the tank.

"What are you doing?" I called out.

He leaned inside the open door. "I'm sure as hell not takin' a car with an empty tank on a rescue mission. Stay here."

I gave him a mock salute then flipped him off.

Ignoring me, he headed inside. The pump finished filling, so I got out to put the handle back in the stand. I saw a man standing at the edge of the building, watching me. I started to flip him off, then glanced over to see Malcolm coming out of the store with a bag in his hand. When I glanced back, the man was gone.

"I told you to stay in the car," Malcolm barked as he approached.

"I saw someone at the corner."

He glanced back toward the building, his back stiffening. "Who was it?"

"It could have been anyone," I said with a sigh. "I'm paranoid."

He kept his gaze on the building, then turned back to me. "Let's go." He handed me the bag and headed to the driver's side and started the car.

I opened the sack as he pulled away from the pump. It contained two bottles of water and an energy drink.

"None of this is going to sober me up," I said, shame tingeing my words. How the hell had I gotten here?

"Maybe not, but I'm hoping you'll at least be an alert drunk." He shot me a glance, then turned back to the road. "And depending on how long you've been an alcoholic, you might be more than semi-functional as a drunk."

"I'm not an alcoholic," I protested, but without the anger that had fueled me at the prison.

He didn't respond.

I popped the top on the energy drink and started to guzzle it. The faster the caffeine hit my system, the better. "We need a plan."

"I'm presuming there's two of them," he said, then glanced at me. "He'd need help with the vehicles."

"Agreed." I told him what I'd learned about all three Sylvester men.

"Hale found out the same shit," he grunted. "If you'd stuck with me, you would have known sooner."

"But then I wouldn't have found out that Chief Larson knew Barry Sylvester warned Stevens. Other than firing him, he didn't do a thing to punish him. In fact, he paved the way for Barry to leave town and get a job with the Little Rock police."

"He has a clean record in Little Rock," Malcolm said.

"That doesn't necessarily mean anything. My partner has a clean record and I suspect he's covered in filth. And hell, Sylvester was dirty in Jackson Creek. You can't get much dirtier than trying to help a child rapist and murderer."

"You can," he said quietly. "You can get a helluva a lot worse, but what he did was heinous and makes me wonder if he was covering for himself or someone else."

"Question of the night."

He cast a glance at me. "Gut reaction?"

"Even if he turned dirty in Little Rock, it started in Jackson Creek. He was covering for someone else with Stevens."

"And who do you think that person is…?"

"His son Danny. I talked to Drew. He told me that Danny exhibited basic psychopath symptoms around the time of Andi's kidnapping—abusing animals and bugs. Plus, they lived a block away from Stevens. Drew says either his father or brother could have known him."

"So did Danny help Stevens or just watch?"

I scrunched my nose. "*What?*"

"That photo he left for you was taken from outside a window. A peeping Tom."

I stared at him, momentarily speechless. I had to admit the angle had looked weird, but I hadn't let myself stare at it for long enough to make the connection. "You think Danny was watching through a window?"

"Maybe it just started that way, and by the end he was participating. Or maybe Daddy Sylvester found the photos and was afraid there'd be blowback on his son, so he warned Stevens. Could be he didn't know how involved his son actually was."

"So Danny Sylvester kidnapped Ava," I said, working the puzzle in my head, which was hampered by the alcohol in my bloodstream. "He was living with his father when the shooting occurred last October. He could have seen my name in the news and found out where I lived."

"Maybe it was curiosity or maybe he was specifically looking for a photo of your sister," Malcolm said. "I'm guessing the latter since the break-ins stopped as soon as he took it."

"Or because he almost got caught."

"He got off on that," Malcolm said in disgust. "But once he had his memento, he moved back to Wolford."

"I still say he couldn't have known I'd come back," I protested.

"And maybe the photo was all he needed until you *did* come back," Malcolm said. "If he was just an observer with your sister, he was a voyeur. Maybe seeing your name dredged up those old feelings and he wanted to experience it for himself. He chose your sister's best friend's kid. He started tormenting you. This is all a big game to him."

I let his words sink in and mulled them over. "You could be right, and I suspect his father is trying to cover for him again. He took a leave of absence a week ago."

Malcolm's head jerked toward me. "It makes sense."

He obviously didn't know *everything*.

"So we should expect two of them," I said. "The real question is whether they'll expect you."

"We'll deal with 'em."

I shook my head. "Not when I'm not armed."

"Once I deem you sober enough, you will be."

"We don't have time to stop by my apartment to get my gun."

"You'll use one of mine." He grimaced. "I'd prefer for you not to be armed, but you make do with what you've got."

"You're admitting you can't do this all by yourself?" I asked in a snotty tone.

"Of course I can, but I'm hoping to do so without harming the kid."

He had a point. "What about a plan?"

"They want you to show up on your own so we'll let them think you're by yourself. I'll pull off the road a few hundred feet away and sneak in through the back. You'll drive up and go through whatever door they have opened for you.'"

I didn't ask him how he'd potentially get in through the back if it was locked up. I presumed he had plenty of experience with breaking and entering. "You don't think I should go for the element of surprise?"

"No, *I'll* be the element of surprise."

"You know they plan to kill me, right? There's no way they're going to let me or Ava go."

"Which is why I'm the backup." He slowed down and started to pull onto the shoulder, putting the car in park. "I'm not gonna let anything happen to the kid. You have to trust me on that."

I looked into his face and decided I believed him. Especially after I'd seen him beat John Michael Stevens. "And what about me?" I asked dryly, the buzz in my head starting to fade.

"Order of priority. The kid, then you. You're a cop. Aren't you supposed to put your life on the line every day?"

"I'm not a cop anymore, and yes. I'm willing to go in there and die if it means saving Ava." Because it occurred to me that this could be a way to atone for my sins. Saving a kid after killing one.

"This isn't a suicide mission," he said, his voice low and threatening. "And if you insinuate any more than you just did that it is, I'll tie you up to the steering wheel and go save the kid myself." He shrugged. "Of course, the risk rate goes up significantly, so the choice is yours."

"This isn't a suicide mission," I conceded. "My life might be shit, but I'm in no hurry to leave it."

He studied me, then nodded. "Close your eyes and touch your nose."

"What?" But I knew it was a drunk test, even if he was administering it the wrong way. I did as he said with both hands, then opened my eyes. "Happy?"

"Not especially, but it'll have to do." He reached into his jacket and pulled out a handgun. "You only have nine shots, so make them count."

I popped out the clip and counted the bullets, then loaded them back in.

"Do you want me to give you some kind of signal?"

"Nope," he said as he opened the driver's door. "I've got it covered." He walked in front of the car and bolted into the woods next to the road.

I got out and walked around the car to the driver's seat, my nerves starting to get the best of me. I'd been involved with a few hostage situations, but never without a team. Then again, that wasn't true. I'd saved that one woman when responding to a domestic violence call. But I'd been sober and had practiced on the firing range the week before.

The last time I'd fired a gun was when I'd killed Dylan Carpenter.

Suck it up, Buttercup.

I needed to save Ava. I didn't have time for this self-pity shit.

I pulled back onto the road and drove the few hundred feet to the old Peterman warehouse entrance. The parking lot was empty except for two cars—a beat-up Toyota Camry and a white Jeep Cherokee.

If I'd had any remaining doubts that Eddie Johnson had been killed by Ava's kidnapper, they would have quickly evaporated.

I parked next to the front entrance and pulled the flashlight out of my glove compartment. After tucking the gun into the waistband of my jeans at the small of my back, I got out of the car, flicked on the flashlight, and walked right up to the door.

I wondered if I should slow down and give Malcolm time to catch up, but decided I wanted to get some answers before they killed me. I suspected whoever had left those notes would be eager to explain.

Or at least I was counting on it.

The front door was locked, but the glass was knocked out. I bent down and climbed through, glass crunching under the soles of my ankle boots.

I'd just announced my presence.

I didn't let that slow me down as I walked through an empty room toward a door. It was unlocked, so I opened it and peered around the corner. It opened to an empty twenty-foot hallway with another door at the far end.

I considered pulling out my gun, but I wasn't any kind of sharpshooter, even at peak performance and sober. My best bet was to count on Malcolm to provide my backup and focus on finding Ava.

Hopefully, alive and unharmed.

Turning off the flashlight, I opened the door and peered into the darkness, letting my eyes adjust. A glow appeared in the distance, and I could make out empty metal shelving that stretched up to what had to be a twenty-foot ceiling.

"Harper, I know you're here, so no use hiding," a deep voice called out. "I have someone here who wants to see you. Tell her, Ava."

"Harper?" a scared voice called out.

Ava had likely never heard of me before, so her kidnapper must have told her something about me.

I headed down a long aisle toward the light and came to a halt when I saw Ava Peterman wearing pink pajamas. Her hair was tangled, and her face was pale. Duct tape was wrapped around her chest, binding her to a rickety old office chair. Her wrists were taped to the chair arms. Her legs were too short to reach the base or the silver pole connected to the wheels, but her ankles were bound together.

A man stood about ten feet behind her, his face and upper body in the shadows.

"Why are you doing this?" I asked, stopping at the end of the aisle.

"Wrong question," the man said ominously. "Shouldn't you be asking *who* is doing this?"

"Does it matter?" I said dryly. "Ava looks relatively unharmed, so let her go and maybe we can call this a misunderstanding." There only appeared to be one person with her, which made me feel a hell of a lot better. We stood a chance, especially if Malcolm made it through the back.

The man began to laugh as he backed up into the shadows. "Let's play a game."

The voice sounded familiar, but I couldn't quite place it.

"Isn't that what we've *been* doing?" I asked, taking a step closer. "All the notes were a game."

"That was fun, wasn't it?" he asked, his voice moving to my right in the darkness. "But you weren't very good at it."

"What can I say?" I said, taking another step closer to Ava and trying to casually look around the room. I was at the end of multiple aisles of shelves. Stacks of pallets were arranged in front of me, spaced about six feet apart, giving Ava's kidnapper plenty of places to hide. She was in the middle, exposed. "I never claimed to be good. Just persistent."

"But you only found me because I led you here. Don't you want to know who I am? Don't you want to know who bested you?"

He wanted me to ask, but I wasn't going to give him the pleasure. He sounded too young to be Barry, but then again, I hadn't expected the father to be the kidnapper.

"Not particularly."

"You liar!" he shouted, his voice moving through the shadows behind Ava.

"If I had to choose between who you are or who helped you, I'd go with the latter. So who helped you?'

"Who says I didn't do this myself?" he demanded, now moving to my left.

"You needed help with the cars," I said, taking another step toward Ava. The hopeful look in her eye was nearly my undoing, especially when tears began to fall down her cheeks. "I'm not even sure you were the mastermind. Maybe the other person was, and you just took credit."

"That's not true!"

"I bet your dad would let you take the credit."

"He never gave me credit for shit. He blamed me for everything!" he shouted.

Ava's eyes scrunched shut and she pulled her shoulders up to her ears.

Danny? Danny fit the profile—outbursts of anger, a record of violence, but something about his voice felt off. Now I wasn't so certain.

"Okay, then," I said. "Tell me why you did it."

"Too late," he said, now behind Ava again, his voice more distant. "We've moved on to the game."

"It's past Ava's bedtime, so what do you say we skip the game and you just let me take her home."

"Here are the rules," he said, ignoring my suggestion. "For every wrong answer, I take a shot."

"A shot at *what?*" I asked, advancing another step toward Ava. We were about ten feet apart now, and she looked terrified. Had he played games with her before? Her gaze dropped to my right, and it was then I saw the blood stains on the floor.

Sweet Jesus. Had he killed Eddie Johnson here in front of her?

"Did you play the same game with Eddie?" I asked. "When he lost, you cut off his thumb." The thumb had been delivered to my car in the police parking lot. Drew would have had access.

"The answer was easy," he said, now to my right again. "He should have gotten it correct the first time."

"What was the question?"

"If he touched her in places he shouldn't have."

"Only one body part?"

"He got it right with the next answer. Once he confessed, I had no reason to keep him around."

"You realize confessions obtained during duress are often false, don't you? Eddie Johnson never touched her. You, on the other hand…"

"I never touched her like that!" he shouted. "But he did!"

Would Danny have touched her? After a quick glimpse at that photo, I believed he would have. So if he was telling the truth…

Blood rushed from my head.

I'd chosen the wrong brother. He was trying to disguise his voice now to draw out the game, but I was certain it was him.

I tried to keep my voice from shaking. "And you shot Eddie after he confessed." I decided to take a chance. "Why'd you kill your brother's girlfriend, Drew?"

He started to laugh maniacally.

Ava's eyes locked onto mine, terror freezing her face.

"Didn't expect me to figure it out?" I asked, my voice tight. Where the hell was Malcolm? "Tell me why you killed his girlfriend. They found her body the night you kidnapped Ava."

Drew stepped out of the shadows. "Because she figured out what I was doing and was going to tell my brother."

"And what was it that she figured out?"

"You really haven't figured it out?" he demanded, his eyes blazing.

No, but I wasn't about to admit that to him, so I'd work through what I knew with this new lens. "You were at the Petermans' house the morning after the kidnapping. You put the photo in my car then. But why'd you steal it in the first place?"

"I didn't take it. My stupid brother did. He moved in with my dad after he got out of prison, and he saw your name on the news. He said he never got a memento from your sister, and he wanted one."

So Malcolm and I had been right about that.

"Did your brother help John Michael Stevens?"

He laughed, but it was dripping with resentment. "No, but he watched through the window. And he took photos. When my dad found the photos, he lost his shit."

"So you lied about not knowing your dad warned Stevens."

"Back then? I didn't know for sure, but I guessed. Before Stevens took your sister, Dad was adamant that Danny would grow out of his weirdness, as he called it. He couldn't let himself see that Danny had always been a little creep. He was friends with that monster, Stevens. I knew the guy was creepy as fuck, but when I told my mom, she refused to listen. Just like our father."

"You could have turned him in."

"It would have killed my mother."

Bitterness oozed from my soul. "So instead, you let him kill my sister."

"My brother never touched her!" Drew shouted. "He only watched."

"Gee," I said sarcastically. "That makes it all okay, doesn't it?"

"I never said it did! My father should have done something, and he didn't. When he found the photos and realized what Danny had been doing, he felt responsible. Like he should have listened to me and gotten Danny help. He was afraid Stevens would rat Danny out when he got arrested, so he warned Stevens about the bust and said if Stevens ever told, Dad would kill his mother."

"Sorry to be the bearer of bad news, but Stevens told me last night," I said. "Is your father planning on killing her now?"

"The old bitch died two years ago," he sneered.

I rolled my eyes in disgust. "Sorry you lost your insurance policy."

"Not mine. My father's. He never would give up on Danny. Not even when he killed that guy in a bar fight."

"So what is happening *right now?*" I asked. "Who kidnapped Ava? You?"

Pride filled his eyes.

"*Why?*"

"I had a chance to gain two things at once. Get my brother put behind bars for good *and* fuck with you."

His statement was like a slap to the face. "What did I ever do to you?"

"Your family destroyed mine. Your mother made mine an outcast after my father left with her gossip and her snipes. And your father wanted to put my dad in jail. He only agreed to stand off after Dad said he'd leave town."

"Yeah, after he warned the man who was responsible for Andi's kidnapping that he was about to be arrested!"

"Then when you toss in what Danny did…" He shook his head. "We never stood a chance."

"I'm supposed to accept responsibility for any of that?" I shouted. "For your psycho brother's bad choices? Well, *fuck you, you fucking asshole!*"

"It's not like you're an innocent. You killed that boy in Little Rock in cold blood. You deserved every bit of this game. *And* what's to come."

"Just like I'm gonna love every minute of the game *we're* about to play," Malcolm called out from somewhere overhead. "It's called sitting ducks. Ever heard of it? Let me explain it nice and simple since you seem to be dumber than a bag of rocks. You're the duck, and I shoot you."

Drew swung his shotgun to point it in the direction the voice was coming from and took a shot.

Another shot echoed off the concrete and Drew staggered back a step, then clutched his right arm. Blood bloomed on his shirt sleeve.

I whipped my gun out from behind my back and held it on Drew. "Drop the weapon."

"Not if you want to play the game," Drew said with a laugh. "You're gonna want to know what your sister said about you right before she died. My brother saw it all."

I stared at him in shock.

Another shot rang out, and Drew fell to his knees, staring at me in disbelief for a split second before his face went blank. Blood gushed from his chest as he fell into a heap.

Another figure stepped out of the shadows, the man I'd seen outside the gas station. He glanced down at Drew, then back up at me. The gun in his hand was still pointed at *his son,* because there was only one person he could be.

"He was going to hurt you," Barry Sylvester said, tears streaming down his face. "I had to stop him. He's hurt enough people."

It was then I heard Ava's whimpering.

"Get her out of here," Malcolm said, walking over to us. "I'll take care of this mess."

I gave him a hard glare. "What does that mean?"

Barry Sylvester tossed down his gun and lifted his hands in the air. "Go ahead and shoot me. I deserve it after everything I've done."

"No one's shooting anyone else," I said, my voice shaky. "We need to call the sheriff."

"No sheriff," both men said at once.

"So what do you plan to do with him?" I gestured to Drew's body.

"I'll take care of it," Barry said. "He's my son. My responsibility."

"Is that why you helped him kidnap Eddie Johnson?" I asked.

He adamantly shook his head. "Drew told me that Eddie helped Danny kidnap the girl. I was just trying to make things right. Drew said he could find out where the girl was if I left him alone with Eddie. And I didn't help kidnap the boy. I only helped move his car and then picked Drew up from the bar outside of town later." He choked on a sob. "I didn't see the girl in here, I swear. I had no idea what Drew was up to. Not until I heard they found that guy in the back of the van. Drew told me if I told anyone, he'd tell them I helped Danny do it."

"Where's Danny now?" I asked.

"Hiding," Barry said, tears streaming down his face. "He reached out to me today, telling me Drew was setting him up. But I'd already figured it out by then."

Malcolm locked gazes with Barry. "Both of your sons are walking pieces of garbage."

"Only one of 'em's still walking," Barry said, his voice breaking.

Malcolm didn't say a word, but the look in his eyes told me he wouldn't be walking for long.

Chapter Thirty-Eight

WE DIDN'T CALL THE SHERIFF. In the end, Malcolm convinced me that Vanessa had hired me to find Ava, and it was my responsibility to get her home as soon as possible. The girl was already traumatized enough, and Drew Sylvester was dead. It was up to the Petermans if they wanted to file a report.

I cut Ava free and scooped her up into my arms, carrying her out into my car. She clung to me, wrapping her arms around my neck for dear life. When we got outside, I pried her loose with the promise that she could see her mother in twenty minutes. She immediately released me and fastened her seat belt, ready to go.

To my surprise, when I pulled up to the Peterman's house, Vanessa was on the front porch wearing a bathrobe—just her How had she known we were coming?

It had to be Malcolm.

She ran down the steps and across the yard to grab her daughter out of the front seat of my car. They both collapsed on the grass, a tangle of limbs as they clung to each other, their sobs filling the cold winter night.

TJ came to the front door and hurried down the steps, trying to get them both up and standing. "You're making a scene, Vanessa."

I stepped between them and gave him a threatening look. "You come one step closer to either of them, and I promise you that I'll take you out."

He must have believed me, because he took a step backward, still seething but letting them be.

After Vanessa settled down, she carried Ava into the house. I followed them in, and we sat in the living room while I told them what I knew, trying to be sensitive to Ava listening. TJ stood in the corner of the room, his face red with anger.

"So this was all *your* fault," TJ said in an icy tone. "You're responsible."

"The man who kidnapped our daughter is the one responsible. Not Harper," Vanessa snapped, then took her daughter up to bed.

"The only people involved so far are Barry Sylvester, James Malcolm, and myself," I told TJ after Vanessa and Ava had left the room. "We didn't call the sheriff."

"I suppose you want me to thank you?" Sarcasm dripped from his words.

"Maybe," I said with a shrug. "If I'd had my way, they would have been involved from the moment you discovered your daughter was missing. Maybe you should fire that PI you hired to find her." I headed for the door. If I never saw TJ Peterman again, I'd be a happy woman.

"Did Malcolm really help save my daughter?" he called after me.

"He did." But now I realized his act hadn't been so selfless after all. Malcolm now had something to hold over TJ's head.

Fuck them all.

I headed home and took a long shower, trying to wash away the stench of everything that had transpired not only over the course of the night, but the past four months. I barely dried off before I threw on a pair of sweatpants and a T-shirt and fell into bed.

The sun was bright when I woke up, again to a pounding on my door, only this time it wasn't my mother. It was Nate.

He took one look at me, and worry filled his eyes. "Are you sick?"

"I just woke up. What time is it?"

"Nearly one o'clock." He gave me an apologetic look. "Can I come in?"

I was in no mood for company, so I started to tell him no, but at the last minute I backed up to let him in. I headed for my espresso machine. Maybe caffeine would help the sledgehammer pounding in my head.

"I've been calling and texting all morning. When I couldn't get ahold of you..." His voice broke. "Sorry I just dropped in, but I had to make sure you were okay myself."

"I'm okay. I'm just taking a mental health day."

He didn't look convinced. "Did you talk to Drew last night?"

I couldn't tell him anything about what had happened last night, but I had to say something. "Yeah. We met at Scooter's and he had a couple of beers. We talked about his father and their relationship, then he left."

"So why did you need to talk to him so badly?"

I studied him for a moment then shook my head. "I..." I wasn't sure what I could tell him.

"Drew's dead."

I sucked in a breath. I'd wondered if Malcolm would try to hide the body. I'd wanted to warn him that a missing police officer would get the state police involved, but then again, he was smart enough to know that. "What happened?"

"The police chief is investigating, but it looks like Danny came over to Drew's house and killed him, then killed himself."

"How convenient," I mumbled to myself. I knew I should be horrified. Malcolm had obviously dealt out his own vigilante justice, but I couldn't bring myself to work up the expected outrage.

"What?"

I shook my head. "Nothing."

"I also heard that Ava turned up in the middle of the night and you were the one to bring her home. What's the story there?"

I grimaced and shrugged. "Trade secrets."

His tone darkened. "What the hell happened, Harper?"

Other than Louise, he was my only friend in this god-forsaken town. Would he turn his back if I didn't satisfy his curiosity? "I can't tell you, Nate. I wish I could, but you'll have to accept that and not ask me about it again, or this"—I gestured between us—"whatever this is needs to end."

He was silent for a moment, then said, "Okay."

"Okay?"

"If that's the only way we can still be friends, then okay. The important thing is that Ava's back home, right?"

"Yeah." But how could someone so full of curiosity just let it go?

He left soon after that and I called Louise to check in with her, using the land line in the apartment.

"I've been calling you all morning!" she exclaimed when she answered.

"Sorry, I dropped my phone last night and broke it. I haven't gotten a new one yet."

"I'm sure you've heard the news about the Sylvester brothers."

"Yeah."

She paused. "What do you know about all of that?"

"All I can say is that Ava is safely back home, and while she's mentally traumatized, I don't think she was molested."

"That's all you have to say?"

"It's less paperwork this way."

I hadn't been off the phone long when there was another knock on my door. I opened it, expecting my mother with her eviction notice, and was shocked to see Vanessa. Her hair was messy, and she wasn't wearing a touch of makeup. Dark circles underscored her eyes, but they were filled with relief.

"Harper," she said, looking me up and down in surprise. "I hope I'm not intruding."

"*Never.* Come in. I was just enjoying the third best cup of coffee in Jackson Creek." I sat down at my small table and gestured to the chair across from me.

She gave me a sad smile as she sat down. "I'll make you the best one anytime you want."

"How's Ava?"

"Terrified. Traumatized. But alive." Her eyes flooded with tears. "She told me everything that happened. I know it was Drew Sylvester."

I nodded.

She started to say something, then stopped. "She told me about Drew's brother and how he was part of Andi's kidnapping." She swallowed, looking close to tears. "I'm grateful it was Drew who took Ava and not Danny. At least he didn't touch her."

Maybe she didn't realize that Drew would likely have killed Ava before he'd let her go free to tell people about her ordeal. I wasn't about to tell her.

"Has she said anything else about the kidnapping?"

"She said she woke up and Drew was next to her bed. He covered her face with something that smelled sweet, then the next thing she remembers is waking up at the warehouse."

"So he *did* drug her," I said.

"Yeah, but Ava didn't know anything about the ribbon."

"That one was for me." We were quiet for a moment. "You're sure he didn't touch her?" I'd told Louise that he hadn't, but I still worried that Drew had lied. "Maybe you should get her checked out."

She vigorously shook her head. "That would involve state-mandated reporting and TJ's not willing to do that."

"TJ's a fucking bastard, Nessi."

She cringed. "I know, but I have no choice."

"That's bullshit and we both know it."

"I can't leave him. I'm stuck. My parents love him. I've been a stay-at-home mom for years. I never even got a job after college. I can't support us. I have nowhere to go."

"You don't have to go anywhere. You get the house, and he pays you alimony and child support."

She made an apologetic face.

"What about Ava?" I asked. "After everything I've learned while looking for her over the last few days, I know he's made her life hell."

It was her turn to flush. "I know, but things will be different from here on out."

"Will they?" I knew I should back off, but I'd needed my father to defend me when I was a kid, and he hadn't. I refused to sit back and let the same thing happen to Vanessa's kids.

"I know I've let TJ railroad me, but I have negotiating power now," she said, her jaw firm. "He needs me for his political career."

"You'll be the dutiful wife if he backs off with the kids?"

"Exactly."

I sighed. "I hope you know what you're doing, Nessi."

She gave me a half smile. "I don't, but fake it 'til you make it, right?"

I smiled back. I didn't believe her, but there was nothing I could do about it. They weren't my mistakes to make or solve.

"Yeah, but if you ever need help kicking the bastard out, I'm your girl."

Grinning, she shook her head, then reached into her purse and pulled out an envelope. "Compensation for everything you did."

I took the envelope and then gasped when I peeked inside to see a five-thousand-dollar check. "Vanessa. I don't feel right about taking this."

"I hired you to find my daughter and you did. You probably deserve more than this, but this was all TJ agreed to."

So much for the negotiating power, but I bit my tongue. "Thank you. It was my honor to find her." But I sure planned on depositing this check ASAP before TJ changed his mind.

"Maybe you can help more people," she said. "Thankfully there aren't many kidnappings, but there are plenty of other strange mysteries and happenings around here. I'm sure people would pay you to solve them."

The idea sparked a light in me I hadn't felt in months, but it quickly guttered out. "I have a job at my father's firm. I'll stick with that for now."

"If you change your mind, you can use me as a reference."

Vanessa left right after that. I knew I needed to talk to Malcolm, but I wasn't sure I could deal with seeing him face to face, so I called him instead.

"What happened to Danny Sylvester?" I asked.

"Haven't you heard? He killed his brother."

"That's the rumor going round. How is their father handling it?"

"Not sure. Haven't seen him since we left the warehouse, and I told him I'd take care of his son. He thought I meant the first one."

It took a second before I realized what he'd just said. "He didn't know."

"We didn't discuss it."

I felt nauseated. "There wasn't another way?"

"It took care of two problems at the same time, didn't it? Besides, the world is a better place with less trash."

"Now I'll never know what my sister told him before he killed her."

"She didn't tell him a goddamned thing," he ground out. "That shit stain Drew was lying through his teeth."

Part of me wanted to believe him. The part of me that still believed magic was real and unicorns existed.

I swallowed the bile in my throat. "You had ulterior motives for saving Ava. You're going to use it to get Peterman to back off."

He was silent for a moment, and when he answered, his voice was husky. "Never claimed to be a saint, Detective Adams. If you thought differently, that's on you."

"A mistake I won't be making again."

I hung up, pissed and feeling used, but he was right. He'd never claimed to be anything but himself. I had to respect that kind of honesty, even if I resented him for it.

By six, my father hadn't come home, and I wondered if he was staying in the local B&B until his secretary found his new place…our new place if I accepted his offer. Which I planned to. I might have a job lined up, but this way I could save money until I figured out what do with the rest of my life.

It occurred to me that I hadn't talked to my mother since my father had dropped his bombshell. Might as well suck it up and get it over with. I was in my sweatpants and T-shirt, and I still hadn't done anything to my hair, but I didn't have the energy to fix myself up to have this conversation.

I knocked on the back door and my mother answered in surprise. She looked me up and down, and I braced myself for her criticism. "Harper, you don't have to knock, you know."

My jaw dropped. Who was this woman and what had she done with my mother?

Her eyes narrowed as she looked at me. "I heard that Ava's home."

"I heard that too."

The way she studied me suggested she knew I had something to do with it. I thought she was about to ask, but then she turned abruptly and headed over to the stove. "I'm sure you've spoken with your father by now," she said matter-of-factly as she started to stir something that smelled like butternut squash soup on the stove. "He said he'd be the one to tell you."

"Uh, yeah," I said in confusion. "He told me yesterday. In fact, that's why I'm here. I thought you would have served me with my eviction notice by now."

Her eyes widened. "Eviction notice?"

"Come on, Mom. We both know you never wanted me to move back home, and now that Dad's left, you don't have to keep me here."

"Harper," she chided, setting her wooden spoon down on a ceramic spoon rest and turning to face me. "Whyever would you say such a thing? Of course I wouldn't kick you out."

Now I was certain this woman had replaced my mother. "Mom, you told me that the only reason I was here was because Dad insisted that I come home."

She waved a hand. "Water under the bridge."

"It doesn't matter. I'm here to let you know I'll be out by the end of the month."

Her face fell. "But…I thought you were taking your father's job."

"I am, but I'll be moving out of the apartment."

Tears filled her eyes. "You're going to leave me?"

I stared at her in disbelief. "I've been home a little over two weeks, you can't have grown that attached to me already." Not to mention she'd acted annoyed the few times we'd interacted.

She walked over and patted my cheek. "You're my daughter, Harper. *Of course* I'm attached to you. It'll just be the two of us, keeping each other company."

That's when it hit me that she didn't want *me* here. My mother had never lived alone. She'd gone from her parents' home to living with my father. The thought of being on her own was so terrifying to her that she'd resorted to begging me, of all people, to stay.

"Mom, while I appreciate the generous offer, I don't think—"

To my surprise and horror, she began to cry. "You can't leave me, Harper. I need you."

I wanted to tell her I'd needed her my entire life and never once felt like she was there for me. But I'd be lying if her words didn't tug at some deep-seated need to be loved and wanted by this woman. I'd always felt second best to Andi, and then after her death, it was like we'd both been erased. I knew I should tell her no, because people didn't change just like that. I knew it deep in my heart, but the little girl in me that desperately needed her mother's love had stirred to life and was clambering to the surface, begging to stay. Begging to be loved.

Maybe this was a chance at a fresh start. Maybe my mother would really love me now.

I'd lied to myself often enough to recognize a lie when I saw one.

Then again, when you'd lied to yourself your entire life, what was one more?

Long Gone
Harper Adams Mystery #2
January 16, 2024

Use the QR code to read a *Little Girl Vanished* bonus
story in James Malcolm's point of view.